crescent

Also by Diana Abu-Jaber

Arabian Jazz:
A Novel

crescent

DIANA ABU-JABER

W. W. Norton & Company | New York · London

Copyright © 2003 by Diana Abu-Jaber

All rights reserved
Printed in the United States of America
First Edition

Since this page cannot legibly accommodate all the copyright notices,
page 351 constiitutes an extension of the copyright page.

Transliterations of Arabic words into English vary greatly; those used here are the
author's preferred spellings.

For information about permission to reproduce selections from this book, write to
Permissions, W. W. Norton & Company, Inc., 500 Fifth Avenue,
New York, NY 10110

Manufacturing by Quebecor Fairfield, Inc.
Book design by Barbara M. Bachman
Production manager: Andrew Marasia

Library of Congress Cataloging-in-Publication Data

Abu-Jaber, Diana.
Crescent / by Diana Abu-Jaber.–1st ed.
p. cm.
ISBN 0-393-05747-X
1. Arab American women–Fiction. 2. Los Angeles (Calif.)–Fiction. 3. Cookery,
Lebanese–Fiction. 4. College teachers–Fiction. 5. Arab Americans–Fiction. 6. Women
cooks–Fiction. 7. Restaurants–Fiction. I. Title.

PS3551 .B895 C74 2003
813' .54–dc21

2002152907

W. W. Norton & Company, Inc.
500 Fifth Avenue, New York, N.Y. 10110
www.wwnorton.com

W. W. Norton & Company Ltd.
Castle House, 75/76 Wells Street, London W1T 3QT

1 2 3 4 5 6 7 8 9 0

For Scotty

Acknowledgments

For their literary wisdom and emotional care, my friends Lorraine Gallicchio Mercer, Michelle Huneven, Whitney Otto, Joy Harris, Stephanie Abou, Alexia Paul, Alane Salierno Mason, Alessandra Bastagli, Stefanie Diaz, Bette Sinclair, Steven Fidel, and Chelsea Cain.

For their patience, generosity, and research, my friends Bassam Frangieh, David Hirsch, and Elie Chalala.

PART ONE

CHAPTER ONE

The sky is white.

The sky shouldn't be white because it's after midnight and the moon has not yet appeared and nothing is as black and as ancient as the night in Baghdad. It is dark and fragrant as the hanging gardens of the extinct city of Chaldea, as dark and still as the night in the uppermost chamber of the spiraling Tower of Babel.

But it's white because white is the color of an exploding rocket. The ones that come from over the river, across the fields, from the other side of an invisible border, from another ancient country called Iran. The rockets are so close sometimes he can hear the warning whisk before they explode. The ones that explode in the sky send off big round blooms of colors, pinwheels of fire. But the ones that explode on the ground erase everything: they send out streamers of fire that race across the ground like electric snakes; they light up the donkeys by the water troughs and make their shadows a hundred meters long. They light up every blade of grass, every lizard, and every date; they electrify the dozing palms and set the most distant mountains—the place his uncle calls the Land of Na—on fire.

They make his sister's face glow like yellow blossoms, they make the water look like phosphorescence as it runs from the tap. Their report sizzles along the tops of the tallest western buildings and rings against the minarets and domes. They whistle through the orchards and blast acres of olive trees out of the ground. They light up the Euphrates River, knock down the walls of the old churches, the ancient synagogues, the mysterious, crumbling monuments older than the books, monuments to gods so old they've lost their names, the ancient walls dissolving under the shock waves like dust.

They erase all sleep. For years.

A young boy lies in his bed on the outskirts of town, still not-sleeping. He tries to calm himself by reciting poetry:

"*Know that the world is a mirror from head to foot,*
In every atom are a hundred blazing suns,
If you cleave the heart of one drop of water,
A hundred pure oceans emerge from it."

Far away, on the other side of town, deep in the city night, behind the Eastern Hotel where all the foreigners stay, there is a pool as round as the moon, where a white-skinned woman waits for him in the phosphorescent water. The night over the pool is undisturbed by bombs, he knows, because nothing can cross into the land of the bright-haired women, their painted nails and brilliant hair and glowing skin. She stands hip-deep and motionless in the shallow end of the water, waiting for him to come to her. Her hair is the color of fire and her eyes are the color of sky and the pool is the round moon above Baghdad. He lies dreaming and awake in his bedroom on the other side of town. He is young but he has not truly slept for years. She can send him to a new place, away from the new president, as far away as the other side of the world, a place where he will no longer have to look at his brother and sister not-sleeping, where he will not have to count his heartbeats, his breaths, the pulse in his eyelids. Where his mouth will not taste of iron, his ears will not ring, his hands and feet will not tingle, his stomach will not foam with the roaring sound that has gotten inside of him and that he fears in his deepest heart will never go away again.

*

Her uncle in his room of imagined books. Everything smells of books: an odor of forgotten memories. This is the library of imagined books, her uncle says, because he never reads any of them. Still, he's collected them from friends' basements and attics, garage sales and widows' dens, all over Culver City, West Hollywood, Pasadena, Laurel Canyon, picking books for their heft and their leather-belted covers. The actual pages don't matter.

"If you behave," he tells his thirty-nine-year-old niece Sirine, "I'll tell you the whole story this time."

"You always say I'm too young to hear the whole story," Sirine says. She carves a tiny bit of peel from a lemon for her uncle's coffee. They're up in the bluish white predawn, both of them chronically early risers and chronically sleepy.

Her uncle looks at her over his glasses. The narrow ovals slide down his nose; he tries to press them back into place. "Do I say that? I wonder why. Well, what are you now, a half-century yet?"

"I'm thirty-nine. And a half."

He makes a dismissive little flick with his fingers. "Too young. I'll save the juicy parts for when you're a half-century."

"Oh boy, I can't wait."

"Yes, that's how the young are. No one wants to wait." He takes a ceremonial sip of coffee and nods. "So this is the moralless story of Abdelrahman Salahadin, my favorite cousin, who had an incurable addiction to selling himself and faking his drowning."

"It sounds long," Sirine says. "Haven't I already heard this one?"

"It's a good, short story, Miss Hurry Up American. It's the story of how to love," he says.

Sirine puts her hands into her uncombable hair, closes her eyes. "I'm going to be late for work again."

"There you have it—the whole world is late for work, and all faucets leak too—what can be done? So it begins." He situates himself in his storytelling position—elbow on knee and hand to brow. "Abdelrahman Salahadin was a sensitive man. He never forgot to bathe before his prayers. Sometimes he knelt on the beach and made the sand his prayer carpet. He just had the one vice."

Sirine narrows her eyes. "Wait a second—you said this is the story of how to fall in love? Is there even a woman in this one?"

Her uncle tilts back his head, eyebrows lift, tongue clicks: this means, *no*, or, *wait*, or, *foolish*, or, *you just don't understand*. "Take my word for it," he says. "Love and prayer are intimately related." He sighs. Then he says slyly, "So I hear Professor Handsome was in today eating some of your tabbouleh. *Again*."

Once again, her uncle is speaking of Hanif Al Eyad, the new hire in the Near Eastern Studies Department at the university. Hanif has come into the restaurant four times since arriving in town several weeks ago and her uncle keeps introducing him to Sirine, saying their names over and over, "Sirine, Hanif, Hanif, Sirine."

Sirine leans over the cutting board she has balanced on her knees and steadies the lemon. "I really don't know who you're referring to."

Her uncle gestures with both arms. "He's tremendous, covered with muscles, and shoulders like this—like a Cadillac—and a face like I don't know what."

"Well, if you don't know, I certainly don't," Sirine says as she slices the lemon.

Her uncle lounges back in his big blue chair. "No, really, you can't believe it, I'm telling you, he looks like a hero. Like Ulysses."

"That's supposed to sound good?"

He leans over and picks up the unsliced half of lemon, sniffs it, then bites into one edge.

"I don't know how you do that," Sirine says.

"If I were a girl, I'd be crazy for Ulysses."

"What does Ulysses even look like? Some statue-head with no eyes?"

"No," he says, indignant. "He has eyes."

"Still not interested."

He frowns, pushes his glasses up; they slide back down. "As you know, if you're fifty-two, that makes me eighty-four—"

"Except that I'm thirty-nine."

"And very soon I won't be here. On this planet."

She sighs and looks at him.

"I would just like to see you with someone nice and charming and all those things. That's all."

*

The grill at work is so wide Sirine must stand on tiptoes to reach all the way to the back. There are bright pans hanging from an overhead rack and magnetic rows of gleaming knives. Her arms are dashed with red slivers of burns, and as she bends to scrape the grill surface she feels its smell passing into her hair and clothes. Even after a day off, she can still catch whiffs of it as she turns her head. There is a ruby haze beneath the heat lamp, vapors rising from the stove, and everywhere the murmurings of the fans.

Nadia's Café is like other places—crowded at meals and quiet in between—but somehow there is also usually a lingering conversation, currents of Arabic that ebb around Sirine, fill her head with mellifluous voices. Always there are the same groups of students from the big university up the street, always so lonely, the sadness like blue hollows in their throats, blue motes for their wives and children back home, or for the American women they haven't met. The Arab families usually keep their daughters safe at home. The few women who do manage to come to America are good students—they study at the library and cook for themselves, and only the men spend their time arguing and being lonely, drinking tea and trying to talk to Um-Nadia, Mireille, and Sirine. Especially Sirine. They love her food—the flavors that remind them of their homes—but they also love to watch Sirine, with her skin so pale it has the bluish cast of skim milk, her wild blond head of hair, and her sea-green eyes. She has the worst kind of hair for a chef, curly and viney and falling all over her shoulders, resisting ponytails and scarves and braids. She is so kind and gentle-voiced and her food is so good that the students cannot help themselves—they sit at the tables, leaning toward her.

Um-Nadia, the owner of the café and all-around boss, is always tilting her hip against the students' chairs, keeping them company—she wears a flowered pink housedress with a deep V in front—all soft cleavage and dangling gold hoops and high-heeled too-small slippers—while her daughter Mireille, and Victor Hernandez, the young Mexican busboy hopelessly in love with Mireille, and the Central American custodian Cristobal, and Sirine the chef are in motion around her.

"Paradise," Um-Nadia likes to say. "This life on earth is a paradise, if only we knew it." Sirine has heard her say this so many times she knows how to say it in Arabic.

Victor Hernandez, who looks a little like a short, Mexican Charlton Heston, smiles and raises his eyebrows at Mireille. Mireille looks away from him and frowns at the refrigerator.

Nine years ago, in 1990, the café had been owned by an Egyptian cook and his wife and they called it Falafel Faraoh. They enjoyed a strong following among the impoverished university students, who would rotate in the Friday Falafel Special with their regular diet of burritos, egg rolls, and hamburgers. But the Americans began firing on Iraq in 1991 when Iraqi president Saddam Hussein advanced into Kuwait. And suddenly—amid all the students in their jeans and T-shirts and short shorts, and a smattering of skinny Middle Eastern exchange students in tight slacks who had quickly discovered that Falafel Faraoh tasted nothing like home—there were two grown men in business suits sitting at the counter every day writing things in pads. All they did was glance at the Middle Eastern students and take notes. A cool, impenetrable wall surrounded these two men, separating them from everyone else and growing by the day as they sat there, drinking coffee and speaking quietly to each other. People started whispering: C.I.A. Gradually the students seemed less enticed by the big specials or the colorful advertising banner draped out front. Business began to falter, then fail. One day, after a month of sitting at the counter, the two men took the cook aside and asked if he knew of any terrorist schemes developing in the Arab-American community. The poor man's eyes grew round, his hands grew slippery with sweat and cooking grease, he squeezed his spatula till it hurt his palm; he saw the twin images of his own frightened face in the dark lenses of one of the stranger's glasses. He'd never heard of such a thing in his life. He and his wife liked to watch *Columbo* at night: that was all he knew about intrigues or crime. He thought he was living in America. That night he called his Lebanese friend Um-Nadia—who used to own a little sidewalk café in Beirut—and asked if she'd like to buy a restaurant, cheap, and she said, sure, why not?

The next month, Um-Nadia found Sirine, they scraped years of yellow grease off the walls, and reopened with a menu that claimed to be "Real True Arab Food." The two men in sunglasses promptly reappeared at the counter, but Um-Nadia, who said she'd seen worse in Beirut, chased them off the premises flapping her kitchen towel at them.

Um-Nadia says the loneliness of the Arab is a terrible thing; it is all-consuming. It is already present like a little shadow under the heart when he lays his head on his mother's lap; it threatens to swallow him whole when he leaves his own country, even though he marries and travels and talks to friends twenty-four hours a day. That is the way Sirine suspects that Arabs feel everything—larger than life, feelings walking in the sky. And sometimes when she is awake in the center of the night, the night cool and succulent as heart of palm or a little chicken kabob, Sirine senses these feelings rushing in her own blood. But she was also born with an abiding sense of patience, an ability to live deeply and purely inside her own body, to stop thinking, to work, and to simply exist inside the simplest actions, like chopping an onion or stirring a pot.

Sirine learned how to cook professionally working as a line cook and then a sous chef in the kitchens of French, Italian, and "Californian" restaurants. But when she moved to Nadia's Café, she went through her parents' old recipes and began cooking the favorite—but almost forgotten—dishes of her childhood. She felt as if she were returning to her parents' tiny kitchen and her earliest memories.

And the customers quickly returned to the restaurant, only this time there were many exchange students and immigrants from the Middle East. Sirine rolled out dough early in the morning in her open kitchen behind the counter and discreetly watched the students sipping coffee, studying the newspapers, and having arguments. Everything about these young men seemed infinitely vulnerable and tender: their dense curling lashes, soft round noses and full lips, winnowed-away faces and chests.

Sometimes she used to scan the room and imagine the word *terrorist*. But her gaze ran over the faces and all that came back to her were words like *lonely*, and *young*.

Occasionally, a student would linger at the counter talking to Sirine. He would tell her how painful it is to be an immigrant—even if it was what he'd wanted all his life—sometimes especially if it was what he'd wanted all his life. Americans, he would tell her, don't have the time or the space in their lives for the sort of friendship—days of coffee-drinking and talking—that the Arab students craved. For many of them the café was a little flavor of home.

At Nadia's Café, there is a TV tilted in the corner above the cash register, permanently tuned to the all-Arabic station, with news from Qatar, variety shows and a shopping channel from Kuwait, endless Egyptian movies, Bedouin soap operas in Arabic, and American soap operas with Arabic subtitles. There is a group of regulars who each have their favorite shows and dishes and who sit at the same tables as consistently as if they were assigned. There are Jenoob, Gharb, and Schmaal—engineering students from Egypt; Shark, a math student from Kuwait; Lon Hayden, the chair of Near Eastern Studies; Morris who owns the newsstand; Raphael-from-New-Jersey; Jay, Ron, and Troy from the Kappa Something Something fraternity house; Odah, the Turkish butcher, and his many sons. There are two American policemen—one white and one black—who come to the café every day, order fava bean dip and lentils fried with rice and onions, and have become totally entranced by the Bedouin soap opera plotlines involving ancient blood feuds, bad children, and tribal honor. There are students who come religiously, appearing at the counter with their newspapers almost every day for years, until the day they graduate and disappear, never to be seen again. And then there are the students who never graduate.

Even though Nadia's Café is in the middle of an Iranian neighborhood, there are few Iranian customers. After the long, bitter war between Iraq and Iran, some of Um-Nadia's Iranian neighbors refused to enter the café because of Sirine, the Iraqi-American chef. Still, Khoorosh, the Persian owner of the Victory Market up the street, appeared on Sirine's first day of work announcing that he was ready to forgive the Iraqis on behalf of the Iranians. He stood open-mouthed when he saw white-blond Sirine, then finally blurted out, "Well, look at what Iraq has managed to produce!" He asked if she knew how to make the Persian specialty khoresht fessenjan, his favorite walnut and pomegranate stew, and when she promised to learn, he returned later in the day and presented her with a potted pomegranate tree.

Sirine wears her hair tied back but still it hangs in damp tendrils all over, in the corner of her mouth, in her eyes. She works and listens to the bells ringing over the door, the door banging, conversations surging into argument and back again. There is always so much noise; there are birds arguing in the tree outside the kitchen window. Life is an argument! Um-Nadia says. When Sirine laughs and asks, what are they fighting about? Um-Nadia says, what else? The world.

Sirine looks up, past the hood of the heat lamp, watching customers fill the tables. More students, stripling-thin, faces narrowed with exhaustion, loneliness, and talking. She is frying onions and working on two dishes at once, chopping eggplant and stirring the leben—a delicate mellow yogurt sauce that needs constant stirring or it will break—and she watches the argument at the latest table. Four of them, including Hanif Al Eyad, have just come in. Rectangles of light pass over them from the windows in the door as it opens and closes. There are voices blurring and unblurring, complicated gestures, winding hands and arms. It sounds like the same sort of argument the students are always having—about America, the Middle East, and who is wronging whom—this time it's in Arabic, sometimes it's in English, usually it's a little of both.

She's noticed that Hanif frequently has an entourage of students in his wake, young men—and some women—who tentatively follow him, asking his opinion of things. Her main impressions of Hanif are of his hair, straight and shiny as black glass, and of a faint tropical sleepiness to his eyes. And there is his beautiful, lightly accented, fluid voice, dark as chocolate. His accent has nuances of England and Eastern Europe, like a complicated sauce.

Sirine has just turned from the leben to the eggplant when Hanif bursts into English, "Of course I love Iraq, Iraq is my home—and there is, of course, no going home—" and then back into Arabic.

She looks at him, the white of his teeth, the silky dram of skin, cocoa-bean brown. He's well built, tall, and strong. He laughs and the others follow his laughter. Um-Nadia has stationed herself beside him. Standing, one hip against the table, she holds her hand out as if she will curl her knuckles right through his hair. She sighs, tilts one foot on its shiny worn heel, then pats the puffed top of her own hair. She looks over, still smiling, to Sirine behind the counter, and says, "Roasted lamb, rice and pine nuts, tabbouleh salad, apricot juice." Then she blows a kiss.

Hanif glances at Sirine. She looks down, quick, a bunch of parsley pinched in her fingertips, rocks the big cleaver through a profusion of green leaves, onions, cracked wheat. Suddenly she remembers the leben and hurries to the big potful of yogurt sauce, which is just on the verge of curdling.

CHAPTER TWO

Sirine's uncle leans forward over their kitchen table, watching Sirine as she scrapes a little more tabbouleh salad on to his dinner plate. "I'm so full, Habeebti," he says. "Really, I couldn't eat another bite."

"You didn't eat any vegetables at all." She stands and places the dishes in the sink. When she turns back, however, he is biting into a large, walnut-stuffed ma'mul cookie. She puts her hands on her hips.

"So," he says quickly, dusting crumbs away as if he could hide the evidence. "Isn't it time for the next chapter of the moralless tale of Abdelrahman Salahadin?"

*

Abdelrahman Salahadin carries himself like a handful of water.

Abdelrahman Salahadin—such a long name. It takes forever to say.

Unusual, granted, but venerable. A name of great compassion and beauty—"The Servant of the Merciful One"—Abdelrahman—and the name of a great warrior and liberator—Salah al-Din.

Abdelrahman Salahadin was his mother's favorite son.

In the day his skin is cinnamon-and-honey-colored. At night he is almost invisible. He moves seemingly without moving, the way the eye moves over words on a page.

There is a small wooden rowboat, rocking and hidden in the reeds. The Saudi slaver waits beside it, eyes downcast, modest as a suitor, come to purchase Abdelrahman and spirit him away, across the Red Sea, to his desert castle.

The slaver helps Abdelrahman Salahadin into the boat. After they are settled, he rows and chats with Abdelrahman, trying to wow him with his studies on the language of the mermaids. Between strokes, he hands Abdelrahman Salahadin his payment: a small bag of gold, a gold anklet, and gold earrings.

Abdelrahman inclines his ear toward the horizon as if listening for something. Finally, after they are well out to sea, surrounded by dark, secret swells, a distant canopy of rumbling clouds, he seems to receive an invisible signal and he stands. The slaver looks at him with something like pleading, perhaps already sensing what is about to happen. Abdelrahman lifts his arms and jumps; he spills into the water like honey from a jar, dense and bright, instantly gone.

The slaver stands, mouth open. The boat rocks a little and he sits back down. He doesn't know how to swim. He appeals to God, to the invisible entities of the earth and sky, knowing as he does that everything is written. He wrings his hands, curses his luck, the ocean, the miserable institution of slavery; he shakes his head. Then he begins to laugh.

*

Classes started last week. The trees around the university are melting late summer blossoms; they smell sweet as water and litter the curbs with chunks of purple petals. Even though this is Los Angeles, Sirine still walks or bicycles almost everywhere she needs to go—which is never far.

It's two miles from the door of her uncle's house to the door of Nadia's Café. And there's a mile and a half between her uncle's office on campus and the door of the café, a path that extends straight down Westwood Avenue, through the student-busy village, across big Wilshire (where "Walk" flashes to "Don't Walk" before you're even halfway across), past the bright showy movie marquee, into so-called Teherangeles, with the beauty parlors and bookstores and food markets and the names of everything in Farsi with its Arabic script and different meaning and none of the Americans can quite get that Arabs and Iranians are "completely different animals," as Um-Nadia puts it. And when anyone asks Um-Nadia why did she decide to locate an Iraqi-Lebanese café (and are the Lebanese Arabs or Phoenicians or Druids or what? Her uncle just shrugs and says, "God only knows," and Um-Nadia hits him on the shoulder and says grandly, "They're not—they're Lebanese!") midslope, right in mid-Teherangeles, she shrugs and says, "God only knows. Where else am I going to put it?"

In the mornings when her uncle does not insist on driving her to work, Sirine wakes early and braves the cars in order to ride her bike from West L.A. to Westwood. She's used to the quick rhythms and physical demands of the kitchen and she likes to exert herself. Then she notices the flowering things around her, the plants with the fluted edges like feathered goblets, or striped pink blossoms floating before a storefront, or the two big twin palms in the Garden of the Birds behind Nadia's café. Their long elegant trunks rub together when the wind comes up.

Sirine's never known any other kind of place. She's seen snowstorms on the TV, read descriptions of biting cold. The buildings she knows usually have an open door, rustling screens and trellises. She knows the smell of jasmine in the air, the silver lick of sprinklers, the gardeners tidying lawn clippings, sweeping leaf blowers through the dust and deep heat.

It's barely the start of September and the afternoon is sultry and still as she and her uncle walk to campus. But when they reach the building door a hot little wind blows down from the mountains; bits of debris are lifted into tiny dust devils, a plastic bag flaps in the air like wings. She came to the reading because her uncle said she worked too much and that, in his opinion, we could all do with more culture. But as soon as they find the seminar room where the reading is taking place, he waves to her and drifts down the hall to his friends in the Turkish Studies Department.

Sighing, she sinks onto one of the metal folding chairs. After a few minutes, a man in a silk tie and a polished cotton jacket comes to the podium. He looks like a suave version of her uncle's academic cronies—graceful, athletic, and sophisticated. His clothes seem European. His dark hair spills forward over his forehead. He pushes it back but it just falls back forward, and Sirine feels a sliver of tenderness toward the man. His paper trembles slightly in his hand as he launches into an introduction of the poet, neglecting to introduce himself. "Aziz Abdo is a wonderful, wonderful writer," he says, his voice taut. He lifts his head so Sirine can see a fine pearly sheen on his forehead. He pushes back his hair again, seems to lose his place on his paper, then reads, "Abdo transforms Arabic, he understands its deepest, hidden nature, its possibilities, he forces the language, as one might force a spring planting into its richest, most vital profusion and budding. He tends to this deep, powerful language, nudging seedlings to light. To quote the historian Jaroslav Stetkevych on Arabic, 'Venus-like, it was born in a perfect state of beauty, and it has preserved that beauty in spite of all the hazards of history. . . . It has known austerity, holy ecstasy and voluptuousness, boom and decadence. It exuberated in times of splendor and persisted through times of adversity in a state of near-hibernation. But when it awoke again, it was the same language.' The same description might be applied to tonight's author. Abdo has manipulated and dreamed this rich language-flesh. He is an erotic poet, a scholarly poet, a holy poet of mind and body, one who understands how to bear us, unconscious, through language, into our purest dreams."

He breaks off and stares at the page in his hands. He looks up as if just remembering the audience, slightly breathless. And Sirine realizes that she too is a little breathless, caught up in his rapturous speaking. She has never heard anyone speak so eloquently and longingly of Arabic before. Suddenly she misses her father. And the speaker looks at her and her mouth opens a little; she has been listening to her uncle's friend Hanif.

He only blinks, however, as if he were slightly nearsighted, and then blinks back down at his paper and she releases her breath. Then Hanif holds out his hand and says, "Please welcome Aziz Abdo."

She lowers her head and tries to listen to the poetry. There is a sound like a murmur somewhere inside the sound of her breath, as if someone were whispering to her. She tries to be casual, inspects her nails, smells traces of butter left over from cooking lunch, an incense of oil and grass. But her mind still veers between the poetry and Hanif. Sirine never reads poetry and can't imagine why Hanif's odd introduction should have moved her so. She pulls her uncle's topaz prayer beads out of her pocket and settles herself by thinking of braised squab: a sauce for wild game with motes of cinnamon and smoke.

The poet, the visiting writer named Aziz, leans into the podium; he switches between Arabic and English like someone wandering along a crooked path. Sirine speaks only a few words of Arabic but the sound of it soothes her. She floats in her seat, sifting through the beads, letting herself drowse to the poetry, the audience breathing, watching the carpet glow and glitter as if it were sprinkled with mica. Occasionally she steals glances across the room, attempting to spot Hanif.

She tries to perk up whenever the poet glances in her direction. His voice ticks like a whisk in a copper bowl. His poems conjure up the image of an old man sweeping the streets in Baghdad, Jerusalem, and Damascus. Sirine sees trees filled with birdcages, sparkling with colored songbirds. She sees sinewy sands, palm trees bending in the sky. These sound like places she might like to visit. She wonders if this is good writing.

Someone settles into the chair beside her. His shoulder brushes hers and a deep warmth races from her shoulder to the top of her head and the bottoms of her feet. And for the rest of the reading, she holds very still, squeezing her prayer beads.

The poet rocks up and down on his toes, pink-faced, lightly glazed with sweat. He places one hand over his heart, holds the other one up oratorically, and closes with a line that he says comes from a famous poet whom he refers to as his spiritual mentor: " 'Let the beauty we love be what we do. There are hundreds of ways to kneel and kiss the ground.' "

Afterward everyone stands up. Sirine peeks from the corner of her eye and confirms that it is Hanif who has been sitting next to her. She nervously stands and walks out of the row, trying to look nonchalant. The conference room opens to a small veranda where there is a long table covered with wine bottles and cheeses, and a small gathering of women with black hair that rolls around their shoulders like thunderclouds, men with blond beards, an elderly woman wearing a silk cape. Hanif stretches and wanders after Sirine to the table, and she tries to observe him without being obvious. His black hair is shot through with glints of gray and there is something pure and regal about the cast of his forehead; it seems like the distinctive, beautifully formed sort of brow that is bred within royal houses for generations. He raises his eyebrows—a question—then pours two glasses. The air is humid, and the little plastic cups of cold white wine mist up as they're poured. Hanif glances at her. His eyes have a vaguely Asian cast to them, the irises smudged, slightly burnt. It is the injured quality of his eyes that sticks with her. She thinks of the heroes in her uncle's stories with the dramatic black eyes.

"Would you like some?" He offers her a glass. Startled, she nods and then lifts it to her cheek a moment. A few students hover around Hanif but he doesn't look at them. "I saw that you had some prayer beads—" He holds out one hand as if imitating her. "The way you held them was very delightful—very American."

"Oh." She feels embarrassed and somehow dismayed. "My uncle gave them to me," she says, as if in self-defense.

"What a wonderful uncle, then," he says.

Then there's a silence that goes on a little too long, both of them frowning at their wine cups. Hanif looks up as if remembering something and says, "Did you enjoy the reading?"

"I really loved your introduction," she says, but then this seems too intimate, so she adds, "I thought it was really wise. I don't even know why." She notices the tips of his ears turning pink and panics. "I mean—oh, I don't know what I'm saying, it always comes out wrong—I always feel like such a fake smart person at these things," she blurts. "Oh—I mean like a spy, not like I think smart people are fakes—"

"Yes, yes, so do I exactly!" he says.

"But how could you? I mean, you actually work here, I mean—you're one of the smart ones."

He looks blank. She hugs her elbow and sips her wine without tasting it. They both stare hard at the ground. Neither of them speaks.

"Well. Then. I suppose—should I let you go?" he says.

"Or—well—" she says. "Um." She bites her lip, swirls her wine.

"Hello, Professor." A woman's voice drifts over Sirine's shoulder. Sirine turns to see a young woman standing there; her head is covered with a black veil, only her face showing.

Hanif looks startled, then frowns; he seems to be trying to remember the woman's name. "Hello there," he says. "How are you—uh—Rana?"

"That was some lecture the other day in class." The woman doesn't acknowledge Sirine; instead she moves up and edges one shoulder in front of her. "The connections you were drawing between the different classical periods were so helpful. You explain things in a way that I can finally understand—unlike some of these people."

"Oh well . . ." He glances over her shoulder to Sirine. "I'm told I'm one of the smart ones," he says with a smile.

The woman turns, following Hanif's gaze, and finally seems to notice Sirine. She nods at her, then turns back to Hanif. "Well, I just wanted to let you know," she says. "I can't wait till the next class." She waves at him so the tips of her fingers—painted crimson—glitter under the edges of her long black sleeves, then moves away.

Sirine inhales. The breeze is picking up a bit and bougainvillea buds like tiny purple lanterns skid across the floor. She tries to think of something to say to reclaim the conversation.

"Ah, there you are, good, good." Her uncle saunters over, spots the cheese and crackers, and snaps off a branch of grapes. "I was looking absolutely everywhere."

Sirine crosses her arms. "Did you try looking in here?" she asks.

"Ah . . . aha! Funny. Oh—did you meet my buddy Hanif Al Eyad, our new hire in Near Eastern Studies? This is my adorable niece, Sirine. Sirine, Hanif. Look at him—look at that face. What a face. Like Ulysses, right? Look at that expression. He's an Iraqi classic just like your old uncle."

Hanif shakes his head and smiles a big, squared-off smile, teeth bright against his toast-brown skin. He looks down, then up again, and she notices for the first time a pale scar that flicks from the outer edge of one eye onto his cheekbone. "Please, just call me Han," he says to Sirine.

"We have met," Sirine says to her uncle. "You've introduced us before."

Han's eyes flicker at her as if checking to see if she's teasing. His hand slides over the back of his neck. Then his head jerks up. "My God," he murmurs. "You're Sirine. From the café. We have met."

Sirine laughs. "You didn't recognize me," she says. "All this time we were talking!"

His eyes are wide and round. "I'm—you—you just—you looked so different outside the café—"

Sirine fingers a few loose spirals of hair that have fallen over one shoulder. She isn't wearing her hair pulled back or her jacket and apron. She smiles at him. "I didn't recognize you at first either."

"You didn't?" He looks at her, then shades his eyes in mock embarrassment.

"You two are having a smiling war," her uncle says.

Sirine scowls at her uncle.

"So anyways," her uncle says, looking around. "Oh, lovely, lovely, look here now is our new star student, Nathan." He signals to him. A young man wearing rimless oval glasses and a square black camera slung around his neck slips through the crowd and joins them.

"I was just about to tell my niece how wonderful our Hanif is," Sirine's uncle says.

Nathan removes the glasses and wipes the ovals with the hem of his shirt, then carefully hooks them back around his ears. His narrow features are melancholy. He picks up a plate and turns back to Sirine. "I'm honored to meet you. You make the famous lentils and onions dish." He is slight and wiry, but up closer, Sirine can see that he's older than he seems. His smile is slightly off-kilter, as if unevenly weighted, his hair shaved down to black stubble. He points his thumb at Han in a jaunty, offhanded way. "He went to Cambridge, did a postdoc at Yale. He's a linguist. He's been everywhere. He had his pick of schools and didn't have to come here at all."

"What's wrong with here?" her uncle asks.

"And he's published extensively on American transcendentalism and has translated Whitman, Poe, Dickinson, and now Hemingway into Arabic!"

"If you can imagine such a thing," her uncle says.

"Nathan—" Han is laughing. He shakes his head. "Nathan here is a wonder—he knows something about everything."

Nathan shrugs. "No. Maybe a little music and photography. That's it. I don't really know anything."

"You've got to see his exhibit next door," Han says. "He's so talented, it's a little frightening to have him in class."

"I'll bet," her uncle says.

"I'm—enthusiastic," Nathan admits with an embarrassed smile, then offers his hand to Sirine. "Nathan Green."

She takes it cautiously. "Well, hi."

Aziz the poet makes his way toward them. He is stopping to speak to everyone, hugging women and men both. Sirine picks up a lilt of spicy cologne as he comes closer.

Finally he emerges; he throws his arms around Sirine's uncle and then Han. Nathan backs up a step but then he too is enveloped. "Excellent," Aziz says ardently. "Excellent, excellent."

He turns to Sirine. Sirine thinks that he looks like a poet. His skin is the color of coffee and milk and his deep-set eyes are satiny. His sky-blue dress shirt sticks to his chest with long swatches of sweat. He wears his hair swept back from his face so it rises a few inches from his head. "Ahh," he says, a long release of breath. "Yes, yes, excellent!"

"Aziz, this is my unattainable niece Sirine," her uncle says to him.

"Oh, wonderful. How marvelous. I love a niece. And this is clearly a niece among nieces." His hand folds around hers and then his other goes on top of that. He seems to be holding her in place. "*Enchanté*," he says. "Seriously."

She smiles and nods but her gaze briefly ticks over his right shoulder to Han, who is watching them.

"Did you love the reading?" Aziz asks. "Be honest."

Han joins them then, puts a hand on Aziz's back. "This guy," he says. "I've moved all around the world, read all sorts of stuff. I thought I'd given up on poetry. I come to Los Angeles, of all places on earth, and I find the Walt Whitman of Syria in the office next door to me."

"An essential poet," Sirine's uncle says, nodding.

Aziz is still holding her hand. Slightly flustered, Sirine says, "Oh, are you famous?"

"She's used to Hollywood poets," her uncle says to Aziz.

Nathan turns toward Sirine in a confiding half-crouch. "He's just got one book out, *Half Moon*, but he has a minor reputation among Arab intellectuals," he says. "Nothing like Mahmoud Darwish, of course, or even Abdelkebir Khatibi."

"Of course," her uncle says, plucking more grapes.

Aziz seems to enjoy the discussion about himself. She can't tell if he's overheard Nathan or not. "Yes, my little book and I do get around," he says. "We were escorted out of Damascus abruptly and for a while we were teaching somewhere on Cape Cod—no one ever told me the name of the town. Then we were living in someplace like Mobile, Alabama, where I was teaching in a private girls' school with lots of intelligent, poetry-loving girls. Then the big school here called and said come. So what do you know, I came."

"I think if you talked to anyone in Syria, even a regular person like a cobbler or a butcher, they've probably heard of him," Nathan adds.

"A cobbler maybe, but a butcher? I'm not that famous."

Nathan glances at Aziz's hand on Sirine's and says, "You could let go of her now, you know."

"Maybe yes . . . maybe no," Aziz says with a tremendous smile.

Sirine resists the urge to tug. "Hm," she says.

"No, really," Han says to Aziz, also with a smile. He puts his hand on Aziz's shoulder. "Why don't you make an attempt?"

Aziz squeezes once, then releases her. "Open sesame," he says, "the spell is broken."

She feels cool sweat on the back of her hand.

Han pats Aziz lightly on the shoulder. "Better that way."

*

As Sirine and her uncle are leaving, Sirine notices the smaller room off to one side. It's empty except for some matted black and white photos on the walls. At first they all appear to be out of focus, but as she moves closer, Sirine realizes that these are portraits of people in varying states of distress or agitation: blurred heads turning away, hands fluttering up in evasion, some appear to be outright shouting or laughing. The images are disturbing yet graceful, filled with languid shadows, as if the photographer were shooting through surfaces. There are small tags beneath the portraits, listing titles and modest prices: *Emily, Omar, Ian.* Sirine is captivated by the faces.

"Well. Some exciting things to look at," her uncle says.

"What is all this?" She stops in front of one image that looks a little like a drowning man trapped beneath the camera lens, his mouth smeared and open, his eyes streaks.

"Nathan? Nate? That American boy? He's a kind of photographer. He won a graduate student fellowship and the School of Arts invited him to do his own exhibit. But when he heard that Aziz was giving this reading, he wanted to show his pictures at the same time. I think he was making a statement. I don't know what." He points to a sign by the door that says "Photography Against Art: Real Seens by Nathan Green."

"These are his?" During the reception she'd noticed Nathan taking some photographs of people bent over their plates, his fingers circling the lens of his camera. He hunched a little before each shot as if bowing in apology.

Her uncle stops by the drowning-man portrait for a moment and smiles as if recognizing a friend. He nods and turns away. "Well, he is an unusual fellow," he says.

The photos bother Sirine: they remind her of times she's known she was dreaming and couldn't wake herself up. She gazes at one particularly dark image: something that looks like a well of light, a person at its center, head tilted back, staring straight up at the camera. The image slips inside her, cold, like swallowed tears.

When Sirine and her uncle leave the building, the moon has come out and she sees her uncle's face in the hard lights that illuminate the front of the building. She notices the tracery of lines covering his skin, radiating from the corners of his eyes and crossing his cheeks. She sees the way his chin has softened and melts into his neck and the way his scalp shows through his hair.

He looks at her and smiles and she says, almost curtly, "Uncle, please, watch the steps!"

And he says, "Ah yes, the terrible, fearsome steps."

CHAPTER THREE

I would just like to point out at this moment, for the record, that accomplished uncles and storytellers are usually rewarded with plates of knaffea pastry. For the record.

Then we can get on with our story.

So Abdelrahman Salahadin, the wily cousin, crawls sideways under the wild, roving waves. He has spent so much time under the sea he wears it like a bedsheet. The gold pieces bump and crawl and stay tied tight inside the bag tucked inside the pocket with its golden button, knotted around Abdelrahman Salahadin's smooth muscle of a body.

The fish turn their heads and theorize that they have seen a phantasm, a pink-palmed jinn, a ghost from one of the drowned cities. The waves throw their shuttered light over his face and limbs and he is handsome as an old-time Egyptian movie star. Jellyfish awake from their dreaming-lives, crabs put away their poetry, shrimps shudder like castanets. He does not swim so much as dance, arms spread, legs flung, head back, eyes open as day. What a being he is.

Every time he does this, he tells himself, it is the last time. It is no career for a young man. It is a bad habit. His mother, my aunt Camille, the freed Nubian slave, wants him to go into dentistry. He likes the idea of it, the sharp and pointed instruments—mallets and pliers and scissors, the numbing oils, and especially the smooth enamel surfaces of teeth, waiting in the dark.

He thinks of teeth as he slips over rocks and other hard objects along the sea bottom. He thinks of himself as a small tongue in the great mouth of the sea.

And who will come to his funeral if he drowns this time? he muses. Surely not his mother, who has told him so a million and six times; not his father, who is so drunk he forgets he has two houses, four wives, and twenty sons, one of whom makes money by selling himself off, then pretending to drown while escaping.

Only his brothers will come to the funeral. They love him the best.

*

Sirine can't sleep. She lies awake in her bed with the shining sleigh frame and the cool white covers. Strange things keep her awake: Aziz's rhythmic poetry, the blurred faces from Nathan's photographs, the dark chocolate of Han's voice. She lets herself stray past the stage of sleep and even past the stage of remembering, and she wanders into the stage of soul-searching. Sometimes when she lies awake her body feels as finely made as a tuning fork. She can hear and smell the most delicate things, the smell and music of thought itself. A intricate breeze blows through the lacy curtains and sets them afloat, and bird cries rustle in the bushes. She listens to the evening sounds. If she lived in a colder place, she thinks, the sound outside her windows might be rain, but it's only the sawing of palm leaves against each other in the breeze.

*

She is, somehow, thirty-nine and a half years old; her parents are dead; she has never married. The memories of all her past boyfriends are so faded, it is as if a magic page had lifted and the tracings of their faces disappeared. None of them managed to interest her in getting married, having children, or even moving away, which she'd somehow always assumed was the point of having a boyfriend. She remembers that one liked to study historical inventions. Another was an expert bridge player. They always loved her cooking—even the ones who'd never bitten into a falafel or scooped up hummus in pita bread before.

Sirine sometimes dates two men at once, and recently somehow there were three men calling her and coming by the house: her uncle's blue-eyed mechanic, an intern at the university hospital, and a bustling chef at the German restaurant on Sepulveda who brought her tins full of fancy butter cookies. But ever since the start of school, she's been too preoccupied with cooking to return their calls. She's always had more men in her life than she's known what to do with. Um-Nadia says that attraction is Sirine's special talent—a sort of magnetism deeper in her cells than basic beauty or charm. She's never broken up with anyone, she just loses track of them, adding new men as she goes. Never, not for a single day since her second year in high school, has she been without a boyfriend or admirer of some sort, and she has never really, entirely given herself to any of them. She knows this—it doesn't seem a deliberate choice to her, it was simply something that never happened. She wonders sometimes if it's a sort of flaw or lack in her—the inability to lose herself in someone else. Sirine has lived in her uncle's calm library of a house nearly all her life; she's never quite understood how people could trade in quiet spaces and solitary gardens and courtyards, thoughtful walks and the delicious rhythms of work, for the fearful tumult of falling into love.

*

Um-Nadia is helping to clean the smoked wheat kernels for a dinner special and singing a song in Arabic about a man who somehow misplaced his lover and who asks a shepherd if he's seen her anywhere.

"I stayed up last night trying to remember things about my old boyfriends," Sirine says to Um-Nadia's daughter Mireille.

"Well, one of them was named Doug. One of your guys. If that helps," Mireille says, watching her mother and Sirine sort kernels. "He was so cute, remember? He wore those striped coveralls." Mireille refuses to prepare food, and only occasionally and grudgingly eats it. Mostly she leans in the kitchen doorframe blowing cigarette smoke out the back door. Now she sighs a plume of smoke and tips back her head; the morning light glows in her bleached hair.

Um-Nadia interrupts her song. "Yes, yes, yes," she says. "Life is an insomnia. And who can keep track of such things as boyfriends?"

"You mean, like, life is an amnesia," Mireille says.

Um-Nadia thinks about it a moment. "That too. But I meant insomnia first. Where you sit up at night trying to think of silly things like, where did I put my old husband, what happened to my blue pants, why does my hand hurt, and so on et cetera." She edges a little closer to Sirine, watches her scraping chopped onion into a pan. "He's here right now, you know," she says, her voice low. "He's right outside."

"Who, Ma?" Mireille tries to look around her mother's shoulder. "Who's 'he' now?"

Sirine knows who. She can see his shadow through the wooden screen door, its shiny latch like a silver tooth.

"He's a *Muslim*, you know." Um-Nadia's voice is half-warning and half-laughter. "Dark as an Egyptian."

"Ma!" Mireille shouts. "Get a grip."

Um-Nadia's grinning like it's one of her old jokes. "And here is our beautiful Sirine, whiter than this." She takes a bite out of a whole peeled onion as if it were an apple. "Finally, a man for her to remember."

*

Outside, there's a new batch of Arab students coming to eat at Nadia's Café again this year—new and regulars. Some of them are already sitting on the front steps before the café has officially opened, before their morning classes. They order the smallest, cheapest dishes: bean dip and garlic; bread and olives and thickened yogurt. Sometimes they bring their own food. Or they sit at the tables outside and play drums with their fingers, the one-stringed rebab, the violin, the flute, Arabic music sailing through the walls of the café so no one working inside can hear themselves think.

Um-Nadia waits until the air is roasted chocolaty, big and smoky with the scent of brewing coffee. Then she knocks the front door latch open. She holds the door wide and lets the older returning students, the immigrants and workingmen in, one by one, morning-shy, half-sleepy, hopeful from dreams, from a walk in the still-sweet air, not so lonesome this early in the day. Nothing a small cup of coffee and a plate of bread and olives can't cure. She makes the younger students wait outside until the others have had their first cup of coffee.

Han and Nathan come in together. Han bows to Um-Nadia and kisses her hand. Um-Nadia's smile deepens to dimples. Sirine watches the way she holds out the chair for him as if he were royalty. And now Sirine thinks he does look different from the rest of the customers. His hair falls in a black arc over his forehead. Sirine stands in the front kitchen and slides the morning pastry out of the oven, fragrant with brown spices, and layered with nuts and sugars and cheese. "Ah, you've made knaffea today," Um-Nadia says as she streams past Sirine. "Who are we in love with, I wonder?" Then her dark, secret laugh.

Mireille perches on the stool next to Sirine, her legs jackknifed into her tight jeans, and peers behind Sirine at Han's table. "Look at them," she mutters. "Probably all waited on since the day they were born."

Sirine glances up at the men. "Do you think?"

"All these guys really want is to get us back into veils, making babies, and I don't know what, nursing goats or something. You watch out, I'm telling you."

Sirine nods and sprinkles hot syrup over the pastry.

"They're like animals—look at them! I swear, men are all half-animals and half-something else."

Victor Hernandez comes in and slides two big canvas sacks of rice off his back onto the counter, then looks balefully at Mireille. "Are you talking bad about us?" he says.

Mireille shrugs and pooches out her scarlet lips, which is Arabic for no or maybe or I don't know and I don't care. She uses one of her long nails to curl her hair behind one ear.

"You know, we're not all the same," he says, resuming the conversation that they have every day.

"Oh, is that so, macho?"

"Yes."

"Hm."

Sirine hits her bell and waits for Mireille to pick up; when she doesn't, Sirine comes out from behind the counter to bring Han the plate of knaffea herself. Mireille and Victor stop talking and Um-Nadia and the customers look up to see this break in precedent, even the two policemen sitting by the TV, eating fried lentils and onions, and watching reports in Arabic about terrorists from Saudi Arabia.

"Some knaffea, sir?" she says, and when Han looks at her the feeling of it stirs inside her like an ache in her neck and shoulders. She has an impulse to sit and feed him by hand.

"Oh, knaffea," Nathan says longingly.

"And you were invited?" Han asks, laughing.

"Of course he's invited," Sirine says. "Everyone is always invited." Nathan's pale eyes swing over her, luminous and grateful, though he doesn't move toward the food. Han's laugh drifts across Sirine's skin. She stares at the sugar container. Mireille bumps up beside her. "I'm the waitress," she says to Nathan. "Don't be harassing the chef. Anything you want, you ask *me*."

Han turns toward Sirine as if he is trying to ask her something in that roomful of people. Her face goes damp and blood-warm, while in the background she can hear Nathan saying sweetly, wistfully, "I always loved knaffea," as if it were now forbidden to him.

"The thing about knaffea," Um-Nadia says, "it is said to be so delicious that it brings even the wild animals home."

"What wild animals?" Mireille asks.

"Sure," Han says. "All those stories about the animals—the *jemel* and *asfoori* and the *ghazal*—oh, what is that called in English again?"

"Oryx," Nathan says promptly.

"Really? Oryx?" He looks at Nathan. "Well, the *ghazal* is always wandering, looking for his lost love, and they say he has to go away before he can find his way home again."

"Ah-hunh, and now what does that mean?" Mireille clicks her nails along the counter.

"No, think about it," Um-Nadia says and lifts one of her arched eyebrows. "It means things."

"Plus I don't see how knaffea enters into it."

"Why do you always have to be against love?" Victor asks Mireille.

"I'm not against love! How is this about love?"

"Are you kidding? The whole thing's about love," says Um-Nadia. "Ask Sirine—she made the knaffea."

They turn to look at her. Han smiles.

"Yuh," Mireille says, "like Sirine knows about love." Then she looks startled and glances at Sirine. "That didn't come out right."

Sirine backs up, hands wrapped in her apron. She shoves through the swinging door to the back kitchen.

Later, Mireille comes in and apologizes. She makes Sirine a pot of sweet tea and says that Sirine knows a great deal about love, much more than Mireille.

*

On the first Friday in September, they close the café early, Um-Nadia hanging a sign on the café window that says: "All gone to Lon's."

Lon Hayden—who throws this party every fall—used to be a movie actor and played cowhands in a string of small-time Westerns, and then he changed his mind and got a degree in Middle Eastern theater and became the Near Eastern Studies Department chairman. His wife is a casting director for big action movies and makes enough money for them to own a grand house with a grove of bearded palm trees with silver-scaly prehistoric trunks. Lon comes to the café once a week for lamb shank braised in olive oil and garlic.

Sirine's uncle picks her up at work and they drive through Westwood, into the lush compound of Beverly Hills. The air is alive with drifting pollens and the scent of fine, rare rains lifting from the ocean. Lon's house is a low, sprawling arrangement, set back on acres of velvet green lawn behind an electric gate tricked out with surveillance cameras. Sirine's uncle waves at the camera and then jumps when the disembodied voice says, "Come on in." The gate swings open. "Americans," he sighs. They roll along the winding drive until they approach a small army of young men in white uniforms; one trots up to them and says, "Valet park," and Sirine's uncle gets nervous and drops the keys in the grass.

There are movie people and university people and Nadia's Café people milling around in little groups, holding tall glasses. Um-Nadia is wearing her wraparound dress and what she calls her ruby slippers; her black hair is piled high on top of her head. She stands with one hand on her waist, her hip hitched up like a question mark. She waves at Sirine and winks at her uncle, smiling her slow smile, eyes half-closed, lined in electric-blue. Then she lifts her chin and says, "I've got to go talk to people." Mireille is also there, in silvery workout clothes and silver heels, and Victor Hernandez stands beside her with his square jaw and distant gaze, holding both their drinks and a plate of deviled eggs.

The house and its grounds are so vast, partygoers seem to appear out of nowhere, strolling around bends in the lawn; there are murmuring, secluded groups of people lounging in bent twig chairs. The beautiful centerpiece of the grounds is the spotlit pool, which looks like a series of five or six loosely connected lagoons landscaped with fronds and bubbling falls and rock steps. Her uncle mentions that most of Foreign Languages and Near Eastern Studies had been invited—Sirine surreptitiously looks around for Han—but the sun has gone beneath the horizon so everyone is partially hidden now and it's hard to make out faces clearly.

She sits on the edge of a cluster of movie people slouched in lawn chairs who are comparing the foods they're allergic to—wheat, dairy, corn, nuts, coffee, chocolate, yeast, wine, onions, eggs—which turns into a conversation about different diets they've tried—Blood Type, Scarsdale, Grapefruit, D.N.A.—which turns into a conversation about their favorite Chinese herbs, aromatherapies, tinctures, and vitamin supplements. The chatter bores Sirine into a buzzing, pleasant sort of trance. She watches Lon and his three teenage sons carry a battered stereo turntable and walnut-stained amplifiers out of the house, dragging what looks like a two-thousand-foot extension cord behind them. "Lon, no!" his wife cries out, her hands going to her hips.

"I remember when he bought that stereo back in college," one of the actors says, a man who played Lon's sidekick in the cowboy movies. "He still likes to haul it out at parties." Lon's amiable, unembarrassable sons set up the stereo. It looks a bit sad and dilapidated on the velvety lawn, but then one of the sons fits a record onto the turntable, carefully positions the arm, and Middle Eastern violins and flutes swirl and swoosh through the air. "Un-oh," says one of the actresses. "Headache music."

The sidekick smiles. "*Simon Shaheen plays Mohammed Abdul Wahab*—I know Lon's favorites."

Sirine sees Um-Nadia put down her drink, grab the Russian Studies professor, Zinovy Basilevich, and start propelling him around the pool in a shimmying, complicated dance. The big, ginger-mustached professor looks frightened and happy. They pass several groups of people, then one person looks up as they pass: it's Han.

Han doesn't seem to have noticed Sirine. He's standing on the far end of one of the pool-lagoons lit by rose-colored spotlights, dressed in a way that seems deliberately American: loose tan shorts, sandals, a fluid yellow shirt. The party has gotten crowded and there's a press of people all around him—she thinks there is something about him that makes people want to stand close. He smiles as people approach and inclines slightly toward everyone who talks to him, as if he were intrigued, a little bit in love with each of them.

She moves toward a small grove of potted palms near the drinks table, heart thumping as if she were being chased. Some graduate students approach Han but he keeps looking around. He walks along the side of the pool, scanning the party, students trailing. The surface of the pool looks waxy, the water bending and flexing. It throws reflections over Han's face and the palm fronds blur before Sirine's eyes. Her throat feels tight, the ground wavy beneath her feet. "Stay away from him," she murmurs to herself.

"Absolutely," Mireille says in her right ear. Sirine jumps. "Look at that—he's so in love with himself he should get a room!"

Sirine glances at her but Mireille is looking in the other direction, halfway up the sloping lawn, where Aziz is sprawled in a lounge chair. Sirine can see the rounded rise of his stomach in a pale silk shirt, his outstretched legs crossed at the ankles, his expression smooth and mild, and his eyes shadowed with thick straight lashes. He's flanked by female students, each of them watching him with adoring faces. He holds one hand up in the air, turns it this way and that, as if he were examining a delicate vase, and all the students watch as if they too could see the vase.

"Oh, that is trouble on a lawn chair," Mireille says knowingly.

"You think?" Sirine asks. "He seems sort of . . . innocent."

Mireille clinks the ice in her glass. "Well, of course—that's you talking."

Now Um-Nadia's laughter chimes up from the poolside. She stands between the Russian professor and a graduate student in ethnomusicology, one hand on each of their chests, as if to stop them from fighting over her. Then she drops her hands and gestures to Sirine's uncle with twirling, swimming motions. He shakes his head and remains in his chair but holds up a glass, toasting her.

"Are you done with these people?" Mireille says. "Let's get out of here, the jungle drums are starting."

Sirine is tired and she feels too shy to stay alone at the party. She starts to follow Mireille, but just as she begins walking, a skinny, loose-jointed young man comes over the hill toward her. "Sirine," he calls out. "Sirine, Sirine!" It's Li Pin Chu, a new engineering student who teaches Taiwanese, one of the many students from overseas who gravitate to Sirine's uncle. He is also deeply enamored of Sirine's cooking.

"Oh, great, now this guy," Mireille mutters. "You're on your own, my dear, I'm done," she says, then fluffs her starchy yellow hair and stalks off.

"Sirine! Here I am. You know the expression: 'From brightest sky—lightning,' " Li Pin says, holding out his arms as if to fold her in an embrace.

"Yes," she says, nodding. "I'm sure that's true."

"Where is your bathing costume?" He has come into the party wearing a terry cloth shirt, geranium-red swim trunks, and flip-flops. He pulls off the shirt. "Ready for swim!" he announces. "What about you?"

Sirine looks down at her jeans and blouse, touches her collar. "Um," she says. "The thing is . . ."

He looks around then, finally noticing that everyone came fully clothed and that no one is actually swimming. "Uh-oh," he says. "This keep happening to me."

A few of the guests standing nearby glance at him. Sirine bites her lip: the invitations—hand-written and xeroxed—simply said, *pool party*. She tells Li Pin she'll be right back and walks out into the maze of valet parking. She finds their car, grabs the old swimsuit she keeps in the trunk, and then scoots down in the back seat and pulls it on. When she comes back to the pool, she sees that there's a lemon-colored shirt tossed on a bush and Han is already in the water, his tan dress shorts flaring out around his legs. He and Li Pin Chu are gamely trying to give each other pointers on how to swim. "I think you lay down with your face in the water," Han is saying.

Sirine watches them for a moment from the slope above the pool, her thoughts hushed and her breathing slow, a sense of something like gratitude rinsing over her. She dives in from the edge of the pool and surfaces near Han. She doesn't feel as shy in the water. It swells around them, and pulls them off their feet. "Sea nymph," Han says.

Li Pin fashions a sort of backstroke by falling backward into the water and propelling himself with just his arms. They watch him do this across the length of the pool, over and over. It's a warm night and there seems to be almost no difference between the temperature of the night air and that of the water. It seems as if the three of them are living in a place completely separate from the party that drifts above them, just a few feet away. The sky has gone entirely dark now; it floats star-smeared over the span of hills all around. They drift on their backs and close their eyes and talk about childhood games, then toys, then the foods of their past. Li Pin Chu tells them that if he could eat one dish every day for the rest of his life it would be sliced pork and egg in palm sugar. Han says he would enjoy some chicken stewed in onion yogurt sauce. Sirine thinks she might like some reheated spaghetti and meatballs—a breakfast that her mother used to make from the previous night's dinner. The water laps over her ears and fills her head with a faint roar; there's a high clear scent of chlorine. She has no idea how long they stay in the water; her fingertips wrinkle but she doesn't get cold. She's comfortable and sleepy and Han and Li Pin feel like people she's known for a very long time. Finally, Li Pin floats over to shake their hands and say goodbye, as if they were the hosts. He climbs out and Sirine and Han hold themselves motionless for a moment, watching the water settle to a molten glow, brimming like mercury with the half-moon light.

Han sighs, then turns and dives under the water. His back crests, then disappears as he moves silently across the pool.

"Look!" Li Pin says, standing on the rock ledge beside the pool, his face lit up as if he were watching something miraculous. "He does know swimming!" Han surfaces at the far edge and waves at them. "Well, what do you know about that," Li Pin marvels. "He is filled with invisible writing."

Sirine waves to Li Pin, then dips back under as well; she notices then that the pool is lit up with small amber lights embedded in its curving floor, so the pool water looks huge and empty. She thinks of night swims in the bottomless ocean when she was a girl and the thrilling cold of the Pacific. But this water is heated, as warm as a mouth. She and Han dive and redive, swimming beneath the surface as if exploring the rooms inside a bright silent house. Sirine's hair twirls and soars over her head. At one point, as they swim around each other, their hands and legs brush and they burst to the surface, gulping air.

"So you do swim," Sirine says.

Han looks pleased. "Perhaps a bit."

"How did you learn?"

He is quiet for a moment, submerged to the shoulders; the rippling pool lights play over his face and neck. "Isn't everyone sort of born swimming? I think it's probably something you either remember or you let yourself forget."

Sirine sinks back into the water. "You mean like riding a bicycle?"

"Essentially," he says and dunks his head for a moment, then comes back up and laughs and says, "I mean, if you were born riding a bicycle."

They drift into one of the quiet bends in the pool that's just a few yards from where her uncle is sitting. He's telling stories to a small group of academics, some of whom look drowsy. Others look confused and bored as they scout around for new party arrivals. "I don't understand," Fred Perlman from the History Department is saying. "This is a true story? Or it isn't?"

"No, that's the gorgeousness of it!" says a dark-eyed woman in a leather dress. "It's just like acting in commercials—you just have to give yourself to it, let yourself be it, and it all comes true."

Sirine's uncle nods and points at the leather-dress woman, then rocks back in the lounge chair, searching for his cup of black coffee. "You see? Now she understands everything." He tries to prop the coffee back up in the grass. "Now, where were we? Ah yes, Abdelrahman Salahadin is consulting with a seahorse...."

Sirine is so warm she doesn't want to leave the water, so she sits on a shallow lip inside the pool to let her legs float. Han props himself up across from her and his head tilts back. She can't make out his expression in the darkness: he seems elusive and far away and yet also quite aware of her. She's exhausted from the heat and the swimming and feels she could fall asleep in the warm water.

He moves to her side. "Look there." Han points to the sky. "An Arab crescent."

She looks at the paper-fine moon. "Why do you call it that?"

"It reminds me of the moon from back home." He looks at her. "It's a good omen." He rests his head against the lip of the pool. They listen to her uncle's story for a while. "Abdelrahman Salahadin," Han murmurs.

"What?"

He raises his head slightly and his eyes are black and shining and still. "Your uncle's story. It's so familiar."

"You've heard it before?"

He doesn't move his head. "Just the feeling of it." He seems to be smiling faintly. "In Iraq, everyone tells jokes and fables. It's too difficult to say anything directly."

They listen as her uncle describes the ways of mermaids. Sirine smoothes her hair back with a wet hand. Her hair feels thick and stiff with chlorine. "You mean like fables are secret codes?"

"In America, you say 'secret code,' but in Iraq, that's just the way things are. Everything's sort of folded up and layered, just a bit more complicated. Here it's all right out there, right on the surfaces. Everyone's telling you exactly how they feel all the time and what they're thinking. Trying to pin everything down."

"Is that bad?"

Han swirls his legs through the glossy water and Sirine feels little underwater eddies along her legs. The soles of her feet are flexed, her legs gently switching back and forth in the water. "Oh no, not bad. It's just different," he says. "Like, here you only need to know one language, but in lots of other places you need extras. I've gotten used to saying several things at once. Just in case any secret police came around."

"So stories about, like, fish are actually about—"

"Could be anything. Maybe about war or birth. Maybe it's a way to talk about a journey, or to reflect on love."

Her laughter bubbles up nervously. She slips below the surface for a moment and opens her eyes. She can see his body, his flickering legs, the angle of his chest rising up to the surface of the water. She's so warm, the water sizzling in little bubbles all over her skin.

*

That night after the party, just before she heads upstairs to bed, her uncle stops her in the entryway. "So?" he says; there are grass stains on his pants and his voice is light and muzzy from too much wine and coffee. "What you think?"

"Of?" She crosses her arms and leans against the stairs' curved railing.

He raises his eyebrows. "You know. *Him*."

Sirine smiles and looks away, but she closes her eyes for a moment. "Oh. I don't know. Of course, he's very sweet. And not bad-looking."

"Sweet . . . doesn't that mean strange and stupid in girl-language?"

"But there's also something complicated about him—it makes me . . ." She wobbles her hand.

"Complicated?" He scratches the stubble starting along his jaw and looks contemplative. "Well, but he's an exile—they're all messed up inside. But I thought girls are supposed to love that."

"What do you mean, 'exile'? Because he left Iraq?"

"Because he can't go back. Because anything you can't have you want twice as much. Because he needs someone to show him how to live in this country and how to let go of the other."

"Lovely. A project." She gives him a little air-punch on the shoulder, but she thinks about this all the way up the stairs. Han seems to have some sort of internal light that makes him intriguing and, at the same time, a little bit hard for her to look at directly: he's so charming and educated and worldly. But it's more than that. Most Arab men have always been eminently polite to her, filled with an Old World propriety, so formal, they seem almost not to see her but to see an outline captioned: *Woman*. Han, she's noticed, looks at her. Even though they barely know each other, she already has the clear, uncanny sense that when he looks, he sees her.

When Sirine goes to bed that night she still feels the buoyancy of the pool water beneath her arms and legs. She lies in bed, floating. As she falls asleep, the sensation of floating mingles with a dream of Han swimming deep below the water. She's swimming near the surface and she can't find him but she knows he's down in the dark depths beneath her, swimming in endless circles.

CHAPTER FOUR

Okay, now it's a typical day in the little port city of Aqaba. Abdelrahman Salahadin has evaded the latest slaver by faking his drowning and swimming to shore. He lies low for a few weeks, and when he thinks the coast is clear, once again he makes his way through the reed-split sands, this time on his way back to market. His feet are sinewy, his soles soft as hands from walking over beaches. No one can tell him who he is. He is Abdelrahman Salahadin, son of a freed Nubian and a burdened Iraqi Bedouin.

Slavery has been outlawed in most Arab countries for years now. But there are villages in Jordan made up entirely of the descendants of runaway Saudi slaves. Abdelrahman knows he might be free, but he's still an Arab. No one ever wants to be the Arab—it's too old and too tragic and too mysterious and too exasperating and too lonely for anyone but an actual Arab to put up with for very long. Essentially, it's an image problem. Ask anyone, Persians, Turks, even Lebanese and Egyptians—none of them want to be the Arab. They say things like, well, really we're Indo-Russian-Asian-European-Chaldeans. So in the end, the only one who gets to be the Arab is the same little old Bedouin with his goats and his sheep and his poetry about his goats and his sheep, because he doesn't know that he's the Arab, and what he doesn't know won't hurt him.

Anyway, Abdelrahman's eyes have the hard, lacquer shine of beetles, and when he laughs people stop their conversations. Now he steps into the dusty clearing of the marketplace and proclaims himself for sale, and everyone looks up.

"Fifty dinars," he shouts, "for this hair, these eyes, the sweat of my shoulders, the width of my chest, fifty dinars to claim me!"

Years ago, Abdelrahman found his wife in bed with another man, and he knew in a flash he'd been right all along: he recalled the dark time before his discovery of the truth, the many nights that she'd whispered he was mad, smiled into his eyes, and convinced him that he was crazy; he'd realized that it is as easy to be mad as to be sane. He left their home vowing never to be betrayed again.

Abdelrahman Salahadin proclaims himself for sale in the market as is his habit. The customer who approaches him now is short of stature with eyes soft as gloves; he is wrapped up in face, headdress, and full robes white as a bird's breast. His voice is pure refinement. "Hello, slave," he says. He looks him over, circles him three times, checks his joints, and inspects the whites of his eyes. Finally he says, "Yes, yes, fine. I'd like to buy you. Pick up your things and let's go."

"My price is fifty dinars," says Abdelrahman.

"I will pay you one hundred," says the covered man.

"I will meet you tomorrow morning at such-and-such hiding place among the reeds at the lip of the Red Sea," says Abdelrahman Salahadin.

"No," whispers the hidden man, whose voice filters through his wrappings like the sound of nostalgia and lost love, and from whose person seems to emanate scents of eucalyptus, cypress, and the Tigris River. "You must come with me now. I am apt to lose all interest by tomorrow morning." With that, he drapes a filament of gold thread around Abdelrahman's wrist and leads him away.

*

Sirine learned about food from her parents. Even though her mother was American, her father always said his wife thought about food like an Arab. Sirine's mother strained the salted yogurt through cheesecloth to make creamy labneh, stirred the onion and lentils together in a heavy iron pan to make mjeddrah, and studded joints of lamb with fat cloves of garlic to make roasted kharuf. Sirine's earliest memory was of sitting on a phone book on a kitchen chair, the sour-tart smell of pickled grape leaves in the air. Her mother spread the leaves flat on the table like little floating hands, placed the spoonful of rice and meat at the center of each one, and Sirine with her tiny fingers rolled the leaves up tighter and neater than anyone else could—tender, garlicky, meaty packages that burst in the mouth.

The smell of the food cooking always brought her father into the kitchen. It was a magic spell that could conjure him from the next room, the basement, the garage. No matter where he was, he would appear, smiling and hungry. And if it was one of his important favorites—stuffed grape leaves, mjeddrah, or roast leg of lamb—he would appear in the kitchen even before the meal was done cooking. When she was a little girl, Sirine thought that this was why her mother cooked—to keep her husband close to her, attached to a delicate golden thread of scent.

Sirine's parents died when she was nine. They were emergency care personnel for the American Red Cross, killed in a clash between tribes while on assignment in Africa. On the day she learned of their deaths, Sirine went into the kitchen and made an entire tray of stuffed grape leaves all by herself. Then she and her uncle ate them all week, sitting at the kitchen table. Sirine sat on a telephone book propped on her chair, legs swinging, eating and watching the back door.

Years later, when Um-Nadia first hired Sirine, Um-Nadia said that she had several dreams in which she and Sirine's mother discussed Sirine's career and that Sirine's mother had said, yes: Sirine is a chef, through and through. "So I've checked your references," Um-Nadia said. Then she also read Sirine's coffee grounds and said she could see the signs written in the black coffee traces along the milky porcelain: sharp knife, quick hands, white apron, and the sadness of a chef. "Chefs know—nothing lasts," she told Sirine. "In the mouth, then gone."

Sirine goes to bed so early sometimes there's still a gray scrim of light in the sky, then she rises before morning light. Um-Nadia says that great food needs darkness. It requires letting the dough inhale the very early morning and letting the kabobs drink up wine and garlic all night long, and—on occasion—it requires stuffing the small birds, squabs, pigeons, and other sweet, wild game under the round moon, "when they have let go of their songs," Um-Nadia says. Sirine dreams of cooking and wakes to thoughts of cooking—even when she can't stand the old smells of rancid butter and oils hanging in her hair. She still wakes too early, to grind and salt the lamb by hand, to fan the parsley over the chopping block.

Her uncle's dog King Babar walks through the sleepless predawn with her; the air is thick and humid. He sits on her bare feet as she prepares some marinades to take in to work and he gazes after her, eyes melting with an expression of unutterable love, as she leaves for work, as if it is all too much, too much, for one poor, ungroomed, mutty terrier to bear.

*

On Saturday morning Sirine feels exhausted; her throat and lips burn as if she's been eating raw sugar. Mireille and Um-Nadia and Victor Hernandez and Cristobal the cleaning man and the early-breakfast students feel it too. Several of them look like they've walked straight from last night's party to work. The police officers are cradling their heads in their hands. Um-Nadia's hair is still up in her frothy bun and her blue eye shadow has drifted above her eyebrows. "Now, there was a party," she says. "I *love* lime rickeys."

The door jingles and Han's student Nathan appears. Um-Nadia turns slowly, holding her temples, to see who's come in. "The American's here," she says.

Nathan comes to the counter and sits across from where Sirine is working. He pushes the napkin to one side and puts his camera on the counter. His skin looks a bit raw, hard-scrubbed. The disks of his eyes are a lush bluish gray, and when he looks at her, Sirine feels something there heavy as velvet curtains, something that he holds back with one arm.

"You can have tea," Um-Nadia says to Nathan, putting down a steaming glass with a spoon in it. "Perhaps someone will eventually make coffee."

"Um-Nadia," Nathan says. He frowns slightly and looks her hair and face over. "You look different today."

She lifts her chin and pats carefully at her bun. "I'm a believer in being different. It makes you younger and younger."

Mireille comes out with a plate of hummus and bread. "Very soon you will be ageless," she says.

Um-Nadia raises her eyebrows. "She thinks I don't know what that means. But I know what everything means!" She takes the hummus from Mireille and puts it in front of Nathan. "Eat," she says. "You look like an Ethiopian." Then she sits beside the police officers to watch her Bedouin soap opera and pointedly turns her back to Nathan.

"I don't think that's p.c.," one of the officers says to her.

"What isn't?" Um-Nadia says. "Ethiopians?"

Nathan moves the plate a quarter-turn. The caps of his shoulders are peaked and bony and look a bit like wings when he raises them. Sirine brings him some fresh pita bread. "Watch the steam when you tear it," she says.

"Thank you for the knaffea—you know—the other day," he murmurs.

"I didn't think you ate any of it."

"I don't really like food much," he says, eyes lowered.

"Mm." She goes behind the counter, then leans over it and pours a little olive oil from a small jug over the top of the hummus; the oil is velvety and green. "Try it like this," she says.

But he shakes his head mournfully. He's so thin everything about him seems pinched and crimped. "Has Han come in yet?"

She wipes her hands on her apron. "Was he going to come by?"

He smiles and raises one eyebrow. She quickly turns away, busying herself with wiping. "What?" he asks. "What'd I say?"

"Just the way you're looking at me."

"Looking?"

Sirine stares at her towel. "I don't know. Like you're taking a picture."

Nathan laughs. He picks up his hot tea, then puts it back down. "I can't help it—when I see a wonderful subject."

She touches her hair, tied back for work in a messy braid. Then she tucks in her towel and starts to look for a pan. "I look terrible in pictures."

"Not at all. You'd photograph beautifully." He tilts his head and turns one hand in the air. "There's something about you that stops the eye. It's a rare quality. People look at you and forget about things." He looks down, face red.

"Is that good?" She unhooks one of the pans from the ceiling rack and slides it onto the range. A crazy-quilt pattern of light slides over the walls, reflected from the glass door, customers coming in and out. "That doesn't necessarily sound good," she says.

"Who cares about good? Good is like nice, pleasant, normal." He frowns. "But it's not just that, it's more than the way you look. Good is . . . blah. You're this—other thing—all complicated."

"I'm boring."

"You're not," he says firmly.

She looks at him. She has the strangest feeling—like a tickling of déjà vu or a premonition—that he wants to tell her something. She looks away from him and starts scraping chopped tomatoes into the pan with a wooden spoon. "To be honest, sometimes I think no one can see me at all."

The door jingles again, more tiny stars thrown through the room. Nathan sits up. "Maybe I should be getting to class." Some other students come in and Nathan looks them over, then settles back down. He stirs a stream of sugar from the container into his coffee. "I registered late for school and Han's class was already full when I showed up, but I talked my way in. Now he says he counts on me being there to say interesting things in class." He smirks and says, "I'm not sure how he meant that."

Sirine pushes back more wisps of hair. "I bet you're a great student."

Nathan glances at her. "No. Han's a great professor. I've never studied with anyone like him before. The kind of teacher you always hope you'll find but doesn't actually exist. Only he does, there he is. You get the feeling when you listen to his lectures that he's taking you apart, piece by piece. All the things you thought you knew have to be relearned. You find out you have to learn a new way of knowing things. You listen with your whole body, not just your head, and you see that he teaches the same way, with his whole being. He teaches Islamic history and Arabic literature but he also teaches about life and art and faith and love. . . . I mean, if you know how to listen for it."

"Which I'm sure you do."

"Of course, I've got an advantage—I'm a little older than the others and I've been out of school for a while, working—out in the world."

"Really?"

He leans forward on his elbows. "You know, I moved here specially to study with him, when I heard he was coming to teach here. I don't know why he lets me hang around him—I think he feels sorry for me."

"Oh, no." She knocks her spoon clean on the side of the pan and puts it down, leans her forearms on the counter. "That doesn't seem like Han's style. He probably just likes you."

Nathan drops his head as if he can't quite meet her expression, rubs the heel of his palm over his eyes, smiles as if laughing at himself. "Hard to imagine."

"So you knew all about his work, then? Is he also famous like Aziz?"

"Aziz!" He waves the thought away. "No, it's just—I've been following Han's career for some time now. I look for his work in the scholarly journals, his articles on Arabic literature and translation, all that sort of thing. I've got a personal interest."

"Personal how?"

He tears off a little piece of bread, holds it just over the hummus without actually dipping it in. "We've known people in common." He looks down at the hummus then and shrugs. And besides—I mean, apart from the personal stuff—I just think he's brilliant."

A restaurant reviewer for the *L.A. Times* once described Sirine's cooking as brilliant; she remembers the suffused glow of satisfaction she felt, looking at that single word. "Do you think he's some kind of genius or something?"

"Oh, well—a genius? That's a funny word. Maybe a sort of genius." Nathan swirls his glass of tea. "I guess I have a few ideas about him."

"Han?" She feels both intrigued and nervous, not quite sure she wants to hear these things. She starts splitting open heads of garlic and picking at the papery skin covering the cloves. "How about—tell me something about yourself instead?"

He opens his mouth, then says, "Oh. Really, I'd rather not do that." He slides a cigarette out of a packet and plays with it nervously, puts it in his mouth unlit—Um-Nadia allows smoking only between three and six-thirty in the afternoon. "I'm mean, there's just nothing interesting to tell about me."

"What do you mean?" She peels another clove. "You're a photographer and everything. You're very interesting."

"No, really, I'm not anything. An overgrown student in search of a life, maybe."

She laughs, a soft exhalation. She shakes her head and flattens the cloves under the side of her knife.

"I used to be . . . better, let's say. A long time ago. But now—sometimes it's like I can hardly sit in this chair, I can hardly walk on the ground. I'm made out of powder. . . ." He looks at her quickly, as if frightened of what he'd just let slip. "Damn. Does everyone do this? Come right up to you and start saying unbelievably weird things?"

She laughs again and says, "Oh, now . . ." But it's true. She's used to men's attentions, their desire to impress her or just keep her listening—a quiet, captive audience behind a counter and a chopping block.

"Anyway—I take comfort thinking it's not just me," he says. "Lots of people are like that." He puts the cigarette in his mouth, takes it back out. "Like powder. Just sort of . . ." He waves one hand around. "I can see right through some people. There's so little there. That's why my photography is what it is. I've got this kind of X-ray vision. And then there's people like you and Han. There's more to you. Layers, surprises. And Han, well . . ." He trails off.

"What?"

"No." He laughs.

She looks at him sideways, wondering what he's thinking. She bites her top lip a little.

"Well . . ." He lowers his voice confidentially and leans forward. "Okay. Have you heard of oryxes?" He takes out a plastic lighter and lights his cigarette. His hands are stained and a little shaky. "Black and white, with long, straight, spiral-carved horns. They're supposed to be something like the inspiration for unicorns. I don't know if that's true, that's just something I heard. And somehow, when I met Han that was the first thing I thought of—the oryx. I don't know why—I don't think they even live in Iraq. Some people say they're gazelles or antelopes, but they're really a different species, larger and rougher. Gorgeous. And they've been just about hunted away to nothing. They're different from all the other animals. At one point I really wanted to photograph them but I never got the chance." He looks at her so closely she feels he is drawing something hidden right up out of her skin. "I always wanted to see one, just to know they existed. I always thought, if I could get a photo of an oryx, I'd have some kind of proof."

Sirine says, "Proof of what?"

He grins, blowing out smoke, and shrugs and says, "I'm not sure yet. Just proof!"

Just then the door to the back kitchen swings open and Um-Nadia comes out and snicks the cigarette from Nathan's hands like swatting a fly. She shakes a finger at him and says, "No smoking till three o'clock!"

When he packs up his books and leaves in a huff, Sirine looks down at the plate of hummus—all the oil looks like it's been licked from the top.

CHAPTER FIVE

Bear in mind, of course, that this is a form of love story in disguise. And who does love stories better than the Bedu anyway? Remember that Bedouin love poem in which the Bedouin is so in love that he says that his he-camel is in love with her she-camel? A classic.

The latest purchaser of Abdelrahman Salahadin—the Covered Man—moves with the charm of birdsong; Abdelrahman watches his slight gestures as they walk together through the crowded souk and he becomes entangled in his own thoughts and snaggled in his emotions. He suspects the man is a jinn of some sort, come to steal him from the water—which is exactly what his mother always told him would happen. He believes that this man has looped a bit of the thread-leash through a corner of his soul.

The streets of Aqaba are shell spirals and, on summer nights, crowded and complicated as a woman's heart. Boys sit on the curbs and wonder about love, women run their hands through their hair, locks dense with sea salt, men unfurl velvet prayer rugs, hands on their knees, they bow, rise, rock into the sea-waves of prayer.

The Covered Man leads Abdelrahman Salahadin to a new harbor at the end of the busiest street, sand-frayed and tangled in reeds, shell, and glass. The complicated waves wind and unwind, surf breaking into backwash, an endless dispute. The Covered Man leads Abdelrahman toward a boat in the harbor, an ancient felucca like the Portuguese used to sail, with an elongated, swannish neck and tapering sides curved like lips. It rocks boldly among the other boats, which creak and thump against its sides. They must leap from deck to deck in order to reach the felucca; it tilts as Abdelrahman steps aboard, then as he shifts it rights itself primly.

For the first time in his life, Abdelrahman looks for the oars, to conduct himself as a proper slave should. But the Covered Man says, no, please sit. He takes up the sweep oar in the aft of the boat and, snapping the gold thread which binds them together, they set off.

*

Nadia's Café is set in an old converted house with three main rooms: the small front dining area crowded with too many tables and a row of swivel seats along a chrome-lined counter; behind the counter, where there's a silver-hooded grill and a workstation with a counter to chop at and a window over the sink; and, through a swinging door, the back kitchen, full of shelves, cupboards, a giant refrigerator, and a linoleum-topped table with wobbly pipe-metal legs and five vinyl-cracked chairs. The walls in the front of the café are covered with strips of yellowing newspaper reviews that say things like, "Aladdin's hidden treasure!" and "The Middle East in Westwood." And there is even a framed and signed glossy photograph of Casey Kasem, who once stopped by the café to eat and proclaimed that they made the best mjeddrah in town.

The back kitchen is Sirine's retreat, her favorite place to sit at a table chopping carrots and thinking her thoughts. She can look out the window at the back courtyard and feel like she's a child again, working at her mother's table. Mondays are for baklava, which she learned to make by watching her parents. Her mother said that a baklava-maker should have sensitive, supple hands, so she was in charge of opening and unpeeling the paper-thin layers of dough and placing them in a stack in the tray. Her father was in charge of pastry-brushing each layer of dough with a coat of drawn butter. It was systematic yet graceful: her mother carefully unpeeling each layer and placing them in the tray where Sirine's father painted them.

It was important to move quickly so that the unbuttered layers didn't dry out and start to fall apart. This was one of the ways that Sirine learned how her parents loved each other—their concerted movements like a dance; they swam together through the round arcs of her mother's arms and her father's tender strokes. Sirine was proud when they let her paint a layer, prouder when she was able to pick up one of the translucent sheets and transport it to the tray—light as raw silk, fragile as a veil.

On Tuesday morning, however, Sirine has overslept. She's late to work and won't have enough time to finish preparing the baklava before starting breakfast. She could skip a day of the desserts and serve the customers ice cream and figs or coconut cookies and butter cake from the Iranian Shusha Bakery two doors down. But the baklava is important—it cheers the students up. They close their eyes when they bite into its crackling layers, all lightness and scent of orange blossoms.

And Sirine feels unsettled when she tries to begin breakfast without preparing the baklava first; she can't find her place in things. So finally she shoves the breakfast ingredients aside and pulls out the baklava tray with no idea of how she'll find the time to finish it, just thinking: sugar, cinnamon, chopped walnuts, clarified butter, filo dough. . . . She's working in the greenish morning light, concentrating so she doesn't notice the tapping at the back door, doesn't even hear it until the door cracks open, a voice saying, "Sirine?"

There's a mist of dust and flour in the light from the open doorway and someone is standing there, backlit. "Oh!" Sirine straightens up.

"Is this okay? I took a chance that you'd be here early," he says, stepping in. And the light softens and turns and she sees it's Han. "I just thought I'd—I mean—I just wanted to say hi." He looks at the counter piled up with filo dough. "I'm sorry. I've barged in at a bad time, haven't I?"

Sirine is looking at his fingers. Remembers the brush of them underwater.

"What?"

She smiles.

There's time for baklava if they make it together.

She hunts in the big drawer for another apron, shows him where to stand, how to pick up the sheet of filo dough from its edge, the careful, precise unpeeling, the quick movement from the folded sheets to the tray, and finally, the positioning on top of the tray. He watches everything closely, asks no questions, and then aligns the next pastry sheet perfectly. She paints the dough with clarified butter. And while Sirine has never known how to dance, always stiffening and trying to lead while her partner murmurs relax, relax—and while there are very few people who know how to cook and move with her in the kitchen—it seems that she and Han know how to make baklava together. She's startled to find that she seems to feel his presence in her shoulders, running through her arms and wrists, into her hands. Her senses feel bunched together like fingers around a bouquet, her skin sensitive to the touch. She feels light-headed. She watches the fluid movement in his legs, arms, and neck, the dark fringe of his eyes. He transports the sheets and she sweeps the pastry brush, losing herself in the rocking movement. She takes in the powerful curve of his neck and shoulders; his skin is silkily brown. There's just a touch of insomnia in his eyes, an inward, solitary air.

He says, "This reminds me."

"It reminds you? Of what?"

He nods. "The kitchen. I never much wanted to be up in my father's orchard. I liked this. I liked the kitchen. The table. Stove. Where the women were always telling stories. My mother and my aunts and the neighbors and—my sister." He smoothes another sheet.

Sirine butters it, then pours a thick filling of ground walnuts, sugar, and spices over the layers. She strokes her palm over the top to level it. "My mother too," she murmurs. "Well, it was usually just her and me. She talked to me while we worked. Told me stuff."

Han glances at her. "Like what sort of stuff?"

She smiles and shrugs, a little shy. "Oh, silly things, like whether you pour hot syrup over cold baklava or cold syrup over hot."

"That's quite serious, that's metaphysical."

She considers this, surprised by the memories that start to come to her—the way her mother's small lessons felt like larger secrets when Sirine was a girl: how instructions in the fine dicing of walnuts and the way to clarify butter were also meditations on hope and devotion. "Yes," she says, a soft, dawning recognition in her voice. "I think so too."

"Oh, definitely. My mother told me that if I knew how to make good baklava I would be irresistible to any woman," he says.

"Ah, so she taught you how to make baklava," Sirine observes.

"No. So she refused to teach me."

Sirine laughs. "But somehow you learned how to make it anyway. Lucky for me."

"Actually, I'm learning how right this second."

Another layer. Butter. She glances at him, then back at the baklava. "You miss it?"

He looks up. "I miss . . . ? The kitchen? My home?" He accidentally tears a corner of a sheet of dough—it's starting to get dry. " 'I miss my mother's coffee / I miss my mother's bread.' "

Sirine raises her eyebrows.

"It's a poem. Not mine." He grimaces, trying to reattach the dough. "No, I miss everything, Sirine. Absolutely everything."

"Tell me something you miss," Sirine says, stroking the butter over the dough. "I mean, specifically."

"Mm, specifically." He peels another pastry sheet. "All right. Here's one—we had a well on our property. It was lined with big, crackling palm trees all around. All the Bedouin used to use it. I would stand in line with them holding two big metal pails and they would bring up the water using an old-fashioned crank and spill the fresh water from the bucket into my pails. And I would drink a cup of the water as soon as it spilled out of the earth—it was so cold it would make my ears ring. And it tasted like—I don't know, it was so good—it tasted like rocks and wind and pure . . . pure *coldness*."

Sirine patches the cracking layer with more butter. She can just about taste the cold sweetness of that water—as if she had tasted it before and knows how good it is—and she feels a wild rush of desire to drink some right there and then. "I can imagine it," she says. "I can imagine just how that would taste."

He carefully lays another pastry sheet down, tugging on the ends to straighten the wrinkles. "There was an old Bedouin who guarded the well for us. He was thin-boned, with glossy hair and liquid eyes—like so many of the desert Bedu—part hawk and part man. His name was Abu-Najmeh, he had a little yellow dog we called Zibdeh, and Abu-Najmeh used to sleep sitting up beside the well with his rifle in his arms and his dog at his feet." Han smiles. "I haven't thought of him in years. He would aim at anyone who he thought was trying to steal the water. Including me and my sister.

But he didn't shoot too often. He used to say, 'There is no greater gold than water, thanks be to Allah.' "

Sirine smiles. She patches another cracked layer, dabbing at it with her pastry brush.

"Once, when he was walking through town, he found two children's bicycles in the trash heap behind one of the big hotels. Just thrown away. Maybe some diplomat got them for his kids while they were visiting and didn't want to bother shipping them home when they returned. Anyway, Abu-Najmeh, who had never even seen or heard of a bicycle in his entire life, somehow took one look at those things and understood exactly the principle behind them. He gave one to me and one to my friend Sami and helped us learn how to ride by running alongside the bikes. Sixty-six years old, his sword bouncing in his belt, his rifle on his back, his head scarf flying, and a handlebar in each hand."

Sirine laughs and pulls a pastry sheet off center, tearing it. She tries to pull it back into place, bites her lower lip. "Do you think you'll go back?"

His back stiffens. "I can't go back," he says. "To Iraq? No."

She tilts the bowl of butter. "Why not?"

"Not the way things are now, of course. It's very dangerous—it was terribly difficult for me to get out of the country in the first place." He tries to patch the last broken layer of dough together. "But even so, it's like there's some part of me that can't quite grasp the thought of never returning. I have to keep reminding myself. It's so hard to imagine. So I just tell myself: not yet."

"How terrible," she says. What Han says reminds her of a sense that she's had—about both knowing and not-knowing something. She often has the feeling of missing something and not quite understanding what it is that she's missing. At the same time, she's not sure what Han means about the dangers or why it was so difficult to leave—but she also feels embarrassed to ask him and reveal her ignorance. She doesn't follow the news and now she feels ashamed that she's taken so little interest in her father's home country. Distracted, she lowers the brush and accidentally swipes his fingers with butter. She blushes and quickly wipes his hand off with her apron. "Oh, I'm so sorry," she says.

His hand is warm and his fingers fumble through hers. "You may butter my fingers anytime," he says, then coughs and looks abashed. The kitchen door swings open and Um-Nadia walks in. She stops in her tracks when she sees them, her eyes wide, the mascaraed lashes like spikes, a brilliant smile opening on her face.

*

After Han leaves, Sirine goes out to the front kitchen. She is prepping for the lunch rush when Victor pushes through the door from the back kitchen with his mop.

"Hi, Chef," he says and swipes the mop around for a few minutes. Then he says: "So—making baklava with Han?"

She lowers her spoon, looks at him. "Nosy."

He grins, head down toward the mopping.

"By the way," he says, mopping around her, "I like your rose."

She frowns then looks into the back kitchen and notices a slip of paper partially tucked beneath the cutting board. University stationery. In one corner there's a funny little drawing of an arcing, winged fish, and beneath this, a phone number and an address. She unfolds it. "Sirine. I am a very bad cook. But I am a good student. Would you be willing to join me for a dinner tomorrow night? Very truly yours, Hanif." Beside the note is a radish carved into the shape of a blossom.

CHAPTER SIX

Sirine comes downstairs late in the evening and finds her uncle eating a big plate of leftover falafels. "Do you know how much fat is in that?" she says. "What about some nice yogurt labneh and cucumbers?"

Her uncle looks at her thoughtfully and puts down half a falafel. "So we are on chapter . . . what, now? Three? Seven?"

She sighs.

"And are there any more cookies left?"

*

Once they are clear of the other boats, the Covered Man sets the sails and they billow with the blue winds. In the twinkling of an eye, it seems, they are at the heart of the Red Sea. Abdelrahman hears the summons of the seahorses, the longing manta rays, the cry of mermaids, mermen. The whole mer-world chants: *Abdelrahman Salahadin! Where are you?*

Invoking his willpower, he shuts his eyes, then stands. But he begins to tremble and he sits down. He has waited too long, he thinks, the sea will drag him away. But then again, what will happen if he stays with this jinn? He stands again but his trembling gets worse, so again he sits.

He does this up and down for a while as the water gets

choppier and the boat seems to get smaller. It just so happens that he's up when the Covered Man sits back and pours them both cups of coffee. Then he begins to speak.

"I am from the Beni-Sakr Tribe. You can tell from the style of my wrappings that I am from a desert people. What you may not know is that the Bedouins were once water people, that where there are dunes there were once sapphire waves."

"So that is why you are such an expert sailor!" Abdelrahman marvels, eyeing the long intricate white wrappings that cover the man's head and face and the red sash at his middle. Then Abdelrahman notices he's standing and quickly sits.

The Covered Man sighs again as if wondering if it is possible for any one creature to truly understand another. He says, "No, unfortunately neither I nor any of my tribesmen remember the sea. It's a forgotten language. But this story begins with the sea, not long after the day of my sixteenth birthday, when I married my second cousin. Some say the point of marriage is the consolidation of wealth and family. But it meant much more to us. I felt when we wed that our souls recognized each other—possibly from previous lives—and clung to each other. After our wedding, we were inseparable."

"But something happened, right?" says Abdelrahman Salahadin. He looks around anxiously at the ominous swells and stands.

The Covered Man seems to smile. "I see you are familiar with the shape of stories! Something must always happen, isn't that so? It can't simply be: and they lived happily together and so on. . . . So be it, something did happen: my mate and I journeyed along the great trade routes of the desert bartering embroidery, spices, and animals in each of the cities we visited. We were in a caravan traveling to the tiny city of Jiddah, tucked on to the shores of the Arabian Gulf. This would have been the farthest any of us had traveled from the belly of the desert; it would be the first time that any of us would see the ocean, and we speculated as to what it might look like. Some said it rolled like a thousand-thousand stones across a low embankment, others that it flowed like melted glass.

"It took three weeks to travel from the Great Desert to the ocean. As we approached, the sand gave rise to a variety of corkscrew plants, camel briars, rasping thistles, and twirling ferns. I paid little attention—I was waiting to see the water. I smelled it first, a high, purifying scent. Then I heard it, a murmur which gradually increased till it was a roar. I covered my ears and looked up and saw clouds bright as satin, then looked down and my eyes were filled with the flaming, churning sea. I instinctively sought out the hand of my beloved but to my shock no one was there. Then I saw someone running down the embankment."

"This was . . . ?" Abdelrahman is impatient, sensitive to the sway of water all around them.

The Covered Man nods. "Of course, my only beloved. The one who, over the course of five years, had become eyebeam to my eye, essential to me as salt and air. And my Rarity, my Rose, my Diamond of Diamonds, was running into the vast blue embrace."

*

That evening when she returns from work, Sirine can hear King Babar whining and crying even before she has the door open. She bends to him and he jumps into her arms and leans against her chest, his nose buried in her hair. The only nights Sirine eats at home—Sunday and Monday when the restaurant is closed—King Babar sits on her lap through the meal. He snoozes, only half-waking to nibble the morsels that she transports to him under the table, and drifts in a sweet dream of love, eating, and forgetting. The rest of the week she eats at work, and goes to bed almost as soon as she gets in for an early start the next day.

Tonight should be an early night according to King Babar's internal clock, but Sirine is putting on new clothes, a green vapor of a dress for the warm evening. King Babar follows her to the front door, staring, his eyes rolled up at her face. She kisses him goodbye, feeling the faintest pang for leaving him behind.

She checks the address that Han gave her and realizes that his apartment is also in West L.A., practically within walking distance. She wheels her fendered three-speed bike out of the front entrance, hikes up her skirt, tucks it in around her legs, and pushes off.

Sirine rolls up the quiet street through a ripple of streetlights. Han lives in a complex that blurs into all the other complexes along the street; they have names like the Del Mar, the Vista, the Casa Lupita, rows of balconies, panels of glass, side-swept with date palms and bougainvillea and banana trees. The street looks shimmery in the moonlight, ephemeral as a mirage. Sirine stands outside his building, the Cyprus Gardens, checks the number written on her hand. She imagines for a moment that if she closes her eyes the neighborhoods will disappear—that's what her uncle says about L.A.: close your eyes and it will vanish.

The intercom in his building lobby is broken, the front door propped open with a flat, speckled rock. It's an older building constructed around a courtyard with a dreamy musky scent of decaying roses, jasmine, and dust. She enters the elevator and its doors rattle shut; it ascends with a myriad of watery sighs and shivers. The elevator groans and shudders its way to the top, fifth floor. Sirine stands outside his door for a moment, inhales through her nose. Number 503. She lifts her fist and accidentally knocks too loudly.

Han immediately opens the door as if he'd been waiting right behind it. He takes her hand and the touch travels all the way to her spine. She's so nervous, her senses all sharpened, she can only take in one detail at a time: the painted edge of the doorframe as he draws her in; stacks and stacks of books piled on their sides; a blue cloth spread out on the floor; the air swirling with the smell of cooking. For some reason the word *Africa* comes into her head. She glances at Han again: he is freshly shaved, his hair polished back with a brush, strands of hair falling forward over his brow: he swipes at it now, absently, with one hand. He looks as if he can't quite believe she's standing there. The apartment smells of thyme and sumac and something with a rich, pearly sweetness. He seems different in this glazed atmosphere, his face softer, as if all his emotions have drifted to the surface of his body, so she can feel all of him in the touch of his hand. He takes a half-step closer and the yellow light flickers.

He says something, his voice so low she has to incline her head to hear. "You are . . . you look . . . "

The blue cloth on the floor is a pulse of color: it flashes behind her eyes and fills her head and for a moment the feeling—an intense, atom-gathering desire—is the same as this sea-blue color at their feet.

She smiles.

" . . . beautiful," he says.

Then he asks something else, but she is looking around, briefly distracted, and has to step back a little from him in order to hear him. He's asking if he can get her a drink; she barely nods. The picture window appears to be full of stars. She's looking and looking. A sound vague as bees or distant bells hums between the black spaces in the sky, then she realizes it's coming from the corners of the room: a woman singing. Han goes out and then comes back with round goblets of crimson wine.

"How lovely," Sirine says. "What a lovely voice she has."

"It's Fairuz," Han says. "I was going to play some American music for you but I guess I don't actually own any. I meant for tonight to be all-American for you."

"But I'm not really all-American," Sirine says.

"Well, then I hope you will tell me what you are," Han says.

Sirine follows him into the kitchen, where a damp wisp is curling out of the top of the stove. She admires the square shape and fit of his hands on the oven door. She inhales and realizes what she's smelling. "Oh! You made meat loaf?"

He slides it out, a sleeve of meat. "Just like mom used to make?"

*

Broccoli branches, mashed potatoes, spools of gravy, sliced pillowy white bread. It slides on to Sirine's plate, glossy with butter. The meat loaf is oniony and dense under its charred crust, dressed in sweet puddles of ketchup. On the counter there's a food-stained copy of *The Joy of Cooking* and a red-plaid Betty Crocker cookbook, both from the library. She's impressed. No one ever wants to cook for her; the rare home-dinners at friends' houses are served with anxiety and apologies. But Han just seems excited—his skin slightly damp and pink from the kitchen heat—and intrigued by the new kind of cooking, a shift of ingredients like a move from native tongue into a foreign language: butter instead of olive oil; potatoes instead of rice; beef instead of lamb. He seats her on a pillow on the blue cloth and then sets the dishes before her on the cloth. He sits across from her, one knee skimming hers. They touch and she makes herself lean forward to reach the bowl of potatoes. Their knees graze again.

Han tastes each dish while looking at Sirine, so the meal seems like a question. She nods and praises him lavishly. "Mm, the rich texture of this meat loaf—the egg and breadcrumbs—and these bits of onion are so good, and there's a little chili powder and dry mustard, isn't there? It's lovely. And there's something in the sauce . . . something . . ."

"You mean ketchup?" Han asks.

"Oh yes, I suppose that's it." She smiles.

"That's remarkable."

Sirine smiles vaguely, tips her head, not sure of what he means. "What?"

"The way you taste things. . . ." He gestures over the food, picks up a bite of meat loaf in his fingers as if it were an olive. "You know what everything here is—I mean exactly."

"Oh no." She laughs. "It's so basic, anyone can do that. It's like you just taste the starting places—where it all came from. Unless of course it's ketchup."

He gazes at her, then carefully takes her hand and kisses her fingers. "Then I think you must be of this place."

Sirine laughs again, disconcerted by his intensity. "Well, I don't know about that, but I think food should taste like where it came from. I mean good food especially. You can sort of trace it back. You know, so the best butter tastes a little like pastures and flowers, that sort of stuff. Things show their origins."

"That must be why you seem so American to me," he says shyly and glances down into his wineglass.

She doesn't completely understand what he means by this, but then it doesn't seem to matter that much. The night clouds ripple past the balcony doors like fish tails. The air smells like desert salt. She finishes her glass of wine and he pours her more. The soft evasion in his eyes draws her in. It's as if he isn't entirely in the room: his gaze subtly refocusing between her face and a hidden, internal place. His eyes reflect both the kitchen lights and the night clouds. Sirine leans closer, her skin warm. She's disoriented by his scent and proximity. "So . . ." She casts around a bit. "So, you don't actually have any furniture, I see. That's sort of unusual."

He looks over his shoulder as if this is a new discovery, then shakes his head. "It's not very comfortable, is it? It's just—it hadn't really occurred to me—I mean, that I would need things like chairs and bookcases. I've moved around so much between schools and teaching posts and about a million different apartments. I haven't had much incentive to buy furniture. I suppose in some way I had the sense that it would be like a commitment—to a place, I mean."

She raises her eyebrows. "But then you never get to really live anywhere that way—you'd always be thinking about where you're going to. You'd never just be somewhere."

"That's true," he says, a tilted grin on his face as if she'd caught him at something.

"So . . ." She touches the lip of the wineglass. "Do you think you could live here?"

"I think so." He looks at her for a moment. "That's what I'm trying to find out."

Her gaze slips then and she is looking at his hand, its smooth palm so much lighter than the skin on back, the crosshatching of dark creases. She comments again on the food and then on the music. She watches his hand as he pours them each more wine. The singer's voice vibrates and seems to translate things loose in the air between them into her intricate song.

Han nods and pours her more wine. "This song is called 'Andaloussiya.' It was a place where the Muslims and Jews lived together and devised miraculous works of philosophy and architecture. All the sorts of things that people get up to when you leave them in the sun for a while."

"Really, the Muslims and the Jews creating things together?" Sirine says; she closes her eyes and sips the wine, tasting cherry and oak and—echo-soft—raisin and tar. "Think of that."

"Oh yes, they were smart," Han says, his voice confidential, as if he were telling secrets. "Have you seen the Alhambra—the climbing spirals and arches? Very smart. It's an extraordinary place—I've visited it several times."

"What happened to them?"

"The Andaloussians? Oh, scattered, chased away, conquered. They were too much for their time."

"It's wonderful, all the places you've seen."

He lifts one shoulder, lets it fall. "I'm not sure it's any more wonderful than just staying home, sometimes, really." Han looks at the crumbs on her plate and then at Sirine. "Did you eat enough? Are you still hungry?" His voice hums along her breastbone like fingertips.

She laughs. She puts down her glass of wine and it wobbles once before she stills it. "I'm fine, really. Stuffed."

He slices off a sliver from the meat loaf in the pan and picks it up with his fingertips. He holds it to her lips. "Come on," he says. "*Min eedi.*" *From my hand.* The thing intimate friends say to express the greatest of care. She opens her mouth and remembers her father feeding her a bite of bread, *min eedi,* he said. And Han places the food in her mouth.

*

They carry dishes in to to his smooth white sink, his little kitchen, and they argue briefly over who will wash and then they end up washing the dishes together, bumping their shoulders then their elbows then their hips.

After the dishes and another glass of wine, Han answers Sirine's questions about Islam—she's curious, not having been raised with formal religion. He describes what the interior of a mosque looks like, its clean, open prayer hall, and—after much coaxing—he recites the *athan,* the call to prayers, to Sirine outside on the floor of his balcony. It sounds like singing to Sirine, but he says no—this is praying, which is pure. He hesitates a moment, as if he can't quite remember, then demonstrates the postures and genuflections for praying—bowing from waist to knees to head. She loves the motion of it and tries to imitate him but her head swims a bit and she has to sit back down on the balcony floor. "It's so nice," she says quietly. "It reminds me of the way I feel sometimes when I'm working, like when I stir a pot of soup, or when I knead the bread dough." She stops and wonders if what she's saying makes any sense.

He sits cross-legged beside her on the floor and rubs the back of his neck. "Haven't prayed in some time. I'm out of practice."

Sirine has always felt comforted by the cool slip of her uncle's prayer beads in her hand, but she has never actually tried to pray before. She doesn't want to tell him this. It's like not knowing how to play an instrument or how to speak a foreign language—something she feels she should know. She watches Han closely, tries to memorize his expression, the way he places his hands on his knees.

Suddenly he stops and looks at her in dismay. "Oh my God, dessert," he says.

"There's dessert?"

"In the freezer."

✳

The moon comes out and turns red. They're back sitting side by side on the tiny balcony, eating frozen chocolate layer cake straight from the box and spoonfuls of vanilla ice cream from the carton, and drinking from one cup of Lipton's tea, which Han says is the great colonial tea bag: "A brown tea bag upon which great white empires are built." Sirine is laughing at Han's stories about places where he's taught, and difficult students and difficult colleagues. He tells her about studying in England, about the house where he lived that was—he swears—the size, shape, and smell of a large brick chimney, in a neighborhood full of large brick chimneys, the smell of roasted lamb and curried goat all over the neighborhood. He tells about his Sudanese roommate at Georgetown who owned a prayer rug with a compass to find Mecca built right into it. "After a few weeks in America, he rolled it up and used the compass to go camping," Han says.

Sirine watches his eyes, then she watches his mouth. She inhales traces of a lemon cologne that reminds her of watching her father shave. "What about old girlfriends?" she asks.

"Who?"

"Oh, I'm sure you've had a few big relationships."

He shrugs, looks as blank as if he'd turned his pockets inside out. "I've spent my life studying like a madman. Then I spent my life teaching and writing like a madman. Honestly, I'm very good at just being inside myself."

"Oh, now . . ."

"There've been maybe three women whom you might could barely call a sort of girlfriend, English girls—there was Miriam and Julietta, and one—it seems I can't remember her name . . ." His face is bright pink. "I can barely remember any of them, when I think of it."

She realizes that her question might have been more personal than she'd meant it to be. She asks quickly, "What about Iraq? Tell me what Iraq is like."

He eases back into himself. Leans against the wall and gazes at the big red moon. The air stirs around them, so mild it's almost without temperature. "Iraq is endless. As a child, I thought it held the whole world," he says. "There's the Euphrates River going one way, the Tigris in another. In Baghdad the Tigris is like a reflecting mirror under all the tall buildings. The gold and turquoise mosques with their big courtyards, all the libraries and museums, the great wooden doors and massive gates. But it's more than buildings—there is a special quality to the air in Iraq. A feeling."

"What feeling?"

He purses his lips. "I don't know how to say this without sounding crazy."

"That's okay—go ahead and sound crazy."

He tips his head back again, closes his eyes, and takes a deep breath. "It's like sometimes I feel like I can sense the ghosts of all sorts of invisible cities and places that used to be there, on that land—the Chaldean Empire and the Hanging Gardens of Babylon and—I know I'm not telling this very well. The night there seems to start two thousand years ago, it's so light and dry—a bit like this night, I think." He looks off the balcony toward an invisible place; Sirine looks in the same direction. "And then there's my parents' house."

He tells her about the whitewashed stone of their small home, his father's olive orchards, the salty, grassy smell of the olives roasting in the sun; he describes the finesse of his mother's embroidery, the precise delicacy of the stitches; he talks about the Iraqi guard—the soldiers with their automatic weapons, the crisp uniforms and slanted berets that he'd seen in the city streets, how he'd been afraid of them when he was a child. He talks about trying to sleep when he could hear gunfire and soldiers in the street, never feeling entirely safe, always wanting to run far away.

She leans forward into her listening and he leans forward into his telling and once again their knees are touching. She would very much like to take his hand. But they are sitting so close that she doesn't know what to do. She wonders if she seems too available. If Han is merely attracted to her silvery blond hair, the bluish translucence of her skin. The Arab men she knows can be giddy and talkative when they're out in public, but then subdued and somber when they come into the café. They kiss Um-Nadia's hand as if she were their mother, and then tease Mireille and threaten to marry her off to their brothers. They sit and watch Sirine surreptitiously or their eyes follow the American girls through the café window. Occasionally one of them will appear with an American girlfriend and all the other students will observe them. But never an Arab girl. Sirine is used to their sweet, mild advances—the way they'll bring her little presents, chocolates, and flowers—but never try to touch her.

"I'd love to see Baghdad," she says tentatively, and as she says it she realizes it's true, though she's never liked to travel.

Han's head stays lowered but he looks up at her carefully. "Have you ever been to the Middle East at all?"

The tips of her fingers tingle as if she were cold and she curls them into her palms. "I've hardly been anywhere," she says. Then she smiles slightly and says, "And here you've been everywhere."

*

She stays too late, drunk on Han's stories and with laughing. At times he seems to lure her forward, as if he would take her arms and pull her into a kiss, and at times she panics a little and pulls back, overexcited and startled by the way he stirs her up. She's conscious of the darkened bedroom just on the other side of the balcony door, so she looks in another direction and watches the trees lined up along the sidewalk, silver-limbed, the hand-shaped leaves swimming through the moonlight. The evening looks mysterious and enticing, beckoning her.

But eventually the curry-colored moon disappears and Han is shaking the wine bottle, trying to pour out the last drops of wine—the goblets are gone and they seem to be drinking from the teacup. The smattering of wine looks inky in the bottom of the cup. She makes herself check her watch. "Oh no. Oh no, it's so late. I have to get home. I get up very early." She unfolds her legs and pulls herself up by the balcony rail.

"Oh, but . . ." He stands. He looks startled. "It doesn't seem late." He looks around at the city-lit sky. "It doesn't really seem much like night at all here. I can barely see the stars with all these lights. In Baghdad, the moon and stars were so clear, like ice." His eyes are black and his skin sleek and African. The crescent-shaped scar near his eye gleams faintly.

*

Her bike is still propped against the wall by Han's door. But he's appalled by the thought of her bicycling home in the dark. "This city is full of every kind of lunatic there is, and every one of them has gotten a car from somewhere," he says. "Or haven't you noticed?"

"Oh no, it's fine. I do this all the time. I can practically bicycle with my eyes closed," she says and flicks on the light mounted to her handlebars; it casts a greenish glow through the gloomy corridor. "Actually, sometimes I think it's easier to ride without the light." She switches it off.

"I'll drive you," Han says, grabbing his keys.

They argue over it in the elevator, sweetly, Sirine tapping on his chest. Han catches Sirine's hand and doesn't let go and then the door creaks open and he has to let go so she can push her bike.

Han's car is parked on the street in front of his building. It's a big, squared-off rectangle with a hood ornament in the shape of an anchor. The white orb of the streetlight hangs over it and beams a sapphire gleam on the car hood. The car interior is so spacious they can practically roll the bike in back without tilting it. Sirine goes around to the passenger side and sinks into the plush seat. "It's amazing," she says, running her hands over the upholstery.

"It belonged to Lon, the department chair," Han says. "His wife gave it to me when I got here. I don't know if she asked him first or not, though."

They pull away from the curb and lights from the street slink over the windshield and through the car as they drive. It's only about ten blocks from Han's apartment to Sirine's house and Han looks startled and disappointed when they arrive. "We're there?" he says. "I didn't realize you lived so close."

"Like neighbors," Sirine says.

He parallel parks in front of the house, moving the car in slow arcs. Its length extends so far over its wheelbase that Sirine thinks she can feel the front and back ends wafting up and down. Han clunks it into park, then sits back and runs his hands over the steering wheel. The streetlights burn through the night with a mellow amber glow.

"I really don't get the geography of this town," he says. "It seems like things keep swimming around me. I think I know where something is, then it's gone."

"It's not so hard," Sirine says. "See, right over there—" She taps the windshield, "That's where the ocean is, and—"

"Show me." He looks at her, his eyes darker than the air. "If you draw me a map I think I'll understand better."

"Do you have paper?" She looks over the empty sweep of the car's interior. "I don't have anything to write with."

He holds up his hands, side to side as if they were hinged. "That's okay. You can just use my hands."

She smiles, a little confused. He leans forward and the streetlight gives him yellow-brown cat eyes. A car rolling down the street toward them fills the interior with light, then an aftermath of prickling black waves. "All right." She takes his hands, runs her finger along one edge. "Is this what you mean? Like, if the ocean was here on the side and these knuckles are mountains and here on the back it's Santa Monica, Beverly Hills, West L.A., West Hollywood, and X marks the spot." She traces her fingertips over the backs of his hands, her other hand pressing into the soft pads of his palm. "This is where we are—X."

"Right now? In this car?" He leans back; his eyes are black marble, dark lamps. She holds his gaze a moment, hears a rush of pulse in her ears like ocean surf. Her breath goes high and tight and shallow; she hopes he can't see her clearly in the car—her translucent skin so vulnerable to the slightest emotion. He turns her hands over, palms up, and says, "Now you." He draws one finger down one side of her palm and says, "This is the Tigris River Valley. In this section there's the desert and in this point it's plains. The Euphrates runs along there. This is Baghdad here. And here is Tahrir Square." He touches the center of her palm. "At the foot of the Jumhurriya Bridge. The center of everything. All the main streets run out from this spot. In this direction and that direction, there are wide busy sidewalks and apartments piled up on top of shops, men in business suits, women with strollers, street vendors selling kabobs, eggs, fruit drinks. There's the man with his cart who sold me rolls sprinkled with thyme and sesame every morning and then saluted me like a soldier. And there's this one street...." He holds her palm cradled in one hand and traces his finger up along the inside of her arm to the inner crease of her elbow, then up to her shoulder. Everywhere he touches her it feels like it must be glowing, as if he were drawing warm butter all over her skin. "It just goes and goes, all the way from Baghdad to Paris." He circles her shoulder. "And here"—he touches the inner crease of her elbow—"is the home of the Nile crocodile with the beautiful speaking voice. And here"—his fingers return to her shoulder, dip along her clavicle—"is the dangerous singing forest."

"The dangerous singing forest?" she whispers.

He frowns and looks thoughtful. "Or is that in Madagascar?" His hand slips behind her neck and he inches toward her on the seat. "There's a savanna. Chameleons like emeralds and limes and saffron and rubies. Red cinnamon trees filled with lemurs."

"I've always wanted to see Madagascar," she murmurs: his breath is on her face. Their foreheads touch.

His hand rises to her face and she can feel that he's trembling and she realizes that she's trembling too. "I'll take you," he whispers.

When he kisses her, the backs of her thighs go soft and her breath dissolves and her eyelids float over her eyes. She wants to press one hand against her sternum. Instead, her hands slip over his shoulders and she moves even closer.

CHAPTER SEVEN

Are you paying attention? The moralless story requires, of course, greater care and general alertness than your run-of-the-mill, everyday story with a moral, which basically gives you the Cliffs Notes version of itself in the end anyway. A moralless story is deep yet takes no longer to tell than it takes to steep a cup of mint tea.

So: tippling and toppling on the blue boat, our poor cousin Abdelrahman Salahadin brushes the salt from his temples and tries to focus on the Covered Man, who blurs and ripples in the transparent sea light as he tells the story of his beloved. The air rises up from the West, runs over the boat, and chills his skin. He looks toward the vanished horizon, paces a bit, then sits back down beside the Covered Man.

"Let me repeat, we felt, upon our first meeting, that we recognized each other," says the Covered Man. "We felt we had existed together even before our bodies were born. We were inseparable from the moment of our union. There was nothing, I tell you, nothing to prepare me for that day when my dear one discovered the sea and ran away over the sand."

For some minutes there is little sound but that of the waves giving up their light and the night spilling into the ocean. Abdelrahman Salahadin and the Covered Man are eclipsed and the wind is full of darkness. His hand tightens on the thin lip of the boat. Then he thinks that he might be afraid of the water at night. The muscles in his back tighten, and perspiration breaks along his temples.

"What happened when your beloved ran into the water?" Abdelrahman asks, his head turned away.

The Covered Man says, "What happened was the inevitable. As you know, all things are foreordained by God, and all things are foretold within the perfect symmetry of His eye.

"We made our encampment on the cusp of the beach. Most of the Bedu were too frightened to go near the water. They slept with their backs to the sea. My mate, however, sat with both feet in its path. After thirty days of trading in town, it was time to go. But my beloved refused, wanting the bright arms of the waves. I told the Bedu to go on, that we would catch up to them later. They tried to convince me to come with them. My beloved, they said, had been claimed by the sea. They said I was no longer married to a human being but to a thing with a floating root like a jellyfish.

"How is one meant to leave behind the object of one's love? I waved goodbye to my compatriots and slept alone on the beach with only the sand for my pillow. I slept facing the ocean as a lonely lover sleeps facing the door through which their dear one has left.

"My beloved no longer came back from playing in the waves. Day and night intertwined and on occasion I could see a flash of a shoulder between the waves. Then one day I woke from a dream in which we had kissed as we once used to do, and in that dream my mate touched my face and then said, let me go.

"I woke and scanned the horizon of water, shouting a name, but it was like shouting into the emptiness between the stars. And I knew then that I had lost my husband forever."

At that, the Covered Man pushes back his wrappings, and—did you already guess it? The he is a she! She stands quickly, a tremor running through the nut-brown hull. And though it is in the very belly of the night, the dial of the zodiac turns above them and Sagittarius's arrow ignites her brow; her beauty flashes before Abdelrahman, blinding him. "I'm sorry to have disguised my identity," she says, "but I could see no other way."

Abdelrahman gropes for the railing but the very floorboards have melted beneath his feet. Nothing in the world is as he thought it was. "Ya Allah," he breathes. *Oh God.*

*

"Where is she?" Um-Nadia cries out. "Where is that Queen of Sheba?"

Sirine is yawning. It was quite late when she finally walked out of Han's big dark car and into her house, too late for her uncle to get up and start asking questions. That night, Sirine had strings of erotic dreams, dream-flesh in her hands, her unknown partners' eyes were closed, their lashes shining black as figs, their legs scissored between hers. When birds began arguing in the trees, she woke, filled with the sense that she'd spent the whole night kissing Han. Now she scrapes up grease like layers of skin and listens to the buzz of students' conversations all around her. She smiles to herself and doesn't talk to anyone. She goes downstairs and rummages through the freezer in the basement, listening to Um-Nadia come in, pace over her head, and call out, "Hello, Queen? Where are you?"

Finally she walks back up carrying a bushel of onions. Mireille is making a shopping list, tapping on a cigarette. "You must've had a good night. Mom's already calling you the Queen of Sheba."

Um-Nadia and Mireille have watched Sirine get coupled and uncoupled many times while the two of them stayed steadfastly single. No one can remember what happened to Um-Nadia's husband or if there was ever a man in Mireille's life. They've been on their own for years. But each time Sirine acquires a new lover, it seems that Um-Nadia can look at her and see it, or read it in the coffee grounds, or wake in the morning feeling it in her bones.

"It's so exciting, this man. If this was the time of Salah al-Din, Han would be a famous general," Um-Nadia tells the police officers as she brings them their puréed beans and bread. "He would be in charge of you both. And Sirine would be his Cleopatra. Or his Queen of Sheba. Also in charge of you."

They raise their eyebrows skeptically.

She turns and catches sight of Sirine's face as she comes up behind her. "What?"

"Could I talk to you a minute?" Sirine says. "Out back."

They go through the back kitchen, past Mireille and Victor, who are continuing their discussion about whether or not men are animals, and out into the courtyard.

"So here we are," Um-Nadia says. "All private."

Sirine pushes a strand of hair back and tucks it under her hair band. "Han and I barely know each other. I have no idea where this is going to go. It's too soon for Antony and Cleopatra."

Um-Nadia's pointed black eyes flicker, as if she were reading something written on Sirine's face. "What's wrong with true love?"

Sirine blinks. "Well, as an idea, nothing."

Um-Nadia folds her arms under her bosom and sighs heavily. "Okay, Habeebti, all right. Listen to me, let me advise you in this, there's no mystery—I could have any man I wanted out there, you know, any second I wanted." She snaps her fingers. "Like this! Look at the way your uncle is always hanging and hanging around. That's no accident. The fact is that there are certain special ways that women have always gotten their men: through cooking, through acts of love, through pleasing the mother, through making a nice baby. What it is up to the woman to do—if she doesn't know it by smell and instinct—is to learn her man up and down, front to back. You have to pay attention, Habeebti. He will show himself. He is like a fish, you already have him by the tail, but he's slippery, he doesn't want to jump out of your hands but he might not be able to stop himself. You need to grab him by the head too."

"I'm supposed to grab Han by the head?"

"That is what you will be paying attention to see, Habeebti," she says gently. "Oh, Habeebti, you know that you are another daughter to me?"

Almost everyone at Nadia's Café, from the students to the work staff, knows that Um-Nadia's important daughter Nadia (because "Um-Nadia" means *Mother-of-Nadia*, so everyone will know you're a mother) is not, as she says, actually living far away in Dearborn, which, to some, is the heaven-on-earth for Arabs in America, with its Lebanese bakeries and daily broadcast of the call to prayers. They know that Bint Um-Nadia (or, *the daughter of the mother of Nadia*) died many years ago, but Um-Nadia won't say the word *cancer*; sometimes she says Nadia died from "the smoke." But usually she just says—to strangers and old friends alike—that Nadia is in Dearborn.

On the day Um-Nadia came into the kitchen at the Café De Venise in

Brentwood to steal Sirine from her old job, Sirine could see the will inside Um-Nadia as clear and strong as a physical thing. She pulled off her apron, left behind half-constructed salads with smoked mozzarella, capers, and sun-dried tomatoes, and went back to making the simple and perfect foods of her childhood. In exchange, Um-Nadia sings to Sirine and kisses her hands and tells her she's *pure beauty*.

In the courtyard, Um-Nadia brings her face in close, so Sirine can see the coffee-colored lights in her irises, her mascara-tangled lashes; she smiles broadly and says: "Habeebti, forgive me, I didn't even see it before—you are so afraid!"

"No, I'm not," Sirine says, feeling dull-witted. She takes a step back. "Afraid of what?"

Um-Nadia claps her hands together, making a *pock* sound, and bright orange and turquoise birds flap out of the trees. "But that's a good sign—it's a wonderful sign, the best of signs."

Sirine's throat feels tight. She glares at the white tiles paving the courtyard, following their intricate designs. "I am definitely not afraid," she says.

Um-Nadia runs one hand over Sirine's braid tenderly. "But that feeling will go away in time. You must be patient a little bit. Like they say in the old song, even the birds wait for love. There is a time," Um-Nadia says, lifting one finger like an exclamation point, "when things go out of tune. It's not all the time. It's not even a lot of the time. But it is some of the time. And then you have to deal with it all. Everything comes out wrong. You dream about goats and monkeys. People start to look at things wrong. Maybe you think the world looks squashed and flat. Maybe you get stones in the bulgur and you burn the smoked wheat."

Sirine sits slowly on the lowest step; Um-Nadia settles beside her.

"My daughter Nadia"—the lifted finger again—"she got herself tangled in one of these knots. That child was pure gold—do you know what I mean by pure gold? I mean every speck of her was all the way alive. But she started to go into one of these wrong times. You want to protect your children, don't you? You let them out of your body but you never let them all of the way out. Nadia started to look at things the wrong way, it was like she was trying to drink the water in a mirage. I tried to bring her water. I would bring her fresh, clear water in my own hands if she would let me, but do you think she would let me?"

Sirine touches Um-Nadia's hand. Her skin is airy and light as a wish.

Um-Nadia shakes her head as if disagreeing with some unspoken argument. Her fingers close around Sirine's. "So warm! Your blood is overheated. I think you're getting yourself worked up." Um-Nadia purses her lips and slivers her eyes. She taps her lips with one finger and then she says, "There's love-crazy and then there's just plain love. If your parents were alive they would have showed you how to be in love. But you've only got your poor idiot uncle, so you've got to learn it all by yourself."

Mireille swings into the kitchen. "We're out of tabbouleh salad!"

Sirine starts to rise, but Um-Nadia waves her down. "Never mind," she says to Mireille. "Make do. Cut a tomato."

"A tomato!" Mireille bangs back out the door, indignant.

"Where was I? Yes! Look at your Han. His face fills a woman up. I hope you don't mind me saying that," she adds coyly. "And he has the kind of nice big spirit that men used to come with. Now they have to buy them or make them up. But there are other concerns."

"About Han? What do you mean?"

Um-Nadia waves her hands, palms up before her as if shining a window. "I look and then I look again. I see Arab men come here from far away all the time. They all come to me because we make something like a home in this country. It helps. And most of them stay." She raises her eyebrows. "But lots of them go."

"That's natural," Sirine says.

Um-Nadia closes her eyes and shakes her head. "The world is full of shadows and X rays and things are upside down when we think they're right ways up. Men especially get confused. Like the husband of my friend Munira—did I tell you about her? She's the one who found out her husband had a secret extra family back in Lebanon. It's classic. Men lose track of where they are. They miss their mother and father and sister. They don't know how to carry their homes inside themselves." She looks closely at Sirine. "You need to know how to do that."

Sirine wraps her arms over her chest, leans back so she feels the edge of the wooden step pressing into her.

Um-Nadia points with her chin and says, "Let's pour you some coffee, Habeebti. Then I'll read your cup."

Sirine shakes her head. "No, I don't like that. I don't want to know."

Mireille bangs back into the kitchen. "We're out of tomatoes! Shall I serve leaves and twigs?"

Um-Nadia raises her eyebrows at Mireille. "Use your creativity."

Sirine touches the brightly flowering bush beside the steps, runs her hands over the petals. "I just think it's too soon for all this. I don't feel right. I feel like I'm getting sick or something."

"Yes . . . yes!" Um-Nadia stands up in her teetery little shoes "You feel like this." She breaks some flowers from the tree and shakes them at Sirine so the petals scatter wildly. Then she pulls some jasmine blossoms from the next plant, crushes them in her hand, and holds them to Sirine's nose. Sirine's head fills with the damp, sweet scent. "You feel like this smells. That's how it works. That's exactly how fast it is. Never mind one kiss." She throws the blossoms into the bushes. "Less than one second is all it takes." Um-Nadia puts her hands on her hips and nods knowingly. "You never knew what love felt like before."

*

By ten that night the customers have all gone. Um-Nadia counts the money in the register and Mireille checks her shopping list. Cristobal and Victor Hernandez clean and swab. On warm nights they all move back and forth from lingering at the tables outside, chatting with a few straggling customers, to the work inside, and then back out again. Um-Nadia leans against the doorjamb sharing a cigarette with Nathan, contemplating the white night and the masses of papery bougainvillea flowers growing in a patch outside her door. "Movie-star flowers," she murmurs. "*Mejnoona*."

It is Sirine's favorite time, when the night turns black as bitter chocolate and the stars pop out. Han walks up just after closing and Sirine can hear their voices out front—Han's is soft and rich, and Um-Nadia is so excited and flirtatious that she's practically singing. She ceremoniously ushers Han in through the back kitchen, delivering him to Sirine. While the others are lingering out front, Sirine stands with Han at the back door. She has just finished making a tray of kibbeh and she wipes morsels of the raw spiced ground lamb from her fingers. They laugh and flirt and whisper to each other words so quiet no one can hear them.

Sirine smiles and shyly trails a finger down the front of his shirt. "I have to work late tonight," she says.

"Are you sure?" He cocks his head and she laughs and nods and then nods again. He touches her hair then and strolls backward for a few steps before turning into the night.

She stays after all the others have gone home. She doesn't turn the lights on but works by the moon and the streetlights and by touch, spreading small brined grape leaves flat on the cutting board, slicing out the tiny stems, wrapping the star-spoked leaves around rice and meat. It's a soothing task she likes to save for the solitary meditations of evening: her first chance to think over the night before in Han's apartment, which seems already somehow much more important than an ordinary first date. But Um-Nadia's coaxing makes her anxious and uncomfortable and she senses again that her feelings are rushing away from her, that it's wiser to pull back a bit, to try and understand who Han is a little better. She sighs and eats a grape leaf straight from the brine, her mouth puckering on its tart, raw taste. The night is so still she half-imagines she can hear the distant music he was playing: now it is ingrained in the faint *shush* of the breeze as she puts the knifepoint to the leaf. She lets the feeling creep over her until it vibrates under her skin, luxuriating in the sweetness of the recollection. At the same time, she is growing conscious of her fear of the dark. She's annoyed with the sense of her own weakness and childishness, and she tries to push the fear away. Instead, though, the anxiety tightens around her like a net. She won't let herself look up at all the creaks and clicks she hears in the old building—sounds that are also there in the daylight, she knows. The prickling moves along her spine, and just when she decides to turn on the lights, she looks up: "Oh my God." She puts down her knife and presses her hands against her apron, her heart pounding.

Nathan is standing just outside the screen door.

"You're still here," he says quietly.

"Oh my God. You startled me."

"Sorry, sorry. Didn't mean to creep up." He turns his face slightly; through the mesh of the screen his gray eyes look like shadows. "It's a photographer's vice, I guess." He tips his forehead against the screen and looks up at her. "I went home but I couldn't sleep." Sirine stares at him. "I thought, just—maybe someone would still be here . . . maybe want to visit," he mumbles.

"Well." She rubs her fingers over her temples. Then she tries to match the knife back to the leaf but her hand slips and she slices the leaf in two. She sighs. "Well, come in if you want."

He pushes through the screen door. "Really, I'm sorry. People tell me I do that. Sometimes I have to remind myself to make noise." He sits across from her at the table, in one of the uneven-legged chairs, and rocks forward, then back. "You're stuffing grape leaves."

She glances at him. "You know about grape leaves?"

"I bummed around the Middle East for a couple years. In Jordan. And Iraq." He rocks some more. "I was studying Arabic—just for the heck of it—and I decided I wanted to photograph the area. Once I started doing that..." He shrugs. "I kind of went crazy over it. I wanted to learn everything I could—the history, the people, the food, whatever...." He clears his throat. "Am I bothering you? Should I just go home?"

She shakes her head but focuses on rolling the leaf, getting each corner precisely folded. "I thought you didn't like food."

"Now. But then, I used to feel like the closer I was to physical things, the closer I got to the soul."

She smiles and looks up, not sure if he's joking, but instantly sees his seriousness—which makes him so easy for the others to tease. She feels a flicker of guilt and says, "Would you like some baklava?"

He touches the point of the grape leaf she's trimming. "A night like tonight, with a big moon outside keeping me up—it makes me sort of sad."

She raises her eyebrows.

"Oh, I'm used to it. What do they say: 'The cure for sadness is called sadness'?" He laughs at himself. "I look at things and I know—how good it would be to taste your food, what a good thing it is to eat baklava. Enjoy the smells and flavors in a kitchen. But it's just, there's not much point anymore."

She puts her knife down and props her chin on her palm. "Why did you say before that you're made of powder?"

He nods. "You remembered that?" He closes his eyes. He is quiet long enough that she thinks he won't answer her, but then he says, "Have you ever—have you ever been so in love with someone that it just takes everything out of you? Where you can't think or move or eat or anything, just carry this big, crazy love around?"

She looks back at her grape leaf. "Well . . ." she says slowly. "I don't guess I ever have, really. Not like that."

He doesn't say anything for a moment, and when she looks back up, he's gazing at her. "I thought there was something about you . . . like that. Self-possessed. You've never let it run away with you. I understand that. It's a kind of innocence, I think. I used to be that way, but going to Iraq shook me loose from who I was. The deep, wild strangeness of the place. The way the air smelled like dust and herbs, the strange slant of the sun. I couldn't help myself. I fell in love with a girl there, I almost think I had to—I was so wide open to everything." He exhales. "When I did—I'd honestly never felt such a thing before. It was like a heaviness that weighed down every part of me, it was so much inside me, in my blood and bones. It pressed on my head and my arms. I'd always thought love made you feel light, but this was exactly the opposite. It was the heaviest thing."

She laughs without meaning to. "It sounds sort of awful," she says.

He gazes at her. "There's something about you, really, that reminds me so much . . ." He barely touches the side of her nose and cheek. "Right here. This place. It's like her. And around your eyes too, just under the eyebrows. . . ."

She ducks her head.

He smiles. "Do I sound strange? I don't have any perspective. At the time, I let it take me away." He tips back in his chair. "I knew it was too much, but I didn't care. It was something that just stripped me clean. I felt pulverized. Like a new man. I loved everything about her and I didn't care about anything else. I loved her wrists and her laugh and her shoes and her teeth. I was so happy I even stopped taking photographs. I was sure I would feel that way, absolutely and completely, for the rest of my life." Nathan rubs his palms over the top of his short-cropped hair. "I don't know if you can understand this. I grew up half-wild. My parents divorced when I was a kid and all I knew about families was what I learned from watching other people. I went into the Middle East without any idea of who I was—there was no needle on my compass, you know? But the people in Iraq—this sounds dumb and romantic—but the thing is, they really seemed to know who they were. They dressed the way their grandparents dressed, they ate the way they've eaten for hundreds of years. And they were so alive—I mean, lots of them didn't have TV or telephones, but everyone talked about politics, art, religion, you name it. They were living under a dictatorship but their inner selves stayed *alive*—do you see?"

Sirine nods, but she feels his words skimming over her skin. She concentrates on each grape leaf, working and listening.

"And when I met this woman—you know it was just an accident—but she was like *true north* to me. When I first saw her in the market it was like I was seeing the truest thing in the world. I would have done anything for her. I remember—she had this long wild hair like yours. She would tie it up in her scarf and every day, by the end of the day, it would all be fallen down around her shoulders again. She used to say, 'I want to be a good Muslim but my hair won't let me.' Then she'd laugh like it was all just funny. She had the most beautiful, beautiful laugh. It rose and fell like music." He takes off his glasses and stares at the ceiling. "I'm sorry. I know I'm talking too much. It's been a long time since I've talked about any of it."

"And you couldn't sleep." Sirine smiles at him. "It sounds like it was a great thing."

Nathan lowers his face and replaces his glasses, hooking them around his ears. "Oh. Well. There're always complications, aren't there? An Arab girl, a Muslim, an Iraqi. And an American, failed-Episcopalian boy."

She begins trimming another grape leaf. "That doesn't have to mean anything."

"Maybe it doesn't. I don't know. But for us, it made everything so difficult—to be together."

"Different sorts of people get together all the time."

"Yes, but then she died."

"Oh." Sirine looks back up at him. And now she can see it—the dark crystal, the shards of black glass inside him—she should have seen this in him right from the start. "I'm so sorry," she whispers. She can hear her own breath. She wants to ask *how*. But now she feels she's said too much as it is. She puts down the knife again.

"That's when I turned into powder." He sprinkles his fingers through the air. "Poof."

She stares at her knife and wishes she were smarter about things. Wishes she knew how to say something wise or consoling to him, something that wouldn't sound frightened or awkward. But then she remembers the time after her parents' death, when people would approach her and try to explain her loss to her; they said things that were supposed to cure her of her sadness, but that had no effect at all. And she knew then, even when she was nine years old, that there was no wise or consoling thing to say. There were only certain helpful kinds of silences, and some were better than others.

But Nathan doesn't seem to expect anything. He stands and stretches and looks as if he's just finished saying everything he would say. He goes to the door, his hand flat against the screen, then he pushes through and goes down the two steps. He pauses and returns, now both palms floating on the screen. He stares at her a moment. "Save me some grape leaves, okay?" he says.

Sirine stares at the door; he's so hard to see, his shadow flickering back and forth. "Nathan? Wait a second. Don't go—"

He doesn't answer.

"Nathan?" She puts down the knife and goes to open the door. But when she opens it he's gone.

CHAPTER EIGHT

The sailboat tips and sways in the deep ocean water. Abdelrahman clutches his heart and the Covered Man, who is now an Uncovered Woman, holds up one hand. Naked to the elbows, her arms are transparencies, her waist casts no shadow. "Your reputation, Abdelrahman Salahadin, precedes you," she says. "Since the day of his disappearance, I have hired swimmers and sailors in hopes of recovering my husband, all to no avail. The years have spilt like oil, and the men tell me there will be nothing left of him but bones." She lifts her diaphanous hands. "I thought, oh Abdelrahman, that if any man could see through the flesh of the ocean, look into the duplicitous minds of the fish, it would be you, famed above all swimmers, a man who has drowned and returned a thousand times a thousand! And yet . . ."

Abdelrahman tries to still his heart, strains to hear what fruit might be dangling off the slender branch of "and yet." The ocean sighs, full of night, and far off, from one of the distant poles of evening, he hears a sound like Satan crying for his lost world. "And . . . yet . . . ?"

She says, "And yet . . . today I have discovered that what I thought was love has become nothing but bones, and what I thought was memory is nothing more than ashes. From the first moment I saw you, oh Abdelrahman, in the marketplace, my soul has seized upon you."

Abdelrahman feels the sweep of a hundred emotions, the scorch of invisible wings! He tries to speak but can only laugh, the laugh of the doomed. The muscles in his swimmer's back flex as he moves to embrace the beloved, she who has reeducated him in both the strength and the fearfulness of desire. He walks forward into the dark boat.

But there is nowhere to go. Because it seems to him that the floor has melted, the railing has shattered, and once Abdelrahman starts falling he cannot stop. But was that the trace of her fingers on his skin? Was that the sweetness of her eyes closing in love? And was that the jealous voice of the ocean shouting his name as the Abdelrahman falls, swiftly, ungracefully, indubitably, in?

He spins in the dead black air of the sea and the last thing he sees through the opaque surface is the face of the beloved crying . . . or is she laughing? And then a crowd of mixed butterflies, merry and inexplicable this far from shore, flutters over the surface of the water.

And he tumbles, lost in the dark sea, love fixed like a great hook in his side. Abdelrahman has been stripped of his powers by the force of love. The earth rotates and the ocean opens its infinite catacombs, its underground dominion of bones, and lets Abdelrahman Salahadin in.

*

Sirine wakes that morning feeling haunted, stirred up by her late conversation with Nathan. She feels as if her own spirit had risen in the night, separate and darkly liquid, barely contained by her body. It's an old, familiar, and uncomfortable feeling. To soothe herself, she thinks of certain heroines from her uncle's stories—warrior women presented with unsolvable fatal riddles. These women conquer palaces and armies, break spells of silence and paralysis, confound sphinxes and jinns, know the seven types of smile, and in the end, just after solving the riddle, they drop their masks, their husband's clothing, their weapons, their pens, and they are simply themselves again. Sirine wants to be this sort of woman and she lets them inspire her but then she worries that she does not have their cleverness or stamina.

King Babar, however, has no interest in Sirine's waking moods. To him, the world is as it is: pure happiness, as long as he can be with the one he loves. He waits for the delicate vibrations of consciousness in the room and then leaps in bed beside Sirine. She kisses him on his purplish muzzle and then dresses.

She hears voices on her way out of the bathroom: one—murmurous, rising and ebbing—is her uncle's, one—clever and sly—sounds like Aziz. They are talking inside her uncle's library and as she enters, the pungent scent of cardamom and coffee is revolving in the air. It seems to emanate from the Persian rugs and the spines of unread books as well as from the bronze coffeepot at the center of the table.

"Hello, Habeebti," her uncle says. "You remember our famous poet friend."

She crosses her arms and grins at Aziz. "You don't seem like the early-riser type to me."

Aziz is lounging in the overstuffed velvet chair by the fireplace—which her uncle calls his too-easy chair. Sirine notes that he has a large plate piled with her gh'rayba sugar cookies in front of him. "It's not early, it's just very very very very late. I haven't been to bed yet. I plan to go home after this midnight snack and sleep until dinnertime."

"Aziz was just now illustrating how Middle Eastern politics are an endless enigma."

"I've never known when to shut up," Aziz says. "I thought writing poetry would teach me that, but I'm a miserable case."

"Join the club," her uncle says. "The Miserable Case Club."

"Oh yes, that club," Sirine says. She pours herself a demitasse of the coffee and sits beside their chairs on the Naugahyde couch. "What happened?"

"Well, nothing actually happened," Aziz says. "This is university life we're talking about."

Her uncle nods and fingers the gilt edge of the porcelain cup.

"I very nicely and sweetly told a woman in my Arabic poetry class that she had to stop saying that contemporary Islam is a woman-hater religion. At least in class she does."

"You did? So then what did she say?"

"She didn't say anything at first. But she did throw a pen at me. And then she said I was trying to oppress her. Me! Aziz! And here I am, the world's biggest feminist and lover of women!"

"Not necessarily the same thing." Her uncle reaches to Aziz's plate and knocks a little sugar off a powdery gh'raybah cookie. "Apparently our dear poet here mixed up some ideas about religion and poetry in the classroom."

"I merely pointed out that there's a tradition of Islamic poetry which uses the notion of the ideal womanly lover as a tribute to divine love. In other words, sexy love poetry that's actually about heaven. And vice versa." He makes a cutting motion with the flat of his hand. "I'm innocent," he says.

"Innocent as a yellow monkey," her uncle says. He and Aziz look at each other. Aziz rolls back in his velvet chair with a laugh that's half-roar and half-wheeze.

"I'm not a professor!" Aziz says. "I never claimed to be! Someone read my little book and called me up and told me to come here and say things to the students. Half the time I don't know what I'm saying. I throw out some thoughts and then hope one or two of them sticks. It's all words to me. When I sit to write I just want to make things clean and clear. Like looking through windows."

"Poor Aziz," her uncle murmurs. "Always cleaning the windows."

"Are you Muslim?" Sirine asks.

He shrugs. "Who knows? I am Aziz, I am large, I contain multitudes. I defy classification. And it just seems to me like Islam has a hard enough time in this country. So, okay, it is the patriarchy and the oppressor and ten million other things besides. That's what religion is supposed to be! But how are the Americans in my class going to learn anything about anything with this woman yelling like a terrorist?"

"Well," her uncle says, "if this poetry-class woman—"

"Rana," says Aziz.

"Rana? She is Arab?" her uncle says.

Aziz puts up his hands. "I don't know what she could be."

"Well, if this Rana-something really had faith in her convictions, then she shouldn't let something like one little poet get her exercised."

"No one's tying her down," Aziz says grumpily. He eats another cookie, then shakes his finger at Sirine. "Yes, yes," he says. "You understand me. Anyone who can make these cookies understands me. It's uncanny how that works. Most women know the true Aziz. I've always sensed that. They see something deep inside of me. You do, don't you? Don't be modest, you read me like a book."

"Maybe like a brochure," her uncle says.

Sirine shrugs but feels flattered that a famous poet would think she understood him. Aziz gets to his feet, takes Sirine's hand, and bows at the waist until he's almost perpendicular to the floor. He closes his eyes and kisses her hand so tenderly it seems she can feel a trickle of warmth beneath her skin.

Her uncle reaches over from his chair, grabs the back of Aziz's shirt, and tugs him back into his chair.

"You do understand," Aziz says after he plunks back down. His grape-black eyes look liquid. "You have redeemed me and I must think how to repay you."

"Oh, now," Sirine says and tries to look demure by smiling at her knees. She notices a little kiss-print in powdered sugar on the back of her hand.

"Truly," her uncle says to Aziz. "In fact, we beg you, no thanks are required."

But Aziz merely winks at Sirine and bites into a cookie.

*

It's slow at the café so Um-Nadia sends Mireille and Sirine out to the Wednesday afternoon farmer's market in Westwood. The two women comb the tables and stalls full of gleaming tomatoes, black-eyed sunflowers, pomegranates full of blood-red seeds. The air smells like burst fruit. Heat rolls in across the neighborhoods, emptying the streets, rippling above the cars. The two women fill bags with knobs and globes of squashes and another bag with garlic and another bag with cucumbers.

"Best walnuts in town," a tanned young farmhand tells Sirine and Mireille. "They're fresh, perfect, and they taste like butter."

Sirine cocks an eyebrow. "At these prices? They better."

He smiles, his teeth impossibly white. "Hey, you gotta pay for the good stuff."

Mireille bats her eyes at him. She's wearing her mother's false eyelashes today and they wobble a bit. "We'll take two pounds," she says archly.

After they get the bag and walk off, Mireille nudges Sirine and says, "I've got an idea, let's go sit in on Han's class."

Sirine's stops and looks up the street to the lip of the campus. "Oh, now," she says. "I don't know. I mean, for one thing I don't know if he'd want us to do that."

"Sure he would! Isn't he teaching today?" Mireille asks. "Let's go up there and watch him. Don't you want to know what kind of a teacher he is?"

Mireille is forty-two, two and a half years older than Sirine, but she can never remember what age she claims to be, so she's apt to tell people she's anywhere between twenty-six and thirty-five. She likes to spend her tips on beauty treatments—facials, pedicures, makeovers—waxes her eyebrows into surprised arcs, and cuts the plastic surgery ads from the paper, preparing for the day, she says, when she's brave enough to get a face-lift. She does half-pushups on the counters in the back kitchen whenever she remembers to.

Sirine hesitates but, as usual, Mireille is able to talk her into doing something she isn't sure she wants to do. The two of them walk up toward the massive campus. Sirine is always surprised by the crowds of students, how lively and free-spirited they seem, and what a world apart the campus is. Sirine and Mireille go into the Languages Building where her uncle also teaches, and they stroll through the corridors; most of the classroom doors are closed, the sounds of teaching muted and watery. But then Sirine thinks she hears the edge of Han's voice around the corner. For a moment she nearly panics, feeling conspicuous and a bit like a spy. But then Mireille grins and pulls her toward Han's voice. Sirine follows, her palms sweat-cool and heart bouncing, and he's there. The door of the classroom is open a crack and she can see Han standing at the other end of the classroom. She's so startled to see him she can hardly believe he doesn't look right up at them.

"Come on, let's go in," Mireille whispers.

Sirine wants to but something holds her back. She feels forward and undignified; she is also caught off guard by the sight of his gracefulness in the classroom. He looks so complete, so perfectly at ease as he teaches—the way she feels when she cooks—that she doesn't want to disturb him.

"So as you all know—right?—Mahfouz was born in Cairo, 1911," he says. His hand is sweeping over the blackboard, making quick, intense notes. "He's written over thirty novels and was awarded the Nobel Prize for literature in 1988. . . ."

He's deep in concentration, his hands moving, his head inclined back toward the class, tender and solicitous. Sirine watches the pretty young women—many of whom look Middle Eastern—sitting in the front rows, so alert, all tiny attentive movements, a crossed leg, a hand sliding across hair.

Mireille whispers in her ear. "It's strange. It's like I can see he's attractive, but he's much too . . . he's too Arab for me."

"Look at all those girls."

She glances at Sirine, eyebrows raised. "They're not as pretty as you."

Sirine picks out one woman in the back of the classroom covered in a black head scarf and dress, so only the pale oval of her face is showing. Her eyes look plush as mink, her lips wide and curving. She is entirely focused on Han.

"I didn't think girls dressed like that in this country," Sirine whispers. "I thought that was just back home."

"I bet their parents make them," Mireille says. "I think that's the one that threw her pen at Aziz. He told me. She walked by the café."

"Her?" Sirine backs away from the doorway and into the hall to face Mireille. "The one that's all covered up?"

"Yeah," she says.

"But she said that Islam is a woman-hater religion—something like that."

Mireille puts her hands on her hips and looks at her as if she were a little crazy. "Sometimes you really don't understand things."

Han's voice rises and Sirine turns back toward the doorway. Han is pacing and scratching things on the blackboard. She remembers that this is some sort of class on contemporary Arab writers; the names Ahdaf Soueif, Emile Habiby, and Naguib Mahfouz are written on the blackboard. "Some critics contend that the Nobel Committee selected Mahfouz because he's a 'safe' writer," Han is saying. "That his style is very Western, very accessible to American readers, somewhat like Dickens, with his large casts of characters, plain prose style, and broad humor."

Two of the women in the front row glance at each other. One tucks her hair behind her ear, then the other one does the same; their crossed legs bob up and down.

"But Mahfouz is an intensely Egyptian author, his writing has reflected the social spectrum of his country—he's been part of creating an exciting new national identity."

His gestures are broad and circular, electric; the chalk streaks over the blackboard. He walks in and out of the columns of light broadcast from the side windows.

" . . . Said commented that Mahfouz is 'a Galsworthy, a Mann, a Zola, and a Jules Romains'—" He draws arrows across the blackboard. Sirine admires his confidence and his easy authority. "It's true—Mahfouz encompasses their social conscience, their attention to human suffering and sensuality as well as their devotion to philosophical reflection."

Han turns to the class, paces back and forth, waving his hand as if he were directing a symphony. "But not everything has to be compared to the West to be impressive." He smiles wryly at the class and Sirine is startled by a burst of laughter from the students. "Mahfouz descends from ancient Arab traditions of art and poetry. Consider the classical Abbasid period—the Abbasids were brave military leaders but they also appreciated the arts and theater. They built tiled mosques and sweeping courtyards, and they developed and refined approaches to education and literature for the spiritual and psychological well-being of their culture. There's an old expression in the Arab world that 'Cairo writes, Beirut publishes, and Baghdad reads.' The Abbasid writers of Baghdad were also readers and thinkers. They were able to evolve a new kind of poetry that broke with rigid pre-Islamic poetic codes by observing and addressing the changes in the contemporary life. Generations later, Mahfouz did the same by going into the streets and alleyways of Cairo and examining the day-to-day life of the people around him." He chalks another arrow across the blackboard. "Mahfouz exemplifies the Abbasid Arab 'Renaissance man,' if you will—both politically and artistically sophisticated and socially aware. . . ." He pauses and looks at the class.

"You might even contrast him with Hemingway. . . ."

There's another smattering of laughter. Some of them nod. The woman that Sirine was looking at raises her hand, doesn't wait to be called on. "I don't see the connection, Professor," she says.

"Ah, Rana," Han says, sighing. He speaks affectionately and familiarly, as if they were old friends. "So impatient—please grant me a minute to make my point."

Rana pretends to pout and Sirine notices two girls in the front row rolling their eyes at each other. "It seems strange," Rana says coyly, clearly enjoying the attention.

"Well, look at it this way—it's all about place and identity," Han says. His hands slide back into his pockets, he takes a few steps in her direction. "Hemingway slipped easily between national identities, traveling all over the world, meeting everyone, having whatever adventures he could, yet he's considered the most quintessentially American writer. Mahfouz, on the other hand, has spent almost his entire life in the same streets and neighborhoods, writing about Cairo and its people, yet he's considered an international author—"

"That's just because he's not an American!" Rana says, tossing her head.

"Okay, but consider this—Mahfouz once said, 'If I had traveled like Hemingway, I'm sure that my work would have been different. My work was shaped by being so Egyptian.'"

Rana allows the barest smile, inclines her head. Sirine is barely breathing as she watches her. Then she feels Mireille's hand on her shoulder. "Come on," she whispers. "We better get back."

Han walks toward the center of the classroom, into a place where the light falls in scalloped waves from a half-turned set of venetian blinds. His hair falls over his forehead and the color in his eyes looks veiled and gold. "The question in the contemporary era is, what does it mean to call oneself an 'Egyptian writer' or even a 'Middle Eastern writer' anymore?" he says, his voice softer now. "The media is saturated with the imagery of the West. Is it even possible—or desirable—to have an identity apart from this?"

Sirine glances back once at the veiled woman before they go. Rana lifts her eyes and Sirine thinks that she is looking at them—or, actually, someone behind them; but when Sirine turns to look, no one is there.

CHAPTER NINE

"Abdelrahman Salahadin carried himself, you might say, like a handful of water," her uncle says. "Which is why his mother Camille, my great-great-auntie Camille, loved him the best. Blue, blue water like the blue-dyed skin of the blue-robed Bedu, palmsful of blueness."

"Blue blue blue!" Um-Nadia mutters. "Where's the story in all this blue business?"

Her uncle sighs, raises his eyebrows. Sirine and her uncle and Um-Nadia sit together in his library of imagined books, visiting after work.

"After he didn't come home from work one day, she knew there was one of two possibilities: one, that her son had been bewitched by a houri, a jinn, or a beautiful woman. Two, he'd finally drowned, just as she'd told him would happen. And being a perspicacious woman, she knew it could also be some unlucky combination of the two. My auntie Camille was a freed Nubian slave—she was no dumb-dumb. For a time, she was the third wife of the Sultan of Imr, a sultana!"

"Oof," Um-Nadia says. "If I had an avocado for every sultan I meet, all of us would have smooth skin."

Sirine's uncle sniffs. "Any old way, the story of how she

tumbled from royalty to slavery is an interesting one which I may someday tell. Now, then. The knob in the spine of this story has my auntie Camille recovering from an unpleasant stint of slavery. She long suspected that her son wanted revenge for her enslavement, hence his endless hidery and seekery with the notorious Saudi slavers.

"Her hand henna-painting business barely paid the rent, so Auntie Camille decided the only way to gather the necessary resources to find her son was—following family tradition—to sell herself back into slavery. But she would not surrender herself to any run-of-the-mill slavers. No, she offered herself to none other than the British explorer Sir Richard Burton—who had none of the sweetness of my favorite Welsh actor, only the same name."

Um-Nadia sighs. "So in other words this is some kind of story about some movie star."

"I just told you, it's the other Richard Burton," Sirine's uncle fumes.

"Sorry, sorry, sorry, Sahib," Um-Nadia says quickly, rolling her eyes at Sirine.

"Fine! So! The reason—as I was about to tell you—that Aunt Camille sold herself to Burton was because she'd heard that the Englishman had found the source of the Nile River."

"Why, was it lost?" Um-Nadia claps her hand over her mouth as soon as she says this.

"May I speak?" Her uncle looks around at both of them. "Or should I just go to bed now?" He stands. Both women protest and he sits back down. "Well. She had a plan to find her son. She thought that if she could convince Richard Burton to take her to the source of the Nile, she could then meet the Mother of All Fish and ask for her help—mother-to-mother-style—in establishing the whereabouts of her son, my cousin, Abdelrahman Salahadin."

"That's how they thought back then," Um-Nadia explains and winks at Sirine. "Me, I prefer to fry my fish."

"All right, then, clearly you don't care about the story—" Sirine's uncle says, standing.

"No, no, please, Uncle," Sirine says, touching his wrist. "We're listening."

He looks for a moment at Um-Nadia, who looks back with a very innocent expression, and then sits down again. "Where was I?"

＊

It takes Sirine a while to fall asleep; her head whirls with bits of stories and advice. She begins to drift, but then there is a sound in her dream like a spattering of rain. She dreams she is floating in a river and particles of rain dust the air around her. She holds out her hands, lifts her face. The rain gets louder.

And then she wakes and it isn't exactly the sound of rain anymore. There's a tick and tick against her window. She nudges King Babar, asleep against her ankles, who grumbles and moans, and she gets up and goes to the window. It's Han, he's standing by the house with handfuls of stones, looking up and grinning like crazy. She slides open her window, laughing and trying to be quiet at the same time. "You're going to wake up my uncle!"

"Hi!" he whisper-shouts. "Hey there."

"What are you doing?"

He smiles, almost demure. "I don't know exactly. Do you mind?"

"What time is it?"

He puts one hand against the side of the house as if he intends to scale it. "Can I come in? Just for a minute—no more than a minute. I just need to see you again."

She goes down to the front door in her tattered blue plaid pajamas—a pair she's worn for years—the cool black air sifting in from the front door, curling around her bare ankles like a sort of magic spell. "Here I am." She's a bit shy. "Um. Would you like some hot cocoa?"

His face is hard to see in the dark. He puts one hand to her hair and her knees weaken again with the memory of the previous night's kiss. "So there you were outside my classroom today," he says.

"You saw us?"

"How could I not? Why didn't you come in?"

She stares at him, stricken with embarrassment. Finally he looks around and says, "And this is your uncle's house?"

She considers that her uncle could be asleep in any of the armchairs downstairs. "Come on," she whispers. "Let's go up to my room."

Sirine has always gone out to meet her boyfriends; she's never before brought a man upstairs into her bedroom. Standing there with Han, she feels as if she has introduced a wild element into the room, the space lit only by streetlights and the stars. Now the room looks different—clean-swept and bare: blank walls, a barely rumpled comforter on her bed. She thinks *spinster* and hugs her elbows. Han leans in the doorway looking in. "Aha," he says. "So, your secret place."

"Secret?"

"Sure—bedrooms are full of all sorts of interesting hidden things."

"I don't have any," Sirine says. "Not that I know of."

"We all have hidden things."

"Then mine must be hidden from me too." She tows him to her bed and they sit side by side. She feels clumsy and excited as a teenager. "Really, I just sleep here. It's boring."

"Did you do all those sorts of American girl things? Have slumber parties and pillow fights and all that stuff on TV?"

"Hardly. I used to stay up half the night watching the news with my uncle or making tea and snacks for his friends. They'd all come over and just talk and talk and talk."

"That doesn't sound very American. Didn't you have, what? A bedtime?"

She laughs and runs her hand over the comforter. "Most of the time I didn't even sleep in here. I'd fall asleep wherever. I remember I liked to sleep on the carpet under the dining room table with the dog. My uncle didn't know exactly how to raise a kid. So we pretty much just made it up as we went along."

"And look how well you turned out," Han muses.

She looks down and pushes out her lips, trying to hide a smile.

He says, "God, I was happy to see you at school."

"I know," she says, not looking up. "Me too."

"I couldn't look right at you, though. I couldn't have finished class." His hand moves over hers, turning it palm up. "Can I give you something?"

Sirine lifts her hand. She is holding a new silver key.

"It's to my apartment," he says. She looks at him, startled. "I would like you to have it. I mean, if you don't mind."

"You want to give me your key?"

"I was just thinking about it." He smiles, holds up his hands helplessly.

"Somehow I was thinking it would make me feel better . . . knowing that you had this."

She stares at him, wondering what to say, but she feels oddly pleased and flattered; a shiver runs over her. He pulls her in closer against the warmth of his rib cage, then lowers his lips to the top of her head. She tilts her head so he is kissing her forehead, then beside her eye, then the outer corner of her mouth.

And then they kiss again, her mouth softening, and their desire is like a blue flash, their bodies moving up against each other. They lay back on the bed as they kiss, bumping up against King Babar, who groans and complains and stays asleep. Sirine's skin is flushed and sensitive, her lips raw, lightly abraded from the start of stubble on his face. His hands move flickering through the thin cotton of her pajama top. She pushes them away, grinning. She feels both daring and chaste. Something inside her resisting, a giddy mixture of excitement and fear. She refuses to progress past kissing, but then they kiss so deeply that they knock their teeth together and laugh and then kiss some more. She squeezes the key in her hand.

*

Sirine wakes at five, her usual time, when the dawn isn't even silver yet and all the birds are asleep. She realizes slowly that Han is beside her, still dressed and sleeping, and King Babar is snug between them, nestled in like a baby.

"Oh my God." She's half-laughing and half-upset, shaking Han. He wakes and looks around, startled. He sits up. His hair has fallen in a glossy sweep over his forehead and his clothes are rumpled, his shirt twisted around on his chest. She covers her mouth with her hand and looks at the door. "My uncle's already up! You've got to go."

He nods, kisses her twice, and strokes his thumb over her cheekbone. "So this is what it is to date a good Arab girl."

"Good Arab girls don't date," she says and looks behind her at her shut door, thinks she hears her uncle in the bathroom.

He gets up and tries to straighten his clothes. He pushes back his hair. "Will I get to see you later?"

"It's Saturday—it's a long workday today."

"I don't care," he says and moves toward the window. "I can wait."

"You can't go through the window! We're up high."

"Just one floor," he says, grinning a little crazily. "So do I get to see you tonight?"

"I don't know yet," she hisses, smiling and annoyed with herself for smiling. "Please don't—you'll hurt yourself."

"Oh, I'm already doomed," he says cheerfully, slipping his legs out. And before she can stop him, he slides all the way out, hangs by his fingertips five feet from the ground, and then drops. He staggers, turns, waving and blowing kisses as he goes.

*

During her morning break Sirine goes to the back courtyard, which Um-Nadia calls the garden of birds. She sinks into the string hammock tied between two bending palm trees, partially hidden from view behind a bower of broad, fan-shaped leaves. She drowses, recalling her night with Han, her body soft with desire and heat; there are bits of birdsong that flit through the air like chips of odd colors. The air smells like olives and cypress and roasting herbs—the lavender and sage and thyme and rosemary, onions and garlic shoots that grow half-cared-for by Mireille and Sirine, half-wild, all around the courtyard. She feels weak and watery-kneed, as if perhaps she's coming down with something, as if she hovers slightly outside of her own body. She only got a few hours of sleep last night and she's starting to drift off when a low rumble of voices moves through the kitchen and onto the back porch.

Nathan and Aziz walk out the back door in midargument, their bodies and gestures buoyant with the energy of their words. Nathan runs his hands over his stubbly cropped head and Aziz's hair is ruffed up like blackbird feathers; neither of them sees her. They sit at the wrought-iron table under the spreading bougainvillea branches, scraping the iron chairs back loudly. They lean forward and crook their ankles around the chair legs.

Sirine closes her eyes and for a moment the traffic sounds and the buzzing electric lines beyond the courtyard all blur into a soft whine like a cicada shrilling.

"But the old-timer Middle Eastern poetry," Aziz is saying, "it's such a bore. It's all nightingales that aren't really birds and roses that aren't really flowers. And the big-head critics say Omar Khayyam wasn't really writing about food and wine, it was more divine love or some other nicety-nice. Nobody can ever just enjoy themselves. I prefer when the prayers turn out to be about sex, not the other way around."

Nathan sniffs. "Why is that so terrible? It's poetry. You know, symbolism."

"It's smoke, mirrors, et cetera," Aziz says. "Let us just say I prefer a little old-fashioned kissing. Maybe a little plain old-fashioned wild sex."

Sirine opens her eyes again and sees the men through a filmy sun-and-leaf haze. Then she lifts one hand for shade and notices Han poking his head through the back door. "Sirine?"

"Over here!" Nathan says, waving.

"I don't think we were who he had in mind," Aziz says

"We're discussing Middle Eastern poetry," Nathan tells Han.

"Oh, well, count me out." Han takes the third seat at the table but scans the courtyard over his shoulder. "I don't do poetry."

Sirine stretches, then decides to wait behind her screen of leaves.

"Oh, I see. And I suppose you prefer something like: 'They went to the bar. And it was good. And they drank a beer, and that was good too.'"

"Is that Aziz doing Hemingway?" Han asks.

"Aziz interprets all the greats," Aziz says. "My Arabic poet can beat up your Hemingway any day." He turns to Nathan. "He could beat up Whitman too. You know there's a great tradition of sensitive yet manly Arab poets."

Nathan puts one finger in the air. " 'I live in the face of a woman / who lives in a wave— / a surging wave / that finds a shore / lost like a harbor under shells.' "

Han taps the edge of the table. "Bravo, Nathan."

"Yes, very bravo," says Aziz. "That's the poetry of Ali Ahmed Said, of course, more famously known as Adonis. I'd recognize that attitude anywhere. So what about this?" He clears his throat, then says: " 'A young gazelle there is in the tribe, dark-lipped, fruit-shaking, / flaunting a double necklace of pearls and topazes, / holding aloof, with the herd grazing in the lush thicket, / nibbling the tips of the araq-fruit, wrapped in her cloak.' "

"Ibn al-Abd!" Nathan says. "That's easy. 'The Ode of Tarafah.' "

"Okay, okay." Han raises one hand. "Let me try one: 'And a red feather

/ Is blown into the air by the magician / Sometimes turning into a gazelle / With horns of gold / Sometimes into a priestess practicing seduction / And the game of the end / In the harem of the caliph / His night is haunted by ghosts and boredom.'"

"Abdul Wahab Al-Bayati!" Both Nathan and Aziz cry before Han is finished.

"'On the morning they left / we said goodbye / filled with sadness / for the absence to come,'" Nathan says.

"Oh, that's, um—that's . . . I know that . . ." Han waves his hand around.

Aziz sits up. "That's 'Leavetaking' by Ibn Jakh, eleventh century. Okay, you'll never get this one—I dare both of you!" He lifts both hands and declaims: " 'If white is the color / of mourning in Andalusia, / it is a proper custom. / Look at me, / I dress myself in the white / of white hair / in mourning for my youth.' " He folds his arms over his chest. "My theme song."

"Sure, that's 'Mourning in Andalusia' by Abu il-Hasan al-Husri," Nathan says. He passes one hand contemplatively over the top of his hair. "Actually, that was a favorite of a bunch of the young writers at the French Council."

Han tilts his head toward Nathan. "The French Council. Oh. Not . . . the little office in Tahrir Square?"

"Yes! You know it? A group of students and writers from the University of Baghdad used to gather there in the afternoons and talk about writing and recite work."

"Why does no one in America recite poetry?" Aziz complains. "They go to the coffeehouse and they just drink the coffee."

"I heard about the French Council salons," Han says to Nathan. His voice is spirited. Sirine sits forward in the hammock so it sways a little and the leaves undulate overhead. "I always wanted to go."

"You should have! There were all sorts of arts societies," Nathan says. "Not just poetry. We met all over Baghdad—actors and singers and painters. Loads of us. Of course, so much had to be done in secret because of Saddam."

Aziz sinks his head into his hand. "Ah, but doesn't the taboo make things more exciting?"

"*No.*" Both Han and Nathan speak at once.

"Well," Han concedes, "sometimes. It did seem exciting to me at the time. But I went away to school when I was still very young, before I could really see any of this for myself. When I was a young boy I used to bicycle past the cafés and try and look inside."

"Oh yeah, the cafés and the clubs were all crowded, full of life," Nathan says. "Of course, people frequently went to each other's homes—especially as there were more and more problems. But I thought the best scene was at the Sapphire Club. Late night. After all the tourists and expatriates went home."

"The Sapphire Club!" Han says. Sirine hears the sweet twist in his voice, as if he were looking at something that he yearned for. Her heart trips. She pushes off from the hammock and tries to get a better glimpse of his face but loses her balance and her hand splashes through the leaves. "Oh!"

Then the back door opens and Um-Nadia is standing on the porch in her gold high-heeled slippers. She looks from Han to Aziz to Nathan. "Where is Chef?" she says and waves at the screen of leaves. "Cleopatra? You are needed at the grill!"

Quietly, guiltily, Sirine steps around the leaves and all three men turn to look at her.

CHAPTER TEN

Sir Richard Burton wandered the Arab world like a speckled wraith. He dressed in native garb, spent hours gazing into Arab eyes. Arabic, in turn, went into his heart like a piercing seed, growing tendrils of beliefs and attitudes. But his tongue was flat as slate. He spoke so many languages that he had no native music left in him. He did, however, like so many Victorians, have an aptitude for ownership, an attachment to things material and personal, like colonies and slaves—he especially enjoyed owning slaves while living in someone else's house. He was an amateur slaver but he was a professional amateur, wearing the robes of so many different tribes, eating the food and entering the land of so many different countries.

Burton had written a book called *The Perfumed Garden*, and after she sold herself to Burton, Abdelrahman Salahadin's mother Auntie Camille found herself in just such a place. Burton's house in Syria, where he was residing at the time, was loud with birdsong, splashy with butterflies; ladders rose into bowers, grapes swayed, trellises swung and vines clung, and the sky arched like the roof of a mosque. And there was Sir Richard sitting in the middle of it, crouching on cushions, fat as a pasha, with his friends and all the local yokels coming and going, talking, eating, forming opinions, messing up the paperwork, et cetera. Not like this so-called America today where they just talk all day long on their phone, their computer, and no one ever lays eyes on each other and no one remembers how to cook a tomato or to bring flowers or to kiss the babies.

Anyway, Sir Richard said to Auntie Camille, yes, it's true I know the way to the source of the Nile, I helped find it, but it no longer matters. I no longer want anything to do with that silly river. You see, Sir Richard's former best friend had grabbed all the credit for himself about finding the source, so Sir Richard's heart was no longer in it.

What does Camille do? Does she lose heart? Not in the least. She sits on a rug on the terrace and starts to meditate on the garden. She hears the sound of leaves on leaves and that sound is a word and the word, she says, is *aujuba*, wonder. She watches the way the nightingales and the hummingbirds spin around the garden like spirits and shadows. She makes a house of the outdoors, a cape of the night. You may have guessed that she wasn't much of a slave, but that was of little consequence to Burton, who, remember, was just an amateur, and enjoyed collecting people just for the sake of collecting. He adorned himself with Arabs, Chinese, and Indians, and he wrote and wrote and wrote, trying to fill the empty space inside him with a layer of ink.

He also happened to be married. It was a marriage conducted at arm's length. But of course, as Chekhov said: if you fear loneliness then marriage is not for you. His wife was an agreeable soul who routinely burnt whatever writing of her husband's was not to her liking.

Well, it could not have escaped the notice of Mrs. Sir Richard that a coal-eyed beauty with shimmering hair had taken up residence on one of their terraces, and when she pointed this out to Mr. Sir Richard, he said vaguely, hm, oh yes, so she is, so she is. And when the Mrs. pressed for more information, he said, oh, mm, she's one of the slaves, dear.

But here is the interesting part. In her slow and very nice and deliberate way, Aunt Camille began to take up space in Burton's imagination. Like a creature leaving a chrysalis, she began the metamorphosis from slave to muse. He found he liked to contemplate her curled up on the lawn while he ate his morning scone and he liked to watch her peeling loquats while he worked on his conjugation of Croatian intransitives.

He was a slaver, an explorer, and a translator, yet he could not quite translate Camille's white Nile of skin and blue Nile of hair into the right sorts of words. She made him ache in seven different places and she taught him the seven kinds of smiles; she filled his sleep with smoke and made his mouth taste of cherries. And one day, after thumbing through some old notebooks, random tales from ancient Persia, Phoenicia, Hindustan, Burton found himself writing the thunderstruck phrase: "And afterwards." He had begun his famous, criminal, suggestive, imperial version of Victorian madness dissolved in the sky over the Middle East—his translation of *The Thousand and One Nights*.

*

That evening after work, while mockingbirds are singing loudly in the branches and the palms tumble over her head in the breeze, their fronds like crossed swords, Sirine walks to the Victory Market.

"Bonjour, honored chef!" Khoorosh cries out as soon as she enters. The shop is small and close, the air damp with a rich influx of spices, garlic, saffron, and clove. Sirine often shops there, even when she doesn't need anything—just to sample a new spice or to taste one of Khoorosh's imported ingredients, dreaming of new dishes located somewhere between Iraq, Iran, and America.

"Chef, these I put aside, just for you," Khoorosh says, as he hurries to the back of the store. He returns with preserved lemons, Turkish honey, pomegranate paste, and a container of tiny apricots, and brings them to the counter. "Look at these beauties," he says suavely. "The foods of love."

"Beautiful. How much are they?" Sirine asks.

"What are you talking about? You're insulting me now."

"Khoorosh, you can't always give me everything."

"No, these are a gift."

"I want to pay for my gifts."

"Never mind. These are a gift from my hand to yours. If you say one more single word about money I'm going to become very upset. I'm developing a headache now."

More customers come in and greet Khoorosh in Farsi, the language rippling fluidly between them. Sirine flees back into the shelves, the intimate smoke of spices mixing with the sound of the customers' laughter.

She enjoys the refined cadences of Farsi, enjoys this eavesdropping without understanding; it is comforting and delightful and deeply familiar—the immigrants' special language of longing and nostalgia. Her childhood was spent in places like the Victory Market, holding her uncle's hand as they wandered in search of the special flavors that weren't in any of the big American grocery stores. It didn't matter if the shop was Persian, Greek, or Italian, because all of them had the same great bins of beans and lentils, glass cases of white cheeses and braided cheeses, murky jars of olives, fresh breads and pastries flavoring the air. And the shop makes her think of Han—somehow, everything seems redolent, brimming with suggestions of Han. When she turns into an aisle full of bins of red and yellow spices and resinous scents that swirl through the air, she is swept by a craving so thorough, she understands finally that she isn't getting sick. It seems that something potent was unlocked inside her during the night, as they shared sleep without quite touching, his breath fanning her face. The intimate proximity of Han's body comes back to her now, the scent of his skin echoed in the rich powder of spices. Desire saturates her, filling her cells, and her sense of reserve instantly gives way. The sweep of her own hand through her hair, the switch of her legs, even the rush of breath through her mouth stirs her. She hurries with her few supplies to the cash register, her head lowered and her hands fumbling with money, and pays for as much as Khoorosh will allow.

Sirine walks out then, forgetting her purchases, and Khoorosh has to run outside with her bag. She laughs breathlessly and tucks the bag into her bicycle basket, knocks back the kickstand, and heads into the star-sprinkled night. She's in a postwork haze, her joints loose, muscles slack, but she pedals until she's sweaty and breathless. She doesn't even know if Han will be home, but then he is there, opening the door and nodding as if in answer to a question. He puts her bag on the counter and looks at her. He moves a few steps closer, then, instinctively, shyly, she takes a few steps back. "Wait," she says. She removes the pint of apricots, plump and exquisite as roses, and offers him one. He takes a bite and puts his hand over hers as she takes a bite, the velvety peel and fruit sugar filling her whole mouth. The air between them is complicated, infused with the scents from the bags: toasted sesame, sweet orange blossom water, and fragrant rosewater.

They finish it and she drops the apricot pit in the sink; Han cups her hand again and licks a drop of juice from her fingertip.

Sirine holds her breath; the ground gets a little wavy. Han slips behind her and runs his hands over the tops of her shoulders. He tilts the top of his head to the back of her head, squeezes, and begins rubbing the muscles between her neck and shoulders. Her head falls forward, captured by the pleasure of it. He presses the heels of his palms along her inner back and squeezes her shoulder blades and rubs just inside them. She lets him work his way down to the small of her back, then back up to the V between her shoulders. He strokes the sides of her rib cage, digs into the tight saddle of flesh over her shoulders, rubs the back of her neck, then runs his knuckles down the length of her back. He interweaves new strokes and pressures. After several deepening, luxurious passes, her body is boneless and liquid.

She turns in to him and they twine their arms around each other. They slide and kiss and Sirine toes off her shoes. She dances him backward into the bedroom, backing down onto his mattress. They pull at each other's clothes, trying to unwrap each other, kicking at pants and tossing shirts. He pauses and carefully removes the yellow plastic barrettes in her hair. They roll over each other, stroke each other's arms and legs; he laces his fingers into hers. She opens her mouth and tastes his skin and tongue. He is amber and caramel and earth-colored. His skin excites her; she inhales deeply, as if she could take in his essence; he tastes of almond, of sweetness. She hesitates a moment, then says, "Do you have, you know—"

"What?"

"You know. Protection?"

His face goes blank and he says, "Protection against what?"

Then he smiles, rolls over to his discarded pants, and pulls a condom out of the pocket. He waves the plastic wrapper by one corner and says, "We're safe!"

The last time Sirine has had sex with anyone was with a tanned beach boy named Danny, over three years ago: long enough for her to have more or less forgotten the feeling of it. But now, when Han rocks his body over hers, the lean weight of his thighs rubbing against hers, it is practically a new sensation, the physical pleasure opening and stirring through her muscles. Her back arches and her ribs seem to unlock. He moves with a deep, almost animal assurance, seemingly without any self-consciousness at all: his body wholly engaged and his eyes steady and focused. She opens her mouth and the only sound is a rushing breath, sweeping through, expanding and contracting the room. They move together, watching each other, hands joined.

At the end, Han's eyes dilate and darken and his mouth opens as if in surprise but he makes no sound; the length of his body holds and contracts, softens and slowly collapses over hers. She presses in against him and then feels that she is falling through her body; her pulse is fast inside her chest. She finally shuts her eyes and feels the last riffling sensations beneath her skin, and then, briefly, has a sense much like leaving her body: rising just beyond their small balcony, seeing rows of balconies, pale streets, plaster houses the color of skin, neat red tile roofs. The violet night streaks across their faces. There are glistening palms, pool-dark salamanders between the houses, patient iguanas. She senses the insect world turning, horned beetles and wax-winged figures taking to the air. She opens her eyes into the damp, fever dream of their embrace.

Han's arms smell like bread and sleep; when he gathers her back, it is like being drawn into a world beneath the water, an undersea cave. She closes her eyes and floats. And eventually, still in his arms, she sleeps.

*

At points, her sleep feels heavy as the ocean, other times she rises near the surface and seems to hear odd sounds: small cries, untuned music. Or she glimpses cloudy faces, unknown apparitions. She feels vaguely that she is being watched.

Sirine wakes after just a couple hours, in the early part of dawn, and the apartment is filled with a silver fog. A country filled with milky canals. She walks to the door and looks back at Han and his face is smooth with sleep. His skin has taken on a bronze patina.

She walks around his small bedroom, naked and bleary-eyed, feeling like she's awakened into someone else's dream. There are objects scattered around: a few books inscribed with gold Arabic calligraphy, a glass bottle filled with colored sands, a string of beads, a folded-up square of silk, a brass letter opener, and beside this, a photograph in a silver frame: a younger Han beside a boy and young woman, each of them with the same nut-brown skin, chestnut-colored eyes. They look happy and complete and Sirine feels a vague jealousy over their apparent ownership of each other. She tries to remember if Han said he had a sister. She replaces the picture carefully beside the letter opener.

Drowsy, she is about to return to the warm cave of his arms and chest, but she pauses for a moment, listening. Did she just hear something? She stands in the doorway that faces out to the balcony and sees how the cardamom-scented fog is everywhere in the streets, as if it rose from the breath of dreamers inside the streets of houses.

She turns to go back to bed but then a glint of something catches her eye. And she turns and it cannot be, but the darkness and the fog create the illusion of a gargoyle face peering into the window, as if someone were crouching in a corner of the balcony, watching.

She catches her breath. But she knows this must be a mirage, part of a dream. She closes her eyes and moves backward, slowly and carefully, until her leg touches the edge of the bed; she lowers herself in and lies there for a while, waiting for her mind to settle, telling herself, it's nothing, there's no one out there. She pulls the covers up tight around her neck crawls in close to Han, and, after much turning and resettling, gradually falls back to sleep.

*

When she wakes again the fog has vanished and it is morning. Han grinds coffee in a heavy copper grinder, stirs tea full of mint and sugar, and cuts up chunks of cheese, ripe tomatoes, and cream-colored avocados for their breakfast. After eating, they drive to Santa Monica and walk through the early postcard-blue streets. The sun at dawn is already roasting the sky, clouds melted down to ribs and fish bones, the palm trees glistening with heat. Sirine and Han stroll past businesspeople, students, café workers, and tourists, a blur of movement.

Then a little boy with wide brown eyes and silky eyelashes says, "Look at them, Mommy." His mother hushes him, grabbing his hand. Sirine glances at Han's hand, the perfect, coffee-colored skin against her own whiteness.

The sun is too hot, so they move into the shade and find a building open at the edge of the park, the senior center. It's shadowy relief inside but a crinkled man in a wheelchair glides toward them over the dim, waxed floors.

"Center's closed," he says. They start to go and he glides closer. "Unless it was the camera obscura you came to see? The key's on the shelf, you can just go on up, then."

They look at each other, turn, and start to climb the squeaking stairs. The air is close and feels heavy with must or mildew like a closet that's been shut up for too long. At the top they enter an unlit paneled chamber, and at the center of the room is a large, colorful disk covering the surface of a round table. It looks like a painting, but Sirine realizes the disk is full of moving light. "It's some kind of periscope image," Han says. He reaches over and turns the camera mechanism and the panorama swirls across the table. "Look, this is a projection from the street outside, close to the building."

Sirine strolls around the big table: it is full of the images of moving cars, strolling tourists, rising seagulls. "Wild." She imagines the room filled with old people from the senior center, all of them crouched over the table, watching people on the streets. "It's a spy camera," she says. "This is better than watching TV. You can see what the neighbors are up to."

"How interesting," Han says. "No one would ever suspect all those senior citizens were hidden in here spying on everyone. Not to mention that this contraption came from the Muslims."

"This camera thing?"

Han turns the periscope some more, studying the image. "A first-century physicist, Al-Hazen from Baghdad—he dreamed up the camera obscura."

She smiles slyly. "Did he envision it being in the top floor of a senior center?" Glancing down, she notices among the projected images on the tabletop what looks like a single immobile figure in the center of all the activity, a man's form, seeming somehow to be staring from his place on the table directly at her. "Look at that," she says, pointing.

Han squints and the images shimmer for a moment and refocus and he is looking just beyond the point where the man had been standing to an empty park bench facing the ocean. The man is gone. "Look at what?" he says. "What did you see?"

"I thought—I don't know—it's too weird."

"Tell me."

"I've been seeing things lately." She puts her hand over the spot where she thought she saw the man and the images move over her fingers.

*

Han insists they walk outside to the place—she remembers the bench, a certain stand of tiger lilies—but the man is gone. Or was never there in the first place. She looks back toward the senior center and now she sees it—the rotating camera obscura, perched on the rooftop under its own little peaked roof, almost invisible.

"Just because he isn't still here doesn't mean he wasn't there in the first place," Han says gallantly. "In fact, that's probably exactly what it *does* mean."

"My uncle says it's the Arab disease. Where you keep thinking the C.I.A. is following you around."

"Having anyone follow me around tends to make me nervous."

She glances at him and for some reason she says, "Nathan does. I mean—follow you around."

"Let's see," Han says, amused. "Could Nathan be C.I.A.? He wears those tight glasses and he's always staring at people and taking pictures. But on the other hand, he's also totally loyal—his Arabic is surprisingly good—he even knows the village slang. He's certainly the hardest-working student I've ever seen. And I think basically he's pure of heart." He sits on the slatted park bench and holds one hand out to Sirine. She sits, sliding inside the crook of his arm. The park is situated high above the beach and they watch the waves spinning in and out. She is taken with Han's phrase, "pure of heart," and thinks to ask what he means by this, but she hesitates and instead she says, "I'd love to be able to speak Arabic." She leans back, the sun warm on her face and shoulders.

He looks pleased, his chin dipping toward his chest. "Really? You'd want to learn? It's a tough language to pick up."

She smiles and shrugs. She grew up around Arabic conversations and she feels the presence of Arabic somewhere behind her mind, like a ghost language—crisp, clear, and ocean-blank. And she feels guilty that she can't speak it.

"You're not really fluent in a language until it's pretty much invisible to you," Han says. "When I translate, I deal with words as conscious things. You stare at the pages and you know what everything means, in both languages, and you wonder how on earth to make both languages—with all their history and innuendos—mean the same thing."

"When you put it like that, it sounds sort of impossible."

He rubs his palm over his forehead a moment. "Trying to translate Hemingway into Arabic is like trying to translate a bird into a river. Not only do you have to translate the words, you also have to try and translate the feelings and ideas for all kinds of things from one culture to another—like what faith or courage is."

"I barely know what those things are in the first place."

Han smiles and looks away, makes a little sound.

"What?"

"I was thinking of myself when I was ten years old. How I could never have fathomed something like this. That someday I'd be sitting in a place like this, with a woman like you."

Sirine tries to imagine Han as a ten-year-old boy, which she finds is a bit difficult—there is some aspect of him that strikes her as eternally adult. Then she thinks of the photograph she found in his room—the younger Han standing beside a child and a young woman. "Where are the rest of your family?" she asks.

He doesn't answer right away. She waits, watching the water. The Santa Monica waves are soft and undulant, lacy with foam. Finally he says, "My mother's side of the family are in Nasra—in southern Iraq. My father's sister Dalal lives in the north. I have some other relatives who're scattered around the Middle East and Central America since the Gulf War. And my mother and brother are all still in Baghdad."

She waits a beat, thinking, and then says, "And your sister?"

As soon as she asks that, she thinks she sees something happen inside Han, an infinitesimally small but distinct sensation, as if a tiny internal organ had collapsed. But he only shakes his head and says, "She's there, in

Iraq with the others." Then he says, "Okay, now you tell me—where is your family?"

Sirine holds out her hand. "Here. That's it—my dad and uncle were originally from Iraq but I don't know where exactly. My mom's from Santa Barbara—you know, California—and I don't know her side of the family. My parents are both dead, I don't have any brothers or sisters. It's all pretty much just been me and my uncle for a long time."

He lifts his hand from her shoulder, touches her loose hair, and looks at her thoughtfully. "Which is why you'll never leave L.A., isn't it?" he says.

She starts to protest, then hesitates. She glances over Han's head and notices the camera obscura rotating under its peaked cap on the building top. The wind rises and shakes the rosebushes and kicks up some sandy dust. "I guess I'm always looking for my home, a little bit. I mean, even though I live here, I have this feeling that my real home is somewhere else somehow."

He shades his eyes with the V of his open hand and for a moment she can't read his expression. "What makes a place feel like home for you, then?"

"Work," she says. "Work is home."

"How American of you," he says, smiling. "And is work family as well?"

She looks at him a second. "It might be."

His breath is light and transparent against her brow. He doesn't say anything. They watch the creep of the far gray water and Sirine listens to the deep two-part pulse in Han's chest. Then she feels him take a breath. "There is something else I think I haven't mentioned," he says softly. "About my brother."

"Yes?"

A flurry of wishcatcher seedpods float through the air, touch his hair. He clears his throat and sits forward. Whatever is in his mind pinches his temples; his eyes lower. He runs the back of his hand over his forehead. She waits, staring at his shoulder blade; she has a rising sense of pressure, like fingertips pushing in against her sternum. "You don't have to tell me." Her voice is very quiet.

"He's my younger brother," Han says slowly. "His name is Arif. I haven't seen him—or my parents, for that matter—in over twenty years."

"You haven't been back in twenty years?"

"I escaped to England not long after Saddam Hussein came to power."

"That must've been terrifying."

He smiles vaguely. "It sounds more interesting than it was. Basically I had a scholarship and no easy way to get to England. Arif was only twelve years old when I left the country, but he'd already begun working, in the grand Iraqi tradition, on overthrowing the leadership—reading and writing mainly subversive poetry—if you can imagine."

"I think my uncle writes some of that. There's lots of rhymes?"

"That's it—rhymes and bold pronouncements." He grins broadly. "I set a bad example. He's almost ten years younger—and he got the idea that I was some sort of daring revolutionary gone into exile. I wanted him to leave the country when he still had the chance, but he refused to go. He said he had his work," Han says, rolling his eyes. "He was arrested and imprisoned before his thirteenth birthday. That was twenty-one years ago. And I can't return to help him."

Her breath feels high and tight in her chest. "Why not?"

"Mm. Why not." He weaves his fingers together, a sort of half-prayer. "There are many why-nots in Iraq. It's a tricky place for Iraqi men—there's the army, jail, torture, hangings. I'm wanted by the government for dodging army duty. For one. There are plenty of other aggravating factors." Han stares at his praying fingers. "The ruler is famous for his ruthlessness. When his sons-in-law returned to Iraq after breaking out of the country without permission, Saddam's idea of mercy was allowing them to apologize for escaping before having them executed. If Arif is still alive . . ." he pauses. "If Arif is still alive, it might make things worse for him if I reentered the country. But then again, perhaps not. Perhaps it wouldn't make any difference at all. That's part of what makes this so painful. The frustration. And just not knowing." He studies Sirine's face again with his meticulous gaze. Then he folds his hands under his chin. "How can I talk about it? I don't even know how to think about it. And now I've probably frightened you with all this drama and intrigue."

"Oh, I don't scare that easy," she says casually, but she isn't so sure. It's so hard for Sirine to imagine—the threats, the imprisoned brother—as they recline in that creamy Santa Monica air. "They would kill you?" she asks.

She slides her hand over his; she has no intention of letting him go anywhere. "For real?"

Han ticks back his head—the sad, Arab gesture. The one her uncle has taught her means something like, aren't you listening? His expression seems a sort of surrender: the loss of a thing that he has already lost before. He looks away.

More questions sift through her mind. But then a sleek black bird perches in the palm just over their heads, yelling at them, and Sirine realizes it's gotten late. The sun is up and the insects in the trees around them hiss like steam kettles. Sirine will be late to work and Mireille will make the coffee, which will put everyone in a bad mood. She looks through the grove of wandering palm fronds, the trunks crosshatched and speckled like gray flannel. A movement in the trees startles her. For a moment she thinks she sees a young man's face, nutmeg skin and clove-black hair; he is moving through the trees, watching over his shoulder and running away from them. But he is far away now, a dot of light between the trees, so far away he might as well not have existed.

CHAPTER ELEVEN

At the stylish home of Sir Richard Burton, the air was full of tiger-striped hornets and bees dangling their gold-pollened legs, and the sky was full of dark blue storms. Aunt Camille had been sleeping and waking and meditating on her Hariz carpet on the side lawn, sometimes joined by a jackal-eared dog named Napoleon-Was-Here. She was waiting for Burton's help in locating her naughty missing son Abdelrahman Salahadin, and at the same time she was in the midst of becoming Burton's unwitting muse and collaborator—a muse, of course, being the ultimate collaborator. She was such a bad slave that she'd come out the other end of her total indifference and emerged as a kind of royalty. All the household waited on her—the servants, the foreign scholars and students, the English explorers, and even Burton himself—bringing her glasses of tea and plates of German butter cookies. Camille had performed a much greater service for Burton than any raft of slaves with feather dusters. Burton was writing about an ancient queen of Baghdad, the famous storyteller of the *Arabian Nights*, Shaharazad, but Camille had been the one to show Burton who Shaharazad might have been, with her patience on the lawn, her indomitable throat, her steely wrists, her supine spine. She demonstrated the height of physical beauty itself: fifty-nine years old, sleeping in the outdoors, the morning long and white as an eyelid, her waking form slicing through his sense of the possible. She woke his imagination and lit his consciousness like a torch.

Burton fell in love with her, even though he was as married as a man can be. But who doesn't fall in love with the wrong one every now and then? The point is that Mrs. Richard Burton, who was by now used to everything—gypsy tribes, worm infestations, wandering in dust storms—this same Mrs. Richard Burton was having some trouble acclimating to Queen Shaharazad sleeping on the lawn. "And who is she again?" she asked her husband as he gazed longingly and lyrically at the not-quite-naked figure in his imagination. "A slave," he murmured.

"A slave. Yes. Whose slave exactly?"

"Well, she's our slave, dear. Presumably."

"Ours. Presumably. But she serves no one. Correct?"

"Correct."

"And—not to put too fine a point upon it, but . . . what does she want?" And seeing Sir Richard's blank face, Mrs. Sir Richard decided it was time to go to the lawn and look into things.

Did Camille tell her? Sirine asks.

My dear, apparently you have not been adequately briefed in how to listen to a story. You have to let the story come to you, you cannot fling yourself upon it. So. To make a long chapter much shorter than it should be for Sirine-with-her-watch: yes, Aunt Camille said to Mrs. Sir Richard, "I want to be taken to the source of the Nile. My payment will be that I will release your husband from his enchantment."

Now, Sir Richard was not too sure he wanted to be released—as imprisoned people always get confused about whether they actually want to get out of their chains. Luckily, his wife was more clear-headed about the whole situation. She called for the African guides.

On the day they left, the sun was a yellow silk ribbon; they had helpers and carriers, lifters and toters, and one jackal-eared dog with glistening black eyes. "Napoleon-Was-Here!" they called for the dog. "Come!"

*

Han begins to come to Nadia's Café regularly: Sirine makes him dinners after everyone else has left and watches him eat, pleased and shy, as he praises her and tells her over and over, this is his favorite meal. They go for walks in the evening or out to the movies, and she goes home with him twice, then three times in a row, forgetting to call her uncle and tell him that she will be out. But when she calls to apologize on a fourth night away, he says, "I already know, Habeebti."

She and Han stay up late in the evenings talking. Han puts aside his books and papers, and they sit spooned together on the carpet in the furnitureless room and try to tell each other, in bits and pieces, who they are and where they come from. Han tells her about the foods they ate in Iraq, the clothes they wore, the animals and plants and winds and rocks of his home. He tells her these things in a plain, matter-of-fact voice, as if it is all something that he's shed long ago, simple artifacts he looks back on with almost no feeling. And then Sirine tries to conjure up her childhood in Los Angeles for him with a similar flux of minor detail: the smell of her classroom, her wool skirts and knee socks, the way she wore her hair in braids, barrettes, ponytails, trying to find a way to smooth it down, make it shiny, straight, and neat. But she finds that she struggles to remember these things, and that certain memories—from the early time before her parents' death—are especially difficult to recollect.

One night early in October, after they have been seeing each other for four weeks and Sirine has stayed with Han for four nights in a row, she decides that she misses her uncle's house. She calls and tells Han that she won't be coming home with him that evening. Then she rides her bike home from work, following the narrow swath of her light through the dense, sugary darkness, the crosshatching of headlights everywhere, and fingers of palm leaves arched over the sidewalk, some moss-soft or stiff as straw and serrated. Edges and holes seem to open up in front of her and shapes loom out of the shadows, aqueous and mutable as fish beneath the water. She whirs past Han's apartment, tires clicking, but, from the outside, cannot quite tell which window is his.

Now it seems the night is filled with shadowy forms floating out from somewhere inside of her—chaotic and full of longing. She hears scratching in the bushes, voices between the buildings, the city rings with noise, everyone is talking.

Her uncle's bedroom door is still and shut. She moves past it quietly. King Babar is sleeping in the middle of her bed with a smile on his face—dreaming of eating ants. He opens his eyes when she comes in, following her every move. Sirine opens the windows in her room. With all of her and Han's talk of lost homes and family she is afraid of dreaming about her parents; she can feel it waiting to unfold inside her. That particular dream. She drapes one arm along the windowpane and wishes she could dream it now, with her eyes open and the night lit up with stars and streetlights, the sky like blue shale and no ghost bodies waiting in the closet.

She doesn't want to think about Han, but now it seems she can't help it; he's already taken over her thoughts, invaded her head. She is caught in his new light, a sea glow that clings to her like swimming in a phosphorescent tide. Han. She feels his name in her mouth. Then she thinks about the covered woman in his classroom, the lovely oval of her face like a rare orchid, and Sirine's heart rate seems to increase. She imagines her lover with his alabaster eyes, an ivory scarf wound around his head and mouth, disguising him, a fiery dust enfolding him as he fights for an extinct empire. Then she thinks of him, alone in his dusty, windowless office, the corridors filled with charming girls—many of them Arabs, like himself—educated, enchanting, each of them, it seems, with more of a claim on Han than herself.

She detects traces of Han's scent on her clothes and in the air. She climbs into bed and drifts through the sheets, and Han's voice is like a river running through the room. She has never felt this way about a man before—her American boyfriends seemed much easier to possess. Now her desire has spread alarmingly, like a jinn flowing out of its bottle.

The air in her bedroom is hot and powder-dry. It hangs over her bed and dusts the ceiling. Mosquitoes drift through her open window like ghosts. The palms along the street give off their high, clean scent, and there's another scent in the air—smoky and earthy, like leaves burning deep in a forest clearing.

She can see King Babar curled in his spot at the foot of the bed, watching her in his usual anxious, vaguely troubled way. His eyes glitter and his exquisite black nose reflects a spot of light. She cannot sleep. She misses

Han. She closes her eyes and an image surfaces in the dark: Han, a young woman, a boy; nutmeg skin, clove-colored eyes.

A breeze picks up and roams around in the curtains. She opens her eyes and thinks she sees a lizard on the ceiling over the bed. She watches it for a moment, then closes her eyes and another memory surfaces: white scalloped edges, black and white, a young woman in a plaid dress, white ankle socks, a round pale face—her mother.

*

Sirine gets out of bed again, goes downstairs to the abandoned-living-room, as her uncle calls it, and locates the heavy photo album on the bottom shelf of the tall bookcase. She slides out the huge album—swollen twice its size with photos—and decides she will take it and walk down to the tiny Italian café, La Dolce Vita, four blocks down the street. The café is lit only with candle stubs stuck in wine bottles, so it perpetually appears to be closed, but Sirine has always found it open, no matter what time she's come.

It's a warm, shimmering night and a few elderly Italian customers in black coats sit at the crooked tables set up on the sidewalk. The single waiter—straight-backed, correct Eustavio—bows, kisses her once on each cheek and says, "*Ciao, Maestra*," then goes to get her a milky cappuccino—the drink that he'd decided years ago to serve her.

Sirine scoots herself into one of the four minute wrought-iron tables, her knees banging the iron legs, and she swings open the album so it covers the whole tabletop. Tucked between the pages are pressed flower petals, old letters, a crayon drawing that Sirine made in first grade of her mother, father, and uncle all holding hands, their hair colored in carrot-orange and their eyes all sea-green. The stiff album pages are covered with black pasted-in corners that anchor the edges of the photographs. The photos are black and white, and Sirine's parents are skinny, grinning like kids. A breeze blows her mother's skirt up and her hair forward as she sits on a driftwood log on the beach at Catalina Island. In another, she and Sirine's father lean together inside an archway cut out of one of the giant redwoods. In another, her much-younger uncle is cavorting, turning a sort of failed cartwheel on the front lawn of their old apartment building, the name of the complex done in iron scrolls visible in one corner, the Avalon. It was painted pink.

She thinks she remembers that building. Or maybe she only remembers the photograph. Pictures of unknown friends, long-legged, laughing, spilling glasses of drinks, lounging in nylon beach chairs on the grass. Some of these people were in the Red Cross with her parents. She wishes she knew what their names were. She turns the pages and then she is there, wrapped tight in a blanket, a furze of white hair like a star on her head, her tiny face crinkled up, her fingers curling around her mother's index finger. Sirine brings her face very close to the images, studying them.

"Ah, the midnight photo album," her uncle says from over her shoulder. He sits across from her at the table, his knees banging into the iron legs. "It's that time again."

She grins at him. "You knew I was here?"

He shrugs. "Makes sense."

Eustavio hurries over, kissing her uncle and greeting him in Italian.

"Sì, sì, sì," her uncle says, the only Italian he knows.

"Uncle, where in Iraq is our family from?" There's a photo of her father sitting with his feet crossed on a desk covered with stacks of papers, a bemused expression on his face.

"The midnight Iraq conversation," her uncle says. "Haven't I told you before? I could have sworn I did, but maybe not. . . ."

"Please, just tell me again?"

"Oh, we were from some little old place. It was called Bab el Shaikh—*the Sheikh's Door*—like it?"

"You never talk about it. You never talk about Iraq at all."

He holds up his hands. "I'm a sentimentalist. Everything touches my tender heart. When you're a sentimentalist such things resist being talked about."

A photo: her parents, arms around each other, her mother's round skirt flying out in a whirl.

Sirine ticks her fingers against her cup. "Why is that?"

"It means talking about the difference between then and now, and that's often a sad thing. And immigrants are always a bit sad right from the start anyways. Nobody warns you when you leave town what's about to happen to your brains. And then some immigrants are sadder than others. And there's all kinds of reasons why, but the big one is that you can't go back. For example, the Iraq your father and I came from doesn't exist anymore. It's a new, scary place. When your old house doesn't exist anymore, that makes things sadder in general."

Eustavio brings them plates of dewy, rose-scented penne cotta. "Wouldn't you say that immigrants are sadder than other people?" her uncle asks the waiter.

Eustavio straightens up and closes his eyes. He answers Sirine's uncle in Italian, then he says to Sirine in his accented English, "Sadness? *Certo!* When we leave our home we fall in love with our sadness."

Sirine's uncle nods as Eustavio walks away. "You see," he says.

Sirine draws her spoon through the thick banks of foam on her coffee. "What was it like? In your hometown?"

He thinks it over a bit. "I'd say pretty much same as here. But small. And no movies. Dry and hot in the summer. Wet and cold in winter. Nothing much going on. There was a vegetable market where they kept the best tomatoes in back. A little white school, wooden desks. Everyone was always getting into everyone else's business, I remember that. Nobody owned much of anything, no cars or TVs. We had some donkeys. Your father and I, we enjoyed rock-throwing wars with the kids who lived up the hill."

"Han's brother was arrested and he's still in prison," Sirine blurts out. "Han says he can never go back again."

A photo of Sirine at two, sitting in a blow-up wading pool, one of her bathing suit straps slipped off her shoulder.

Her uncle stares at her, closes his eyes. Finally he rubs his fingertips over his eyes. "Oh no. Terrible. Yes, now, that, you see—that place is a different Iraq you're talking about. Different from the one that I and your father grew up in. I'm so sorry for Han." He presses his knuckles against his mouth and thinks for a moment. "Is there that picture of the two of us? When we first got here, we used to be skinny as Frank Sinatra used to be."

Sirine finds it: knobby elbows, spindly necks, knobby knees, their pants hang two inches above their ankles, their arms thrown across each other's shoulders. "We grew the biggest mustaches we could. We were pretty sure that would make the girls go ape."

Sirine traces one finger over the photograph; touches her father's mustache.

"Habeebti," her uncle says, his voice curls around her head like a wisp of smoke. "What's got you all jumpy? Is Han scaring you? All those stories of his?"

"Oh no—" She starts to shake her head. *Yes.*

"I think we're all safe over here, my dear. Why look for Saddam Hussein in the broom closet?"

Sirine folds her arms over her chest.

"Habeebti," her uncle says, "you can do this fine. Your uncle is the scaredy-cat in the family—your father wasn't. He was brave. You can tell just by looking at him. Look at that mustache! Nothing frightened him. He would go anywhere. . . . He fell in love with your mother like jumping into the lake."

Sirine looks at the photograph, the dim faces, and she wishes she could remember what her father's voice sounded like. She thinks it might have sounded like her uncle's voice. She takes a bite of the custardy penne cotta and it melts into a dozen separate flavors. She can smell oranges and lemons, cherry and wood, and even the soft silk and wool of Persian carpets, the smell that she thought came from Iraq.

*

Back at home, Sirine falls asleep on the living room floor, the big photo album under her head like a pillow. Her uncle drapes a blanket over her, and King Babar tucks himself up tightly beside her. She dozes and her dreaming shades into remembering, a bit of memory spinning above her head, unraveling, as it often does, into a thing that she thought she'd forgotten.

Perhaps she was four. The little girl might have been the same age as Sirine, and Sirine stared at her through the glass eye of the TV screen. The screen was round and curved. When the TV first arrived, Sirine thought it was a fish bowl and she was disappointed when they turned the light on and people were inside.

But she grew to like seeing the people too. She looked at the little girl on the TV. She touched the glass of the screen and electric sounds crackled against her hand. "What is her name?" Sirine asked.

"I don't know," her uncle said. "Perhaps it is Meena?"

"Yes," Sirine said. "It probably is."

The little girl looked at Sirine. Sirine could tell she was seeing her. Her eyes were shaped that way. Even though the TV was black and white, she could see the little girl's color. She pressed her wrist against the little girl's face to see the difference between them better. "Look," she said. "She's col-ored-in. Like Baba."

"Yes, like your baba."

Sirine sat about eight inches from the TV and put her finger in her mouth. The little girl had a swollen belly and there were flies crawling at the edges of her eyes. Sirine wanted to ask about these things but she didn't. Then a big word was there and her uncle said the big word was *Bangladesh*. "Mama and Baba," Sirine said.

"Yes, Habeebti," her uncle said. That is what they all called Sirine, Habeebti. *My dearest*. "That's where they are."

"Do they know Meena?"

"Difficult to say. We'll have to ask them when they get back," her uncle said.

When they turned off the TV, the little girl turned into a tiny point of starlight in the center of the screen. Sirine put her finger over it.

Later, Sirine and her uncle sat on the Hard Couch and watched the news. The news had two serious men and their names were Huntley-and-Brinkley. And their music before the news was frightening and loud and it ran through Sirine's body like rain. After that, there was a show about Perry Mason and his music was long shadows.

But when they listened to the loud music and looked at the serious men, Sirine knew they were looking for her parents. Her parents were always in the places that the men talked about. And even though she never saw her Mama or Baba on the TV, she knew they were inside of the box, somewhere.

CHAPTER TWELVE

So Aunt Camille makes ready to set off on her trip to the Nile. But this raises an interesting point—namely, that a trip is never just a trip and a place is never just a place. In some Arab countries, if someone talks about Malta, well, they're talking about the far side of the moon. If something is so beautiful that you can't bear it, you say it's sent you to the Garden of Paradise. If you claim that you're willing to travel to the source of the Nile, then you're actually saying that you will wait forever and a day for what you want. And people who've fallen madly in love? They say they've moved to Baghdad.

*

The morning at the café is bright as chrome, jangling into Sirine's nerves, so deeply hot: the peculiar sort of late autumn Angeles heat that smells of bone meal, lime, and dust, clothes baked dry on the lines, seaweed and ocean salt dried and hanging like a high-water mark in the air; even the roar of airplanes seems lower, soaked into the heat like the sound of rising temperatures. If her dreams came, they left her clear and scoured out by morning—she remembers nothing. She had awakened with a crease in her cheek from the photo album that she'd dragged into the bed, King Babar sitting at her feet, watching her with his jealous, liquid eyes.

She starts the coffee for the café breakfast crowd, inhaling the rich aroma: usually this scent is a comfort, but somehow today it is a small knot under her chest. She goes to the back kitchen and pauses in the doorway, looking out onto the courtyard: the sky is filled with arrowhead clouds, streaks of cobalt and powder-blue, a whiskery wind.

Mireille is doing her chin-tightening facial exercises in the mirror of the open bathroom door. She has drawn cat-eye edges at the corners of her eyes with liner. Victor Hernandez is wiping plates and looking at Mireille in his usual way—a little heartsick and lost. Sirine should be chopping tomatoes but instead she steps out on the back porch, nursing a peculiar and delicious loneliness. She sits down on the cool back step. Um-Nadia comes out with a pot of coffee and a cup and sits down next to her. "What are you thinking and thinking of, Habeebti?"

Sirine rests her chin in her hands and stares at the flowering bougainvillea with its bold sprays of colors. "What do they call that again, the crazy woman tree?"

"The *mejnoona*. Love-crazy."

*

All morning Sirine winds the bread dough in and out of itself, spins cabbage leaves, fat and silky, around rice and currents. She puts new ingredients in a salad, a frill of nuts, fresh herbs, dried fruit. Um-Nadia samples her salad, which tastes of ocean and beach grass, and she seems startled. "It's so good," she murmurs.

Sirine hums and stirs. She sifts through bags of wild rice. While Victor rushes around, assembling the usual plates of hummus and tabbouleh, she makes a mustard out of crushed grapes, a cake with lashings of cinnamon and pepper.

That afternoon, Nathan and her uncle come in and he is telling Nathan about the seven kinds of smiles: "There's also the Smile Through Tears, which is up and down, when you're trying to be noble; the Innocent Dog Smile, when there's something to hide; the Pretty Face Smile, for when you want everyone to admire you. . . ."

Sirine starts to pour some tea, but Nathan shakes his head.

"Nathan's an excellent chaperone," her uncle says. "He listens. Much of the time." She brings her uncle a plate of ma'mul cookies stuffed with dates. Her uncle holds up one cookie, "Look at this. Arabs will stuff anything—a tomato, a cabbage leaf, a cookie. Both the medieval cookery manuals—the *Cookery Book of al-Baghdadi* and the *Kitab al-Wusla Ila'L-Habib*, also known as the *Book of the Link with the Beloved*—contain recipes for savory eggplants stuffed with meat. Did you know that Shakespeare's favorite food was stuffed eggplant? And there's some who say that Shakespeare's name was actually Sheikh Zubayr." Her uncle waves at Nathan. "There's a nice thesis topic for you."

He finishes his tea and gets up to go, saying he has a class to teach, but Nathan remains at the table. Sirine notices he's wearing his big camera on a strap slung around his neck and his overstuffed book bag takes up the chair next to him. He puts his camera on top of the bag next to him. Then he changes his mind and puts it on the table.

In the afternoons, Nadia's Café tends to be a place for students; the faculty usually go home to wives and families. Each time a professor appears, a current runs through the café. The students get interested. And it seems that through his association with the faculty, some of this mystique has rubbed off on Nathan as well. The students glance at him. Abdullah, a stem-thin young engineering major from Yemen, gazes at Nathan's camera, and Gharb and Jenoob, new students from Egypt, try unsuccessfully to draw Nathan into an argument about the legality of taxes.

Sirine finishes deskewering six plates of lamb shish kabobs and three plates of chicken, drizzling oil over ground beef and hummus, over smoky puréed eggplant, over a bowl of olives, and splashing four tabbouleh salads with lemon. She wipes down the counter, then leans against it, looking at Nathan.

"Nice camera," she says

His gray eyes swing up to hers, then move quickly away. "Yes," he says. "Isn't it?" He holds it up lovingly in both hands. "Want to see it?"

She shows him her hands, which are glistening with onion juice and garlic skin. "Thanks, but . . ." she says.

His gaze is still and direct and terribly serious, his expression intent and overheated. Then he looks back at his coffee, stirring it left-handed and pouring in sugar with his right. "I have some new prints I just made up. Perhaps you'd like to see," he says casually. He pulls a folder out of his book bag and slides a photograph out of the folder. It's big as a sheet of typing paper, glossy and muted, snowy-gray tones, and it takes her a moment to register what it is: an image of Sirine and Han standing just inches apart, their faces shining, slightly out of focus; they look like they're moments from kissing, but they're both holding plates and plastic wineglasses. Sirine wipes off her hands carefully and takes the photograph by its edges. She thinks for a moment that the paper feels warm like the coil on a range, the sensation sparking through her body. It is such a sweet image: as if someone had managed to take a photograph of the moment of love, a prismatic mist caught shimmering in midair between them. "Oh my," she says. Then looks up at him. "When was this? I don't even remember this."

He shrugs, modest and embarrassed. "I hope you don't mind. I don't ask for permission—I mean, I can't. My photos sort of come over me, it's like, when the spirit takes me. I see something and then, that's it, I've got to get that shot." His eyes glow behind his glasses. He touches the photo. "This one was at the reception for Aziz. You were just standing there talking and I was sort of hidden in the crowd. And you both looked so—well, like *this* . . ." He gestures toward their images. "As you can see. But I mean, I don't mean to intrude—if you don't like it—" he adds hastily, reaching for it.

"I love it," she says, holding it closer. She feels a pang of discomfort that their personal lives should be so public—so seeable—but then it seems that this must be more a result of Nathan's ability—that he sees what others can't, like a doctor or a priest—someone you trust to be blasé and professional about intimate information.

"You do? Honestly?" His lips are pale, his eyes lowered, his lashes dense as pieces of felt.

The door jingles open just then and Han comes in. Nathan quickly slips the photograph out of Sirine's finger's and back into his bag. When he looks up, his eyes seem to take on light and depth, as if this were just who he'd been waiting to see. He lifts his book bag in Han's direction. "I developed some old rolls of film today and there's some prints I thought you might like. . . ."

Han smiles at Sirine as if Nathan were their private joke, but Sirine looks at the bag, her curiosity snagged despite herself. "Please," she says.

Nathan carefully withdraws another folder, swings it open, and spreads a number of large black and white prints over the table. The images are charming and graceful: men with long rifles, long swords, fringed, elaborately wrapped headdresses. There are backdrops of sweeping white valleys, photos of older men with peaked faces, younger men with fine, triangular cheekbones.

"God," Han breaths, sifting through the prints. "Look at these." He picks up a shot of a lonely, long-shadowed caravan across a watery horizon of dunes. "These are the Iraqi desert tribes, aren't they? Bedouin."

"Exactly, exactly," Nathan says. "There may be a few of the marsh Arabs in here as well. Maybe some Kurds."

Han picks up a shot of a solitary laughing man, one hand in his lap, the handle of his scimitar pressed against his chest, the whitest teeth inside a dust-dark face. "These faces," he says softly.

And Sirine is struck as well by the steady, patient gaze of these subjects, as if they'd spent lifetimes watching the horizons, as if distance and time were built into their very bodies. She admires a shot of camels, their disdainful, intelligent faces.

"You've really captured something here, I think," Han says. "It's remarkable."

Nathan looks down, pleased and seemingly a bit disoriented by the praise. Han turns the photo of the laughing man. "This could practically be the brother of our well-keeper—Abu-Najmeh. He had this same kind of laugh—that took up all of his face. And he always put his hand like this, over his heart, like he was taking a vow." Han looks at Nathan. "Did you live with these people?"

Nathan gazes into the black eye of his coffee cup, shakes his head. "Only visited. I traveled all over Iraq but I kept moving. The more I saw, the more I wanted to see. Until I finally stopped in Baghdad for a while." He glances at Sirine.

Han shuffles through more prints and stops on one of mountains filled with folding cloud shadows. "Here," he says. "This landscape?" He shows it to Sirine. "I loved this place."

Nathan nods. "Oh, the Masrah Valley."

"My father has family there. We used to go visit them in the spring. I can almost smell it," Han says. "The air smells like dry caves and roasting weeds and bones."

"And salt and olives and coffee," Nathan says. "And the air is white dust." Nathan gathers up the prints and slides the folder to Han. "Please, I want you to have these."

Han hesitates and glances at Sirine.

"It's nothing," Nathan says. "I have the negatives. There are plenty more where these came from. Please."

Sirine looks away; she pulls another print from the folder and stares at it in surprise. It's a city scene: a brash swipe of neon across twilight, carpets hanging from towering windows, arches and keyhole doors, streaks of cars and motorbikes, stacked-up apartments, a scribble of Arabic and English, people cutting between cars, a boy carrying a silver tray, everything looks soot-stained, tilted, dizzying. A crazy place: she holds it with the edges pressed into her fingertips as if it might catch on fire. It tugs at her, makes her feel she is falling forward, as if, if she held it a moment longer, she would tumble onto that gray asphalt.

Han glances over. "What are you looking—"

Nathan notices. "Oh, I'm always getting my pictures mixed up, that's Baghdad." He starts to pull it out of her fingers when he stops and looks up, frowning. "Sirine, is there . . . smoke?"

She finally looks away from the photo and realizes there's a dark curl of something burning seeping from the back kitchen. She shoves back her chair and bangs through the swinging door. It's the big cauldron of rice—she'd left it on a low flame and forgotten about it. Now the back kitchen is filling with smoke and the top of the rice pot is a streaming black cloud.

Sirine hefts it off the stove and hurries out into the back courtyard, hoping that Victor hasn't gotten around to replacing the café's sprinkler system batteries. Um-Nadia, Mireille, and Victor are all standing around in the back smoking. They squint at her as she lugs the cauldron down the steps and sets it on the slate tiles. "I thought I smelled something," Mireille says.

Victor lifts the lid and waves at the great wash of smoke with it. "Whoa," he says. "Somebody burned the rice."

"You burned the rice?" Um-Nadia asks; she looks astonished, even excited. "You never burn the rice."

Sirine rubs her forehead. "What a mess. What a mess."

"You never burn the rice," Um-Nadia says again, now openly smiling. "What an interesting thing to do."

By the time Sirine goes back into the kitchen, Nathan has left and Han tells her he has to get to class. After he leaves, she notices something is propped beside the grill. It's the photo that Nathan took of her and Han, one of its edges singed from its proximity to the heat; she can smell the burnt paper. On the other side of the photograph there's an address and a notation that says simply, "Nathan's studio."

Khoorosh the grocer is sitting at a table eating lunch. He looks up from his plate of stuffed cabbage and gestures with his fork. "That American boy left that for you," he says. "He is a little disordered, I am here to tell you. Sometimes he comes to the Victory and takes pictures of stuff."

"What kind of stuff?" Sirine asks.

Khoorosh wipes off his big mustache in two swipes with his napkin. "Crazy stuff. Boxes of tissues, baby food, celery. He makes me too nervous. I said he'd feel better if he ate some food instead of making pictures of it."

"How weird."

"He's one of these types, likes to argue, asks a million opinions—how do I feel about this president, that dictator, Shah versus Ayatollah, Iranian Jews, Iraqi Jews, Palestinian Christians, Muslims in Hollywood—I don't know what," he says, waving it away with one hand.

Sirine looks at the door. "What do you say?"

He takes a big bite of cabbage and shrugs. "I say I'm a small businessman. I don't have time for politics, I don't have the money, I don't have the energy, and I don't have the special interest. Plus, I enjoy most of the people in the world just fine."

"Well, then. Lucky for us," Sirine says to him, leaning on the counter.

He grins at her, spears the last forkful of stuffed cabbage, holds it in midair, and says intensely, "You, I love."

She spends the rest of the day with her elbows tucked to her sides, barely looking up from the food or the stove. The dizzy picture keeps coming back to her, tugging at her thoughts: *Baghdad*. She never wants to go anywhere, she thinks. She never wants to leave her home.

But that night when work is over, she goes back to Han's apartment again.

CHAPTER THIRTEEN

Aunt Camille, Sir Richard Burton, Mrs. Sir Richard Burton, and a dozen or two carriers, trackers, runners, guides, and all-around helpers crossed the shifty, brassy Sinai into Mother Africa, made a left at Cairo, and accidentally took the long way down the Nile. Burton made a better translator than explorer and a better party-thrower than translator. But you know how some people are, they're good at one thing so they think they must be good at everything.

They followed the sparkling, sprawling water into places where it turned into spun silver and milk. But it's strange the way these water names worked—the Blue Nile doesn't look blue and the White Nile isn't white, and you might not think the Dead Sea has much personality but it bites and scratches the minute you get in and leaves a crust all over you if you don't take your shower.

Anyway. Finally, they headed toward the source of the Nile—Lake Nyanza or Tana or Albert or Tanganyika—also called Victoria—depending on which direction you're coming from and whose villages you're pillaging. But does the river care about the names of its sources? Even the Lebanese can't make up their minds to be Arabs, since some Phoenicians were in the neighborhood two thousand years ago.

Nevertheless, they came to a crossroads, at which point there was a tremendous *mishkila* about which lake was the truest source of the Nile. Sir Richard argued for the largest source and the Missus argued for the oldest, but Aunt Camille was looking for the soul of the river. Eventually she decided—as these decisions are so often made—not according to science or history, but according to the dictates of the innermost voice. She would go to the lake with the most elegant name, the word that unfolded like the layers of begonias—Tanganyika, the same lake that was also named after a mustached and sour-faced old English queen. Tanganyika/Victoria would be the best of both worlds, she thought, North and South, Africans and colonists, chickens and eggs, and so forth.

So that is where they took her, to the steep green bank of Lake Tanganyika. The water spread itself out like a ball gown before her; it unscrolled its deep green waters, fish hung suspended in its currents like bits of jade and topaz. They left her alone there, with one young African bearer and one jackal-eared dog, and eventually the bearer realized that no one was really watching him and he slipped away into the cracks of the jungle. Which was fine with Aunt Camille. That night the water looked languid and bottomless, specks of light bobbed on its surface like metal scales. She saw things out of the corners of her eyes and heard things out of the corners of her ears and she unfurled her Hariz carpet and slept full-length under every star in the sky, crickets chiming all night long.

The rest of the story is hearsay and conjecture, but this is what she reported: she was awakened early the next morning by a voice like a bell in the back of her mind. The air was filled with a shimmering curtain of insect buzz and the voice came like threads of honey looped over a bowl of milk. "I am guardian of the Nile," the voice reportedly said. "And I hear you're looking for me."

*

Sirine bicycles to Han's apartment that evening. She's worn out from work, her mind soft. Nathan's photograph of the two of them is in an envelope in the basket attached to her handlebars. She sees a bar of light under his door and knocks quietly. He opens the door, breaks into a wide smile. "Sirine," he says, as if he hasn't seen her in years. "I missed you last night." He circles her with his arms and hums something with the rising and falling of Arabic music, and they move around the living room floor—not quite a dance, but more than a shuffle. They laugh and turn over the beige carpet, past the stacks of books, pages and pages of notes, pencils, index cards, pads. She sees things in swipes—coffee rings on papers, rumpled shirts, loose socks. The orderly, precise room of their first date is gone. They dance around open books, open music cassettes, a few plates covered with crumbs, coffee cups stuck to saucers, over a couple of crumpled student papers, and finally into the bedroom.

She's all giddy laughter. A tiny voice in her head warns her that she should just slow down for a moment—try to get her bearings. But instead she lets him pull her on top of him as he falls back on the bed, the two of them rolling around each other like rolling together down a hill. He holds her close and they start kissing so deeply she can barely catch her breath; colored lights flash behind her eyes. Han tugs at his shirt, ignoring the buttons, lifting it straight over his head. She hikes her skirt around her hips and skims her panties off. She climbs on top of Han but then he flips her and lifts her hips, entering her from above, their lovemaking intense and silent, the giddiness spilling away. When she comes, she closes her eyes and feels again as if she is flying forward through the length of her body. Then they make love again, barely resting in between. They make love too many times until both of them feel burnt and half-skinned. She inhales the scent on the inside of his neck and inside his hair. The smell of salt. They rub their feet against each other, kiss and shift around and can't find a place to put their arms. She is buzzing with her desire, from their stream of kisses, from the exotic night in a still-strange room, the two-horned moon framed in the balcony door, tipped and waiting like a goblet to be filled. And when they finally fall asleep it is like falling into a well, echoing, bottomless, and dark.

Later, Sirine wakes in the early morning fog again and she is holding Han's hand. The clock radio says it's already five-thirty and she has no sense of having slept at all. She gets up to go to the bathroom and the fog is like a gauze against the dark windows. She sees the books, the letter opener, some opal prayer beads with a silver tassel, but the photograph of Han and the boy and young woman is gone; oddly only the empty silver frame remains.

Han is awake when she comes back, waiting for her. He opens his arms, reaching for her. "Come back to bed."

"I can't. I really have to get going. I've been getting to work too late."

But then she climbs back into the warm bed and lays her head against his chest, combs her fingers through the curling hair.

"*Ya elbi, ya hayati,*" he murmurs.

"What is that?"

"*Elbi* means 'my heart,' *hayati* means 'my life.' *Ya eyeni,* 'my eyes.' " The words shimmer over her. "Say more," she says.

"*Ya wardi,* 'my flower,' *ya thahabi,* 'my treasure. . . .' " It is like a litany of body parts, pieces of the earth and air and things physical and metaphysical—*my rose, my seventh heaven, my fig tree, my gold, my senses*—as if everything were tied together inside this love-talk.

"It's like a poem," she says, strumming his chest with her hand. "It sounds more like love in Arabic."

"Than in English? Oh, I don't know about that. Romeo and Juliet came from England. Though they're Italian in the story." He yawns luxuriously, skims one hand over her hair. "The Americans would say you're ethnocentric."

Sirine laughs. "What would the Arabs say?"

"Probably that you're right." His eyes ripple over her. "My American Queen of Sheba." She draws her fingertips down slowly over his face and he closes his eyes for a moment. "Sometimes I look at you and feel that I'm free-falling," he says, then opens his eyes. "Like falling out of the tops of trees or something."

She blinks. "How do you mean?"

"How do I . . . ?"

"What about me makes you feel that way?" She feels bold to ask this, to ask in such a direct way. But he has described exactly the thing that she also feels—the sense of plunging, so fast and so far.

He shifts on to his elbows and holds her, holds himself poised over her, looking, his breath stirring in her hair, so quiet and intent on her face that for a moment she thinks he won't answer. But then he finally says, "You are the place I want to be—you're the opposite of exile. When I look at you—when I touch you—I feel ease. I feel joy. It's like you know some sort of secret, Hayati, a key to being alive—to living. . . ." He kisses each of her fingertips, saying, "Right here and here and here and—"

She laughs and says skeptically, "I know that?"

"Partly, it's in the way you know things. For most people, if they know something in the way that people think they're supposed to—like owning or capturing it—then I think they don't really know it at all. But somehow, for some reason, you're different. You're able to let the knowing just exist inside of you, or around you, or on the surface of your skin. It's like knowing how to hold still enough for wild birds to come and sit beside you."

"And are you the wild bird?"

He smiles slowly.

She remembers something then and tells him to wait a sec. She pulls on his shirt, soft with his aftershave and sweat, and goes to her bicycle, propped up by the living room door. Then she comes back with Nathan's photograph and hands it to him. "This is for you. You didn't see this yesterday."

He turns on the bedside light and stares at the photograph, turns it slightly, marveling. "My God," he murmurs. "That's us. Where did this come from? I have no memory of this being taken."

She nods. "Nathan took it when we weren't looking. On the day we first met."

"That devil." He tilts his head back. "He sneaked up on us?"

"He says he doesn't ask permission. Does it bother you?" Sirine asks, wondering if she should feel bothered.

He props the photograph against the bedside lamp, gazing at it. "I suppose it should. But it doesn't. It's beautiful, the two of us together like that."

He starts to hand it back but she shakes her head. "Please, you keep it," she says.

He nods and looks at it for a long moment as if reflecting, then gets up. "And there is something I want to give to you," he says and goes to his pile of books and picks up his prayer beads and the silk scarf. He hands her the folded scarf. "I want you to have this."

The material is so soft between her fingers it feels like dipping her hand into water. The material floats and gleams in her lap. She's a little afraid of it and she doesn't unfold it. "Thank you," she says. "But this is—this is too much. I really can't accept this."

He curls his hand around the edge of her hair where it falls into her face, draws it back. "Please," he says intently. "I want you to."

She smiles, fingering the material. "Where did it come from?"

"They sent it to me after I'd escaped. They wanted me to have a reminder."

"Of what?"

He gazes at her and she has the impression that he doesn't know what to tell her. Finally he says, "I never actually had much time with my family. When I was a teenager, I went to boarding school in Cairo. Then when I was twenty-two years old, I left Iraq for good. My parents had very little money to help me get out and it was dangerous for me to leave. But it was dangerous to stay. It was 1980 and Saddam Hussein had declared this terrible war on Iran. I would have been conscripted or imprisoned. Most people were too frightened to try to escape from the country, but they would help me. Everyone helped me escape—my family and friends. People brought money, they charted my route. Abu-Najmeh gave me his short dagger for protection and I ended up using it as a bribe for a soldier who stopped me outside of Baghdad. My friend Sami found a cabdriver who took me forty miles in the middle of the night out into the desert. I had to escape through the desert into Jordan where my family had friends, first in an open jeep crowded with other refugees, and then on horseback with a group of Bedu, and then finally on foot for two days."

"You crossed the desert on foot," she says, amazed.

He rubs the back of his neck. "Well, the smallest corner of it. But yes, it was the desert and I was most definitely on foot. I'd been warned by the Bedu that there were armed men everywhere, Saddam's guards, mercenaries, Kurdish guerrillas, all sorts of soldiers hidden in caves and trees. The sane ones were bribable, but the crazy ones were only half-bribable. I had a few foreign coins that a friend had given me so it would be harder for them to count. I didn't eat and barely drank for those two days. It was a hundred and ten degrees before noon and freezing at night, and I never knew when a soldier or border guard might appear from anywhere. All I had when I left were the clothes I was wearing and a bottle of water. And this—wrapped around my shoulder, under my shirt." He holds up the prayer beads so they run between his fingers; they look to Sirine like a necklace made of blue tears. "These misbaha beads were from my father. They're lapis stones. To help me say my prayers," he adds. "But I found that my prayers had left me, so I used them to worry on instead. And this was from . . ." He touches the silk scarf, then frowns as if he can't quite remember. "This was from my mother. I kept it on my bed in England."

He slides the shirt off her shoulders, then opens the veil and slowly drapes it across her reclining body; the silk floats over her skin. It is about four feet by four feet, black with faint shifting tones of gray and rose, embroidered along the borders with a precise, intricate design that makes her think of red berries. "This is the traditional pattern of my mother's village in the south. All the villages have their own design. If you study them, you can figure out where a certain embroidery stitch has come from." He hands it to her. "She used to wear it over her hair."

Sirine lifts it and drapes the silk on her head as she has seen the veiled Muslim women do, winding the ends around her neck.

"Yes," he says. "Just like that, exactly. Ah ha. Now I see an Arab woman in you—an aristocrat, ancient royalty. Here and here . . ." He touches her eyes and lips. "And here." He runs his hand along her naked body, then slides it around the cusp of her hip. "It looks exactly right on you."

"You mean being veiled?" She touches the edge of the scarf against her throat. "Or being naked?" She pulls one edge of the scarf down over her face. "Like this?"

He touches her cheekbone and kisses her softly through the material of the scarf. "Mm-hm. Either/or."

She fingers one edge, then slides it off. "It's a beautiful thing. But really—"

"No, please." He pats the scarf back. "I have my beads." He holds up his hand so she can see them looped around his fingers. "I have these. But I want you to keep the scarf."

She wants the scarf but there is also something about it, a vague sense warning her away. "It's your only memento," she protests.

"*Ya elbi*," he says. *My heart*. He wraps the scarf around her shoulders and sinks back into the bed beside her. "Look at you, just look. It was made for you. It's necessary that you keep it." He ties two corners together. "My mother was wearing this when my father fell in love with her."

Sirine leans toward him but doesn't touch him. She needs to face him, the tide of his memory. She touches the veil, then she asks quietly, "Do you miss your family?"

He studies her, his expression quiet and contemplative. "I do and I don't. It's hard to get information from Iraq, so few letters get through, and the ones that do are usually so heavily censored that they don't make much sense. I suppose my brother is still in prison and I hope that he and my mother are still alive. But I have no way of telling for sure. And there's no way for me to know if I'll ever see them again." He pauses. "I always think about them."

She can't help it; she asks, "And your sister?"

He waits, still watching her. And then she feels it again: the sense that the two of them are inside the story together. It feels like something unraveling. Sirine breathes high in her lungs; she and Han are so close together, their arms interwoven. But he doesn't answer her. Instead he says, "And you, Sirine? Do you miss your parents?"

Her shoulders ache, tensing upward. Light comes through the window in bright spots like clean white sailboats. This is something she never talks about. She looks back at his face and then down into that cracking light, the memory.

Slowly she begins talking. She tells him about her parents' jobs as relief workers. How they were often away from home, always in the worst places, the most dangerous, war-torn, ruined. She tells about her father's belief that most of the world's greatest contemporary problems could be traced to the American obsession with commerce, and her mother's certainty that Americans were just as devoted to nature, religion, friends, and family as the Arabs were.

She watches Han as she talks. He holds her hand and his eyes follow hers. And her voice doesn't tremble, so she goes on and tells him about sitting with her uncle and waiting for her parents, watching the news and waiting. She tells about the way she sometimes thought there wasn't really enough room in her parents' relationship for her—they were so focused on each other, they traveled together and refused assignments that would split them up: and they left her behind.

"It wasn't the same thing as crossing the desert," she says softly. She leans back against the wall behind the bed. "But in a way that's sort of how it felt. Waiting for them to come home. Looking at the days on my calendar as something to be crossed off, blanked out. I remember asking my uncle almost every morning: 'Is this the day they come home?' And he would say things like, 'Not until the afternoon before the morning of three and a half evenings in a row.'"

Han laughs and strokes her hand. "Your uncle . . ."

She closes her eyes, feels his fingers run between hers. "I think I wished half my childhood away waiting for them. And then one day I stopped. I got up and made us breakfast and I forgot to ask if this was the day. And it was such a relief that I kept on forgetting. I just stopped waiting. My uncle was the one who would talk to me and read to me—not them. He loved me just the right way."

Han nods, watching her. "Meaning, he was there," he says.

"That was the biggest thing. Just that." She looks past Han's shoulder to the white, glimmering window. "I even stopped feeling excited when my parents came home. I tried not to show it, but I can remember when I started not wanting to go to my parents' house when they came back. They'd be gone, sometimes a month, sometimes more—which is forever to a kid. After a while I felt like I barely knew who they were. They were these adults who seemed to think I was supposed to love them. Like I owed them my love." She lowers her eyes, surprised to feel her face going hot. Her throat tightens, the memory cold beneath her skin. "My mother used to seem . . . sad—sort of confused, I guess. She'd be so excited to be coming home, she'd be crying as they walked in the door, and she'd squeeze me so hard. And I'd be . . . just . . . limp."

*

Sirine tells Han: She must have been seven years old when her mother began having her nightmares. Her parents' first few nights home would be calm, almost uneventful, considering the dramatic things they'd been doing—a month of treating burn victims in India or helping starving women and children in the Sudan. But then there would be a night when Sirine would awaken—at first she wouldn't even understand what was waking her—her senses befuddled by deep sleep. It was a sound like something tearing the night into two pieces. Sirine would be so frightened she'd be pinned to her bed, paralyzed as if the breath were punched out of her chest. Then the sound of her father's voice, calling through her mother's scream: "Sandra! Sandra!" as if he were calling to her from another shore, calling her back home. But she never woke from her screams: sometimes they intensified, and sometimes they dwindled immediately. Sirine's father would stand in Sirine's doorway a few minutes later and whisper, "Habeebti?" But for some reason, she would keep her eyes closed, her breath soft and shallow, as if she were frightened or embarrassed to have heard her mother's cries. In the morning, no one would speak of the screams at all.

When Sirine was nine, the screams stopped but instead she began to hear her mother crying at night. "I can't bear it," she heard her saying. "I can't do this. I can't do this."

And her father's low murmur in answer: "You can, Sandy, you can." And then one night, when the crying continued, she heard his voice saying, "All right, all right, all right . . ." A few days later, Sirine's mother told Sirine they were going to stop traveling. They'd asked to be transferred to office positions in Los Angeles and they would be staying home. With her. They had just one last job away, to help an African village with its rebuilding. Then they would be home for good, she promised, squatting, almost kneeling as she spoke, searching Sirine's eyes as if asking for forgiveness.

They left and Sirine never saw them again.

*

Sirine believed that she had wished them out of existing.

"Well," Han says. He cups her hands carefully, as if she were made of eggshell. "Children think they have these mysterious powers, don't they?"

Sirine shakes her head. She doesn't know what she knows: she doesn't allow herself to think of such things—she hasn't in years. She tucks her chin in toward her chest and feels the start of a body-deep sliver of pain—the dark space that yawned open when she realized that her parents died. She can't say any more then; she looks at Han and he looks back and she sees that he understands the thing exactly. He reaches over, draws his scarf around her, and gathers her into his arms. She feels the delicious luxury and safety of enclosure, lays her head against his chest, and breathes.

*

Later that day, back at work, Sirine drapes her scarf over a peg in the back kitchen where it won't get dirty. She would wear it tied around her waist but she wants to protect its mild, elusive fragrance, afraid of smothering it in the kitchen smells, the frying onions, garlic, lamb, and oil.

During the afternoon stillness when the heat concentrates in the air and the palm trees turn to glass, Sirine is sitting with Um-Nadia in the back kitchen when the phone rings. Um-Nadia picks it up and Sirine can tell by the way she says, "Yes? Oh-ho. Oh no, you bad man—yes, yes, you bad thing—no, no, *you* are, you bad, extra naughty . . ." that she's talking to

Odah the Turkish butcher, who's had a crush on Um-Nadia for at least as long as Sirine's known him. Um-Nadia always tells Odah that she is saving herself for the mysterious Mr. X. Now she cups her palm over the receiver and tells Sirine, "He says he's put aside some special legs of lamb and for you to come and pick the best." Sirine unties her apron; she considers wrapping the scarf around her neck, but the window thermometer reads eighty-nine degrees. Everyone has been saying what a warm autumn it is.

Sirine walks along the lip of Westwood Boulevard. The big street looks cooked and yellow as a lizard skin in the late afternoon; there are Iranian restaurants, markets, and bakeries up and down the block, quiet now but mobbed at the dinner hour. This is a scene that she's looked at almost every day for over eight years. There's the swoop of traffic over the hill, the gray curbs, cement-busted sidewalks, and the busy jumble of Persian businesses—Shiraz Beauty Salon, Victory Market, Shusha Bakery, and Shaharazad Drugstore, with their shop signs written in English and Arabic script, and long, velvety-looking sedans and scrappy little compacts parked nose to nose along the streets.

Sirine doesn't quite come to the corner; she waits for a break in the cars and then runs across the middle of the street. She walks past an open fruit stand where they give her free kumquats, past a fallen power line, power company workers, and some police who ask her what tonight's special is, past the Persian Marxist Revolution Bookshop, where the clerks wave to her, down to the Topkapi Butcher Shop at the bottom of the street. It's a compact place, sleek and enameled as a tooth. No one can speak much above a whisper in there or voices will clatter and echo all over the place. Odah's shop is always crowded with Turks, Arabs, and Persians, as well as Italians, Poles, Bosnians, and Russians; almost all of the customers are identically dressed women in black babushkas and heavy black shoes. Sirine's uncle calls it the old lady store.

Usually Odah has one of his countless sons or nephews just run the shipment of meat up to Nadia's Café. But Sirine doesn't mind coming in to look over the wares and to watch Odah and his handsome sons hustling from the case to the scales, handling the big joints, the meat with its fresh bloom of marbling and blood.

She is somewhere deep in the ragged line that starts at the door and leads up to the counter, watching a tiny woman who apparently speaks no

English gesture to one of Odah's sons—trying to demonstrate the cut of meat she wants—when someone stumbles into the line. The old ladies gasp and their purses swing on their arms. Sirine turns and recognizes the back of the man's shoulders. He seems to be half-crouching, trying to hide himself behind the line of customers. "Aziz?"

He turns, peering around anxiously, a film of sweat beading over his temples. "Who?" He pauses and finally recognizes Sirine. A big smile breaks across his face and he says, "It's Cleopatra!" He scoops up her hand and kisses it.

There are loud grumbles and several of the elderly women shove Aziz out of line. Behind them, one white-haired woman with electric-blue eyes shakes a knuckly finger at him and says, "No budging!"

"Who are you hiding from?" Sirine steps out of line. She looks out the big front window and spots the edge of a woman's black veil whipping up the street. "Hey. Isn't that that student?"

Aziz's eyes go round and innocent. "Is who what student? I have no students, only assassins." He drags a handkerchief out of his pocket and mops his face, then pulls his damp blue silk shirt away from his chest. Then he scans the room once more and says, "No, really, I'm just experiencing a little technical difficulty. A complication, as they say. Having more fun than one Aziz can handle." He smiles his gigantic smile and takes Sirine's hand again. "It's good as can be to see you again, my dear. Look at how lovely you are without an apron on."

Sirine ducks her face. "Oh, now."

"Where are you spending your free time? Is that Han monopolizing your life? You know, he doesn't write poetry."

She sinks her hands into her pockets, tries to think of something that she's done with herself. "Well. I've been working on things," she says defensively.

He raises his black eyebrows. "You sound like my students, they're forever working on things. Why don't you come to my office and I'll teach you how to write poetry? I can tutor you." He leans over her, brings his face close, and she can smell something like licorice on his breath.

"Well . . ." She wraps her arms around herself, grabs her elbows. "English was my worst subject."

"We'll write everything in classical Arabic," Aziz says.

"I don't know if Han would appreciate you giving me private lessons."

"Han?" He sounds as if he's never heard the name before. "Why?"

"Sirine of my dreams!" A voice bursts in echoes over the white tiles of the shop. All the old ladies stop their arguing and turn. Odah emerges from his side office. "Sirine of the trees!" Odah is about five-foot-three, built with thick wide shoulders, no neck, and a big head covered with woolly black hair. His big soft nose looks squashed against his face and his eyes are huge and dolorous. The happier Odah is, the sadder he looks. "Sirine, come in back here! I want you to see!" He grabs her hand and they hurry behind the counter, Aziz following. They go down a hallway and through a door into the refrigerated room behind the store. Their breaths turn to steam. Long, uncarved sides of beef hang from the ceiling. Odah leads her to a small silver cooler, the size of a footlocker; they lean over it and their breaths make pale spirals. Aziz says, "Open sesame!"

Odah looks at him. "Who are you supposed to be?"

"That's just Aziz," Sirine says.

He sticks out his hand. "I'm Aziz the poet," Aziz says.

"Oh, a poet." Odah doesn't seem to notice Aziz's hand. "Never mind about that." He squats over the cooler and it opens with a gasp. He tilts it, showing off a row of bright pink lamb legs. "You get first choice. The very best spring lamb."

"But it's October," Aziz says.

"In New Zealand it's spring!" Odah's voice ricochets off the shining gray walls. He puts his hand delicately to his chest, then recovers and bends back over the meat. "And this," he says, tenderly cradling a few cuts propped in butcher paper, "is for my rose, Um-Nadia. You tell her, yes? Special from Odah."

After Sirine has selected the lamb and gone back to the front of the shop, Odah presents her with Um-Nadia's package of cuts, wrapped in gold foil with a single pink ribbon. He taps it, then taps his chest, saying, "Remember, from me."

"Now, there is a true romantic," Aziz says, watching as Odah disappears back into his office. "He must be married."

"No, he's divorced. A bunch of times."

"Ah, no wonder. A chronic romantic. But romance is one of the fundaments of life, a crucial element, like bread and water, wouldn't you say?" He looks at her closely, his smile easy and soft, and Sirine notices for a moment how smooth his tan skin is and the brightness of his dark brown eyes. Then she realizes he is holding her hand again. She releases herself and plunges her hand back into her pockets. She feels her blush starting all the way at the center of her sternum. "I guess. I never thought about it that way before," she says.

"Perhaps you're not meeting your minimum daily requirements," he says. "You look a bit pale to me. A bit anemic. Dr. Aziz thinks you might be needing more poetry, more music, more kisses, more laughter, and also more dancing in your life. And he is prepared to write the prescription."

She's trying to think of a response when the white-haired woman who'd stood behind Sirine in line—now on her way out—taps Sirine's shoulder with a white-papered packet of meat, raises one finger, and shakes it at them vigorously, saying in broken English, "Monkey business!"

Suddenly there's a wild clattering, a juddering noise that fills the tight space like roaring water in a drum, and a vivid blue blur spins around them: a bird has somehow flown into the shop and it batters itself against the plate-glass window trying to escape. The old ladies scream in twenty different languages, dropping their packages and straw baskets and wheeled carriers, and run out of the shop, as do Odah and his sons. Aziz drags Sirine out as well, laughing. "Oh no, oh dear!" he cries, laughing and shaking his head. "They think it's the Evil Eye."

"It *is* the Evil Eye, you idiot poet!" Odah rumbles at him as they shove through the door. "Do you realize what this means for me? All new charms!"

Sirine's heart is speeded up and she's out of breath. She presses one hand down against her chest as if she could slow herself down, and she peers into the window. The poor bird is still spinning its wings against the window, a crazy, round blueness. Odah turns to her, bows, and then takes the pink-ribboned package from her. "I am terribly sorry," he says, his wide eyes shining. "But it is impossible now. I can not allow Um-Nadia to have this under the current circumstances."

"Why not? We left the shop—it's okay."

Odah shakes his head ominously. "Something—or someone—" he eyes Aziz—"has allowed the Evil Eye to enter my shop. Everything is tainted. Believe me, if I find out who is responsible—"

"Time to go check on my poetry class," Aziz says, and begins walking backward away from Sirine and Odah. "I left them writing something. It's been lovely, you two." He turns and strides up the hill toward campus.

Sighing, Odah puts the meat on top of the mailbox like it's a special delivery package. "Fine," he says and crosses his arms.

*

While Sirine and all the customers are still gathered on the sidewalk, two young officers pull up in a cruiser. Odah tells them that the Evil Eye is inside his store. One of the officers puts his hand on his gun and the other says, "I think we should call the fire department." Then everyone stands there awhile watching the bird pinwheeling through the shop, and Odah sighs heavily several times, occasionally crying out, "Oh, the bad omen!" Finally, Sami—the smart son—thinks to prop open the door. And just as suddenly as it came in, the bird flies out the door, then rises calm as a sigh into the trees. And watching it go, Sirine feels some tension slip out of her body as well. She walks back from the butcher shop feeling oddly peaceful. When she turns the corner, she thinks she sees a flash of blue in one of the bushes and she moves closer, wondering if it might be the escaped bird. But then she hears Mireille call her name from up the street. And she backs up, thinking perhaps it's best to leave the Evil Eye alone.

CHAPTER FOURTEEN

The story that you are not going to believe goes like this: There was once an Arab empire that dominated the world. The glorious Abbasid Empire reigned from the eighth until the thirteenth centuries—five hundred years. And Baghdad was its celestial capital. Now you blink: it is seven or eight centuries later and the world has turned upside down in its usual way. The Abbasid Empire dissolved. But a few Arabs have a long, long memory and like to believe that someday the world and everything in it will be returned to them. Most other Arabs would settle for a little bit of peace, less fighting in the backyard, getting to keep the backyard, et cetera. And then there are the Arabs who feel that no matter what it is they want—the world or a little peace and quiet—America seems to be dedicated to keeping it from them.

So Aunt Camille was waiting on the banks of Tanganyika, hoping for an audience with the Mother of All Fish. Was she thinking about the end of the Abbasid Empire? Possible. Not likely. Like most Arabs, she assumed that the late morning in 1258 when the Mongol hordes came to the doors of Baghdad was when the party was pretty much over. Or perhaps she felt that the day in 1492 when the Moorish prince of Granada handed over the keys to the city to King Ferdinand, well, that was the end of that!

Aunt Camille had just heard a rich bell-like voice ask if she was looking for her—a singular, unearthly voice that she joyously took to be the voice of the Mother of All Fish. Imagine her surprise, then, when the vines swayed and the bushes trembled and the branches crackled and not the Mother of All Fish, but a great jinn with garnet-colored eyes and skin the color of powdered cocoa bean stepped forward and cried out, "Halt! I am the Lost Secret King of the Abbasid Empire and I demand to know your business."

This jinn was no dumb-dumb; he was aiming to upset the emotions of each and every Arab he met by saying this. The Arab Abbasid Empire had enjoyed the same sort of glory as that of the Roman Empire and had achieved the depth of the Greek; it had spanned continents and hemispheres, produced libraries, inventions, and celestial insights—and then it was gone and the Arabs had to go back to being regular people. Except here was this jinn with crackling gold sandals and gleaming emerald rings on his middle toes; his chest was covered and clankling with medals from all the kings and generals he'd eaten, his nostrils were opened wide and his eyes were opened wide, and his hair and beard were standing up in every direction, take your pick. The Lost Secret King of the Abbasid Empire! He was offering them the bitter brazen hopes of renewed glories and a nibble of nostalgia besides. The lost king come to reclaim the Arab throne! It was like coming face-to-face with Charlemagne or the white ghost of Elvis.

But Aunt Camille was a cool customer; she took him in from head to toe, and finally she said, "I've never heard of any lost Abbasid king."

"Well," hissed the jinn—and his breath smelled of just-struck matches and boiling oil and the last cried wishes of a thousand dying creatures—"that's why I'm the Lost *Secret* King of the Abbasid Empire, now, isn't it? When my disappointing father the Moorish prince gave away the Muslim city of Granada, my grandmother sent me into hiding—which, as everyone knows, has a way of stopping time. I stayed in a cave for a hundred years and when the floods came, I was forced to roam the world like a nameless wild man with only a wild donkey for a companion, letting my hair flow down my back and my beard flow down my front and my mind fill with electrical thoughts. This went on, along with all sorts of mayhem and adventures, until I was found and adopted by the Mother of All Fish, who taught me how to pray and who set me on the path of life again."

At the mention of the fish-mother, Aunt Camille perked up and cried, "That's exactly who I came to see!"

The jinn rolled himself out to his full seven feet two inches so his hair shimmered and his toes glimmered and he said in a voice that carried the low rumbling notes of the roaming Nile and the silky crisscrossings of the braiding Euphrates: "HAVE YOU GOT AN APPOINTMENT?"

*

That evening, just before Sirine leaves to go home, Mireille stands by the window and whispers, "Look at the moon, it looks like a baby."

Um-Nadia frowns, turns, and says to Sirine, "Something happened at the butcher shop!"

Sirine, who'd forgotten all about the bird, looks up, startled. "Did Odah call you?"

Um-Nadia squints at her. "It's all over your eyes—they're like *this*." She waves her fingertips in a fringy, sliding motion. "And you didn't bring home any lamb."

"Well, there was one thing," Sirine ventures. Um-Nadia's eyes sharpen. Sirine tells her the story of the trapped bird in the market and Um-Nadia slaps her hand to her chest. Then she has Sirine slowly turn her head to either side, checking her face, and she examines Sirine's hands closely, turning them over. "Okay, all right," she says at last, apparently reassured. "You be extra careful tonight—things are in the air," she says, pointing at Sirine.

But Sirine feels calm and clear, light and fearless. After she closes up the café, she bicycles to Han's through a night rich and warm as cashmere. The bougainvillea crazy-woman plants shake their papery buds. Clouds foam in the sky, the moon is low and almost vermilion, and the stars sail along in their private orbits. Sirine feels the thought of Han as if it circulated within her own body, as if he were the fundamental element that Aziz spoke of—as purely necessary as air and bread. She feels drawn to Han as if she were under the sweetest spell.

He is waiting for her in the front of his building, standing still under the long, violet shadows. He smiles and takes her bike. He kisses her neck in the elevator. Then he steps back and looks at her, his expression blurred in the fuzzy light. "Here you are," he says. "Let me see you. Are you really here?"

"Well," she says, "are *you* really here?"

"Sometimes I'm not sure," he says gravely. "Have I dreamed all this or is it real?"

They walk, arms scooped around each other's backs, into his apartment and go right into his bedroom. A plate of chopped fruit is positioned on the bed. They eat and sip some wine and then they make love; a recording of the Lebanese singer plays in the background, faint as a hand drifting over her hair.

Afterward, Sirine lies with her cheek against his chest, the sound of his heart thrumming in her ear, and behind that the sound of the music. She sinks into the vibrations of his body, the liquid quality of his voice stirring inside his lungs. The long stroke of his caress repeats, warm and hypnotic, and she drifts to sleep.

But they swim apart during the night. Her sleep is fragmented, sprinkled with odd dream-sounds: a baby's laugh, musical notes, a low vibrating moan. She bobs near the surface of unsettled sleep, frequently waking. There is no moon and the night through the window is plush and pincushioned and too dark, squeezing out everything, even the stars.

And she has the sense again of being watched, so real it is like an actual presence in the room. She feels she could simply open her eyes and see the staring figure bent over their bed. She struggles to wake herself several times, dreaming that her mind is awake but her body sleeps. Finally she manages to open her eyes in the dark—just a sliver—but no one is there. Just Han asleep, his breathing soft and regular. She turns on her side, watching him. He looks different in his sleep, his features swept clean. She slides her knees toward the edge of the bed and then pauses and looks back at him, wondering if it is possible that she already loves him.

She lifts her feet out of bed soundlessly, rising, drawn again to the dresser across the room. There are the same objects, but somehow they seem altered: the bottle with colored sand looks poisonous, the letter opener looks like a dagger. She searches for the photograph of Han and the boy and girl, but it's gone. She is looking for something like a clue, some small key. She needs to know more about him, to know if it is safe to feel this way about him. Her hands go carefully, carefully, to the top drawer in his dresser. It hisses open, revealing the soft, bundled shapes of clothes. She slips her hands between them, glancing back once over her shoulder. At the bottom of the drawer she feels something and pulls it out carefully: a letter.

Trembling, she takes it into the bathroom and eases the door shut. She has never snooped around a boyfriend's room like this before and she is amazed at herself—where did she get the nerve to do this? What if he wakes up? Yet she cannot seem to stop. The letter is addressed to Han at a school address in England, forwarded several times, the outside covered in scrawls and corrections. Inside, it's dated April 1999, six months ago. There are a few sentences in Arabic, then the rest is written in a cramped, tilting English:

> *So now I switch to this language, in hopes of evading censors and prying eyes, you understand. Thank heavens for my time in the Aaliyyah Girls' School—at least it taught me something useful. Still, the mail service here is undependable, and who knows if you've actually received a single one of my letters. At least half the reason why I write anymore is to hear myself think, since no one else will listen. We are a nation of thinking-out-louders, and Baghdad is the city of the dead.*
>
> *I hope you received the veil I sent last year.*
>
> *I frequently wonder what your life is like there in such a cold, distant place. I cannot quite manage to imagine it. And most probably you can no longer imagine ours either.*
>
> *As of today, here is what we have: the air over the city is electrical, stirring with chemical dust and ashes. A gray soup, land laid to waste. Life progresses in fits and starts. The vegetable seller opens his stalls but there isn't enough milk for the children, and the children are everywhere, all over the streets, their eyes too*

big and their knees and ankles and wrists all knobs. If you give one a banana, he will run just out of range in case you change your mind, and then eat it peel and all. The carousel in the amusement park next to the Baghdad Zoo is still crowded with children. They run and climb over the painted horses, and their laughter is something that freezes in the air, already an echo when you hear it. Our young women, like our men, march in formation through the streets wearing their veils and carrying long, black guns. Our fine, beautiful country is gone. We can't get away from the smell of burning. Terrible chemical fallout, starvation, no medicine, the usual catastrophe—so dull being a victim. There are many diseases, cholera, malaria, typhus, and rickets. How ridiculous to be struggling with outdated diseases! Our ancient night flashes with bombs. The Americans still bomb Iraq on nearly a daily basis. I'm told that during the Persian Gulf crisis these displays were compared to fireworks on American television.

Your mother talks about you all the time, as if you'd just stepped into the other room for a moment and will be right back. I'm writing to you now to tell you, very simply and very sadly, that your mother is not well. She has of course been sick in the past, but now it is something different. I don't know if it is possible to die from sadness—living here among such loss and grief—but I have started to think that it may well be. Your mother eats less and less. She doesn't like to get up from her bed and she no longer sits with the other women. I see a kind of darkness rising inside her like the darkness rising from the bottom of a well.

I tell you this now, my dear, not to hurt you but to let you know that if you want to see your mother again in this lifetime this may be your last chance. There is no way to undo the murder, of course, and we live in fear of Saddam's ruthlessness. But it may be that you can still find a way to come home again.

I think of you daily and, God willing, we will find each other again in the next life, if not this one. Do you remember, when we were both in school, you telling me that you never missed saying your prayers? Your faith, you said, was what shaped your character and mind and gave you hope for the future. I wonder, Hanif, do you still say your prayers every day?

There's a line in Arabic. Then:

With my enduring love, D.

*

Sirine's hands are shaking. *What murder?* She is paralyzed, thinking, I have to ask him. But if she asks she will reveal her sneakiness, the betrayal of his trust. She feels the presence of a dead person rise over them, ineffable and irresistible, a navy-eyed ghost in the corner—perhaps the staring intruder she felt in her sleep.

She creeps out of the bathroom and quickly slides the letter back under his clothes in the dresser. Now she thinks she hears strange, minute sounds all around the apartment, odd ticks and crackles that make her heart leap in her chest. She has trouble making out his form in the dark: she needs to see him. Is he planning to return to Iraq? Had he killed someone? Her mind is blurry with confusion but she is too frightened to try and unfold and reread the letter. She looks around.

And who is this letter from? The letter writer called him "my dearest." And then, surfacing like a creature hidden in the murkiest water, she recalls Um-Nadia's stories about women betrayed, their faithless men. She stares at Han's sleeping form and it seems at that moment as if he were nothing more than a shadow, a ripple of ink running over the sheets. And all of this—everything that seemed to be starting between them—was just a story she told herself.

Sirine thinks of the way her parents disappeared into the Sudan when Sirine was a little girl, as they had so many times before—into Turkey, Africa, India, into famines, civil wars, and earthquakes, sometimes leaving Sirine with weeks, even months, of silence, no addresses, the phone lines destroyed. The last time they disappeared, Sirine and her uncle didn't know what happened until several days after their death. And unlike the families of victims on the news who speak of premonitions, unsettling forebodings, Sirine had no inkling at the time that anything was wrong.

Sirine feels dizzy and weak-kneed. She sinks down onto the bed. What if he's planning to go? Han might be married, she thinks. Perhaps he has children. And perhaps he has killed someone. She lies perfectly still, watching the rise and fall of his chest. If she leaves now she will never return: it is too much for her. She begins to do what she always did when she was a little girl—she looks for a sign, any sign. She used to do this so she would know her parents were still alive when they went away: a blue car or a child with a toy or a bird in the tree kept them alive in her mind. And now she knows it is childish and impossible but she is waiting, even as she shakes her head, trying to clear it. Her heart feels diaphanous. Her hands close into fists, her breath caged in her chest. It is too much, too hard. She senses her feelings for Han contracting, retreating to a locked, distant star within her center. Just as she is about to get up, find her clothes and purse and bicycle key, she hears him murmur and turn toward her.

"Sirine."

"Yes?"

But he is asleep. His hands strum across the bed. "Sirine," he murmurs, "Sirine."

She turns, eyes wide, and her gaze falls on the silver frame—he'd moved it to his bedside table and she sees that now it holds the photograph that Nathan took—of Sirine and Han and their lustrous, held gaze, the opalescent moment of love.

Everything inside her holds and then whitens and dilates and she is closing her eyes, listening to his voice, the helpless truth of sleeping. And for that moment, it's just enough: a way to believe in him.

*

It's Sunday, Sirine's day off. They sleep late and make a breakfast from the fruit trees and garden in the building's courtyard: sweet oranges, tangerines, tomatoes, grapefruit, avocado. They sit on a fold-out aluminum love seat on his balcony with plates and knives and a bowl of salt. A trail of juice runs along her fingers and Han kisses her palms.

Looking at him in the sheer morning, the air billowing like curtains, she feels hopeful and restored, as if recovering from an illness. The memory of the letter in the night seems more manageable in the light. She thinks there must be a way to ask about it. They are being tested, she tells herself—though she isn't sure why—and the only way to pass this test is to hold very still.

Han breaks a tangerine into sections and feeds them to her one by one. Then he cuts a lemon in half, sprinkles a spoonful of sugar over the cut top, and bites into it. Sirine looks around at the wandering palms and the dusty street. Just that morning the radio weatherman had said it would be an Indian summer scorcher. She slices open an avocado and sprinkles it with coarse salt before handing it to Han. "Oh, Leila used to do that," he says softly. "Salt on the avocado."

She looks at him. "Leila?"

A point at the center of his eyes freezes. He puts down the half of butter-colored avocado. "My sister, Leila."

"I didn't know her name."

"I didn't mention it before?" He touches the pale avocado on his plate but doesn't pick it up.

She feels pricked by the sense that somehow she's missed something. "Not actually. You haven't said much about her at all."

"I haven't, really?" He smiles, but his smile looks half-broken. He puts his hand on the back of his neck and sighs. A crisp breeze kicks the dust into spirals beneath the balcony. Then he tries for a better smile and says, "I suppose I haven't. She's younger. She's with my parents. . . ." His voice trails off.

His eyes are dark and brilliant, almost phosphorescent. He takes her fingers in his, sifting through them one by one. The abandoned fruit peels have already started to curl up on the plate, dried like little jewel-toned palms; there is the mild incense of oranges and lemons in the air. "Sirine forgive me this terrible question, but—do you trust me?"

She immediately feels guilty. She looks down, then back up. "I think I do."

He nods. "Of course. We're still in the beginning part of learning each other, I know that. I need—if you can manage this—I need a little more time. There is more I need to tell you, but just—not yet. But I will if you can wait. I promise. Is that . . . can you do that for me?"

She leans forward, opens her mouth, wanting to try and ask him more, but she also feels a sort of warning, a sensation like leaves skittering across her chest. Maybe she doesn't want to know everything yet either. So she simply stands and begins picking up their dishes. The silverware rattles in her hand. She carries everything quickly in to the kitchen sink and feels so light-headed she wonders if she got enough sleep last night. She lets the hot water run hard into the sink so the steam courses up around her face. She picks up the sponge in one hand and a plate in the other and looks toward where Han is still sitting on the balcony. He has pulled his blue prayer beads out of his pocket and clicks through them, rubbing each bead over his forefinger with his thumb.

She leaves the dishes and goes back out on to the balcony. She feels a tension inside her pressing out like a tide. She sits beside him on the love seat, crosses her arms over her chest, and says, "Is it true that Muslims can have four wives?"

He laughs, startled. "What's this?"

She feels foolish but the question is in the air now. "Just something I heard," she mumbles. "Something I've always wondered about. Mireille says they do."

He extends his arm along the back of the love seat. "All right. Well. I guess technically, if you go by Islamic code, then yes, four wives. But there's a big catch: Muhammad said, if you marry more than one woman you have to treat them all equally. Which lots of religious scholars say is pretty much impossible."

"Why impossible?"

He curls his arm around her shoulders. She feels the rise and fall of his rib cage. "It's human nature to have favorites," he says quietly, stroking her hair.

"Do you feel—" She stumbles, guilty and anxious, thinking of the hidden letter. She squeezes her palms together. "I mean—do you believe that your religion—that Islam—defines who you are?"

She can feel him hesitating, his head moving as if to try and look at her. "That's an interesting question," he says guardedly. Her palms grow damp and she wonders if she's given herself away. But when she doesn't speak, he sighs and says, "For me, it's more complicated than that. I've heard of people defining themselves according to their work or religion or family. But I pretty much think I define myself by an absence."

She dares a glance at him. "What absence?"

"Well, I'm no longer a believer but I still consider myself a Muslim. In some ways, my religion is even more important to me because of that."

"How can you be Muslim if you don't believe in it?"

"I don't believe in a specific notion of God. But I do believe in social constructions, notions of allegiance, cultural identity. . . . Oh." He looks away and Sirine is quickly afraid that he's impatient with all her questions or he thinks she's not intelligent enough for him. But then he says, "The fact of exile is bigger than everything else in my life. Leaving my country was like—I don't know—like part of my body was torn away. I have phantom pains from the loss of that part—I'm haunted by myself. I don't know— does any of that make any sense? It's as if I'm trying to describe something that I'm not, that's no longer here."

"I think I can get it," she says timidly.

"Exile is like . . ." He sits forward, elbows on his knees, his prayer beads wrapped around one open hand, his hands grasping for some sort of form or image. "It's a dim, gray room, full of sounds and shadows, but there's nothing real or actual inside of it. You're constantly thinking that you see old friends on the street—or old enemies that make you shout out in your dreams. You go up to people, certain that they're members of your family, and when you get close their faces melt away into total strangers'. Or sometimes you just forget this is America and not Iraq. Everything that you were—every sight, sound, taste, memory, all of that has been wiped away. You forget everything you thought you knew." He drops his hands. "You have to."

"Why?"

"You have to let yourself forget or you'll just go crazy. Sometimes when I see some of those homeless people on the street—you know, the ones walking around talking to the air, shuffling around, old torn-up clothes— sometimes I think I've never felt so close to anyone as those people. They know what it feels like—they live in between worlds so they're not really anywhere. Exiled from themselves."

Sirine feels a sensation like ghost fingers trailing down her spine; she shivers and hugs her elbows in close. "So—is that what you did? I mean, you let yourself forget?" she asks, hoping he'll say yes.

But he says, "I'm trying to." And then, "Sometimes it's so hard. I had no idea, none, when I left my country, what a life-changing thing it would be. It's much harder than I'd ever thought could be possible. I wasn't prepared for how much I would miss them—and for how much worse simply knowing I can't return makes me feel. And of course there's no way I could have known any of this before I'd left, when I was so young and excited and thought I was ready for anything at all."

Sirine gazes at him, waiting for him to return to the balcony, put his arms around her, to say that she's more than made up for all this loss in his life. Instead, however, he closes his eyes, his shoulders lowering heavily, and he clicks through his prayer beads.

CHAPTER FIFTEEN

Aunt Camille had finally found her way over the broad back of Egypt, to the door of the Mother of All Fish, only to be stopped by the lack of an appointment. Wouldn't you know it?

So Aunt Camille's delicate shoulders slumped and Napoleon-Was-Here lowered his heavy dog-head and the crocodiles wept and the jacaranda blossoms fell out of the purple sky. "No," she admitted to the guard-jinn. "I don't have an appointment."

Now, this was not a hard-hearted jinn. He was a big softie in actual fact. But the Eternal Golden Rule is: an appointment is required. After all, the world was filled with all sorts of hungry-eyed fisher sorts who thought there was no sweeter, milkier dish than a fillet of Mother of All Fish with a garlic-lemon sauce on the side. And these sorts always came without an appointment.

The jinn had to try and navigate between being a Mr. Softie and having a jinn's natural love of rules. He was a nephew of the Sphinx and second cousin once removed of Rumpelstiltskin. He considered asking her one of the vintage jinn, gate-guarding riddles, unsolvable to all but the hero. But he immediately divined that she was the co-hero of this story, giving her a clear, natural edge.

Instead he hemmed and hawed and made small talk—as best a scarlet-eyed jinn can make—and essentially blocked Camille's way until the muezzin of Lake Tanganyika had time to climb his tree and begin his call to prayer. At that moment, time stopped and Nature looked up; the birds stopped twittering and the leaves stopped rattling, in order to let their souls be diverted by that sweet, drifting call, onto the path of prayer. Relieved, the great jinn grabbed her hand in his meaty, sweaty paw and said, "Let us pray!"

Aunt Camille knelt and said her prayers, which consisted largely of: Dear God, please let me get past this jinn. After a respectable interval, then, she finished her prayers and all the other woodland creatures and spirits and entities finished theirs. Everyone sighed and then went back to work. All but the jinn, who just bowed and prayed and prayed like there was no tomorrow and no today. It occurred to Aunt Camille that he might just pray until the next call to prayers was announced in a couple of hours, and that he could, in fact, keep this prayer business going indefinitely, thus blocking any and all progress toward the fish-mother. So she made another plan. She called to her loyal companion, Napoleon-Was-Here, crossed her fingers, and said, "Do you smell if this crazy jinn has a *mutbakh*—also called a *kitchen*—anywhere around here?" Well, the dog put his long educated nose into the air, twirled it around, and sure enough, off they went.

*

It's late in the day, the light red and burnished as if it is coming from far away. But there're still a couple students waiting outside of Han's office door—both young women in short skirts, with backpacks and chewed-up pencils. Sirine sits with them and listens to the voices behind the door with its frosted glass: one low and languorous as a dark river, the other younger and milder, sparked with feminine laughter, ringing like a spoon in a glass of tea; their shadows ripple in watery slivers over the window. Han pokes his head out the door then, spots Sirine, and smiles. "I'll just be a few more minutes. . . ." He indicates the waiting students.

He stands in the door and the student he was speaking to slides past him—Sirine notes—so she brushes very slightly against him. "Thank you, Professor," she says, eyes lowered, a faint smile on her lips. It's the covered woman, the veil tucked tightly in at her chin, just framing her face—but Sirine wonders, isn't she wearing lipstick and eyeliner? Han calls another student in and closes the door. The covered woman turns to go—Sirine is trying to remember, is this the one who threw the pen at Aziz?—when she turns and says, "Aren't you Sirine?"

Startled, Sirine sits upright. "Do I know you?"

The woman's eyes are black with wine-colored flecks and her lashes are so long they have a slight dip, like a canopy. "My family used to eat at Nadia's Café all the time—when I was just a girl. I used to love watching you work inside your kitchen. That was years ago—I'm a student here now," she says. A modest smile. "And Hanif—I mean, the professor—has often mentioned you."

"He's mentioned me?"

"Oh—not like in class. Privately." Now she covers her smile with her fingertips, as if she's revealed something. "I mean, during office hours, of course. He speaks of you . . . very warmly. He said something about me wearing the *hejjab*"—she indicates her veil and black coat—"and we just started talking about it. So few of us wear the veil in this country. And he told me that you seem to show a bit of an interest in Islam."

Sirine isn't entirely smiling. "He told you that? Privately?"

Now the student pulls up a chair and sits across from Sirine; her expression is level and a bit intense. "If you think you'd like to learn more, I belong to a group. . . ." She tears a scrap of paper out of a notebook and begins writing on it. "Women in Islam. We meet once a week. Please come. If you're the tiniest bit interested. It's so important to have women like yourself attend, you're such a model to the younger women." Sirine stares at her. The student's face is open and polished as a shell. She reaches over and fingers Han's scarf, which Sirine has wrapped around her neck. "That's great. These stitches. You look so . . . almost Arab in it. You're Iraqi, aren't you?" she asks.

Han must have told her that as well, Sirine thinks. "Half," Sirine says. "My father."

"Like Han!" She grabs Sirine's hand. "I wish I were Iraqi. I love Iraqis. They're the best of the Arabs. Baghdad is the mother of the whole Arab world. Now you really, really have to come. There's a meeting this Sunday afternoon—are you off from work? I'll look for you." She stands then quickly bends and places a tiny kiss on Sirine's cheek. Sirine smells jasmine and clove perfume.

She disappears out the door and Sirine sits there, hands in her lap, her heart booming.

*

That evening in bed, Sirine pulls back from Han. Shadows from turning headlights crawl through the bedroom, making low, black furrows, the white foam of waves.

"What is it?" he says, pushing a dangling lock of her hair behind her ear.

"I think I want to go to that meeting," she says. She's aware that she's testing him, but not sure what his response should be. "The Women in Islam meeting your student told me about."

He hesitates, looks amused. The black of his eyes blends into the black of his lashes like melted chocolate, dark slants under folds of skin. A soft wing of stubble covers his lower face. "Well, sure, if you like."

"You don't have an opinion?"

He doesn't respond right away: the longer he is quiet, the more she thinks she wants to attend. He lays back in the bed and she slides over him. His lips are pale and soft, his hands unfold. "Well, it's fine either way." He fills his hands with her hair. "That's what I like about this country," he says. "You can do whatever. A meeting is only a meeting. There doesn't have to be anything more to it than that."

*

The meeting is in a big hotel downtown. Sirine turns a corner, following the concierge's directions along an endless, winding corridor. Each of the rooms along the corridor have gold plates inscribed with their names: the Santa Ana, the San Gabriel, the Sierra. She finds the Shasta Room at the end of the corridor and when she pushes through the heavy door, it's a burst of white-paneled walls and ornate crystal chandeliers. The walls and carpet are all the same creamy white and seem to fade away from the center of the room. There's a podium with a spray of yellow roses, and huddled at the center of the big room, a loose ring of chairs and perhaps seventeen or eighteen women. A handful of the women are fully cloaked in veils and floor-length black dress; the rest are dressed in pants and cardigans, jeans and blouses.

The carpet feels spongy beneath Sirine's feet and the voices of the women are absorbed into the walls, so it's hard to hear anything clearly until she's actually sitting inside the ring of chairs. Only her pulse amplifies, filling her ears. Sirine is regretting not having brought Mireille along for support, but when she invited her, Mireille said she was "against religion, period." Sirine came thinking that there might be something important here she could learn about Han—the pieces of things he didn't seem able to tell her about. But the longer she stands in the room, the more uncomfortable she feels. This reminds her of a conference meeting she once catered: a small, aggressively officious group called Women Mean Business. She wonders if she turned and tried to tiptoe out, if anyone would notice. But every face is turned toward her now. The student who invited her doesn't seem to be anywhere in sight and she freezes for a moment, wondering if it's a sort of secret society. Then one of the women in black beckons her in and says, "It's okay. We don't bite."

Sirine perches at the edge of the seat, as if she might need to spring to her feet at any moment. The women resume chatting with each other. One woman is working on a crossword puzzle; another, whose hair is covered with a black head scarf, is plaiting the hair of a woman in a fuzzy pink sweater. A number of them smile at Sirine.

A woman in a knitted gray cardigan and a pair of bifocals on a pearl chain stands and welcomes them. She asks for everyone to introduce themselves briefly—Sirine wonders if this is being done for her benefit—and some of the women just shyly murmur their names and their nationality. One woman says, "I'm married to Hassan Almirah and my children's names are Tonia and Tamim," before someone reminds her to give her own first name. But many of them offer some sort of testimonial or request: "I used drugs to try and clear my soul, but then I found Islam." Or: "I am praying to get a job and get back on my feet." As it gets closer to Sirine's turn, her heart begins hammering and her mind goes blank. Then everyone is looking at her. "Sirine," she manages to say. "I cook." A covered woman sitting behind her touches her shoulder and leans over. "I didn't think you'd really come," she whispers.

Sirine turns—the woman's face is covered except for her eyes, which are hooded black marbles, the sort of eyes Um-Nadia would call Cleopatra eyes. She removes the veiling covering her mouth and nose and Sirine realizes it's the pretty student from Han's class. "I'm Rana," the woman says to the group. "As most of you know. From Saudi Arabia. And I don't have a husband and I don't have any kids, all right?"

*

The secretary reads minutes, announcements, then opens the floor to a group discussion over whether they'll participate in a campus sit-in to protest the occupation of the West Bank, whether they'll donate baked goods to the Lutheran fund-raiser, and whether they'll appear on a local TV news show to discuss the negative portrayal of Arabs in Hollywood films.

Sirine watches the faces of the women around her: about half of the group have fair skin and light eyes, including some of the covered women. Some are in white head scarves and some in black, and each scarf seems to be knotted or fastened in a slightly different way: the ends tucked in at the side of the face or elaborately swept around the neck or pinned under the chin. A number of the older women there have darkened their eyes with scrolls of eyeliner and dramatic red lipstick.

Suddenly Rana leans forward, elbows on her knees, and says she has something important to say. She is wearing a gold ring on her thumb inscribed with what appear to be Roman numerals and Sirine watches her twist it around as she speaks about the war in the Persian Gulf, her voice gathering intensity: "Nine full years after the war—it's the total destruction of Iraq's economy and people . . . targeting women and children . . . the American embargoes . . . biological weapons, rocket launchers, nerve gas. . . ." Sirine's concentration flickers—she takes in snatches of Rana's words, but she is distracted by her transported expression and voice: "American Muslims must do everything they can to show support for their Iraqi brothers and sisters. We can demonstrate, write to Congress. . . ."

The girl in the pink sweater snaps her gum and bobs her foot. A number of the women light cigarettes while Rana is speaking and the group leader looks nervous and waves her hand at the smoke. "Whoever sets off the next smoke alarm," she interrupts, "has to find the next meeting room."

Rana pulls up indignantly and sends a scathing look across the group.

One of the older women sighs and folds her arms over her chest, rocking her body back in her chair. "Rana, I'm sorry, but do you always have to be at the top of your lungs all the time? People like you make the Amerkees think Muslims are always angry." She adds something in Arabic so a number of the other women shout, "English, English!"

Rana looks dazed. "How can you talk like that, Suha?" she demands. "Do you know the effect of an American rocket on an Iraqi tank?" She lifts her hand. "The Americans were firing after the Iraqis had already *surrendered*, they were retreating."

Suha sniffs. "I don't even know why you expect us to know about all these political things," she says. "We just want to be Americans like everyone else."

Rana points at Suha. "Do you see? This is exactly the attitude that's the problem! You want to know where terrorists come from? They come from passivity—from well-meaning people! Americans want big cars, big houses—they don't care what their government does to put cheap gasoline in their cars, to make all these big, expensive things happen. Fine, but don't be surprised when the terrorism ends up right back here."

"How can you say such a thing about your own country?" Suha asks, her face darkening with indignation; a number of the other women nod. "You were even born here."

"How can *you* be so indifferent to human lives? These are your brothers and sisters we're talking about!"

Suha holds up one hand and says, "My brothers and sisters are in Orange County where they belong."

*

After the meeting, Rana turns to Sirine, gripping her hands. Rana's palms are warm—her whole body radiates heat and the bright lighting seems to sap away the pink of her skin. Her eyes look enormous and unblinking. "Sister," Rana says, and even her voice is hot. "You're a natural Muslim, I can see it."

Sirine stands still, letting Rana hold her hands in her fiery grip. She is a little afraid of Rana and inspired by her and she feels a sudden reckless impulse to confide in her, to ask some of the questions that have been worrying her. "I was wondering . . ." Sirine begins tentatively, then shies away, startled by the way Rana's eyes widen. "I mean—well, just, thank you for inviting me."

Sirine smiles but now Rana's eyes seem to be ticking over her, a faintly ironic expression on her face. "I hope you got something out of it. Sometimes I'm not even sure if there's a way for a Christian to comprehend a Muslim," she says speculatively. "May I ask what faith you belong to?"

Sirine looks down at her hands and notices a fine crease of flour between her fingers and under her nails. She stuffs them into her pockets. "I suppose I don't actually have one," she ventures. "I mean, my parents didn't, so . . ." She trails off. But she's afraid Rana will be disappointed by this, so she adds, "Well, I believe in lots of things."

"I see." Rana looks less than impressed. "That's interesting."

Sirine thinks she sees a dart of wickedness reflected behind the surface of Rana's eyes. It ripples through her slender frame like suppressed laughter. And still, Sirine can't help admiring Rana, her intense beauty and her fierce mind. In her presence, Sirine feels as if her own mind is a small, dimly lit place.

It seems the air-conditioning has kicked on in the room. Sirine runs her palms over her prickling arms. "Are you cold?" Rana takes the wide cotton scarf from her own shoulders and wraps it around Sirine. It reminds Sirine of the one Han gave her. This one is black with a blue embroidered border in the shape of petals. And for an instant Sirine wonders if Han has given them each a scarf. But Rana is bending over her, saying, "Please. Please keep it. I insist."

Through the window Sirine can see the hot mountain wind stirring sand and dust into the air. "Oh no, no, I couldn't possibly," she says.

Rana embraces her, holding Sirine inside the scarf and kissing both her cheeks, then she whispers in her ear, "My sister."

CHAPTER SIXTEEN

It's a lesser-known fact about jinns that, while they do not have living rooms or dining rooms or studies or bathrooms or even very comfortable beds, they do like a nice kitchen, to satisfy their sweet tooth, maybe bake a little knaffea, brew a little coffee, have a few people over—that sort of thing. The river jinn's *mutbakh* was situated behind a crack in a great stone wall along the bank of the lake and Napoleon-Was-Here and Aunt Camille had to squeeze themselves through the crack one by one to get in. The kitchen wasn't much more than a seven-sided marble room with a twelve-foot-high domed ceiling, a stolen Roman mosaic floor of a winged antelope, a mossy boulder for a table, four chairs of twigs, a teensy firehold in the rock with a permanent fire, a cold corner and a pantry, and a very large pile of bones—which Camille preferred to ignore, but which intrigued Napoleon-Was-Here. She checked the cold corner and found seven mice, two squirrels, one crocodile toe, and a few gray *wut-wut*, or bats. In the pantry she found a jug of olive oil, several bulbs of garlic and onion, some ripe tomatoes, half a lemon, several dates, a big cabbage, some rice, jars of cardamom, tea, pepper, green wheat, sugar, turmeric, salt, nutmeg, fenugreek, dried mint, saffron, cinnamon, oregano, sumac, lentils, and powdered coffee. And behind all this, glowing and sweating, smooth and satiny, black as onyx and fat as a baby, she found an eggplant.

Aunt Camille held it up high in the air with both hands like a midwife holds the newly caught infant and announced, "The answer to our prayers!"

Thus ensued some scooping and scraping, some slicing and dicing, some stuffing and some baking. She found a few raisins here, a few pine nuts there, did some frying in *aliya*—the fat of the lamb's tail. She had to experiment a bit with the heat in that fire-hold—and before you knew it, there was a magnificent dish of stuffed eggplant presented on a cobalt-blue glass platter.

The fragrance of the dish filled the kitchen and wafted around them as she carried the platter through the forest to the jinn. He hadn't stopped his prayers once in all this time, but as Aunt Camille drew closer, the rich, garlicky, buttery, nuttery, eggplanty flavor swirled around his head until he felt his senses would be lifted right out of his body. He rocked back on his heels, spied Aunt Camille with her dish, and promptly thundered, "I COMMAND YOU TO GIVE ME THE EGGPLANT!"

"Not so fast," said Aunt Camille, holding the dish behind her back. "I wouldn't want to interrupt a pious jinn in his prayers."

"Hmmm, yes," said the jinn, looking hungry and trapped.

Suddenly she looked distracted. "That is . . . unless . . ."

"Unless . . . ?"

"Of course, unless you're one of those who believe that honoring the body and pleasing its senses is one of the best ways to give thanks to God."

The jinn leapt up in relief. "Why, that's it! That's it exactly!" he cried, and his tongue unrolled and his fingers stretched out toward the eggplant.

"And you know what they say about such sorts of holy men?" she continued, still clinging to the dish.

"Well, no, no, not exactly," said the jinn, his eyes not moving from the eggplant.

"That they are the sorts of holy men who never stand on ceremony and who never insist on an appointment."

At this, the jinn's hunger got the best of him—and if you're ever in a standoff with a jinn or any other sort of bully or gatekeeper, it's best to remember this: their hunger will always get the best of them. He jumped up and cried out, "Forgive me, Mother of All Fish!" and, grabbing the dish, the

Lost Secret King of the Abbasid Empire and the Holy Man of Eggplant spirited off into the black forest with his new religion.

*

Sirine watches the early morning news from Qatar on the TV mounted over the counter. A serious-looking man and woman sit at a desk reading from a sheath of papers. Behind them are small, boxed images: burning oil fields, a starving baby, U.N. trucks crossing muddy rutted streets. Sirine wonders how someone like Rana manages to make sense of this, these stories that seem to have no beginning or end, no boundaries, sliding—as the news does on the screen—from Iraq to Bosnia to Ireland to Palestine. The dire broadcasts fill her with free-floating anxiety, a dread of the world beyond Westwood Boulevard.

The students filter into the café, go to the same chairs at the same tables. They come so early—and the sun is rising later—that there are still long clouds scraped across the sky with a pink scrim beneath them. The air smells of fire and chocolate, black tea and a brassy scent of earth. All of them have stacks of textbooks but they unfold newspapers from home, printed on pale green and yellow newsprint. They rattle these open, poring over the columns, the yellow paper flickering like small flames. News from Algeria, Bethlehem, Baghdad. Sometimes she's seen them in the campus library, studying Internet news on the terminals. She knows that the news is at the center of their lives, reports of the home places they had to leave, the frightening things that may have happened to their families and friends.

One young student sitting at the counter is holding his paper open and upright so that Sirine can see a photograph on the front page. It is grainy, a bit smeared, like something from a half-forgotten nightmare: a group of figures with sacks over their heads. Necks yanked. Toes pointed. Their feet don't touch the ground. She stands, staring at the photo, her hands pressed flat against her apron, not moving. A cold feeling passes through the middle of her chest, an iron spoon clanging in an empty iron pot. It is almost the same as the way she felt when she read the letter in Han's room. Finally the student lowers the paper slightly and looks up. High, delicate cheekbones. His glasses flare white against his skin. He looks vaguely familiar—she's seen him in the café before—he seems too young to be in college. He looks at her.

"What is that?" she asks tentatively, pointing to the photograph. "What's happening there?"

The student half-shrugs, so skinny she can see the knob of his shoulder through his thin shirt. "Just Saddam Hussein. Making an example. He says these people were in collusion with the Americans to overthrow the government." His voice is ironic and mournful for such a youthful face.

"Were they?"

The student pushes up his glasses with one finger. She can't quite see his eyes. And she doesn't know what country he's from. "It's possible. Or it might have been something else. He has all kinds of reasons, they come to him or he can make them up at will." He glances at the photograph again and shrugs. "This is nothing special."

"Nothing special?"

He pushes up his glasses once again, but this time looks at her very carefully and closely. "What do you care?" he says finally.

She's taken aback; without thinking, she moves one hand to her chest. "Of course I care. Why do you say that?"

He reopens the newspaper, folding over the front page so she can't see it. "You're American," he says.

Later, on break, she searches the front sections of the American papers at the newsstand up the street: the *Los Angeles Times*, the *New York Times*, the *Washington Post*. There is no photograph; today, no mention of Iraq. Nothing at all.

*

That evening Sirine leaves work early, right after the busiest part of the dinner rush, just as the sky is starting to darken. She bicycles across Westwood Village, along the edge of the campus with just a hastily jotted address on a scrap of paper, into a warren of student housing, fraternities, and condos. She has to ask several people for help along the way. The full night seems to fall as soon as she moves away from the banks of streetlights, the darkness so dense that the stars pop right out at her. The sky is complicated with glowing planets and recognizable constellations—the bull, the Pleiades—that her uncle used to show her from the roof of his house while they waited for her parents to come home. She stops now and she can almost see a freckled light behind the stars—no moon, just a deep dimension of stars behind stars, adding layers like chambers opening in a black room.

She consults the address again by the blue light thrown from someone's living room TV onto the sidewalk. For a while she's convinced that she is lost. Then she turns a corner and realizes she's on the right street. The address leads to a shack tucked in between a couple of sedate two- and three-story apartment buildings. Its clapboard sides are rotting away, moldy, and part of the structure is made from unmatched plywood boards. The lawn is crabbed up with thickets of weeds and even the two banana trees look stooped over and stunted, their broad fronds split and curling brown. An electric power line droops sizzling over the sunken roof. There isn't a house number and Sirine can't see any lights inside—it looks uninhabited.

She dismounts her bike and cautiously walks it up to the porch. There's an acrid, foreign smell in the air. She stares at the door slightly askew in its frame, and decides to abandon the whole ridiculous plan, turn around, and ride home. She's just folded the address into her pocket and walked back to the street when she hears a door creak open behind her, turns, and sees Nathan standing there. "Oh my God. Sirine," he says. "I thought I heard something out here." He drops his arms to his sides and grins. "You came."

"Hi. I . . ." She stumbles, unsure if she was even invited. "I saw some photos today—they were in the paper—I don't know. I started to think about you—and—"

"Please, please." He holds his arm out, welcoming her, and she goes to the crooked door. "Forgive me. I spend so much time in the darkroom that I miss day and night. They just aren't there for me anymore. I've gotten used to living without turning any lights on." He flips a switch in the room—more of a night-light than an actual lamp—that barely casts enough light for Sirine to make out shapes: empty cups, boxes, cans, all sorts of odds and ends floating around oversized furniture.

"Come, this way." He leads her through the room—she follows, bumping into unidentifiable objects. "Please forgive the—" He kicks something out of the way. "I hardly ever get actual company." He opens a door in the back. And here the smell is the strongest—metallic, sour, and acidic, nearly dizzying. The room is bathed in a powdery bronze-red light and more half-seeable objects loom in the corners and hang from the ceiling.

"Welcome to my bat cave." There are various pieces of equipment, a metal folding chair, a long table set out with trays full of solutions, and a stack of negatives that he's been cutting apart.

"This is where you work?" She feels shy. Both of them speak in lowered careful voices, as if there were people sleeping nearby.

He holds up some negatives, then moves to the trays. "I was just doing some prints. See—this one is developer and this is stop bath and . . ." His expression is obscured in the red light. He holds up a pair of silver tongs. "Do you want to see?" He slides a paper into the tray and gives it a little slosh, then chuckles. "I really can't believe you're here. Really—no one ever visits me." He pauses, then asks, "Did you tell Han you were coming over?"

She smiles archly. "No. But I think it's okay." She picks up a canister, puts it down. The room is cramped and Nathan seems to hunch instinctively, moving between the trays. Nathan says, "Watch." He slips the paper into a tray and after a few moments Sirine can see ghostly shapes rising on the pages in the plastic tub. She tries to get a closer look: a woman's hair, face, and feather-white arms lifted at right angles, swimming across the surface of the page; her legs look oddly bent, her feet bound together—a fishtail? He flicks it into the next tray.

Nathan bends back over the trays: more exotic images emerge from the chemical bath—people laughing—wedges of bright teeth in darkened faces. They look like beings from another planet.

"What are these pictures of?"

"Oh, I never really know." He holds up another negative. "I used to label everything, put dates on my film and keep it all in order. Then I found out that it was better to just forget what it was that I photographed and let it come back in this new form. So I could really let myself see the images." He bends over the trays with such concentration that Sirine senses that she has just flicked out of his consciousness. His breathing is heavy, unselfconscious, with a thin wheeze like a bird's cry. She scrutinizes his profile; his hair looks as if he'd chopped it away with a kitchen scissors or a knife; his narrow jaw clenches and unclenches.

"What's this?" She points to a machine with a dial like the setting on a stove. She touches it and the red overhead light goes out, throwing the room into dimensionless darkness. She grasps the edge of a table. "Oh!"

"The timer." The red light comes back on. Nathan's hand is on her forearm. Gray ghost eyes, all pupils. "You okay?"

"Fine." She laughs weakly.

"You sure?" He looks at her, squints. "You don't look completely fine."

She sits on the metal folding chair beside the table and wonders if the fumes are making her dizzy. She closes her eyes and opens them and his face looms close to hers. For a moment it seems as if he might kiss her. Then he straightens up and turns away.

"Would you like some water?"

She stares at his back. She would love to figure Nathan out. It's like a tickling sensation just beneath the surface of her skin. It seems that he wants something from her, but not really the sorts of things that men usually want. This feels more like a type of impossible and endless wanting—the kind that cannot quite be satisfied. She notices the tender swath of exposed neck, the pink ridges of his ears, and the back of his cropped head, and she senses that he is waiting for something like validation, absolution. "Nathan," she says slowly, "how long did you live in Iraq?"

He turns back; she can see he didn't expect this question.

"It's just—you seem to know so much about it," she says. "I know it really makes Han happy to talk with you about it."

"Does it?" He picks up a pair of tongs and turns them around. "You know, I wasn't supposed to be there."

"You weren't?"

"There's a ban on travel to Iraq. But I went with a friend who was doing relief work, smuggling in food and school supplies for children. Totally unsanctioned by our government. When I was in Baghdad, I was approached by an American man in a business suit who told me I had two choices: leave the country or hand over my photographs."

"Oh." She feels her eyes widen. She's heard a few of these sorts of stories before from the students—about being called upon for questioning—the C.I.A., F.B.I.—the invisible men who seemed to have the power to do just about anything to whomever they choose. "What did you do?"

He squints at her painfully. "I was in love at the time, I couldn't leave."

"Oh." She blinks, her breath caught in her throat like a hiccup. "What were your photographs of?"

He shakes his head, mouth set and grim. Then he says, "Just people. Nothing important. I didn't think there was anything important there. The man asked me to write up a report of my experiences and I refused to do that. I wouldn't give him any names or that sort of information. I took off, left my apartment in the city, and went to stay with the family of the woman I loved. I slept in the fields outside their house. I knew there wasn't any way the man could find me there."

"Were there any photographs of her that you gave the man? Of the woman?"

He stares hard at the silver tongs. "Several." He turns away and dips his tongs into one of the plastic tubs. Sirine watches the images coming up from the bath: blackbirds, bare trees like pencil drawings, people talking, but there's something not quite right about each—a man seems to have too many fingers on his hand, a single horn protrudes from the center of a deer's head.

"Did—did anything happen?"

He shakes his head, rattles the tongs in the tub. "It's too much to explain. To be honest . . . it's hard for me to think about, that old stuff. It all happened years ago. I've already said too much as it is."

She waits, hoping he'll go on. When he doesn't, she finally asks gently, "Do you have any pictures of her?"

A child whose hair looks dunked in tar, slicked against his head. A woman with eyes like tar, deep holes filled with liquid.

"I can't find any," he says. Then he looks up at Sirine, his expression pleading. "Please, don't tell Han about this. About the man or the photos or any of it. I didn't have a choice," he says intensely. "I couldn't leave her and I couldn't bring her with me. I didn't know what to do, I was desperate. Please don't tell Han, please, I don't think he'd understand."

"I'm sure Han wo—"

"Please, just promise me."

She nods. "It's okay, it's all right, really. I won't tell anybody anything."

Nathan shakes his head. "I feel lousy that I told you any of this. I'm always saying too much and I don't mean to and I don't even know it until a day or two goes by and I've had a chance to realize how crazy I sound. I'm sure people think I'm nuts."

"Really—it's—"

He cuts her off, "Why do people have to talk about everything all the time anyway? Talk, talk, talk. Why can't we just let things go? As far as I'm concerned, this is all I need." He gestures toward the prints. "It's what I can see, which is plenty for me. Why do people have to go digging back behind the edges and scratching up words and things, trying to get at stuff? There's nothing else there. Or nothing that anyone needs to know about. I know enough of what's inside of me, and that's all I need."

"Isn't that a little . . . lonely?" she murmurs. She glances around the room. Somehow, from beneath the chemical layers, she believes she can smell his breath or his skin—a musty sort of mix of sesame and burnt sugar. And his voice, so low-modulated and trembling in her ear like the voice from inside a shell, from deep beneath the sea. Suddenly it all feels too close; she doesn't want to be there any longer. But Nathan is holding up another photograph, saying, "It's like you can see just where their soul is. Tucked inside some part of them."

She glances at the image: a dark-skinned man sitting in a chair in front of an office door. His legs are crossed and his head is slightly turned, his posture and the slope of his shoulders gracefully canted in a fine, calligraphic arch. His expression is yearning and grief-stricken, as if he'd been crying and only just stopped before the photo was shot. "How sad," she says softly. Her heart seems to rise in her chest; it's such an odd, stirring image. "Who is this man?"

Nathan chuckles, then stops and looks at her. After a moment he says, "Well. That's Han, of course."

*

She stands waiting in Nathan's doorway. In the half-moon light she looks out across the neglected lawn; she can see pears hanging red as roses in the leaves, soft-winged moths, sulfurous and turquoise, flapping past. She smells the lemon leaves and myrtle and berries roasting in the hot night. The late darkness softens the house and the yard, makes it look quaint and romantic.

"Here it is!" Nathan comes back into the front room, holding a photo with a white mat board frame around it. "I meant to wrap it first, but . . ." He slips it into her hands as if it were a shared secret. "Thank you for coming over here. And letting me go on about—you know—all that. It meant a lot to me."

She takes the photograph without looking at it and pauses for a moment. She rubs her fingers along the edge of the mat board, then looks up. "Nathan, what would happen to Han if he were to go back to Iraq?"

He turns his head slightly. "Why? Has he said something—"

"No, oh no, I'm just wondering, you know, what would happen if he did."

"I think we'd never see him again."

She holds his gaze a moment longer, then steps back and glances at the photograph: a blur of cars, a little boy in one corner with smudged lips that Sirine can tell, even in black and white, are cherry-colored, a hand pulling him out of the frame, a shop sign in sloping Arabic letters. It's a street scene, the shops between Nadia's Café and the butcher shop, and at the center, there's Sirine with her face like a question, her hair white as a torch blowing away from her face, on her way to somewhere.

CHAPTER SEVENTEEN

So where were we? Waiting with Aunt Camille on the banks of Lake Tanganyika, hoping that the Mother of All Fish will meet with her. The Tanganyika is a wild, curling, crazy water, a lakewater giving into the Nile River, filled with every manner of aquatic beast. There were Big Eyes and Yellow Fins, Whirling Lanterns and Fat Mouths. Fishes with wrinkled foreheads and stubby fingers like angry accountants and fishes with smirks and scheming minds like college students, and fishes with long streamers like hair and long hanging fins like legs and goofy freckled faces like the kids from across the street.

And in charge of all the fish babies in the deep, sapphire-blue waters was the old, old, old, old, old, old mother. And she loved all her fish, even the one who looked like the goofy neighbor kid, because that's how mothers are. No objectivity on the subject. Even when they say they're objective, don't you believe it.

And the Mother of All Fish, you might be surprised to learn, was a tired, tiny, salty little sardine of a fish with a flat little nose and a drab little dress and a tiny little babushka knotted under her chin, like all the old Russian and Greek and Italian and Arab ladies got their ideas of how to dress from her. Her bodyguard, the cocoa-skinned jinn, had abandoned her for exactly one stuffed eggplant, so there was nothing left for her to do but take pity on the foreign traveler, wandering lost along the bank, and rise to the occasion. She poked out her dainty fish nose and said, "What now? I am the Mother of All Fish. Now what did they do?"

Aunt Camille arranged herself on the very edge of the lake and wrung her hands and said, in her softest, loveliest voice, "Oh, Dear Mother! I too am a mother, perhaps you've heard of my son. His name happens to be Abdelrahman Salahadin—"

Suddenly, the mothers of the slugs and the frogs and the otters and all the lake beings, along with the Mother of All Fish, rolled their eyes and shook their heads and sighed theatrically. "Abdelrahman Salahadin. . . . Funny," the Mother of All Fish said, "somehow you don't think of a boy like that as even having a mother."

"I know," Aunt Camille said. "He's a naughty boy and I tried to bring him up right and teach him what he needed to know, but he's still naughty. And for some reason I love the worst one the best of all."

Here again, the mothers of the lake beings all sighed in unison, feeling empathy on this point.

"Still and be that as it may," Aunt Camille continued, "the fact is I must've spoiled the boy. If I told him once, I told him a thousand times, no more fake drownings! But did he listen? No! He'd turn right around and do exactly the opposite. Fine. Never mind. The problem is this: exactly what I said would happen has happened—he faked his drowning so many times that he forgot how to swim. He's been missing for months . . . maybe it's years, I lost track. Dear fish-mother," she pleaded, "you're my only hope. I appeal to you, mother to mother, can you tell me what has become of my youngest and favorite son Abdelrahman Salahadin?"

The Mother of All Fish meditated for a while, pensively blowing bubbles, then she bobbed back up and said, "Well, this is a breach of protocol, but out of respect to the Solidarity of Mothers, I will answer you. I know what it feels like to lose a son. I have lost uncountable children in nets and on lines, in droughts and during famines, and a mother feels each loss as keenly as if it were her only child in the world! I do indeed know what happened to Abdelrahman Salahadin. He was abducted by one of our many maritime enchantresses, called afreet or mermaids or selkies or sirens.

Alieph, this particular no-good mermaid, amuses herself by pretending to be a grieving widow in search of her lost husband and luring innocent Bedouins out to the ocean and other such places where they have no business being."

"An afreet!" Aunt Camille exclaimed, and she shook in all her bones. The situation was graver than she had thought.

*

Now the days are rich with a light like the light thrown off the setting sun, a last, potent breath before the long night. Everything is vivid and colored-in. Thanksgiving is the first of the lonely student holidays. Nadia's Café will be closed and there will always be a couple of foreign students who forget or just don't know what day it is, who go to the door and tug and peer in through the darkened window. Then they see the sign on the door written in English and Arabic; they notice the smoky quiet in the streets, the dullness of the shop windows, the click of the traffic light above Westwood Boulevard, and they walk home twice as lonely as before.

Sirine and her uncle try to invite over anyone who needs a place to sit and have a bite and a conversation. At work, Sirine announces that this year will be an Arabic Thanksgiving with rice and pine nuts and ground lamb in the turkey instead of cornbread, and yogurt sauce instead of cranberries. Mireille sulks and says she doesn't like yogurt and Sirine says, annoyed, why can't we ever do things differently? And Um-Nadia says, girls, never mind already, we can have the for-crying-out-loud rice stuffing and I'll bring the can of the red berries sauce.

"I'm going to start doing five hundred or so sit-ups every day," Mireille says, checking the waistband of her black jeans. "I plan on losing weight in honor of Thanksgiving."

In the past Sirine would be absorbed for weeks with thinking about what she would cook for Thanksgiving. It was her mother's favorite holiday and the traditional American foods always made Sirine think of her, the warmth of their table in the fall; it was among the earliest and best of her memories. But things are different now. Her mind has been taken up by Han. She hears his voice in the fabric of things, in running faucets and motors and in the courtyard garden of the birds.

They spend their nights together and Sirine learns about the way Han sleeps. She discovers that he has nightmares, dreams that shake him so he kicks at the covers or cries out so loud she's startled awake, heart pounding. If she tries to wake him, he'll stare at her without seeming to recognize her, or say a few unintelligible words, then slip back into sleep. She thinks perhaps if he talked more about Iraq perhaps he wouldn't have so many bad dreams, that maybe there is a way to talk it out of his system. But she doesn't say this to him—she just lies awake and watches him. Sometimes he sleeps badly, tossing and waking, and Sirine will wake at midnight in an empty bed and hear him roaming through the unlit apartment, from one window to another.

One night, she wakes and creeps to the door of the bedroom and watches Han sitting by the window. He is frowning, gazing off as if he were trying to remember something. His face is shining, a spot of light falling from the window over his blue-black hair. The city night seems to be lowering itself, the light enriched and intensified, overbright. There are smudges against the sky, like veils of rain hovering over a faraway city.

*

Nadia's Café presses in on them too much—a bell jar in which everyone is watching and listening. So on days off, Han and Sirine drive east on Wilshire, north or south on Westwood, explore the endless city streets or nose their way into unknown neighborhoods or find the distant, far-flung suburbs and adjacent towns: Pasadena, Corona, Malibu; everything they see is new to them. The tall apartment buildings, glass-sided offices, balconies, and sliding doors lean toward them and they gaze up through the windshield. They drive from the stucco walls and red tile roofs in West L.A. all the way to downtown. They watch the bankers and secretaries filter away in late afternoon until there's nothing but long blue shadows and empty corridors. Or they drive into the garment district, down streets crowded with stalls of clothes and toys and strings of chilis and green curls of bananas, places that Han says remind him of the streets of Cairo. Sirine buys sweet, dense Mexican candies, pastel-colored Korean candies, crackling layers of tea leaves, lemongrass, kaffir leaves, Chinese medicinal herbs and powders, Japanese ointments and pastes. She tastes everything edible, studies the new flavors, tests the shock of them; and she learns, every time she tastes, about balance and composition, addition and subtraction. Han watches, eyeing the strange foods. When she offers him a taste, he closes his eyes and shakes his head.

They visit the half-abandoned city park zoo and gaze at the skeletal remains of old cages, flakes of straw, the spirits of forgotten animals. They stroll along Melrose, Sunset, Rodeo Drive, glancing in the glinting jewelry and dress shop windows. Han wants to buy Sirine presents but she won't even go inside; the empty, luxurious spaces make her anxious. They wander along granite-colored streets, litter loose in the air like ashes, and then realize they are walking over scuffed stars, worn-down names, handprints in the cement.

Sirine asks Han about himself. She asks about his parents and his memories of school and friends. He comes up with chips of details, bits of recollections of the chalky roads in their village, the grassy green olive oil on their kitchen table, the coal-colored falcon that haunted a tree beside their house. He tells her about going to the desert that started just a few miles from his uncle's farm—the same desert he would eventually cross when he fled Baghdad, the wind-cut miles of hot, dense sand, and a great map of clouds overhead.

One day in mid-November when they have been dating for almost three months, they are sitting on the grass in front of the big Languages Building where Han teaches. They are enjoying the clear day, talking. And Han says to Sirine, "I'm not sure if it's how it really happened or if it's just how I remember things—the way I want to remember things. It seems like life was infinitely simpler and easier, a slow, steady movement through the day. We worked, we ate, we talked. We did small things to entertain ourselves. My mother and the neighbor women traded each other for whatever they needed, thread and buttons, eggs, olives, light bulbs, chickens. My mother traded her embroidery. And she taught reading and writing in exchange for food and clothing, sometimes sheep. Once someone gave her an old stone tablet that she said was ancient, inscribed in Ugaritic, which is supposed to have been the oldest recorded alphabet. She said our own family used to have a castle in Babylon and that it was lined with mosaics of animals conversing with humans, humans with horns and wings, rooms without ceilings, and floors made of water. And the scent of night-blooming jasmine was rubbed into the stone." He smiles. "Family lore."

The sky is a glassy turquoise, warm enough for Sirine to feel lulled and sleepy. She leans back on her elbows and lets her neck spill backward, drinking in light. It's a Sunday so the campus is quiet and there's a hushed, chapellike quality in the air. She squints up at Han then, and realizes that his eyes are shut, his face contracted with grief. "Han, what is it?" she asks, alarmed. It is that look, she is beginning to recognize it: the look of his sleepless nights.

He turns his face away and for a moment he doesn't answer. Then he sighs and says, "It's the light, the air."

She squints at the sky.

"For a moment—for a moment, I forgot where I was. I forgot that this was America. I was on the banks of the Tigris. I could see the sun through my eyelids. My sister was about to call me in to eat. It's like the light broke into me and brought it all back and then I had to return to this place."

She nods, but her throat aches. She brings her face close to his and throws her leg over his, as if she could press herself down into him and the two of them into the earth, into that place and moment, and hold them both there safe and sound.

"I don't understand it," he says. "I don't know what's happening to me."

"Maybe . . . it's a little like . . . like the way death is," she says carefully. She isn't exactly sure how to say what she means; she goes slowly, trying to pick her way through her thoughts. "There's nothing about being alive that lets you get what death is. I mean—when someone close to you dies, there's no way to really understand it, is there? You can sort of know it in your head, but all your body knows is that you're not seeing them or touching them—so all that means is they might just be down the block or in another city."

He nods. "Yes."

"And it's so hard to let yourself know that you'll never actually see or touch them again. To let yourself take in that thing, that you'll only be able to know them through your memory now."

"Yes, yes. And for me it's even worse, somehow," Han says. "This is a terrible thing to say, but I feel it would be easier if I knew they were dead. If I knew I'd only have to go through with the experience of leaving them once and never again. Lately, I've started waking up and feeling like it was just yesterday that I left. Or just an hour ago." He rolls up to a sitting position and holds his head, his fingers spread through his hair. "Twenty-two years ago when I left for England, it sort of felt like I was anesthetized for surgery . . . like falling asleep—"

"You were letting yourself forget," Sirine says.

"Only now I'm afraid," he says.

"What are you afraid of?"

He rubs his temples. "That I haven't forgotten any of it, nothing at all. I'm starting to think that it's all been there inside me all along. And since I've met you—it's starting to return. I'm beginning to feel it and see it. Every time I turn a corner lately, I seem to turn onto Sadoun Street or the Jumhurriya Bridge. Every person I talk to turns into the vegetable seller or my grade school teacher."

"Since you met me?" she asks in dismay.

He takes her hand. "No, it's good; I've been talking and thinking about things I haven't thought about since I left Iraq. Having memories that I'd pushed so far aside it's like I didn't even know I'd lost them. It's like I want you to know everything that I know, I want to take you through my history, so it's inside of both of us, so you know who I am—really know." The sun whitens the sky and he shades his eyes with one hand. "But sometimes when I start remembering . . . sometimes I'm afraid I won't be able to stop." He pauses briefly. "Abu-Najmeh used to say you have to go away three times before you can really get away from anything." He smiles. "I've only left Iraq twice so far."

Sirine watches Han and for a moment it seems that she can actually see the ancient traces in Han's face, the quality of his gaze that seems to originate from a thousand-thousand years of watching the horizon—a forlorn, beautiful gazing, richer and more seductive than anything she's ever seen. And that somehow corresponds to a sensitive and silent element inside herself. She has a moment, like a flash of recognition that flares in her, and then she closes her eyes.

CHAPTER EIGHTEEN

Old stories and memories—especially the old stories that gather in the collective unconscious of a family—are like mirages. Illusory and fantastic, and yet they are frequently based on some reflection of reality. You want to know if Aunt Camille was really talking to a fish? Very possible. She was that sort of person. Was it the Mother of All Fish? Well, perhaps it was just a distinguished-looking fish. Perhaps it was just the conjurings of loneliness, after Camille had been trapped as a servant in an Englishman's chilly house in the desert. Maybe there was no wicked seductress-mermaid, but perhaps there really is a perverse compulsion to go to places where one does not belong. The thing about listening to a story like this, Habeebti, is not to fret over chasing down the details, but to let the spirit of things show themselves. Learn how to just let it be.

Let the tomato be a tomato.

So the Mother of All Fish called up the local lady of the lake, a Tunisian mermaid named Kan Zamana, who stretched indolently on the rocks, her spangled tail scales gleaming and her soft brown shoulders glowing, and Kan Zamana told Aunt Camille what happened to her son. She said that Abdelrahman had been transported to the mermaids' undersea cave in the Land of Na, a pleasure palace for abducted sailors, guarded by the Nisnas—half-formed monkey creatures with one leg and one arm. And that was fine for a while; Abdelrahman was a model prisoner, handsome, well behaved, pleasant company. But it came to pass that another Bedouin arrived at the undersea cave shortly thereafter, this one named Jaipur al-Rashid, but whom people called Crazyman al-Rashid.

It seems that before being abducted by the mermaids, Crazyman al-Rashid had had his own remarkable experience—but no one would listen to his story, and when they did, no one believed it. He claimed to have been abducted by some sort of desert version of space aliens. Crazyman al-Rashid had worked himself into such a lather trying to get someone to listen to his story of camelless carriages and fiery angels that when the mermaid named Alieph finally agreed to hear out his tiresome story, he got so worked up while telling it that he walked straight off a pier. The merfolk—who can't tell the difference between up and down, much less right and wrong—dragged him down to the inky blue cave where Abdelrahman Salahadin was kept and there the Crazyman proceeded to agitate his captive audience of one by filling his head with crazy stories. The Crazyman went on at such length and in such flamboyant detail that he infected Abdelrahman Salahadin with his madness. Abdelrahman became obsessed with the sights and sounds the Crazyman spoke of, convinced that he had to see them himself.

Upon hearing this report, Aunt Camille became excited. "So my son is there now?"

"We had to let him go," Kan Zamana said. "Nobody could stand him. The Crazyman eventually settled in quite nicely, eating peeled sea grapes and parboiled seaweeds and sleeping till noon. But after brushing up against this undesirable, Abdelrahman Salahadin had lost all his manners and all his couth. Worst of all, he inherited the Crazyman's obsessions. The two of them were forever yammering on about Fil'Imm this and Fil'Imm that. And something called Hal'Awud. And the Dar'Aktr, always with the Dar'Aktr!"

But what were these auspicious words? Aunt Camille wondered. Fil'Imm, Hal-Awud, Dar'Aktr. Were they some variety of angel or jinn? Apparently they were entities so powerful and yet so tedious to hear about that Alieph and the other sirens decided they would rather give Abdelrahman back his money and set him free than listen to another word.

"Then he isn't with the mermaids at all!" Aunt Camille cried with equal parts relief and dismay. "Then where, pray tell, is he?"

The lazy mermaid propped herself up on one elbow and pointed. "Last I heard, madame, Abdelrahman Salahadin has gone to Hal'Awud, in the terrible and frightening land of the setting sun."

*

Six thirty-eight A.M. on Thanksgiving morning, Sirine is in the kitchen mincing garlic and King Babar lies at her feet. The kitchen is overheated and fragrant with the scent of roasting turkey. The night before, Um-Nadia came over with her small wooden box stuffed with handwritten recipes, dishes Um-Nadia hadn't prepared or eaten in the thirty-five years since she and Mireille had left Lebanon. Some were recipes for simple, elegant dishes of rice pilafs and roasted meats, others were more exotic dishes of steamed whole pigeons and couscous or braised lambs' brains in broth. And they discussed ingredients and techniques until late in the night. Um-Nadia eventually fell asleep on the hard couch in the living room, while Sirine's uncle dozed across from her in his armchair. But Sirine stayed up all night, checking recipes, chopping, and preparing. She looked up Iraqi dishes, trying to find the childhood foods that she'd heard Han speak of, the sfeehas—savory pies stuffed with meat and spinach—and round mensaf trays piled with lamb and rice and yogurt sauce with onions, and for dessert, tender ma'mul cookies that dissolve in the mouth. She stuffed the turkey with rice, onions, cinnamon, and ground lamb. Now there are pans of sautéed greens with bittersweet vinegar, and lentils with tomato, onion, and garlic on the stove, as well as maple-glazed sweet potatoes, green bean casserole, and pumpkin soufflé.

It's still hours before the first guests will arrive and Um-Nadia and Mireille move through each room with rags and furniture polish, vacuuming, dusting, and sweeping. At one point, Mireille comes in, leans on the speckled kitchen counter, and observes Sirine as she works. "Something smells good," she says. "What is that?"

Um-Nadia stands in the door and waves one hand so her bracelets ring. "It's like the old-time Arabs' cooking."

Sirine smiles, tilts her head, and chases some bits of celery and onion in a frying pan with the tip of her wooden spoon.

*

By noon there is: Han, Mireille, Victor Hernandez and his cousin Eliazer, Aziz the poet, Nathan, Um-Nadia, Cristobal the custodian, Shark, Jenoob, Abdullah, Schmaal, and Gharb—five of the lonely students from the café—Sirine, and her uncle. King Babar greets each of them, standing on his hind legs and putting his dusty paw prints on their pants.

Mireille is setting the table and Um-Nadia is serving mazza in the library. But the students and Aziz go straight into the abandoned-living-room to watch parades and football on the ancient fibrillating TV with its cap of bent antennae and crinkled aluminum foil. The students lie on the three layers of carpet, about three feet from the TV, complaining at some length in Arabic because there isn't a remote control—as Aziz translates to Sirine. Aziz sits all the way at the far end of the room on the couch and asks them to explain everything about parades and football, and they don't seem to mind, patiently instructing him. "Who is that floating man?" Aziz asks.

"That isn't a floating man," Schmaal says. "That is the Giant Bird."

Aziz smiles at Sirine. "Three years in this country and this is my first of all parades." He sighs, then squints at the light-washed screen. "It's a bit like a demonstration, isn't it?" he says.

"Only no rocks," Schmaal says.

"And with music!" Gharb says.

Sirine goes into the kitchen to check on the turkey. The windows are bright as coins, the room saturated in light. Everything glows—the butter, a handful of chopped tomato, a bowl of parsley—ripe colors clear as a painting. She feels the light passing through her. She is stirring gravy when a pair of arms come up from behind her and circle her, and she hears Han murmur in her ear, "I missed you."

She smiles, blows a strip of hair up from her forehead, and leans back against his solid chest. "I've been working all night."

"I can tell. And what is this aroma?"

She leans her head back, smiling. "Do you recognize it?"

Han lowers his nose to her neck.

"You made me meat loaf, so I wanted to reciprocate." She gestures at the pans. "An Arabic Thanksgiving. It was my idea—what do you think?" She lifts the lid from the pan of smoked green wheat kernels and dips in a spoon. "Here. Taste."

He holds the spoon in his mouth for a moment. She knows what he is tasting, how the broth is flavored with pepper and garlic and lustrous, deep smokiness. "And try this," she says. Vibrant vegetable greens, garlic, and lemon. "And this." Herbal, meaty, vaguely fruity.

He places the spoon on the counter. He closes his eyes and inhales. "Han?" She laughs and places a hand on his chest.

He touches his lips.

*

Thanksgiving dinner is vast and steaming, crowded over the tabletop in hot platters bumping against each other. There are three open bottles of wine, all different colors, and there seem to be far more plates and silverware than are actually needed. Among the guests' contributions, there's a big round fatayer—a lamb pie—that Aziz bought from the green-eyed girl at the Iranian bakery; six sliced cylinders of cranberry sauce from Um-Nadia; whole roasted walnuts in chili sauce from Cristobal; plus Victor brought three homemade pumpkin pies and a half-gallon of whipping cream. Nathan wants to keep his camera on the table, even though with its bulky lens it's as big as a soup tureen, so Um-Nadia and Mireille and Victor all scold him until he moves it.

"Well, look at us," Sirine's uncle says, "sitting around here like a bunch of Americans with our crazy turkey. All right, now, I want to make a big toast. Here's to sweet, unusual families, pleasant dogs who behave, food of this nature, the seven types of smiles, the crescent moon, and a nice cup of tea with mint every day. *Sahtain*. Good luck and God bless us everyone."

They nod and clink glasses.

"Is that for Christmas?" Jenoob asks. "When you say that part about God bless?"

"Really, it's nice for any time," Aziz says.

"What are the seven types of smiles?" Eliazer says.

Victor waves his hand in a discreet don't-ask gesture.

Han sits across the table from Sirine and Nathan sits next to Han. King Babar roams from one set of knees to the next, accepting crumbs and table offerings. Sirine only half-listens to the dinner talk; she tries to focus on the food, professionally evaluating her work, but the table is so lively and busy it's hard to pay attention to much of anything. She feels the electricity of Han's presence across from her. His foot slides lightly across the floor till she can feel his instep touching hers. Nathan sits beside Han, watching his exchanges with Sirine.

Sirine puts a forkful of sweet potatoes into her mouth. The potatoes are soft as velvet, the gravy satiny. It is as if she can taste the life inside all those ingredients: the stem that the cranberries grew on, the earth inside the bread, even the warm blood that was once inside the turkey. It comes back to her, the small secret that was always hers, for years, the only truth she seemed to possess—that food was better than love: surer, truer, more satisfying and enriching. As long as she could lose herself in the rhythms of peeling an onion, she was complete and whole. And as long as she could cook, she would be loved.

Bowls are passed, clattering, and the conversation levels off into a buzz. Then Gharb leans forward smiling and says, "This is bizarre."

Everyone looks at him.

He waves his hands. "All these guys and girls all together."

"Yes, imagine the possibilities," Aziz says. He is sitting on the other side of Mireille, who is sitting beside Sirine. Victor Hernandez stares at Aziz from across the table, his lips tightening.

"That's what I mean," Gharb says. "In my village, the guys and women eat apart from each other, to stay out of trouble. This is the first American house I've really eaten at, so I have to get used to it. I like it, of course. I do!"

"American?" Nathan says.

"You're talking about Egypt!" Um-Nadia announces from the head of the table. "In Beirut, it's always boy-girl, et cetera, et cetera. Much more sophisticated."

"You know that's not necessarily the case in Iraq either," Sirine's uncle says. "In our village, the big parties always separated men and women, but for just regular meals the family and friends always ate together."

"Ours as well," Han says. "Everyone together."

"But, yeah, but that's dangerous," Schmaal says from his end of the table. Everyone turns to him. He shrugs. "What? All I'm saying is you can do that boy-girl in America 'cause that's how it is here, right? But like in

Kuwait? You're just asking for it, man. You sit with a girl and you're asking for trouble."

Several people tick their heads back, make the disagreeing *tch* sound. "Wrong again," his friend Shark says. His name is actually Sharq, which means *East*, but he has asked all his American friends to call him "Shark" instead. Sirine can't hear the difference in pronunciation, but he assured her there's a huge difference. "That's the whole *mishkila*, the problem, of it," he says. "That attitude. All the Arab kids are so uptight and freaked out about what's the family gonna think, they're afraid to act normal or anything."

"Normal?" Abdullah asks, laughing. "What's that?"

"You know—normal-regular. Like how stuff is no big deal if you don't make it one."

"Oh yeah? The year before I came to the States—my sister Maisoon?— she went for a ride with her boyfriend in his car. She totally wasn't supposed to have a boyfriend, of course. But anyways. They parked way out in the country where they thought they were secret. Of course, some Bedouin or someone saw them kissing. . . ."

Looks are exchanged across the table.

"Actually, worse than kissing. What is it? Making out?"

"Whoa," Schmaal says. "They should've, like, known not to do that."

Abdullah slaps the table so the forks jump and Um-Nadia makes a disapproving sound. "Big deal, they were kissing! How many American girls have you kissed?"

"Hey, I'm not saying I agree or anything," he says. "Just that that's how it is. And zero, to answer your question. Americans, non-Americans, whatever. Especially in public in cars."

Nathan leans forward and gazes at Abdullah steadily. His face is flushed pink and he holds a glass of wine. "What happened to your sister?" he asks.

"My dad wanted me to beat her," Abdullah says. "You know, 'cause, like, I'm the older brother and all. I'm supposed to teach her some kind of lesson or something."

"Whoa," Schmaal says.

"What did you do?" Nathan asks.

"We jumped up and down."

Aziz starts laughing.

"We closed the bedroom door and I said, let's jump. And we started jumping and hitting the walls and I was shouting all kinds of stuff like slut and whore and stuff. And Maisoon was screaming like I was pulling all the teeth out of her head. Then she messed up her hair like crazy and tore her shirt. Then we came out of the bedroom and my mother shoved me so hard that I fell on my butt and she grabs Maisoon and she's like, you didn't have to beat her so bad. And my father's like, you're tougher than I realized, son. So you can tell me anything you want about normal."

Sirine bites her lip. She feels Han's foot press against hers.

"That is really a pretty sad story," Nathan says, his voice dark. "Really, I mean—there's the treatment of Arab women for you, right there. The whole attitude."

*

Han seems to hover just outside the conversation, his attention wandering between Sirine and his plate of frekeh. He eats slowly, one small forkful at a time. Sirine asks if he wouldn't like some turkey and cranberry sauce, maybe some stuffing, but he merely smiles and shakes his head.

The conversation at the table meanders through the rest of the meal. While Nathan becomes moody and withdrawn, the rest of them talk about the foreign but not unpleasant experience of eating turkey, and the pleasures of the rice stuffing, the stuffed squashes and grape leaves, the creamed spinach and glazed sweet potatoes, the smoked frekeh and the baba ghannuj, and Um-Nadia's sliced canned cranberry sauce. They gossip about the café customers and the students and professors at the university and then they start to talk about Middle Eastern politics, which upsets everyone, so Aziz tries to calm them down by speaking at length about his political theories, relating cultural politics to cultural poetics. "Consider the difference between the first and third person in poetry," he says, pinching his thumb to his forefingers. "It's like the difference between looking at a person and looking through their eyes."

"That's how I feel about eating," Sirine interjects, and some of them laugh.

Aziz lifts his chin and lowers his eyes silkily. "Please tell us more."

"Well, I mean . . ." She fumbles for words and tears apart a slice of bread, trying to think what she means. "Something like . . . tasting a piece of bread that someone bought is like looking *at* that person, but tasting a piece of bread that they baked is like looking out of their eyes."

"Fabulous metaphor," Aziz says.

Nathan lifts his head. "That's giving other people power over you."

"No more than usual," Aziz says. "Somebody's always going to have the power, and somebody's always got to bake the bread." He turns and smiles suavely at Sirine. "You've got the soul of a poet! Cooking and tasting is a metaphor for seeing. Your cooking reveals America to us non-Americans. And vice versa."

"Chef isn't an American cook," Victor Hernandez says. "Not like the way Americans do food—just dumping salt into the pot. All the flavors go in the same direction. Chef cooks like we do. In Mexico, we put cinnamon in with the chocolate and pepper in the sweetcakes, so things pull apart, you know, make it bigger?" He gestures with his hands, opening his palms. Mireille looks at her plate of turkey suspiciously but Sirine's uncle laughs and nods and says, "Yes, that's very good. It wakes you up. Somewhere in the Quran, I maybe think the prophet says something about that—that food should make you optimistic."

But then Jenoob asks how do you say in English what is the opposite of optimistic? And suddenly somehow the conversation veers back to politics. Schmaal brings up the U.N. and nuclear weapons inspections, and Gharb talks about the starvation in Iraq and crime and prostitution, and Nathan says that Iraq is suffering prefamine conditions and is still being bombed regularly by America, who was recently selling them helicopters, and does anyone care, and then they all get quiet and stare at their plates.

"They think we're all terrorists anyway," Aziz says cheerfully, scooping up a forkful of mashed potatoes.

"Who's 'they'?" Victor says. He clicks the tines of his fork against the plate so it makes a dangerous ticking sound. "*I* don't think that."

"You? Oh, big deal. If you and I were out shopping at the mall do you think any of the white guys there could tell the difference between us? They'd think you were one of my terrorist buddies."

"Yeah, if I was out with you. Which I wouldn't be."

Nathan picks up a plate of hummus. "The real irony of today is that this sort of all-American feasting and gorging is going on when back home they're starving—"

"Whose back-home you talking about?" Schmaal says.

"Why does it always have to be politics and fighting with you people!" Um-Nadia cries.

"I agree. The Americans need to hear our poetry and stories and this and that sort of stuff," Gharb says, then turns to Aziz. "Why don't you ever write political poems?"

"That's not what I mean!" Um-Nadia says.

"She means Americans need to know about the big, dark, romantic soul of the Arab," Sirine's uncle says, a bit intensely.

"Believe me, I used to be so political, I made Mahmoud Darwish look like Little Orphan Annie. I made Edward Said look like . . . Edward Scissorshands," Aziz says, thumping his chest with one hand.

"Who is this Little Orphan?" Shark asks.

"But listen, I got fed up with all the harassments. Do you think I got nice letters in the mail when I read my political poetry? I did not. I got letters saying, no, don't tell such unhappy stories about the Arabs. I got calls saying, no more bad news, write about hearts and flowers and happy, happy Arabs being so nice to each other. And from who did I get these letters? From the Arabs who are always complaining that there's not enough truth about Arabs in the magazines and TV."

"Of course," Jenoob says. "All we see on the TV or movies about Arabs is they're shooting someone, bombing someone, or kidnapping someone." He counts them off on his fingers. "Those are the choices. The only lines they get to say are: '*Shut up and sit down!*' " he shouts, fingers cocked like a gun.

Um-Nadia grabs her ears. "That is enough!" She turns to Sirine. "Okay, fine. Now we should be looking into the matter of dessert."

"Oh yes," Sirine says quickly. "I'll go get it."

Sirine's scarf is still folded on the kitchen counter. She picks it up. She is planning to wear it for dramatic effect while bringing in Victor's pumpkin pies. She is standing in the cooling and darkening kitchen, among the silver shells of pots, looking for a pie knife, when there are footsteps. Nathan stands in the doorway, his face solemn. "Sirine, I was hoping to talk to you about our conversation the other day. There were a few things that I—" He stops suddenly, moves closer, his head slightly canted to one side. "What is that?"

"This?" Sirine opens her hands so a swath of material bells out, reveals the delicate berry-colored stitches. "My scarf."

Nathan lifts his fingers and stops just short of touching it. "Is this from Han?"

"Do you like it?" She unfurls the whole scarf and swoops it over her shoulders.

"Oh," Nathan says in a voice that is barely audible.

Sirine says, "It's very old. It belonged to Han's mother."

Nathan's face darkens. He doesn't speak for a moment but just stares at her and the scarf. And then he says, unsteadily, "He told you that?" He doesn't say anything more but simply stands there for another moment. Sirine slips the scarf from her shoulders. She opens her mouth, but Nathan says, "I—can't—I—forgive me. I'm sorry," and quickly leaves the room.

Sirine starts to go after him, but then Um-Nadia and Mireille come into the kitchen and there is a lot to do with pies and putting on coffee, and that's all that anyone can think about.

*

Everyone has returned to the library for baklava, knaffea, cookies, pumpkin pie, and stories. The late afternoon sun comes into the library and infuses everything with brilliant orange and rose color, setting chairs and walls and the Persian carpet on fire. Schmaal holds up one hand and the tiny web of skin between his fingers glows. King Babar leans back into a stretch with his front legs straight out and his head craning back. He yawns hugely, so all that is seen of his face is teeth and an unrolling tongue.

"This is chapter four—or is it five?" Sirine's uncle asks Um-Nadia. "I hope you're keeping track."

"Wait, we need background here or something," Victor says. "Where are we?"

Her uncle shakes his head. "You aren't anywhere. It isn't that kind of story that begins in one place and goes directly to another. It's the kind of story that keeps going and going. And it's completely without a moral. It's a moralless story. You can visit the story for a while or you can go drink your coffee in the backyard and watch the finches. Which is also nice."

"So," Um-Nadia cuts in impatiently, "chapter four or five or six or what have you."

"Yes." Sirine's uncle straightens his collar and takes a sip of coffee. "Chapter what-have-you."

Eliazer, Cristobal, Gharb, and Shark are all asleep on the carpet, in between the furniture. Jenoob and Schmaal sleep on the horsehair couch, and one room away there is the sound of King Babar snuffling through their jackets on the foyer bench, searching for food.

*

Sirine leaves the library to try and find Nathan. She looks in the living room, the backyard, the dining room, the kitchen, then starts heading upstairs. She is going to insist that he speak with her and tell her what is going on. Instead, she runs into Aziz as he is coming out of the upstairs bathroom. "*Tisslam eedayki,*" he says. *Bless your hand*—the compliment to a cook. He takes Sirine's hand and kisses the backs of her fingers, then he turns it over, kisses the center of her palm, and folds her fingers over the kiss like wrapping up a present. "Yes. Such a lovely old home. Isn't your bedroom somewhere up here?"

"Like I'd tell you," she says. "But the guest bathroom is downstairs, for future reference."

"You know," he says, his voice full of melody and suggestion, "I've always thought it was such a mistake for a beautiful woman to tie herself down to just one man."

She raises one eyebrow. "You'd better go find that woman and let her know."

"Are you sure that Han is so innocent?"

She folds her arms over her chest. "Are you saying that you know something I don't know?"

He lifts one of her hands away from her elbow and kisses the inside of her wrist. She can smell his cologne—sweet lemon and grass. "So many things to let you know! You will come out with Aziz one night soon? Just on a friendly friend date? Just the two of us, just to play. No monkey business. Nothing funny. Heaven forbid there's anything funny."

"Yes, heaven forbid."

He bends as if to kiss the inside of her elbow but she withdraws her arm. "Not above the high-water mark," she says.

She hears some footsteps coming up the stairs and she instinctively steps back from Aziz. It's Victor, his eyes piercing and his arms tensed. He pulls up short when he sees Sirine and Aziz and looks back and forth between the two of them. "I thought I heard—I heard a woman's voice and his—" He gives Aziz a withering look then turns to Sirine. "And I thought it was . . . I don't know."

Aziz cranes his neck around to look over first one, then the other shoulder. "Nobody here but us chickens," he says.

Victor glares at him.

"I'm sorry, Victor," Sirine says. "I haven't seen . . . anyone else up here lately. Have you tried the kitchen?"

Victor finally breaks from glaring at Aziz and starts to stomp back down the steps. She hears him mutter, *asshole pendejo.*

"So about our fun-free date." Aziz turns back to Sirine. "When shall we—"

"Can't right now," she says, slipping past him in the hallway. "I'm looking for someone."

"And that someone is not me?" he says mournfully. "No one is ever looking for me. Of course. All right."

"But thank you for the lovely lamb fatayer you brought today."

He stops and bows, clearly pleased with himself. "That was made from the last of those beautiful lamb cuts from Odah."

"What lamb cuts?"

"Remember when the Evil Eye came to the butcher shop and Odah took back the lamb? Well, when the police arrived, he left the lamb on top of a mailbox. I thought it was a shame for that beautiful meat to go to waste. So I came back and grabbed it, then I brought it to the bakery and the green-eyed girl made it special."

"But he said that meat had . . ." she trails off, considering.

"The Evil Eye?" Aziz shrugs. "I smelled it first. I didn't smell any kind of Eye on it." He waves and goes downstairs.

*

Finally, Sirine collapses into the lawn chair beside Han in the backyard. They sit quietly for a while, watching King Babar watch the neighbors' butterscotch tabby eat the berries off a bush. Every time King Babar approaches, the cat fluffs to twice its size, then melts back down as soon as Babar backs away.

"You're coming home with me, yes?" Han says hopefully.

Sirine sighs and looks at the kitchen window just above and behind their heads. "I shouldn't," she says. She can perfectly visualize the mountain of cups and saucers. Every dish and pan in the house has been used in one way or another. She hears the faucet running and knows that Um-Nadia and her uncle are standing at their places over the sink.

"Are you worried about the dishes?" Han says softly. "Dishes are eternal. They just keep getting dirtier. Let's leave them."

The back door creaks slightly, as if someone had been standing there. Sirine looks up, then rubs her arms and hugs herself. "What do you think of Nathan?"

He shifts his weight in the chair, tips it back slightly. "Nathan." He chuckles faintly and murmurs something to himself, then looks away, distracted. "That dog of your uncle's is unearthly, I tell you."

The air stirs and picks up around them and leaves rasp along the ground. Sirine is utterly bone-tired, wrung dry, dizzy and headachy from no sleep, and so she agrees to his plan that they sneak away without saying goodbye to anybody. They pull on their jackets furtively as criminals. Then they tiptoe past the kitchen with the splashing dishes and pyramids of foam, past the abandoned living room with the blaring TV, past the silent imaginary library, down the long hall, and out the front door.

Chapter Nineteen

Aunt Camille learned that she'd gone all the way to the source of the Nile for nothing. After boring the entire undersea world with his stories of Hal'Awud, her son had up and headed to the Land of the Setting Sun.

She and the jackal-eared dog named Napoleon-Was-Here dusted themselves off and started walking toward the sunset. What a ridiculous thing, Aunt Camille thought, to be walking toward the sunset. How will I know when to stop?

Unfortunately for her, she decided to put her faith in her dog's sense of direction. This is because he had helped her find the jinn's kitchen—which was not very far away—and because dogs have humans bamboozled into thinking that they always know the way there. King Babar, for example, bamboozles on a regular basis. But in reality dogs are only reincarnated monks who didn't say their prayers right.

Napoleon took the lead and Aunt Camille followed. So it was that they began walking in wide, desert-flung circles. Years passed in this manner. The Bedu and townspeople gave them food and blessings and assumed they were on pilgrimage to Mecca. In that time, Aunt Camille was courted by an Egyptian prince who entertained her in his desert caravan and gave her a tiny slave girl to keep her company. Aunt Camille named the slave girl Hanan, which means kindness and tenderness, and she raised her gently, lulling her to sleep at night with the story of the search for Abdelrahman, my cousin. And when she set Hanan free on her eighteenth birthday, they still hadn't found Abdelrahman Salahadin and Hanan went away disappointed.

Camille walked in wide, desert-spun circles all over the shoulders of Africa until a nearby tribe got curious and drifted down from the hills to take a closer look at her. These were extremely conceited Bedu, very vain of the fact that they traded in frankincense and not in goats or camels or the usual smelly beasts of the Bedu. Their hair and skin was tinted dusty blue and they smelled of their incense and they spoke Italian and Arabic as well as a sweet and lively chirping language that the ancient Sumerians had called Lulubulu or the Language of Birds. They took a liking to Camille and she discovered that they too were out of place. They were tribesmen originally from the Dhofar Mountains on the Arabian Peninsula. They too knew about Hal'Awud and Dar'Aktr and were very much against them. As it turned out, Dar'Aktr was a person, loud and very white—inordinately white—with bristling eyebrows, hair like a briar patch and a way of speaking that was like the wind beating against the desert. Dar'Aktr was, in fact, the reason why they'd found themselves in this place so far from home. He had moved them here, they said, to do his strange bidding.

"Moved you?" she asked, incredulous. "How?"

They only shook their heads and made signs against the Evil Eye and said Allah only knows, truly it defies all explaining. He had done his strange bidding, which apparently also defied explanation, and then left them with no way to get back home. They were not unhappy with this arrangement, they added, but it was inconvenient. Camille could see that once you got to know these people they were really fairly agreeable. She told them, in turn, about her naughty son, about how she warned him, about her walk down the Nile, about her talk with the fish. Camille also told them about the time she spent as a slave to the famous explorer Sir Richard Burton, and the tribesmen became excited and said, yes, yes! Ar-Rashad Bur'aton! The frightening, hollow-eyed white man! He was there too! And they all felt somehow vindicated, as if this meeting were meant to be. And it was agreed that if they could help Camille find her way back to her home, Camille would help the tribe find the way back to their home on the Arabian Peninsula.

*

The day is a sunburst of smog and mist; it shines in the straight-arrow streets and brown wandering canyons and azure reflecting pools. It's in the wild-field spindles of lavender and heather. It touches the baking rooftops, scaly chicken-foot streets. The spiked plants growing in ditches and open fields. Yellow things sharp as skeletons and horned devilish plants and hard blue scrub gnarled as knuckles. It rises and crosses a semi-lunar horizon, great open page of sky, faintly salty, traces of fruit, citrus, water in the wind.

Sirine has awakened before Han. She props herself on one elbow, studying the brown colors of his skin in the morning. As she does this, she remembers a dream in which Han was leading a double life and had a secret family back in Iraq. His wife was a kind of enchantress who had him under a spell—a woman who looked something like Rana, passionate and brilliant and capable of anything—someone who would summon him back to the Old Country, to his true identity. She dreamed this woman threw off her black veil and underneath she was wearing a garland of yellow flowers in her hair, a red dress like a burst of flames; she looked at Sirine and started laughing.

Sirine rubs her eyes and tries to clear her head. She carefully slides out of bed and goes into the white-tiled bathroom. She peers into the tarnished mirror on the medicine cabinet, turning it and trying to catch the light. She stares at the portrait of herself in the metal-framed mirror. All she can see is white. She is so white. Her eyes wide, almond-shaped, and sea-green, her nose and lips tidy and compact. Entirely her mother. That's all anyone can see: when people ask her nationality they react with astonishment when she says she's half-Arab. I never would have thought *that*, they say, laughing. You sure don't look it. When people say this she feels like her skin is being peeled away. She thinks that she may have somehow inherited her mother on the outside and her father on the inside. If she could compare her own and her father's internal organs—the blood and bones and the shape of her mind and emotions—she thinks she would find her truer and deeper nature. She imagines her parents, young, expecting their first child, expecting, perhaps, a true amalgam of their two bodies. Were they disappointed, she wonders, to have an entirely fair-skinned child?

She tries to creep back into the bed soundlessly but Han opens his eyes. Sirine notices flecks of gold in the black surfaces. He looks for her and smiles and her heart bumps. She thinks it is a sort of smile she has never seen him smile before, more intimate and yet removed, not precisely meant for her. "Hey?" he murmurs. Then, "Habeebti? What is it?"

Sirine smiles back and asks what he would like to have for breakfast. He yawns and sits up, and asks almost timidly, "I don't suppose you could make some more of that frekeh?"

The dish of smoked wheat kernels with olive oil and garlic. She sits still, the sunlight from the balcony skimming through the bedroom. There are bags and bags of frekeh at her uncle's house, pounds of it at the café, even the Indian market a few blocks away from Han's apartment sells it in bulk. But she takes a breath and frowns and says, "I'm not sure if I can find more right now."

She tells Han to sleep a little longer and she walks down to the Indian market by herself. But when she comes back with her groceries she doesn't have frekeh. She makes scrambled eggs and bacon for breakfast. She stirs dollops of heavy cream and cheese into the eggs, letting the bacon grease soak into the egg, slicing squares of buttered toast in half, filling the glasses with orange juice. She serves this to Han while he's still in bed and he smiles and eats it and doesn't say anything more about frekeh.

*

Later that morning, while she's at work, Sirine realizes she can't remember where she's put her scarf.

"Your beautiful scarf? You lost it!" Um-Nadia cries.

"I didn't *lose* it," Sirine says, rattling through the cabinets and shelves in the back kitchen. "It's somewhere."

Um-Nadia tells Victor and Cristobal to look everywhere, then she calls Sirine's uncle at home. "Tell us the scarf is there," she cries into the phone.

She waits and waits and then listens and nods as if confirming the inevitable. She puts one hand over the receiver and says, "No. Vanished."

Mireille turns to Sirine. "When do you last remember wearing it?"

But Sirine doesn't have a last memory. There is only something hazy from yesterday about bringing out dessert, something about draping the scarf on a chair.

"I don't think I saw you wearing it at all," Mireille says.

"Actually . . ." Victor says, "I might have seen it on the floor in the kitchen."

"That is our Sirine," says Um-Nadia.

Nathan stops in for baklava and coffee. He looks hungover and somehow wrung out, his eyes hollow with fatigue, and he doesn't have his camera with him. He apologizes for leaving dinner so suddenly but says he was suffering from a terrible headache.

"Have you seen her scarf?" Um-Nadia asks, throwing up her arms.

"You didn't lose it?" His eyes are dark as lead. "I saw you with it right there in the kitchen. I remember. Where did you put it?"

*

Sirine makes everyone swear they won't breathe a word of this to Han. She bicycles straight home after work. She turns over all the pillows and cushions in the living room. Looks under the chairs in the library. She goes through the laundry basket. Then she thinks she spots it folded on the counter in the kitchen, her breath rises in her chest, but it's only a kitchen towel. "I didn't lose it," she says to herself. "It's definitely somewhere."

Her uncle looks behind some books in the library. "What are you doing?" Sirine asks. "It's not there."

"This is where things are hidden in the movies," he says.

She almost doesn't bother to look upstairs, but then decides to do it just for good measure. The bathroom (she has a sudden, wild hope that Aziz was trying it on) is empty, the towels hanging straight as soldiers. Her bedroom looks blank and empty as well: there's the dark cherrywood sleigh bed, the clean walls, the cream-white comforter. She makes a circuit around the bed, looks back toward the hall, and then hears a sound like crying under her bed.

She drops to her hands and knees. It's King Babar, crying in a high, strange whine, as if he were injured. He's stretched on his belly under the bed—a place he rarely goes unless he's done something like pull over the Christmas tree or eaten all the dinner rolls.

Sirine squints under the bed. "King Babar," she says gently, holding up the edge of the comforter, "what's wrong, honey? What did you do?"

He's in the middle of the floor under the bed. He rolls his big guilty eyes toward her. He sighs and moans and she reaches under the bed to try and console him and then realizes that he's lying on top of something. She reaches under him while he complains, then he growls. Surprised, she says, "Babar, no!" and slides out a white legal-sized envelope. It's old and just folded over, not sealed shut, and inside there is a color snapshot.

She slides it out. A close-up of a girl—a young woman, really—with brilliant spice-black eyes and long, curling black hair that flies in thick locks around her face. She is laughing and pulling the blowing hair away from her face with her hand—or trying to. Her skin is glowing amber and something about her smile ignites the whole shot.

Sirine holds the photo in both hands, the girl's laughter rising into the air, chiming in all the corners and singing in the hallway; her hair—dark but wild and curly as Sirine's—rises and falls, and her eyes fix directly on Sirine.

She looks away from the photograph but then looks back again. "Where did this come from? Where did you get this?" she asks the dog, who's leaning against her leg now.

She studies the photo closely: the grain of the girl's skin, the crease at the corner of her smile, at the edge of an eye. Slowly she starts to realize: this is the same woman she saw in the photo in Han's bedroom. His sister? For some reason this strikes her as vaguely alarming. How did it get there? Her breath races in her chest.

"What is this?" she asks, urgency tightening her voice. King Babar stares at her, panting, smiling.

The feeling comes from outside her body, like a vibration in the air, trembling in the ground. The hidden picture seems like a type of dark magic. She thinks of the hexes that she's heard from Um-Nadia: the ribbon tied to the crib leg to protect the baby, the special string of beads to invoke certain spirits, the mirror that provides a passageway for spirits. For a moment the photo shimmers, obscured by the light. It doesn't feel safe to touch it. She hides it in the bedside drawer.

That night she stays over at Han's house again. She almost says something about the photo but then decides against it. She dreams that Han has a hidden wife who has stolen her scarf; the wife taunts Sirine with it, running just ahead of her, too fast, the scarf rippling behind her like a banner. She runs into the ocean with it, the waves throwing off long violet spools of foam.

*

Very late that night, the phone rings and wakes her up. Sirine feels Han ease out of the bed and creep into the living room. He speaks in Arabic, his voice falling and rising softly. Even though she can't understand the words, she hears something so gentle and imploring in Han's voice, she can almost see the lights above the desert mountains and smell the currents of the Tigris River. She thinks of the photo tucked in her nightstand, singing with laughter.

Sirine lies very still, eyes wide open, taking in darkness. Her breath is tucked tight inside her, her hands curled shut. When she was a little girl, she would lie awake and alone in the extra bedroom in her uncle's house when her parents were traveling for their work. There was a particular grade of loneliness to those isolated nights, her parents as gone as if they'd never really existed at all. She would lie awake and try to imagine who she would be when she was grown up—thirty, forty, fifty years old. It was like trying to look through the sky, layers of yellow haze, to a faraway location. She would speak to this future self, conjure those selves up that she felt somehow already existed around her. When her parents returned, they would always be excited to see her and would usually have an odd little toy for her from one of the countries they'd worked in—once it was a straw doll from India, another time a sort of puppet from Thailand, drawn on paper and propped up on long sticks. Sirine always wondered if the toys had belonged to sick children. Her mother would squeeze her a bit too hard and too long and her father looked as if part of him were still back in the places they'd just left, his eyes empty, not quite focusing on Sirine. Later, she always stuffed the presents to the bottom of the garbage can out back.

But now Sirine dozes, half-listening to the shushing, water sounds of Arabic drifting into the room. She thinks longingly of her old life before Han, of sleeping in the safe narrow bed, King Babar warming her feet. Her uncle with his favorite tomato salad and Um-Nadia with her tea with cardamom and everything is fine, the way it always is.

*

When Sirine wakes again, the sun still hasn't risen but the light is on in the kitchen. She gets up, dresses, and goes out. Han sits at the kitchen table studying the *Los Angeles Times*. Sirine sees more dark photos in the pages and looks away from them. Then she notices pale yellow newsprint underneath a stack of student papers. "What's that?" she asks, touching its edge.

He pulls it out, shows it to her. "Oh. That's the newspaper from Jerusalem."

"I didn't know you read that."

He smiles as if a bit surprised himself. "I don't usually. I just get curious sometimes, I guess. I picked it up at the newsstand on campus."

"Did you read it? Is there anything interesting in it?"

He looks at her now. "Not really. I mean—the usual atrocities. Do you pay attention to foreign politics?"

"Oh, I don't know. I mean, I know I should." She stares at the yellowish newspaper, half-curled on the kitchen counter, the smeared photograph, Arabic spidering across the pages: a secret code for something. She twists her wrists, pulls on her hands—an old habit from childhood when she used to wipe her hands in her apron while hoping that the baklava will be crisp or the lamb will be tender or the grape leaves will hold together. Han watches her a moment, then gently places his hand over hers. "Habeebti, what is it?"

She looks down, twists her hands over her elbows.

"Please, what?"

Finally she looks directly at him. "I need you to tell me more," she says, her voice shaky. "I don't know enough about you yet. If we're—if we're going to be—whatever we're going to be. I need more."

He holds up his hands as if in offering. "Of course. Anything. Tell me what you want to know."

She avoids his gaze and says, "I need to know about the women in your life." He takes her hands and she squeezes tightly, as if he is holding her up, holding her head above an invisible line. And she almost expects him to laugh or look shocked, or at the very least to shake his head and say, what are you talking about, what women?

But instead he nods as if in recognition, as if he'd been waiting for such a request, and says, "Of course I'll tell you—as much as there is to tell."

PART TWO

CHAPTER TWENTY

"When I was a child," Han murmurs, "when I was very young, my friend Sami and I were always looking for ways to entertain ourselves. We lived in a small village at the edge of Baghdad and my father owned a few acres of orchard land where we grew lemons, figs, and olives. But we also lived close enough to the city so that when the well-keeper Abu-Najmeh gave us the bicycles, we discovered it was easy to pedal into the town and explore the neighborhoods and markets. Sami and I got more adventuresome and we began to coast down alleyways and squeeze through shrubs. I couldn't help myself. I was afraid of the unknown but I was constantly lured by unfamiliar streets. That was how we discovered the swimming pool at the Eastern Hotel...."

*

His family wasn't wealthy—they didn't have enough money for his textbooks or to send his sister to school. Han sat under the street lamps outside to do his studying because they couldn't afford electricity. Sometimes he watched birds passing overhead in the night, gulls with sharply articulated wings and blackbirds with long tailfeathers. He ran his fingers over the vocabulary words in his notebooks, writing down his favorites: *shelaal, asfoor, mismar, shemsiyya* . . .

In the Iraq of his childhood, everything went slowly. It took a lizard the entire course of the sun to walk from one side of his bedroom ceiling to the other. Even the morning took its time, slowly easing from grays to blues to greens to yellow light. Han was impatient, however, constantly imagining all the places he planned to journey to, the lives he planned to have.

And then one day he and his best friend Sami were out biking in a busy, unknown section of town and they noticed, quite by accident, rows of emerald-green trees pruned into the shapes of boxes. Creeping closer, they glimpsed a blue slice of water between the leaves. Han felt he'd awakened into one of those new times and places he'd dreamed of.

Sami hung back, but to Han the colorful flowers and graceful palms were as familiar as his uncle's tales about the adventures of Sinbad. Sami cried, "No, no, Han!" as Han slipped in between the shrubs and found himself transported to a world of long legs, red nails, crystal eyes, rows of pale women on chaise lounges arrayed around a perfect full moon of blue water.

Slowly, Sami followed his friend through the shrubs. Then the two boys, aged eleven, stood there staring, frozen in place. At first none of the women moved, and Han wondered if they were real.

Finally one of the women gradually reached up, startling the boys, and slid her dark glasses a half-inch down her nose, peering at them. He watched her gleaming lips crook slightly and then she broke into laughter that sounded as though someone were ringing a tiny dinner bell. Suddenly all the women were laughing, the air filled with the sounds of bells, their hair and skin shimmering like jewels.

The woman with the dark glasses reached toward Han and he moved to her side obediently. Her hair shifted and reflected light like a flame. "So, my little man," she said in English and took his hand. "Do you like to swim?"

He'd studied English in school; he was a good student. He realized he understood what she'd said and his eyes grew wide and hopeful. Han looked over his shoulder. He'd swum the Tigris River and he'd read about enchanted swimming pools in the *Arabian Nights* but never before had he seen one. It looked a bit like a pond, but a pond that had descended from heaven, a liquid sapphire set in marble. "Yes," he said in a small voice. Sami gaped as if he'd never seen Han before—he was actually speaking to them! In their own language!

"What a fine, handsome boy," she said. "What is your name?"

"Hanif," he said, again in the small voice.

"Well, Hanif," she said. "You've got beautiful eyes. Look, Kay." She turned Han to face the lady on the next chair. "Look at the eyelashes."

Han couldn't tell if the friend was even looking at him behind the big black glasses. "Darling," the friend said in a lazy drone, "I could gobble him up."

"Go ahead," the woman with burning hair said. Han realized she was speaking to him. She lifted one long, glowing leg—the first bare woman's leg he'd ever seen—and pointed to the water with her foot. "Go on, someone ought to make use of this ridiculous thing."

Han looked at Sami and then looked back, round-eyed and speechless. He knew how badly Sami wanted to run away. But Han wanted to stay.

He slipped off his white shirt, folded it, and placed it on the grass. The women lay motionless on their chaise lounges, a few of them rippling through magazines, languid boredom rising from them like steam. He circled the pool, the marble inlay warm from the sun, infinitely smooth, but there seemed to be no starting place to the thing, no sloping bank or rocks. He lowered himself, squatting, to the edge, ignoring Sami's whispered pleas, and extended one foot toward the blue. But a shadow in the water—a cloud? an airplane?—distracted him and he lost his balance. His foot slapped flat against the water's surface, which shattered into a million flaming tiles, and in he went.

Eyes open, ears open, mouth open, hair waving on end. His head filled with the weird pulse of the underwater and the sound of his own beating body. His aunt had told him that the water—like the air and fire—was filled with its own kinds of jinns. But when the bubbles cleared, all he could see—his lungs bursting, sinuses aching—was the perfect world, clean and cold and crossed with slanting veins of light. He surged to the surface, coughing, throwing back his hair—a ring of bright droplets—and cried to Sami, *it's great!* Sami walked to the edge and, staring at Han, he jumped in.

They came every day, sneaking away from the other boys. The two of them would carefully fold their shirts on the grass, then spend their days in the water. They became acrobatic and entertained the women with handstands and cartwheels. They made running leaps into the pool—knees tucked up into their arms, sailing high in the air—that sent arcs of spray over the lounge chairs. The women shrieked and held up their hands; one or two would flap their magazines angrily and slip on their robes.

*

Han got to know the women arrayed in their chairs around the edge of the pool: Helga, Houlani, Dee Dee, Sarah, Dot, Gina, Kay, Renate, Connie, Dominique, Margaret, Ginger, Lisel, Pehar, Farnaz, and Janet. They were the wives of diplomats, visiting dignitaries, politicians, and businessmen. Most of the women at the pool had no jobs or income of their own. They oiled themselves and read romance novels and tilted mirrors under their chins. Han had trouble imagining that they could be of the same species as the women in his village—women constantly at work clearing rice, threshing wheat, sweeping the floors, embroidering sheets, their skin toughened, eyes radiating lines from years of looking across fields and high walls of camel thorn climbing into the sun.

The women at the pool seemed half-formed to Han, caught between childhood and adulthood—they were clearly older than he was, yet as slender as children, their skin tender as larvae. And they had the petulance of children—they would egg on Han and Sami, coaxing them to do their tricks in the water, until inevitably they grew bored and turned back to their magazines.

Janet never looked bored. She watched Han closely, or so he hoped—more closely than Sami, who was also bright and diverting and good at English, though perhaps not as fluent or clever as Han. Each day when the boys finally came out of the water the sky looked swollen and shadowy and the late summer air was still hot. The boys' skin would be shriveled, their shorts sagging around their skinny hips. Janet brought out extra towels for them—soft and thick as cream, embroidered with the monogram of the Eastern Hotel.

She took an interest in Han. She was different from the other women, though perhaps at first she seemed the same, with their air of both expectation and boredom. But he noticed the way her eyes narrowed when he told her stories of his life outside the swimming pool—he saw that she listened.

Sami would lay back in his towel, onto the crackly, sunburnt lawn that had been so painfully grown and fertilized and trimmed in order to circle the marble patio, and he would doze in the sun. But Han sat beside Janet's chair, cross-legged on the marble, and told her about the intricate embroidery work his sister did on linens, his mother's painstaking sift through the lentils, the daily pounding of spices—sesame, thyme, sumac—the air filled with a fiery mist. He told her that his mother, like Janet, also lived in a society of women apart from their men—who had other sorts of work and different kinds of relaxation.

Janet laughed and tossed her brilliant hair and said, "Do you think I live like this all the time?"

And Han blinked, uncertain, because it was all he knew of her, so that is what he'd assumed, that she lived in an eternal summer season, in her bathing suit by the pool.

But after two months of this daily pleasure, one day Han and Sami came to the pool and some of the women were gone, their chairs folded and put away. When Han asked about them, Janet sighed and propped her head on one hand and said, "It's nearly the end of the season, thank God. We're going home."

And by the following week, all the women were gone, including Janet—vanished without a trace or a goodbye. The boys stood on the blank marble ring, the chaise lounges empty, just the cold crystal of the water clear and unbroken as an alien sun.

Han returned to the pool several times after that—even though the air was turning distinctly cooler and the days were starting to shorten. But the women didn't return. Eventually the chaises disappeared and a wrinkled black covering was spread over the top of the pool. Han and Sami went back to their old gang of friends. But something inside of Han had been altered. He felt impatient and dissatisfied with his friends, even with school—which he'd previously loved. Though he dressed the same and looked the same, he had changed.

*

Winter came and went; Han passed his twelfth birthday and some of the boys in his school were taken out to help their fathers with their work. Han was to help his father in the orchards that summer—he had been looking forward to it. He would finally be old enough to work among the men. Then he was to return to school in the fall. His father and mother both recognized Han's unusual gifts. There was even talk of eventually sending him to the University of Baghdad—though the money would be a problem, his mother pointed out. Oh, money is always a problem, his father responded.

Han began working in the orchards, climbing the highest, softest branches for the olives. Early one morning before work, Han was between sleep and waking, dreaming of plucking the hard, black olive berries, when there was a tapping at the window. Han got up, yawning, and Sami was there. "The ladies," he said, his cheeks pink with sweat. "They're back!"

Han sneaked out of the house and he and Sami made their way to the pool in the dim predawn. They crept through the hedge and there they saw the folding beach chairs, once again arrayed in a circle, a pair of sunglasses on one, a pair of delicate green sandals beside another—and, soft-gray and shimmering, the pool, its cover peeled away like an old skin, the water clear and still as thought.

But there was a problem—Han and Sami were twelve now and their fathers expected them to be at home helping in the fields.

Han concocted a story about a special meeting at school, so he was able to leave the orchards early that day. That afternoon, he bicycled straight to the pool and greeted Janet. Then he told her, his voice trembling, that he would not be able to spend the summer with them again.

But Janet merely opened a straw bag by her chair and pulled out an embroidered cotton purse. From this, she removed several bills and said, "Could you teach me to speak Arabic?"

When Han's father saw all the money and heard what Han had to say, at first he was stunned and even indignant—struggling to imagine why a wealthy American woman would pay a twelve-year-old to teach her a language. He asked Han, "How did you meet? When? How did you come to speak to each other? What does her husband say about this?"

Han looked at the ground. He had never met Janet's husband—though she wore a ring, he wasn't even sure if such a man existed—and he couldn't bring himself to lie to his father anymore. Perhaps she was not married, Han admitted, but her female friends were always with her.

"How many friends are there?" his father asked.

Han thought it over. "Perhaps fourteen or fifteen?" he said.

His father burst out laughing. "Fourteen or fifteen friends? Have you stumbled into a harem?"

And Han—who'd never actually seen such a thing as a harem, who'd only heard stories of them in books like the *Adventures of Sinbad the Sailor*—wondered if he had.

Luckily, his father was not like ordinary fathers, who might have refused to spare their sons in the fields. His father knew from one glance at all that American money that his son would make many times more teaching this woman than he would barefoot in the olive trees. And even better—he would be working with an American: this, he sensed, might unlatch more important things for his son. He let his questions go unanswered.

*

Han steered his bike with one hand, dodging down narrow alleyways, cutting around stray dogs and chickens, water-bearers and jewelry vendors, knife-sharpeners and fruit sellers, women carrying trays of bread on their heads, boys carrying silver trays full of tea glasses and pots of hot tea. In Han's other hand he carried a tablet of white paper, two pencils, an Arabic-English dictionary, and a thick Arabic grammar book to teach her the beautifully shaped characters of Fus-ha—or classical Arabic—the language of the Quran.

Sami was not as fortunate—his father kept him at work in the fields, and Janet had not offered Sami a handful of money to teach her. So every day, Han climbed all alone through the hole in the hedges to meet with his student.

For a week, maybe even two, Janet copied the exercises Han assigned, trying to curve her fingers around the swoops and dashes of *Alieph, Baa, Taa* . . . trying to curve her lips around the guttural sound of the letter *Eyn,* the rasping *Ghayn,* and the heaviness of *Dahd.* Inevitably, though, after fifteen minutes of struggle, she'd start gossiping with her friends about the embassy parties. And Han would be back inside the pool, diverting the women with flips and dives.

They attained an ideal world this way. Han swam or laid on the grass on a hotel towel, listening to the women speak, basking in the sun, dazzling afterimages of water and chlorine fog passing over his eyelids. There were women there from what seemed like every country in the world, and in their company he developed his aptitude for languages. He was able to spend a few weeks listening to conversations in German, Hindi, or Italian, and discover the rudiments of the languages taking hold in his brain. Some of the women spoke to him in English and some in their own language, and he found that if he listened closely enough that the words' meaning would eventually reveal itself, glimmering through the sounds like fruit on dark branches.

After two weeks of half-hearted exercises, Janet pushed aside the books and papers and said to Han, "Maybe it would be better if we just practiced talking instead."

Han was relieved: it was always a huge task to get Janet to practice her alphabet and each time he taught her a new letter she seemed to forget the letter that had gone before.

But the extent of her Arabic seemed to go no further than the hotel lobby: she could ask for fruits, ice cream, hairdresser, car, maid, towels, vodka, nail polish, flowers, blankets, and dry cleaning, and could say in almost perfect Arabic, "I want," as well as "give me." But no matter how much he coached her, he could not seem to expand her vocabulary. The conversation lessons were set aside like the writing exercises when Janet decided that their time would be better spent perfecting Han's English and that she would continue paying him a stipend for the pleasure of doing this.

When Han returned to school in the fall, the language teachers were amazed by his advancements in English, Italian, and Farsi. And Han's family had enjoyed the wages he'd brought in all summer. There were treats on the table like sesame candy, and pressed apricots, and frekeh with smoked pigeon breast, and an extra sheep in their stock. Han's father was content to allow this arrangement to continue through the following summer as well. "As long as your friend needs the lessons," he said, silencing Han's mother.

Sometimes the desert winds kicked up and swirled sand from miles away into the air, and sometimes thunder boiled in the sky. But mostly there were long, hot, transparent days of swimming and talking. Janet seemed fascinated by what Han told her of his life outside the pool and she asked him many questions. She in turn talked about her life in a place called Lincoln, Nebraska, about table-flat fields filled with rows of corn, planted acres that started just outside her back door, and how the open desert reminded her of the plains.

By the end of their third summer there was starting to be discussion of revolution in Baghdad—the rulership was said to be corrupt and the Iraqis had an idealistic hope for a new regime. But Han's father was not convinced that the new party would be any more just or effective than the last and he said so at their table and in town. The neighbors, in turn, began to talk about the fact that Han did not have to work in the orchards like the other boys. Han's family, which had always been regarded as a bit aloof, was now viewed with open suspicion and resentment: why was there another sheep in their field? Rumors started flying about the place that Han was bicycling off to every day, and his friends started calling him Eye Spy.

Janet seemed more fretful and distracted when they met again in the summer of Han's fourteenth year. Her husband was thinking of moving them to a new seasonal post—the political situation in Iraq was unstable. Janet and her friends whispered and looked preoccupied. Several of the other women hadn't returned that summer and the mood at the pool was different. And Han had begun to change. He'd started to grow, and the full days of swimming had given him broad shoulders, a strong back, and a long, sinewy waist. He was beginning to look more like a man and less like a boy. He noticed the women watching him when he climbed out of the water—not just when he dove in. Some of them had started to wrap themselves with bathrobes when he walked by, while others uncovered their legs. He saw that his shadow was wider and longer, the flat wet imprint of his feet larger.

Something was happening inside his head as well. He talked with Janet in their usual way—she lounged on her chaise, glistening with drops of baby oil, and he stretched long-legged on towels on the ground.

But Janet's eyes frequently looked soft and glossy, and she developed a habit of twirling a lock of hair around the tip of her finger as she talked with him, like a hypnotist swinging a watch on a chain. And Han found that when he left her in the evenings to go back to his family, he continued to think about her. He remembered her eyes as being wider and darker than they actually were. And instead of the pool, for some reason, he thought of the big green ocean, its roving peaks and white veins, its deep wells and silky waves and its faraway gaze.

*

One afternoon late in the summer, Janet placed her painted fingertips on Han's wrist and quietly asked if he would come back to the pool that evening. There was something important she had to speak to him about.

He had never gone to the pool at night before and once again he had to invent a reason in order to get his parents' permission to go out. They would never agree to his meeting with a woman after dark. So Han came up with another story—this time that his friend Sami was sick and Han wanted to go look in on him. His hands trembled as he spoke and he hid them behind his back. It was a reckless lie—easy to uncover. His mother raised one eyebrow and glanced at his father, but Han's father merely nodded.

So Han left in the evening just after dinner, when all the families were home together, the boys already in bed to prepare for their long hours in the fields and orchards. Han took his bike down the slanting blue corners and alleyways of Baghdad. He saw eyes blink in the darkness, the street lamps illuminating a single hand or mouth.

He passed through the city night trembling, but soon he spotted the small opening in the hedge, dismounted his bike, and crept in.

It took a moment for his eyes to adjust because, as dark and seamless as the night was around the pool, the water itself was glowing like a small planet. Lights placed around and inside the rim of the pool sent turquoise beams through the water. He instinctively looked toward Janet's chaise lounge but it was empty and he thought for a moment that she had only been teasing him and hadn't really meant to come at all.

After a moment of standing alone and surveying the empty rows of chairs, however, Han had an intimation that crept over his shoulders and along the nape of his neck, as if someone had snuck up from behind and blown on his skin. Then he heard his name called out in a voice as golden and mellow as if the moon herself had spoken. He turned and there, arms adrift in the far end of the pool, was Janet, her hair loose, the ends trailing in the sapphire water.

He had seen her in American-style bathing suits summer after summer, but never, in all that time, had he seen her in the water. He crouched at the edge of the pool, the two of them watching each other. Then, without warning, she dove under, and the sound of the ocean that he'd been hearing for weeks, perhaps for years, rose in his ears. And seemingly without any say in the matter, he dove in after her.

He was fourteen years old. He swam to Janet—he had no idea what age she was—twenty-three, thirty, thirty-five? Their first kiss was under the water in the deceptive lights. Han burst to the surface, his heart and lungs hammering, dizzy with excitement. He swirled around her, encircling her with his arms, and she let him pull her off her feet, her arms tight around his ribs. It was hard to know if they were playing or serious, even when she untied the strings to her swimsuit so her white belly and small breasts flashed in his hands. Even while she was guiding him inside of her, still in the pool, showing him how and when, and he mistakenly whispered his feelings in Arabic and she shook her head and said, *no, speak English*—even then it all seemed a kind of play.

Only afterward, when they laid sprawled on the chairs, his leg hooked over hers, her arm draped on his shoulder, did he look closely at her face and see that it had not been a game at all.

Her husband was being transferred, she said. It wasn't safe for them to remain in Baghdad—soon the monarchy would be overthrown and the American consul warned that the consulate couldn't vouch for their safety. She didn't know, she whispered, how much more time they had remaining in the city. Han looked around but all he could see was the perimeter of the fence, the dense shrubbery, and the porcelain moon. It was too soon for him to grasp her sadness; he was still electrified by lovemaking, his mind felt scorched, his body smoldering in the places where they'd touched. "*Habeebti*, my darling," he said, but he felt as if he were just trying on the words he'd heard in songs. It seemed that he had no language at all for what had happened. He felt as if he might melt away, that air and rain could pass through his flesh. "I am so happy," he finally managed to say.

"Happy? But this wasn't meant to happen!" she suddenly cried, sitting up.

He lifted his head. "What do you mean? What wasn't meant to happen?"

"Oh God." She covered her eyes with one hand. "Don't you understand, Han?" she said. "I'm a happily married woman, and you—you're just a boy."

He sat up. He stared at her.

"But when I realized that I might never see you again, it's—well, I couldn't stand it. And then I saw you standing there by the side of the pool—you looked so tall and handsome, you reminded me of my husband when we first met. The two of us were barely older than you are now."

He wasn't sure then if it was the night breeze sweeping his damp skin, but he began to shake. His teeth rattled. Janet's unblinking eyes looked like smoke and her skin was so pale it didn't seem like skin at all. She asked what was wrong with him as he slowly contracted, removing himself from her hands. She pushed up to one elbow as if her legs would not carry her and perhaps it was shock but there seemed to be a vague smile on her face. "Where are you going?" she asked, as if she couldn't believe he was leaving.

He was shaking so badly now he wasn't sure he could get back through the hole in the hedge. He felt how the bicycle trembled, the wheels rasping, the handlebars loose; but when he got on, his shaking started to subside and the bike sailed him through the shadows.

*

His father was disappointed to learn that the American's language lessons had abruptly come to an end. Han told him that his student was now quite proficient in Arabic and had learned everything that he could teach her. His father was incredulous and protested that scholars had dedicated whole lifetimes and entire libraries to the study of Arabic. Han shrugged and said that he was the one who required more study, then. His mother, who'd had an uneasy feeling about this business right from the start, held out her arms and lowered her son's head into her lap. She stroked his hair and said to his father, *khullus*, it's finished with, and so much the better. We need him at home where he belongs.

The next day and all the days after that, Han woke thinking of Janet and the pool, and then it would come back to him, her ghostly eyes and shattering words. Slowly the sound of the ocean surf receded from his consciousness until it was nothing more than a distant pulse.

He would get up even before the early summer sun was out and pull on his work clothes and go out to the orchards. But every day as the sun climbed overhead and roasted the silvery leaves and dark olives, Han would eventually drift back indoors and creep into the kitchen, where his mother and sister sat with the neighbor women, patting dough at the table and preparing dinner, all of them laughing and telling stories. Leila's face lit up when her brother appeared at the door and she shared her chair with him; the two of them were narrow enough that they could just manage it. The women's voices soothed and comforted him.

His father and mother knew that he was neglecting his duties, and without Han's previous income he was needed in the fields. But again they allowed him some leeway—it was clear to them that he had been suffering from some sort of an internal wound ever since the end of the language lessons, something he could tell neither of them about.

*

One night at the end of the summer the moon hung hot and round and orange in the sky. The family had just finished dinner but instead of picking up dishes, all of them stayed at the table talking. Their father was telling them the story of their uncle Amoon, who had walked halfway across the desert to Mecca, then gave up and decided to walk back. They heard the sound of winged insects chirring in the dark and a wildcat crying like a baby.

Then there was a knock on the door. "I'll get it," Leila said.

Their father said he would see who was there. It was too late for girls to be going to the door.

It was a woman dressed completely in *hejjab*—a thick black scarf covered her head and face entirely, and a black coat cloaked her from her neck to her ankles; she wore white gloves and black boots as well. Han's father invited her in and it was immediately clear that this was not an Arab woman—she was too tall and she didn't move like an Arab. When she began speaking in English, Han realized that it was Janet.

They sat her at the dinner table, glancing at each other, hastily clearing away dishes, asking if she would have something to eat or drink. But she refused all offers, her voice taut and urgent, and said she had a critical matter to discuss with them.

Han sat frozen at the table, his knees weak and palms prickling with sweat. Although he knew little of how such things occurred, he wondered if she might be pregnant. Or perhaps she'd considered the meaning of their night together— as Han had, over and over—and decided ... what? That she'd been violated or abandoned, even raped? Or perhaps she wanted him back again.

His heart thudded as he listened to her speak. He was so anxious it was hard to hear what she was saying. But his parents only spoke a little English, so—feeling stunned with embarrassment—Han realized that he had to translate for her. And as she talked, he came to understand that she was there to make them some sort of offer.

First she identified herself as the woman that Han had been tutoring.

Han has a great mind, she said, he is a fine, noble teacher, he is unusual and his talents should not be overlooked.

Han murmured these words in Arabic, blushing deeply while his parents nodded, pleased but unnerved by this amazing visitor. So, she went on behind her veil, she and her husband wanted to start a scholarship fund to send exemplary students like Han to the special private school in Cairo—a place where kings and diplomats sent their sons to learn about politics and society and to prepare them to attend the world's great universities.

Han's hands squeezed the edge of his seat as he translated. His arms and back grew rigid. His mother put one gentle hand on his shoulder and his sister laid a hand on his arm.

"Well," his father finally said to Han in Arabic, "tell her this: You've certainly given us a lot to think about. We are overwhelmed by your generous offer, it goes without saying. But this is not a step to be taken lightly. Cairo is very far from here and Han is still young—he has never been away from home. There are many things to consider, not the least of which are Han's own wishes in the matter." Han translated all this with a bowed head and burning face.

Then his mother smiled as if remembering something, looked up, and, also speaking Arabic, said directly to Janet, "Han tells us you've come to the end of his knowledge." She paused a moment, as Han translated. Then she raised her eyebrows, leaned forward, and asked, very slowly and clearly, "How is your Arabic?"

Han fell silent, not translating, holding his breath, teeth gritted together. Janet turned from Han to his mother and finally, cheerfully, asked in English, "What?"

*

The family remained seated at the kitchen table while Han showed their guest out. He had no intention of accepting this strange offer and planned not to say anything more to her beyond a polite good evening. But when they reached the door she shuffled him outside and pulled the door shut behind them. Then she whispered, "My husband saw us in the pool."

Han's chest flooded with air and his eyes opened wide. The night sky seemed to double in size, popping with huge, pointed white stars.

"Don't worry." She touched his arm and an electric current ran through him; Han jerked away. "He was watching from one of the hotel windows and he wasn't sure of what he saw. He thought that it was just two kids playing around in the water, but afterward I walked in wearing my wet bathing suit."

Han stared at her, enraged with himself for imagining something like a romance ever could have happened between the two of them. He was only fourteen years old but he felt at that moment as if he had lived a thousand years. He had an inkling that she had been using him, in some way, all along—though he didn't understand how or why.

"But he didn't see your face," Janet continued. "He could tell you were Iraqi, though. And this time he's sworn to find out who it was—no matter what I tell him."

"This time?" The stars swirled in the sky, left long white tails.

She smoothed out the seams of her *hejjab*. "Do you think it's easy for me, living this way? Spending months and months all by myself in godforsaken places like this?" She looked around at the assortment of little village houses, the unlit street. "There've been other men in my life," she said mildly. "And he knows it. But I've never seen him so upset before. Perhaps it's because you're an Arab," she mused. "He's been obsessed with finding out who you are. He could make a lot of trouble. And we hear things are going to be changing in this country. We hear—someone new is coming to power, another coup. It's best that you go away from here for a while. Let me send you to the school—I've got plenty of money, that isn't even a concern. Please." She touched his hand and this time he didn't manage to pull away. "This is something I want to do."

He said, "And you always get what you want, don't you?" He turned to go, but she grabbed his hand with surprising force. "Han, please!" she begged. "The situation is more serious than you realize. What do you want? Just tell me what you want and I'll do it."

"What I want?" He smiled as if this were a whimsical idea. "All right then, what I want is an answer. Tell me why—of all the men out there—and all the boys—did you have to do this to me?"

She pushed back the hood of her veil and uncovered her face. In the shadows her eyes looked inky. She lifted one of his arms so the moonlight spilled over it. "Look at you," she said in a weightless voice. She raised his arm as if it were a precious artifact, a dark wash of skin inside her curved white fingers. "Just look!"

*

Sirine studies the curve of Han's back in the early morning light as he sits facing away, fingers threaded through his hair. He's fallen silent.

"What happened?" she asks softly.

"What happened . . ." He turns to her but she can't make out his expression, just the rise and fall of his shoulders. "Nothing. The rest of my life." He pauses. "In the end, my father decided for me and my mother stayed silent and my sister cried through the summer until the day I left. Things were changing, we knew. The Ba'athist Party was pushing to incorporate all aspects of our lives—from the media to the arts to the schools—the schools were especially under surveillance, and my father worried over what would happen to a young man like myself, fluent in other languages. I might have been imprisoned—more likely I would have been recruited into the party. The week after Janet's visit, our mathematics instructor was removed—we heard rumors it was because his wife was a member of the Islamic Feminist Movement. He was replaced by a man who had no mathematics training, but was a staunch Ba'athist supporter.

"So I went away to the private school, and that was my first escape from Iraq. My school was filled with children from wealthy families. I never felt like I had a choice in the matter," he says, his voice suddenly dry. "Just like the night at the pool."

"How did you like it there?" She feels the brush of his fingers at her temples, then sifting through her hair.

"It started everything for me. It wasn't so much like or not like. It was more a sort of force of nature. Big and inevitable. The school had British and American faculty, classes were conducted in English, and the history classes were the history of the West, literature was the literature of America and Britain. I didn't question any of it. I wasn't from a rich family, but I felt much older and more worldly than any of those other children—they seemed so soft and formless. I think I was even a little jealous of their innocence. And I was ashamed of what had happened between Janet and me—I felt that somehow it had been my fault."

"Your fault! You were fourteen years old."

He seems to smile a bit. "I was trained to believe that men are always the seducers. Really I was shocked at myself—that I could have done such a thing, with a married woman, no less—and not felt any remorse. Once I got to school, I worked hard at my studies—I think it was my way of trying to repent. The teachers recognized my abilities and encouraged me. I guess I grew out of the curve of my family and home. Maybe I turned into something different than I was born to be. I don't know. I've wondered about that."

Sirine tries to touch him. She reaches toward his face but he shifts and her fingers graze the air. "You seem just right to me," she says.

"I never did see her again," he says quietly. And he looks away into the corner of the room and Sirine knows that he is talking about the American woman again. "Sometimes even now, I still dream I'm back in my room, back in Iraq, and Janet is still in the pool, waiting for me. But I never return."

CHAPTER TWENTY-ONE

Camille and Napoleon-Was-Here were semi-stranded in the desert with the equally lost blue Bedu. They tried all the way-finding tricks that the Bedu knew—navigating by sun, moon, stars, water, wind, shadows, even following the tilt of the camels in the morning and the slant of the campfire flames at night. But somehow the paths never quite led where they expected them to lead. They were out of their depth, too far from their trade routes. After months of fruitless wandering, it seemed that they'd never find their way back home. Just when they thought all hope was lost, Camille sighed and said, "If only that naughty mermaid, Alieph from the Land of Na, hadn't decided to steal my son, none of this would have happened!"

At this, one of the oldest Bedu, a man who was so old that nearly all the blue had leaked out of his skin, and who had a long whispery face and runny little eyes, piped up, "Alieph from the Land of Na? I also know a certain Alieph from the Land of Na! You don't suppose it's the same one, do you?" Well, and he had good reason to ask. After all, you know how that goes, you tell someone in Azerbaijan that you're from Texas and they say, you're from Texas? Do you know Joe Smith? He's from Texas!

But the old Bedouin got Camille's attention, and she said, "If this Alieph you know is a wily and shape-shifting mermaid, then we must be talking about the very same one."

"Then that's her, all right," said the old Bedouin. "And if she hasn't changed addresses, I happen to know she lives not far from here."

He explained that she'd left the Land of Na to retire to the elbow of the Sinai, and that she'd wedged herself into a cozy cave dwelling between the desert and the sea.

Off they went, Camille, the dog, and the Bedu, on another long walk that took days and nights and nights and days. Until they came to a place that fit right into the hinge of the Sinai where towering walls of sandstone cliffs rose vertically from the Red Sea. And they knew it was the right place because when the waves rushed in you couldn't hear a thing. But when they crept out, there was a sound like a velvety shimmering that chimed and echoed in the violet-colored caves studding the cliff face and covering the whole of the earth.

Everyone's eyes got big and their bones began to dance in their bodies and their hearts seemed to be drawn right up out of their chests. "That's her," the old Bedouin said. "That's Alieph from the Land of Na. And she's calling for us."

Camille had never heard the like! And though her mind told her to run away as fast as she could, instead her hands started climbing and her legs started following. Just as it is when you become involved with certain romantic entanglers and entanglers, no? The mind says one thing and the body is in strong disagreement.

Without even realizing it, Camille had fallen under the spell of the siren's call: the sound that contains the scent of berries, chocolate, and mint, that tastes of salt and oil and blood, that sounds like a heart's murmur, the passage of clouds, the call to prayers, the beloved's name, and a distant ringing in the ears. She went with her wits about her, though, because Camille, don't forget, was a bit of a siren herself—and she knew a few tricks of her own.

While the blue Bedu hung back sweating bluish beads of sweat, Camille and Napoleon began hunting. They found a thin ledge that wound along the cliff face; it offered just the narrowest purchase, crumbling and climbing between clumps of sage and burning rocks. And at the crumbliest, sheerest, steepest point, she looked up and spotted the opening to the blackest, deepest cave. The smell of roses was shaking in the air and Camille had to hold on to Napoleon's bony head to keep her balance and restore her courage.

The air was thinner here and the sound was even brighter and Camille might have turned and run right then and there, but she was watching the face of the cave, which was only a few meters away now. Up until this point, she had been reassuring herself with the thought that there was actually no such animal as a mermaid. Of course, there's a Mother of All Fish, because everyone has to have a mother. And there're jinns and nymphs and sylphs, because, well, they're everywhere. But a mermaid? Preposterous! Until, as I say, she happened to look up and see unrolling from the lip of the cave a glimmering, opalescent, sea-green tail.

*

It's not exactly that something has changed, Sirine thinks. That's too definite. She hopes that she's wrong—she hopes that nothing has changed. When she'd asked him to tell her about the women in his life, she thought that might reassure her. And he did tell her, as simply and clearly as someone with nothing to hide. But that night, after he tells her about the American woman named Janet and the pool at the Eastern Hotel, she lies awake at night after Han has fallen asleep, wide awake, listening to the silence in the room, staring in the darkness. It isn't necessarily a bad or ominous feeling, nor is it necessarily expectant or hopeful, but it is definitely a heightened, vigilant state, a kind of waiting, her concentration hovering at the surface of her body like a dragonfly.

Throughout the next day at work she catches herself thinking about the woman in Han's story and suddenly she realizes that her heart is pounding and her breath is speeded up. She walks into the closed screen door at the café, trips over the slightly raised threshold between the two kitchens. By the end of the day, her arms are covered with small red scorch marks from the grill and there are knife cuts on both her thumbs. She avoids Um-Nadia for fear that she will take in Sirine's injuries and add them up like a sum. But that evening as she's closing up, the café deserted except for Cristobal swabbing the back kitchen, Sirine bangs her forehead against a hanging pot—a pot she has walked around almost daily for years. It makes a dull ringing sound that resonates all the way to the back of her skull. She puts one hand on the counter, the pain starting to flicker through her forehead. And suddenly Aziz is there, sliding behind the counter; he takes Sirine by the hand, leads her to a chair, and finds a cold rag to hold to her head.

"What are you doing here?" she asks while pressing on the rag, too embarrassed to look directly at him.

He squats and angles himself so that she can't avoid facing him. "I came to get you a cold rag."

"Thank you."

"Are you all right?"

She waves one hand at him. "It's . . ." Her voice trails away. "Happens all the time."

"Actually, I came to ask if you'll go see some whirling dervishes with me."

And maybe it's the bump on her head, maybe it's Aziz's kindness and the gentleness in his hand as he tends to her, but Sirine smiles at Aziz and says sure, I'll go with you. Why not?

That evening she asks Han if he'll come with them, even pleads a bit, but he smiles absently and tells her to please enjoy the whirling without him. There's finals to grade that week, and he must research his new book if he ever wants to get tenure. He tells her to go on, have a good time, to enjoy herself, and to watch out for that devil Aziz.

*

On Friday when Sirine and Aziz drive to Santa Monica Community College, she is already regretting her decision to go. She tries to keep her knee from bumping his in the little car and she keeps her hands tightly clasped in her lap. They're going to see the Mevlevi dervishes, also known as the whirling dervishes—a thing Sirine has heard of but never imagined actually still existed. She and Aziz sit in the bleachers at the college's gymnasium with about two hundred other people—some wearing conservative suits and dresses mixed in with others who wear dashikis and dreadlocks, sandals and braids, many of them hugging each other and calling out greetings. She can smell traces of a previous night's basketball game—the scuff of rubber-soled basketball shoes, wisps of old sweat and salt and floor varnish, as well as hints of patchouli and jasmine oils. The program tickets cost fifteen dollars—"A small price for a glimpse of heaven, don't you think?" Aziz asks as he pays for them both.

Rumi the poet that Aziz called his spiritual mentor, turns out to have lived a thousand years ago. Sirine reads in the program notes that "Sema" is the name of the whirling prayer ceremony, that Rumi was the founder of the dervish order, and that Sema is "a journey through the universe before God, a spiritual intoxication that takes one to the true existence by means of ecstasy." She scans the audience, feeling expectant yet skeptical about this impending journey. She hasn't thought about issues of the spirit since her visit to the Women in Islam group—which didn't seem to have much to do with spirituality anyway. It seems that whenever she tries to deliberately seek out something like God, she gets distracted, her mind winds back to her body, and she finds that instead she is thinking about something like stuffed grape leaves rolled tightly around rice, ground lamb, garlic, onions, currants, fragrant with green olive oil.

The audience settles down, Aziz sighs happily, and a troupe of musicians climbs onstage. A man steps forward and intones one of Rumi's poems, repeating the line, "Don't go back to sleep."

There is more poetry then and some music and song in which the singer's voice rises and trembles in place like a body of water, transfixing Sirine with its dignified, unearthly sound. She hears snatches of lines: "Listen, if you can stand to . . . the soul lies down in that grass . . . the musical air in a flute . . . a rose lost in its fragrance."

At last about twenty dervishes emerge from a door in the back of the room. They walk to their places, aligned in a circle, and then very slowly they begin to turn. The music gradually intensifies as the dervishes spin faster: eyes closed, heads tilted, their arms gradually lifting—one palm up and one down, their long skirts billowing around their ankles, floating about the floor as they move so they appear to be footless.

Some of the dervishes are hopping a bit, some are smiling, heads slightly canted to one side, but all seem to be enraptured, fixed on some unmoving, internal object: in all that whirling, a point of stillness. Still spinning, they begin to move around the floor in a circle. Then they fan out and cover the floor.

Pinned between listening and watching, Sirine feels transported, in the presence of something like a miracle. She leans forward, forgets to think about anything. All that matters is the swirl of the movement, so familiar to Sirine, giving thought over to the body: repetitive, sustaining. Like stirring a pot.

At the end of the evening, the dervishes line up, still and solemn—none show any sign of dizziness. Sirine thinks they are going to shake hands with the man in charge. (Aziz whispers that he is the sheikh.) Instead, as they approach the sheikh, each dervish bends an arm, elbow forward, so their hands are raised, and clasps the sheikh's upraised hand, and, sweetly, they simultaneously kiss the side of each other's hand.

*

After the closing ritual, she feels that she is waking from a dream. She sighs and then realizes that her arm and leg have drifted somewhat, and that she's been touching Aziz.

She pulls back. "I'm sorry," she says.

"Oh, come back," Aziz says. "It's lovely."

She looks away, her face and neck hot.

*

They walk down the street, Sirine still buoyed by afterimages of the dervishes, their hypnotic movement. The wide sidewalks bordering the campus are shuttered with panels of streetlights and Sirine and Aziz walk through flickering boxes of light. The air is balmy, filled with a mystical quiet, and even Aziz seems subdued. The performance has thrilled and disoriented Sirine: she can't tell if the muffled roar around her is from cars or the ocean or the wind. They walk a bit aimlessly, hands in pockets, not talking, past the parking lots, past shops and alleyways. She feels happy and easy to be walking beside Aziz like this, and then she wonders if she shouldn't be wanting to get right back to Han. But she doesn't really.

Eventually the sidewalk runs out. It ends at a vacant lot bordered by rows of light bulbs strung up between poles, like a defunct car lot. The lights swing in the breeze and scatter wild shadows over the lot. "Well," Aziz says, surveying the scene, "I guess it's the end of the line."

But Sirine still feels restless, not quite ready to go back home. So they go into a small café with just a cobalt neon cup over the door that they'd passed earlier. The place is empty and echoey, its floor covered with black and white tiles, and a mosaic of antelopes in a field covers the counter. The woman at the counter has sleepy black eyes and curtain-straight black hair sliced across at her eyebrows and above her shoulders. She looks at Sirine as if she recognizes her, then bows her head while taking their orders, the shining hair swinging forward in blades.

Sirine sits at one of the wrought-iron tables and rolls herself forward, elbows on the table so her hipbones don't press so hard into the ironwork chair. The silent woman brings them their lattes in blue ceramic bowls, swirling with steam and a faint drift of nutmeg. Sirine cups both hands around hers and gazes into it like into a lantern. She remembers the line, "Don't go back to sleep," and smiles.

"What?" Aziz tilts his head to look under the cascade of her hair.

She pushes her hair back and sits up. "What we just saw—that's a sort of Islam?" she asks.

He looks amused. "Depends on who you ask. Some think so."

"Were they really praying?"

He seems to be thinking about an answer, but it might just be an excuse to let his gaze wash over her. His skin looks coppery in the café light and his lips plump and sensitive, curved into an eternal smile—as if it were his natural expression. He draws his index finger around the lip of the cup and Sirine notices he's wearing a rosy gold ring with a green stone on that finger. There's a faint mark, like a margin, circling the base of his finger and for some reason this sets off a frisson inside her.

"My scholarly opinion is, you're looking especially radiant and enticing tonight."

She laughs and folds her arms, but she finds she wants to spar, push back at Aziz. His eyes on her are shiny and bedeviling.

"Don't be bad," she says, smiling.

He shrugs. "It's who I am. I am Bad Aziz. I was born this way. Might as well ask a cat not to cry."

"Well, thanks for the warning, then," she says. "I never knew your true identity."

"My true identity is there for the knowing." His calf brushes hers under the table and he grins. "I'm an open-and-shut case. Ask me anything. What do you want to know?"

She looks into her cup, barely sipped. Some part of her mind is caught in the memory of the floating skirts, outstretched arms. "All right. Where are you from?"

"The Mother of the Arab World, of course. Damascus. The fancy part of Damascus, where the intelligentsia live. By the city gardens."

"How long in this country?"

"Five long years."

"Favorite music?"

He ticks them off, bending each finger with his index finger. "Cheb Khaled. Oum Koulthoum, of course. And Abba."

"Age?"

"Verrry late thirties, meaning forty-eight."

"Um." She thinks for a second. "Bad habits? Smoking, drinking, running around?"

He grins broadly, waves at her. "D."

"D?"

"All the above."

She lifts her eyebrows. "Oh my. You are bad. Should I be afraid?"

"Afraid?" he says. "Of me?"

She smiles and closes her eyes and there are the pale, serene faces of the dervishes, the white robes rising open and the whirling filling the room like a snowstorm. But then she opens her eyes and Aziz is close to her, holding his hands over hers, his eyes daring and romantic with long, inky lashes. He is saying, "Aziz is quite harmless."

And she only waits for a second before she withdraws her hand.

*

Sirine has her key out before she's even reached her door. Do not look at him, she tells herself. Do not look. A normal woman wouldn't have done this, she suddenly thinks. A normal woman wouldn't be out at night alone with this kind of man. Or perhaps she means a good girl? She tries to remember how many blocks away Han lives, but she can't. And Aziz is behind her, placing his fingertips on her shoulder, and there it is, she can feel the pull of attraction inside her again, quickening in her throat.

"What was the line from that poem?" Aziz murmurs, half to himself. "Now, why can I never think of such things when I need them? It's something like, 'We have the taste of eternity in our mouths.' That's it, isn't it?" He is grinning and stroking her arm. "Come on, lovely Sirine, my siren, don't you want to know what such a thing tastes like?" He pulls her a little closer, a little closer, a little closer. " 'Dissolver of sugar, dissolve me.' " His head tilts slightly; his eyes are just a dark fringe of lashes, and there is his curling upper lip, a soft exhalation of breath. She closes her eyes for a second, just a quick second, as if she is drowsy. She holds her breath, pulls back, but her breath slips and Aziz's scent fills her head, sweet orange blossom and almond, and his breath rushes against her face and it's like giving way to the force of an ocean current and the next thing she knows, her hands have fallen open, helpless at her sides, and they are kissing.

CHAPTER TWENTY-TWO

Back at the lip of the cave of the mermaid Alieph from the Land of Na, Aunt Camille had just witnessed the unrolling of a great green tail. She stood, but could not feel the ground under her feet; she gasped, but could not feel the air in her lungs. The air filled with a sound of shimmering and humming, and the humming rose and converged until it was a voice, a voice made of honey and husks and roses and prayers and weeping and wine and ocean waves and desert light, and the voice was saying, Camille, Camille! Come closer, closer!

Now poor Aunt Camille began to shake in all her bones and Napoleon-Was-Here was shaking beneath her hand, and despite herself she crept closer along the edge until she cried out, "Good Queen Alieph, have mercy on us!"

And then she heard a laughter lighter than dragonflies and a small white pointed hand slipped along the opening of the cave. Then she saw a glowing, pearl-tipped, golden barnacle-encrusted crown emerging spokes-first. This crown was entwined with long tumbling seaweedy locks of gold and copper and bronze. And then finally the curtains of hair fell back and there was a face. And oh, what a face! White as marble in one light, black as onyx in another, the eyes wide and hooded as Cleopatra's and filled with the color and the movement of ocean waves. And her mouth, pure and rare and small as a tropical orchid, opened in laughter and was filled with the sounding roar of the incoming tide.

"Oh, great Alieph!" Camille cried out and fell on her knees and her face and the dog did the same. "Please have mercy!" she cried again.

The mermaid fixed her with one of her terrible, beautiful, speckled eyes then and sighed. Camille opened her eyes. And after a dramatic pause Alieph said, "All day long people are coming to ask me favors! Do this, do that. Does anyone care what it's like for me?"

Camille sat up then and peeped carefully and said, "What do you mean?"

The mermaid arranged herself on the lip of the cave and Camille settled herself on a ledge. Stretching out from tail to crown along the rocks, Alieph sighed again and said, "Imagine if you will the loneliness of the mermaid. We first open our eyes within the womb of the sea, born without the benefit of parents or childhood, eyes full of the green strands of the waves, only sargassum for our clothes. Born without language itself, until the blue whales take pity on us and teach us to sing and the narwhales teach us to embroider.

"We live in exile from both people and fish, at the center of the center of the sea, where no one goes except crazies and wild men, whom we are then obliged to kill by luring them onto the storming rocks. This is our only form of entertainment and usually we don't even mean to do it exactly—we're just curious by nature."

"How many of you are there altogether?" Camille asked.

"Twenty-eight. Alieph, Ba, Ta, Tha, Jeem, Ha . . ." and she went through the whole alphabet. "Some of course are nicer than others."

"Yes, typical sisters," said Camille. "Family gifts are not always evenly distributed."

"Isn't that so!" Alieph marveled. "Some are witty and ironic, some are literalists, some are grouchy, and some are beautiful hosts and make a lovely tea tray. By day we swim hand in hand in hand, all twenty-eight, through sheets of light and topaz schools of fish. By night we make our way back on to the rocky shores of the Land of Na."

"What is that place like?" asked Camille.

"It is black and jagged, made of mahogany, shale, and silver. The rocks turn to ice under the moon and sometimes it thunders so loudly the whole island shakes. Other times huge silent green veins of lightning flash and flash and flash all around and the island glows like a mirror. And sometimes, when it's very quiet, we can just barely hear the sounds of the great missing civilization that is said to be lost somewhere in the distant heart of the center of the center, where no one ever goes."

A good place to visit, Camille thought, but she wouldn't want to live there.

*

Sirine wakes early the next morning and checks the other side of the bed, patting at it in the dark to confirm that she didn't let Aziz come inside. She had pulled out of their kiss last night, saying, "Han is your friend!" and he'd smiled broadly and said, "Yes, and your lover!" It's so early it's still dark out, but last night's flirtation with Aziz has already dwindled away to a wisp, an unfortunate figment of her imagination. Her face feels damp, as if she's just awakened from a fever. She gets up and dresses quickly, missing Han after their night apart. She calls him, eager for the sound of his voice, but no one answers the phone.

She tries not to let herself wonder where he might be so early in the morning. She peeks in her nightstand drawer and the laughing woman in the photo looks at her. She pushes the drawer shut. She will not think about it. No. She drops back on to her bed and closes her eyes. She tries to recall some of the lines of the poetry last night, but can only remember what Aziz said about the taste of eternity right before he kissed her. Did he make that up? King Babar jumps on to the bed and she opens her eyes and he gives her his slightly wise and slightly cockeyed look that seems to say he's known her through a thousand previous lifetimes. She is pervaded by guilt—though she tries to convince herself now that it was all innocent, a deep uneasiness seeps into her bloodstream, the memory of the previous night tainting the air and unsettling her mind. She gets off the bed and gets dressed.

On her way to work, she swerves at the last second and bicycles to Han's apartment. Just before she knocks, she holds her breath and presses her ear to the door. Does she hear voices? She knocks and the interior sound seems to hush. She calls his name. No one answers.

*

All day, Sirine waits for Han to appear. She calls twice during her breaks and there's no answer. Every time the phone rings, she looks up, but it's never Han. It seems she can still taste Aziz on her lips. She squeezes the handle on her frying pan till her knuckles ache, one thought in her head: *Han knows.*

That night, Sirine stays late at work hoping that Han will still come or call her. Tomorrow is the start of Ramadan, a month of daily fasting, broken by an *iftar,* a special meal after sunset and a bite before sunrise. Han has told her that the idea behind the fast of Ramadan is to remind everyone of the poor and less fortunate, a time of charity, compassion, abstinence, and forgiveness. And even though Um-Nadia claims to have no religion and many of their customers are Christians, they all like to eat the traditional foods prepared throughout the Middle East to celebrate the nightly fast-breaking during Ramadan. There are dishes like sweet qatayif crepes and cookies and creamy drinks and thick apricot nectar. Sirine decides to distract herself by looking up some of the more unusual dishes in honor of the month. She stays up late that evening, mixing batters and thumbing through old recipes, until she realizes that the moon has set and it is hours later than she had planned to go home.

Her bicycle is parked in the kitchen courtyard. The moon looks heavy and luxurious, almost full, and there is a dense drizzle that disperses a salty fish scent through the night. She pedals as fast as she dares, afraid of skidding, and sometimes the edges of sidewalk-planted palm trees scrape at her face and soak her hair and hands, the street puddles flinging mud up to her knees. She's riding back to Han's house.

She turns the corner and notices several blocks ahead a couple strolling together under the streetlights. Their backs are toward her, but there's something about the way they move, a familiar tilt of the head, a swing of the arm, that is enough to make her slow down, squeezing her hand brake and squinting through the mist. She gains a little more ground on them and it comes to her that she is looking at Han, and that the person at his side is covered in a head scarf and black robe. The water thickens the air, refracting the light; she can't see clearly. She catches her breath. They appear to be holding hands.

It seems the air itself has turned liquid, impossible to breathe, impossible to see through. The couple's hands appear to touch, then separate. They incline toward each other, then move apart—at one moment vaguely formal and aloof, in the next playful and familiar as lovers.

Sirine dismounts and walks closer with her bicycle, silently easing forward. Her feelings are molten, a pure, ancient heat, like nothing she can ever remember feeling before. She is shaking and sweating. The couple turn toward each other and seem to stop. Sirine stops, squeezing her handlebars, three blocks away, her whole body shaking, the night around her as cold and gray as lead. His hand seems to go to the woman's face. He lowers his head. It's hard to see. Are they kissing? Could such a thing be happening? The streetlights seem to get brighter and more intense, a blue and white flash, and suddenly Sirine senses the terrible delicacy of their bodies, of her own body, her knees trembling, her skin just a membrane of sugar; she looks down at her own hands, knuckles white on the bars, pale and tiny as starfish.

She thinks: he belongs with this woman.

She waits alone under the drizzling streetlight long after they've walked away.

*

She thinks about going to her uncle's house, to her bedroom with the shining sleigh bed, with the window at the foot of the bed, with the one nightstand, with the linen drapes, with the little dog waiting at the center of the bed. But she doesn't want to go back there. She waits until almost all she can feel is the damp and the cold in her bones and then she climbs onto her bike at last and goes to Han's apartment.

It's well past midnight but she doesn't knock and she doesn't listen for voices. She lets herself in with her key. If the woman is there now, at least then Sirine will see her face. But when she opens the door Han is sitting alone cross-legged in the corner, surrounded by books and pages of translation notes. He's not looking at any of it. Sirine is at once both relieved and oddly disappointed. She hears the intricate currents of sound in the corners of the room: he is listening to the beautiful Lebanese singer. He looks up when Sirine enters, but doesn't seem surprised. He looks at her slowly and dreamily, as if only half-recognizing her. Then he smiles, pushing himself up off the ground with one hand. "Habeebti, I was so lost in the music. For a moment I thought you were someone else."

She is panting and shivering. She notes that his hair is dry and he is wearing a dry, white sweater: the man she saw under the streetlights had on a dark suit. Had he changed his clothes?

"Han." Her hair and jeans drip a small crescent on to the floor. "I'm sorry it's so late. I got lost in this old recipe book, I got so involved in the descriptions, and I—I . . ." She trails off, staring at Han. Then she says, "You didn't call me all day."

"I know, I know, I wanted to, but . . ." He fans his hand over his books and papers. "Students have been hounding me over their finals. I finally slipped out of the office and spent the day hiding in the library, working." He holds out his arms to embrace her, then exclaims, "You're soaked!"

She steps back. "I thought I saw you."

"You were in the library today?"

She looks down. "I thought I saw you outside, walking home. With another woman." She waits and hopes he will speak. She tries not to say anything more but then she does anyway: "You were kissing."

"Kissing! I was? Kissing who?" His face is clear, wide, and open. He moves toward her and his hands slide around her shoulders, gently, as if she were a glass bird. She wills herself not to move. He draws her up close and kisses her and lowers his face into her hair.

She tries to back away. "Han—"

He lifts his head. "I've been thinking about you all day. I was going to call you as soon as I got back but I hadn't realized how late it was and the café was already closed. I still sat up hoping that you would come over." He runs his hands over her arms. "You're so cold!" The heat from his palms is dry and soft.

But she pulls out of his grasp. "It looked just like you."

"Sirine, you can't be serious. How could I ever kiss another woman?" he says. He encircles her with his arms, his breath warm and intimate. "How could I kiss anybody but you? I'm yours. I'm utterly lost to you."

She frowns, stares at his stacks of papers.

"Come on." He leads her into the kitchen. "Look what I bought for you today." There are small bags on the counter. She opens them and looks inside before reaching in: chocolate-covered almonds, a bottle of lavender-scented wine, a small silver fish with a blue eye on a silver chain. "To keep you safe," he says, handing her the amulet. "See? The blue helps protect against the Evil Eye. And fish, of course, are good luck."

*

They go to bed, just a few hours left in the night, and Sirine lets him hold her inside the arc of his arms. She lies in a state of half-sleep for some time, replaying what she thought she saw in the street—the set of the man's shoulders, the back of his head—wasn't it Han? His bedroom closet door is half-open and she sees the dark, block shapes of suits. If she touched them would one of them be damp? She feels crazy and guilty and turned around. Everything she sees seems to be distorted by her own guilty conscience. She considers waking Han and telling him about kissing Aziz. But she thinks she doesn't have the courage. She argues with herself over what to do, and eventually she drifts into a half-dream, a childhood memory: the image of the African girl on the TV set, the way Sirine held her arm against the little girl's arm on the screen, comparing the difference in their color. She tries to say something to the little girl; she knows there is something important that she must tell her.

CHAPTER TWENTY-THREE

Curled on the cool stone floor of the cave, the dog Napoleon-Was-Here pressed against her legs, Aunt Camille listened to the mermaid Queen Alieph talk about her life in the ocean and her home on the rocky, fantastical Land of Na.

"It was essentially a mundane, domestic life. We spent all our time sewing clothes that we couldn't wear and tricking and tormenting sailors. But then one day all that changed for me."

Alieph reached back and produced a fat, water-warped book from a shelf inside her cave. "I found this," she said, "in one of our shipwrecks." It was a tattered volume of the work of Herman Melville. "I'd seen chests of gold doubloons and yellow sapphires and turquoise rubies, but nothing quite like this before. I didn't know what it was, so I brought it to a narwhale friend, who, with his blackboard pointer built right into his forehead, is the most scholarly and learned of all fish. I had already learned the language of the whales, of the jellyfish, and of the seahorses, and the narwhale grudgingly agreed that I should understand both sides of my nature—the oceanic and the terrestrial—so he was the one who taught me how to speak and read Arabic."

"I was wondering where you got that accent," Camille said.

"Yes, everyone thinks I'm from Malta!" she said, slapping her fish-thigh, and the two of them got a rise out of that. At last, Alieph sighed and checked that her thick spindles of hair were covering all the necessary parts. "I left my sisters and my land," she said. "Because after the narwhale and I read that book I realized that in my heart of hearts I was a poet, not a shipwrecker. I came here to try and write but people keep bothering me about special favors. Half of them are working on their novels, the other half on their memoirs. No one ever wants to see what I'm working on, so when I get impatient I end up luring them onto nonexistent ledges where they plummet to their deaths. The poor men—they're especially easy to lead astray. One needs only to call and they follow."

"Well, I'd love to see what you're working on!" Camille announced.

Alieph's face lit up. "Oh no, not really," she demurred. But when Camille insisted, Alieph's cheeks filled with blood and her oceanic eyes gleamed. So they went into the cave and passed a delightful day, reading and commenting on Alieph's poetry. Camille made some editorial suggestions, as the narwhale had taught Alieph a highly idiosyncratic punctuation and grammatical system. They drank cups of thick seaweed tea and munched on cuttlefish fritters with squid ink sauce and at the end of it, Alieph said, "You know, no one has ever asked so many questions about me before. I have thoroughly enjoyed myself and I have decided not to kill you after all. Instead I shall tell you exactly how to get back to your home and your bad, bad son Abdelrahman Salahadin, and you will tell him to work on reforming his wicked ways." Because even though Aunt Camille never once mentioned the reason for her journey to Alieph's cave, mermaids and sirens always know the unspoken wishes in people's hearts.

Alieph pointed out a winding, hidden back way, a path that snaked across sandy outcroppings and threaded through weeds and hid under streams and climbed over boulders. It looked wild and treacherous and impassable, with brambles and briars and sharp rocks and hidden rivers, but this was their one and only chance. Camille and Napoleon-Was-Here and the blue Bedu all braced themselves and then they went into the golden bush. After seven days and nights of bad spills, itchy rashes, cuts and scratches, and nasty bug bites, they found themselves at an isolated, wind-blown station for the Transjordan train, the train that would take all of them all the way home again.

*

Um-Nadia has Victor Hernandez stand on the shaky ladder and string Christmas lights around the inside of the café. She stands beneath him, giving a lot of instructions ("That doesn't look like Christmas that way. Put it higher—*higher*—make it go in circles") and holding the slump-legged ladder in an offhanded manner, so it wobbles every time he reaches up with another length of wires. Finally, Mireille comes out and nudges her mother out of the way and Victor looks down and smiles at Mireille. Mireille pretends not to notice, but then she can't help herself and smiles a tiny, one-sided smile up at him.

Nathan comes in. His hair is unwashed and stringy, his eyes dark as peppercorns. "I've been working nonstop," he tells Sirine and Mireille and Um-Nadia. He gives them black and white postcards. On one side is a grainy image of a child, hair flying and hands out, either running or about to fall. The other side announces a photo exhibit called "From a Small Village." "It's my term final project. The official one. The first one in the beginning of the year was just to warm up," he tells them. "It's starting in an hour. I was too shy to give these out to anyone till now."

Um-Nadia studies her invitation after Nathan leaves, then fans herself with it, watching him walk back up the street. "Poor thing. No color, no in-focus, no nothing. You can hardly even see what it is. It's like having a headache. Like Aziz with his no-rhyming poems. I keep telling Nathan he should go see my cousin Basil the plumber. He'll train him, get him rolling, the whole works." She studies the Christmas lights critically for a moment, then says, "All right, let's close the café and go to his party. It's a charity case."

*

Nathan's exhibit is being held in an orange brick box of a church that no one remembers noticing before. The tall, plastic-lettered marquee out front says: "Dynamo Church!" on one side and "The problem with taking mental notes is that the ink dries so quickly" on the other. It is located on one of the busiest stretches of Santa Monica Boulevard, without any sort of nearby parking, so Han and Sirine and her uncle and Um-Nadia zoom past it in Han's big car several times before finding a space on the street. They have to walk seven blocks from the parking space to the church, Um-Nadia in a teetering pair of high heels that she insists were not made for walking in. When they get there, they see a xeroxed sheet of paper announcing the photography exhibit nailed to the front door. "Look," says Sirine's uncle, "Martin Luther was here."

Inside it smells of glue and drywall, as if the building had been constructed that morning. The decor is spartan: a teal-colored linoleum floor, several wooden folding chairs scattered around, and a blackboard up front haunted by the ghosts of erased words: "Success! How to be the CEO of your SOUL!"

There's a series of matted black and white photographs on the walls. A few graduate students linger in front of the wine table clutching plastic cups. Nathan stands at the center of the room holding a plastic cup of Lambrusco and talking to an elderly woman in a magenta wool coat and a mink stole with a hinge-jawed head biting its flank. "Hello!" she says to Sirine's uncle cheerfully. "I'm Dewey. I just came in to see what these young church people had gotten up to today. Every day it's different. Always something. Take a look at these lovely photographs. They're very, very different. Very unusual and artistic-looking. My granddaughter is a photographer too, you know, for the LaBrea High student paper."

Sirine's uncle confers with Dewey while Sirine and Han and Um-Nadia go over to look at the photos. Um-Nadia just glances at one or two before whispering to Sirine, "This is bad news. No improvement at all! I don't know what can be done."

But Sirine finds that she likes the images very much, they're perverse and revealing and even a little pretty. The first shots seem to be of food—rows of crinkling onions at a stand, some people holding up a massive watermelon, and the back of a woman's head and shoulders as she bends over a bushel of walnuts at what looks like a street fair or a farmer's market. Sirine is trying to get a closer look when she hears Han make a muffled sound beside her. He's gazing at a shot of children running in the street. The camera seems to hover twenty feet above them; their hands are outstretched, the silk of their hair flying, and one boy is looking straight up, a fierce accusatory expression on his face.

"How odd," Han murmurs, tilting his head. "Look at how he looks at you." He moves on but Sirine lingers over this and then several more photographs of children—a boy holding a surprised rooster, two little girls in front of two cats. The images aren't at all charming: the animals look matted and filthy, one cat seems to be missing an ear. There are many photographs of adults as well: a woman with bruised-looking eyes leans intently toward the camera; an elderly woman lifts one hand. There are no horns, mysterious fish tails, or floating smiles—but there is something disturbing in the mood of the shots, an ingrained murkiness, rolls of smoke on the horizon, descending from the sky. The faces look wan and starved, the cheeks sunken, eyes like black marbles. All of them peering out as if gazing through the print at the world. As if knowing the onlooker, in some more comfortable place, could sense her complicity as she stared back.

A few more visitors file into the small church, clutching their invitations uncertainly.

"Hello, everyone?" Nathan says in a loud, crowd-gathering voice, though there are only ten people in the room. He stands on a chair. "Yes. I'd like to make a speech? This won't take long." He blushes suddenly and intensely; he looks down as if regretting the decision to stand on the chair. "Um. Maybe *speech* isn't exactly the right word here. Okay, a confession. More of a confession-speech."

"All right, go ahead and say it," Sirine's uncle says from the side.

"Well, first I'd like to thank the Dynamo Church for their progressive vision and support of my project. Um. I'd like to thank Pink Dot for their donation of thirty-five plastic cups—"

Sirine's uncle makes a funnel with his hands and says into it, "Where's the speech?"

Nathan glances at him. "Yes. Okay, then." He takes a deep breath. "So, when I was twenty-one, I didn't know about the world at all. But I had this idea about cowboys and Indians and submarine commanders and Russian spies. I used to be unhappy because I thought that all the bad guys were already caught and there wasn't much excitement left in the world. And then one day I went to see *Black Sunday*. You know—the one with Bruce

Dern where the terrorists take over the Goodyear Blimp? But I came home thinking, oh, good, there's still terrorists!

"So I thought of that as my mission. I mean, don't we all want to have missions? I started dreaming of going to someplace like Lebanon or Iraq and hunting down terrorists." He hangs his head a moment and laughs sheepishly. Everyone remains silent. He lifts his head again and looks around. "You know, like James Bond?" He looks around. "I mean, doesn't everyone want to be like James Bond?" He pauses a moment and Sirine's uncle sighs. "Okay, well, anyway. I had this thought about going over to the Middle East and uncovering terrorist spies. I would take their photos and send them to the C.I.A. or someplace. Long story short, I graduated from college, got over that whole idea, and instead I just decided to travel and take photographs of what I saw.

"And when I finally got there, you know, to the Middle East, I traveled through all these different countries, and this amazing thing happened—the people there were really nice to me. They didn't drive around in huge cars talking to each other on phones. They invited me right into their homes. We sipped tea and talked all day long. Maybe to you that sounds boring, but to me, I felt like I'd finally found something real. Like I'd regained my senses. I ended up taking pictures of a really beautiful world. A very, very lovely and complete place. There were terrible sights to see—starving children and poverty and broken buildings—but today's exhibit is meant to be a celebration of the beauties I found and my own process of education. I never found my terrorist, though, unless"—he hitches one eyebrow, lowers his voice ominously—"it was me."

"Okay, nice speech! Nice speech!" Sirine's uncle says, clapping. "Now it's over."

Everyone scatters quickly and goes to look at the photos. Nathan stands there a moment, then climbs down, saying, "I wasn't done."

Sirine returns to the photographs, looking for clues in the clothing or landmarks to tell her where these shots were taken. They're gray dreams, full of accusation and a lingering sense of emptiness. Sirine notices that the other people in the room seem to bend and look closely at the images, then quickly step back. The murmuring gets louder; people look unsettled.

Nathan drifts into place beside Sirine. She's studying a photo of a young woman in an orchard of silver leaves incandescent with light and rainwater. Smoke roils over the treetops. "Well?" he asks.

Her uncle pulls up on her other side. "This is a celebration?" he asks.

Nathan's knuckles brush the back of her hand and he quickly tucks his own hands up into his armpits. "They're wild," Sirine says. "They're hard to look at."

"Yes," Nathan says fiercely, ardently. "That's it, isn't it? This is exactly what Americans don't want to look at. They don't want to be made to *see*. They don't want to know what is happening out there." He gestures toward the door and several people look over. "What is done to others, in our name, for our sake, so we might live like this." He rolls his hands out to the sides as if he were surrounded by splendor.

Han is standing in front of another photograph of a young woman; she has a shawl that lifts from her shoulders like raven wings and the sky above her is the color of bone. He turns from the photo and says quietly, "Where did you get these?"

"Well, I—I want them to be universal, you see, not just limited to—"

"None of these people gave you permission, did they?" There's an edge in his voice. "Just like all your photographs—you just shot them without asking, didn't you?"

Sirine takes a short breath. "Han?"

"These people would never have agreed to let you do this!"

"But . . . you can see—" Nathan holds one hand toward the photos. "None of them is turning away from me or hiding or—"

"This is my cousin Lamia!" Han says, tapping the frame. "This woman, right here. She lived on our road. She was the daughter of my mother's youngest sister."

Nathan nods, puts one hand on his chest like a pledge. "Han—I was going to tell you—I thought you would like it—"

Sirine stares at the photograph, startled by this unexpected thing.

"This is an absolute violation," Han says loudly enough so several people look up. Sirine wants to touch his shoulder but she's also afraid. "It's a violation of her privacy and it's a violation of my family's privacy. I don't know what you hoped to accomplish by doing this. I don't know if you thought this was clever—some sort of practical joke—"

"No, please, Han!" Nathan pleads. "You don't understand."

"Nor do I wish to. It's not bad enough that your country is bent on systematically destroying mine? Must you also use my family for your personal amusement as well? Or is this strictly about advancing your career?" And then Han sidesteps through the group and leaves the church in six paces, its big front door dropping shut with a bang. Nathan's face is shocked red, his arms loose at his sides. All the air seems to have left his body. "I was going to tell him," he says. "I meant this to honor them." His voice is gray and toneless.

"My, my," says Dewey, the old woman. "There's a temper on that one."

"Arabs," Um-Nadia says, rolling her eyes.

Sirine glances once more at the photo of the woman in the field and scans the other images, wondering who else might be in these photographs. Then she goes outside.

The sky has grown overcast and the light looks satiny behind the clouds, flat and photographic. Han is walking down the street away from the church, away from their parked car. "Han!" she cries. "Han?"

He walks for another few paces. Finally he stops and pauses for a moment before turning around. A wily wind is kicking dust into the air and blowing his hair into his face. Sirine holds hers back with one hand. She walks closer to him and he stands there and waits for her, hard-eyed and still.

She tries to be casual, to not sound alarmed. "Han? Are you okay?"

He continues to stare at her, not speaking, traffic rippling around them, exhaust and soot blowing into the sky. His skin flashes, a metallic glint in his eyes. "Where is it?" he says.

She has trouble hearing him and moves closer. "Where is what?"

He looks at her, still waiting, then says, "The *scarf*. What did you do with the scarf I gave you? Why don't you ever wear it?"

Her mouth opens but she stammers, her voice rattling in her throat. "I guess—I just—I haven't had—"

"I want to know something," he cuts her off. "And I want you to tell me the truth. Can you do that much for me?"

She closes her mouth. Nods.

"Did you lose my scarf?"

She doesn't speak.

"I trusted you with that one thing. Just that one small thing, Sirine."

He looks away from her. "How could I have been such a fool?" His eyes return to her and now they are flat, sharp stone. "How could I have trusted something so precious with someone like *you*?"

Stunned, she opens her mouth again, trying to think of what to say—something, anything—but nothing comes. She can feel the traffic rumbling in the pavement and concrete beneath her feet. She stands silently for a moment, looking back at him. And then he walks away.

*

That evening, after she's had time to imagine a dozen different responses, Sirine calls Han's apartment, but there's no answer. She tries twice more before she goes to bed and barely sleeps that night, imagining Rana comforting Han in his book-lined office. She sees Rana's hand covering Han's, remembers the way the couple's faces seemed to flicker toward each other under the streetlights. Sirine replays the conversation she had with Han afterward and it seems that he had never explicitly denied being with Rana. She turns over and over in her bed and hears the laughter rising from the drawer in her nightstand.

The next day at the café everyone is talking about the way Han stormed out of Nathan's opening. All sorts of opinions and rumors move between the tables.

"He was puffed like a bull," says Um-Nadia. "Hair standing up like this. Eyes steaming. Everything."

"I heard he pushed over a table of wineglasses," one of the police officers says. "They said there was broken glass everywhere. And that he tore up some of the pictures."

"That could well be," Um-Nadia muses.

"Ma!" Mireille says. "They had plastic cups."

"What happened to Nathan?" The police officer asks.

Um-Nadia moves her hands, fingers spread, as if clearing away mist. "Gone. The poor thing melted away from shame."

Sirine is so tired she works in an almost hallucinatory state. The bottles and containers in the kitchen hum as if there are insects inside them, the empty bushes in the garden of birds seem to twitch, and she feels the customers stare until she looks back and then they glance away. By the end of her day, when she senses someone is standing in the courtyard staring at her through the dark kitchen window—she has to look twice before she realizes he's actually there.

It's Aziz. He is waving, carrying a basket of apples that glimmer bronze in the porch light. She tugs open the window over the sink and Aziz holds up his basket. "I come bearing fruit!"

Sirine looks again despite herself: the apples are so lustrous they look like something from a fairy tale. She goes out and sits on the back porch where the moon is twice as big as usual and Aziz sits beside her, the basket of apples on his lap. She hasn't seen him since the night of the dervishes. And the kiss. She holds one of the apples in both hands and studies it to avoid looking at his eyes.

"How have you been, my dear?" he asks. "I have the sneaky feeling that you've been avoiding poor Aziz—you don't have to answer. You can just say yes or no."

She bites her lips. "I'm in trouble with Han," she blurts out.

"What? You are? That's not right! How could that be?"

"Did you see him on campus today?"

He thinks for a moment. "No. Which is unusual. No matter how I might hide and seek at that big overgrown school, Han always finds me. I suppose he would say I always find him. Even when I don't know that I'm looking."

"Was Rana around?"

"Ra—" His eyes widen. "My student? How do you know Rana?" He scrutinizes her more closely. "Wait a second. What are you asking me here? What is going around in your mind?" He reaches for Sirine's apple but she holds it away.

"I thought these were for me," she says.

"Yes, but this one is the sweetest. Look." He slips it out of her hand and bites into it. "I'm just taking one bite all the way on this side here. It's like the other side of the planet. That way our lips will never touch." He returns it to her.

She looks at the apple a moment, then looks back. "So was she?"

"In class?" He shrugs. "Come to think of it, nobody threw anything at me today. So no, I don't believe Rana was in today."

Sirine bites into the apple, then Aziz takes another bite on his side. She gazes into the bushes across from them, wagging in the wind.

"So—you think that means exactly . . . what? Han isn't around, Rana is out, hence and so they're having an affair?" he asks.

His eyes reflect windowpanes of moonlight. He looks patient, even kind. Sirine takes a deep breath and says, "I think Han is really mad at me. Because I lost something he gave me. And . . . maybe because of some pictures he saw—and now I don't know where he is—and all of a sudden everything is awful and it's just getting more and more and more awful!"

Mireille pokes her head out the door. "Sirine—is everything all right? Oh." She stops short at the sight of Aziz.

Aziz waves her back inside. "We've got the entire situation under control."

Mireille scowls at him. "You have exactly nothing under control, my friend," she says archly, and waits until Sirine waves and nods to her before she goes back in.

"All right." He stands briskly. "You've been working too much and this place is boiling your brains. Come." He pats his pockets and fishes out some car keys. "We need a scenery vacation."

Sirine stands and peeks through the lit square of the back door window: Mireille is phoning in orders; Victor and the cleaning man are mopping floors. The café is closed for the night; she should go back in and prepare for tomorrow, mix the dressings and sauces and marinate the kabobs. But she also feels as if none of it really matters at all, the work will all get done—tonight or tomorrow or the next day. No one notices. She can work for hours on a dish that will be eaten in minutes. She feels she could walk away right then and there and never return and no one would even notice.

She stands.

They leave the basket of apples on the back porch. And one apple core.

*

The ocean is so bright under the glimmerglass moon that Sirine can see everything. There are scatterings of young Mexican couples curled together on the beach, listening to radios or watching the water; a webbing of taut moonlit fishing lines radiates from all along the pier. It's been years since Sirine has been to the beach at night and seen its transformation. It makes her sentimental, thinking of night excursions with her parents to the beach, the foam white as curd against the black waves. And it reminds her of the night in the pool this past autumn, when she went swimming with Han.

They walk slowly along the beach just above the reach of the waves for nearly an hour, saying little, just listening to the murmuring ocean, until they reach the wooden pier. Then they turn and walk all the way out to the far end of the pier until they can go no farther and lean against the railing. Sirine sees a current of fish in the water, sparkling like gold coins. Aziz props his elbows on the railing. "This is where I like to come when I need to do some big thinking. Or if I feel poetical."

The moonlight is thick and milky. She can see glistening red threads in Aziz's hair, and the black disks of his irises at the surface of his eyes. There's a wind that simmers up, then dies down and swirls in her hair; she brushes it out of her eyes. Finally he says, "Sirine, you know I have nothing but respect for you. My feelings for you are pure and refined." He looks at Sirine timidly. "And naturally I feel the same way about Han, he's an extraordinary being. He seduces you with his goodness and his quietness and the next thing you know, you're telling him your deepest secrets every second of the day." Sirine leans over the railing. "You've simply fallen under his spell. It's natural. You're just an American and you've got no natural defenses."

"Aziz," she says. "I really don't think—"

He holds up one hand, then drops his fingertips, trailing them along the curve of her arm. "Do you know the story of the zebra and the virgin?"

"You mean the unicorn and the virgin?"

"Yes. Same thing. The zebra with his sad, romantic eyes, he can't speak. He can only look sad and romantic all the time, so all the single virgins who are crazy for that sort of thing get caught by him and taken away in cages and he keeps them in his house."

"I don't think that's how it goes," she says, but the brush of his fingertips along her inner arm is coaxing and the ocean air sways around them under the voluptuous moon. The jellyfish tendrils spiral at the surface of the water, and everything is so big and bold, it presses up against her and awakens her senses like anemones to the whirling sea.

"Why are you here with me?"

"I wish Han were here right now," she says, looking down.

"So do I." He holds her hair away from her face. "Now I know how the poor zebra feels around all that terrible beauty, unable to speak and unable to run away."

Some Mexican fishermen with transistor radios and buckets full of bait and catch walk by. She holds her breath until they move past. Then she looks up and Aziz's face is close to hers. She notices the fine, precise shape of his eyes, black as Han's and for the moment just as vulnerable; his lips are full and crescent-curved. She feels light-headed with the lilt of his breath on her face and she feels herself sliding, weakening, intoxicated with the pleasure of attraction. The wind picks up and roars over the water.

She puts her hands on the railing, tries to hold on to the plain, silvery smooth wood. She holds as still as she can, even when he lifts his fingers to her face and she can feel the vibration of desire begin its delicate tattoo, rising to the surface of her skin. She takes another breath and lets its long, steady force settle her.

For a moment they simply watch the waves wind and unwind, surf breaking into backwash. And then she lets go of the railing. Aziz holds out his hand and Sirine takes it. The wind picks up, full of sparkling points of rain; they lower their heads and run. The car is warm and close with the smell of damp wool and breath and somehow her hand stays inside his. She lets Aziz take her back to his studio apartment in Culver City. Her mind is blank as a window shade. The rain shuffles and rattles against the windows and streams down in beads. They kiss, then make love on a couch that pulls out into a bed, and the sound of the city traffic drowning out her thoughts. Afterward, the warmth of the sheets draws her into a half-sleep. She dreams of being lost in a dense forest where thundering footsteps come rushing toward her, and she wakes with her heart hammering, disoriented by the slippery pillows and their spicy perfume. She wakes Aziz and makes him drive her back to her uncle's house even while he tries to talk her into spending the night.

"Probably we shouldn't let Han know about us right now," Aziz says tentatively as he pulls up in front of the house. "You know these Arab guys. They get jealous and murder people with their bare hands."

She grabs the door handle. "This will never. Ever. Happen again," she says and refuses his handshake. She runs into the house, and takes a steaming shower and rubs at her skin with a hand towel until it stings all over, her pale skin turning rosy. Then she sits stony-eyed in her bedroom window for hours before falling asleep.

*

She answers the phone out of instinct; it's six-thirty, she's had an hour and a half of sleep. "Mm?" she says.

"Sirine? *Rouhi*, is that you? I wanted to catch you before work."

"Han?" She pushes herself up in bed.

"Aziz just called and said you liked my apology."

She catches her breath and the whole night comes back to her, thunderous then leaden; a sickening sensation, like being awakened by nausea. The physical memory of the softness of his mouth. The wrong mouth. She closes her eyes, inhales deeply through her nose.

"Sirine?"

"I—I'm here."

"So you liked it? The basket of apples? I saw them at the farmer's market and thought they were prettier than roses."

"Apples?" The bronze-colored apples. She recalls their juice, the cool snap between her teeth. "But—Aziz—"

"I was afraid if I brought them myself . . . I don't know. I thought you'd still be mad. So he volunteered to do it for me. I didn't dare call you, I felt so bad about the other day. I can't even explain myself in a way that I can understand. Maybe it was like being possessed. What is it that Americans say: something came over me?"

"Oh, Han." She covers her eyes with her hand. "It's all right."

"I keep going over it—yelling at Nathan and you and storming out of there like that. I thought—it's crazy—but I wasn't ready to see those images. It was such a shock—to see my cousin's face like that. I wasn't expecting it. I hadn't seen her or any of my family in twenty years. And there she was, and it was like I'd just left yesterday. She and her mother and sisters came to our house the night I left and they gave me some bread and olives. That was the last time I saw any of them until Nathan's exhibit. It startled me so that I didn't know how to react. But later, when I calmed down enough to think about it . . . I realized how moving it was to me—to see her again, after all these years."

She makes a sound, then stops herself: she wants to confess.

"Sirine," he says. "Do you forgive me?"

"Han." Her throat feels snagged. She takes a breath. "There's nothing to forgive. Not for me anyway," she adds quietly, a sort of pulse inside the movement of her voice. She hears a tapping outside her windowsill and looks up, startled. A redheaded bird is pecking at the frame, its wings open and fluttering. She says, "Han, about the scarf—I didn't—I—"

"No, no," he says. "Don't even say anything. Sirine, none of it matters. That scarf was just a thing. If you lost it or not, things are things and that's it. A scarf is a scarf is a scarf, right? You, on the other hand, are the whole world."

CHAPTER TWENTY-FOUR

Did I ever tell you about the way your auntie Camille once offered a necklace of tears to the Queen of the Camels to carry her to the confluence of the Tigris and the Euphrates? Because everybody knows that the difference between people and animals is that animals can't cry and people can. But the Queen of the Camels refused because that particular confluence is considered by some to be the cradle of civilization, the place where Adam and Eve lost their innocence, and hence the place where the camel first took up her burden.

To recap: Aunt Camille gave birth to my felonious cousin Abdelrahman Salahadin, who sold himself to slavers and escaped by faking his drowning in the Red Sea. She tracked him down by seducing the terrible Sir Richard Burton. She walked to the source of the White Nile, conferred with the Mother of All Fish, struck deals with jinns and mermaids and the blue-skinned Bedouin tribe.

And did you also know that when Camille was an old, old, *old* lady and finally learned to read and write, she discovered that her naughty son Abdelrahman had changed his name and moved to California? I'll tell you what happened. Remember the part where the blue-skinned Bedu are all talking about Hal'Awud and Dar'Aktr? That was in 1960.

In 1959 a director came to Wadi Rum, in the south of Jordan, to think about how he would film his new film called *Ben-Hur*. Of course it all ended up getting filmed in Italy, with American-type actors. But he had this idea to use all sorts of local Arabs to ride through his big war and caravan scene. He discovered the handsome Crazyman al-Rashid shoeless in Wadi Rum— this was before the Crazyman had been kidnapped by the sirens in Aqaba. The director invited al-Rashid to be in his movie, along with several Bedu tribes he'd relocated for extras. Their part, of course, ended up on the cutting room floor. But anyway, this was the start of the Crazyman's obsession with angels and flaming chariots, lights, and cameras, and action—all of which he described to Abdelrahman Salahadin while they were both prisoners of the mermaids.

So what happened to Abdelrahman?

Abdelrahman Salahadin may or may not have been the true name of the movie star Omar Sharif. We'll simply never know for sure. But who really knows anything for sure in this strange and notorious world?

Omar Sharif!

Mm-hm.

And all that talk, that Dar'Aktr and Hal'Awud, those were . . .

Arablish. Dar'Aktr is Arablish for *director* and Hal'Awud is—

Hollywood.

Yes. And when the blue Bedu talked about Ar-Rashad Bur'aton, they weren't talking about the English explorer and slave owner Sir Richard Burton, they were talking about the Welsh, drowned-Arab of an actor, plain old Richard Burton, who also happened to be hanging around on the set, since he was about to start in his great role in a different movie as Marc Antony, and wanted to take in a little desert atmosphere. They just got the words all scrambled up. You see, the Bedu can never leave well enough alone. They love to improvise, improvise, improvise!

*

At the café, Sirine and Um-Nadia become preoccupied with the special *iftar*—or fast-breaking—menu for the month of Ramadan. Muslims all over town hear about it and more customers crowd in, loitering outside and waiting for tables—Iranians, Saudis, Palestinians, Lebanese, even Malaysians, Pakistanis, and Croatians. They come early in the morning, before sunrise, then later after the sun goes down and the day's fast ends, ordering special treats like killaj pastry, qatayif pancakes, zalabiyya fritters, and ma'mul cookies. Sirine no longer has time for anything but cooking and baking. She thinks, in brief, unguarded moments, about what happened between herself and Aziz. She hasn't told anyone—and prays that Aziz won't either—but she carries the thought of it around with her, like a wheeze in her breath. Her anxiety is a bone stuck in the center of her body. Um-Nadia and Mireille treat her like she's sick; they keep a discreet distance, watching her in worried glances.

They get so busy, Victor Hernandez starts to help out as a sous chef, chopping up bowls of onions and garlic and peppers, making salads and mixing marinades. He brings in a bagful of chili peppers one day, some long and narrow and shriveled as old fingers, some petite and glossy as young fingers. He roasts them under the broiler and in a dry skillet, then slides off the charred outer skins. And Sirine uses slices of the soft inner hearts puréed into the baba ghannuj and marinades for the kabobs.

"They say that pepper is good for love," Victor tells her, then raises his eyebrows at Mireille, who turns pink. "It brings heat to the blood."

But Sirine accidentally smears some of the chili oil on her fingers and they burn even through her calluses. She runs cold water over her fingers till her bones ache.

*

Han apologizes to Sirine all week long, bringing her gorgeous fruits with spikes and horns, edible peels and blood-red seeds, baskets of berries from the other side of the world. But the presents only increase her guilt and anxiety, so by the end of the week she can barely eat anything, her stomach knotting against food. He can tell that she's unsettled and he asks if it's because of the scene at Nathan's exhibit, or the fact that he didn't call her right away, or because she thought she saw him with another woman, or some other reason altogether. All of which she denies. One day, after serving the tremendous *'id* meal that celebrates the end of Ramadan (including a whole stuffed lamb, baklava, and knaffea pastry with sweet cheese), she comes out of the café on a break and discovers that there are branches of scented jasmine and flowering bougainvillea twined and wired around the rim of her bicycle basket. She laughs for the first time in days, and when she bicycles to Han's apartment that evening she picks up the scent of cooking food from all the way down the hall. He stands waiting for her in the doorway.

It is like the first night of their love affair again. There are plates of food set out on a blanket on the floor of his living room. Even an azure cotton tablecloth and a pitcher of yellow daisies, a fragrant steam in the air.

She stands above the setting. "What's going on? What is all this?"

Han takes her hands, turns and kisses them. He says, "A simple offering." He seats her on the floor and flourishes one hand over the food. "An *'id al-iftar* for the Queen of Sheba."

"And her army," Sirine says. There is a platter of Moroccan chicken tagine with preserved lemons, couscous studded with pistachios and currants, rice covered with butter-fried almonds. "This is incredible. I didn't know that you could cook like this."

"Well . . ." Han seats himself across from her. "I can't. But it turns out that Um-Nadia can."

"I can't believe it. She never cooks anymore."

"She brought all the ingredients over today and I helped her," he says. "Well, I chopped things. Are you impressed?"

"*Impressed* is not even the word. . . ."

"I wanted to try to do something." He gazes at her helplessly, touches her fingers. "You've been working too hard. You look thin and tired, Hayati."

"Oh, Um-Nadia's always worried. She must've told you that."

He ticks his head back. "I can see for myself."

Han fills Sirine's plate and feeds her a morsel of lamb from his fingers, as if food is their private language. They talk about school and work. The words flow into the eating. And she eats and eats. The flavors are intense in her mouth, the sweet-almondy fruitiness of the pistachios beside the smoky sour taste of the sumac, delicate saffron, and herbal notes of olive. Her stomach starts to ache, unused to so much food. Han eats little himself, instead bringing bites of meat and spoonfuls of rice to her mouth.

When, finally, she cannot eat another bite, she sits back, laughs, and fans herself with one hand. Han will not let her help with the dishes; he tells her to relax, relax, and begins stacking everything himself, the dishes clattering.

She sits back against the wall and watches the stars from the balcony doors awhile: their fine heat and color seem to pass right through her. Some of them glitter and some of them wither or wink out into the darkness. She stretches, then carries some dishes into the kitchen, where Han stands in front of a sparkling pyramid of suds.

"Did you want to save the rice?" she asks.

But his back is to her and the water's running. When he doesn't respond, she puts down the dishes and goes into the bathroom; she washes her face and smoothes her unsmoothable hair. Adjusting the medicine cabinet mirror, she examines the clear green glass of her eyes, checks their corners for wrinkles, then notices how gray strands are starting in her hair, barely discernible against the blond. While she is looking, she notices a faint, fruity perfume. She frowns and inhales, and then it comes to her: the scent of ripe berries. Han's scarf. Eyes wide, she turns, inhaling, hands out like a sleepwalker. She checks the towels, looks under them, and sniffs. There are two worn towels folded on the glass shelf beside the shower, both embroidered with the initials "E.H." She looks in all the drawers and cabinets and even behind the shower curtain. But no sign of the veil. And then the scent begins to dissipate, as if it had all been in her imagination. She grips the sides of the sink with both hands and looks into the mirror and tries to will the fading scent back. Cold perspiration breaks over her forehead and she is struck, horribly, by a wave of nausea. She lowers her head, tries to breathe slowly. But her mouth floods with saliva and she flips up the toilet seat, then she is vomiting hard, her stomach clenching. Her shoulders bunch and her eyes stream and her nose runs and she is helpless to do anything but hold herself over the toilet. It shudders over her, knotting her stomach tighter.

When it finally passes, she sits down, then lies on the bathroom floor, presses her cheek to the cool tile. For some minutes she can't quite think or move, lost inside the hollow chamber of the bathroom.

Finally, she flushes the toilet and brushes her teeth and tongue twice. She has to come out and she feels miserable, thinking of the beautiful meal, wondering how to explain this to Han. But once in the kitchen, she sees he's had the water running all this time—he hasn't heard anything.

"Hayati," he says, smiling and taking her in his arms. He puts his nose to her hair and says, "Where were you?"

That night they make love; it is quick and silent. She feels frail, her bones are glassy and brittle inside her body, and her stomach feels caved in.

She has guiltily avoided sex with Han ever since the night she slept with Aziz. When they begin making love, Sirine feels herself frowning, as if she were concentrating on a dangerous, secret activity. She waits for him to detect her betrayal, to see it in her face. But he closes his eyes, his expression faintly imploring. She is surprised by how easy it is to do this, how available betrayal is. Afterward, she lies on her back and Han cradles her in his arms. She feels weak and loose-jointed. He touches her forehead and runs his fingers along her sternum, then runs his hand down to her stomach and the cradle of her pelvis bones and rests it there.

Later that night, somewhere lost between late night and early morning, the phone rings. Han gets it and she hears him speaking Arabic; he seems to be arguing with someone. She hears the words *Iraq* and *Baghdad* and at that moment rising out of the logic of dreams she feels with a startling clarity—the clarity of the obvious and the long-denied—that something is coming to claim him.

*

The next morning, Sirine sleeps through the alarm and when Han tries to wake her, she can barely open her eyes. He feels her forehead, then calls the café and talks to Mireille, who tells him to keep Sirine at home, she and Um-Nadia will cover for her. Sirine listens to Han and the muffled voice on the other side of the receiver and she knows that Mireille will be worried. It is the first time in nine years that Sirine hasn't come in to work. Han has to go to school but he pulls a heap of covers over her and stacks several Hemingway novels by the bed and then kisses her three times on the forehead. She listens to him pull the door shut behind him and thinks it will feel strange to be alone in his apartment without him. But then the sleepiness quickly reaches up like an undertow from the back of her head and pulls her back down.

When she wakes again, it is after one in the afternoon. She sits up in bed facing the balcony and watches the wind ruffling over rooftops and trees. It seems as if the silky palms are being swept around by a kind of light: she can see it glittering in the sky and rinsing over everything. She realizes slowly that it is raining. She sinks back into the blankets and listens to the drizzle, soft and dense as moss, furry over the roof; it fades and then builds until it sounds like it's seething. The apartment rings with the rain hiss. She takes in the odd emptiness of the things around her, Han's clothes hanging collapsed on their hangers, the bedsheets crumpled and half-warm on the bed. She enjoys the sense of such total isolation; it's a sweet, dull ache like a toothache that she wants to press against.

It will be her fortieth birthday this year. She closes her eyes and imagines that, instead of her fortieth, it will be her hundredth, imagines the loose fit of her skin and hair, her body floating away from her. Then she imagines her own deathbed, dying, the gentle ease of spirit from her bones, her body caving in and melting. First she feels fear and grief, the consciousness of pure oblivion, then that dissolves, turns into something almost pleasurable; some center of tenderness rises to the top of her solar plexus, as if she could feel the shape and outline of her own soul. She thinks of the billowing skirts of the whirling dervishes and is just starting to sink into this feeling when there's a knock at the door.

Sirine sits up and lights flash behind her eyes. She wraps herself in Han's bathrobe, creeps into the next room, and stares at the door. She pads toward the door, stopping partway, her pulse ticking so loudly in her ears she can barely hear. For a moment, she wonders if it's Rana knocking. Then there's the sound of a dog whining and snuffling and she says, "King Babar?"

Her uncle calls out, "Habeebti? Are you there? It's only us chickens out here!"

She opens the door and King Babar bounds in. She picks him up and he pushes his hard head against her face, licking her mouth and eyes and whipping his tail against her arms. "We were very concerned when we heard you'd called in sick. We decided to come check up on you."

They come in and her uncle looks around and says, "Where's the furniture? Habeebti, you're living like a Bedouin in a goat-hair tent."

Sirine is flustered and embarrassed. "Oh, I know, I'm sorry, there's nowhere to sit, really."

"It's all right," he says. "It's very interesting." But when he tries to sit on the floor, he makes a groaning noise and gets stuck about halfway down. He struggles back up.

"Wait." She constructs a chair and table out of stacks of Han's books. Before sitting, her uncle looks at them and says, "Let's see, *The Iliad* and *The Collected Works of Shakespeare*. That will do nicely."

She brews a pot of black tea with mint and finds a plate of date-stuffed cookies and sweet cheese knaffea pastry left over from last night. She brings out the cup and pot and pastries, and her uncle says, "Now, now, I won't eat without your company."

Sirine looks at the food; she knows she should be hungry. She stacks up her own book pile to sit on. "As you can see," she says, gesturing around the place, "I'm fine here."

Her uncle picks up a copy of *A Farewell to Arms,* squints at the title, then shakes his head. He sighs over his cookies then and says, "No, I'm glad—here you are, creating your life like you're supposed to. Of course, Babar and I miss you. It's a lonely business, eating alone. I never met that someone that I was meant to eat my dinners with. Not like—" and then he stops. Sirine waits, thinking he will say: not like your mother and father. But he doesn't finish his sentence. She looks at him closely. She always thought that her uncle and father looked alike, but over the years it seems that her uncle's features have come to replace the memory of her father's face. There are things that she doesn't like to see: the way his hair, once wavy black, has gone gray, and the old-mannish slip of his oval glasses down his soft nose, and the way his irises have lost pigment, turning tea-colored. There were times when she was still a little girl, after her parents had died, that she would forget, and call him *Baba,* "Father." Then he would hold her and say in his gentlest voice, "Now, Habeebti, don't forget, I'm your *Ummo.* Don't forget about your *Baba.*"

Sirine senses that her uncle knows more about love than he lets on. Like the flirtation he carries on with Um-Nadia—only going so far and then veering away. His life seems like an oasis of meditation and tranquillity, even though she knows this isn't fair, that he is a person like herself, after all, and there must be many things she has never known about his private life. And sometimes the thought comes to her that perhaps he never married because his life became entirely and unexpectedly taken up with raising a young girl. Just as Sirine never went to college or managed to marry, but devoted herself to learning to cook her uncle's favorite foods. She would like to ask her uncle what he really thinks of Han. If he believes that Han is a good man for her. But the questions are too personal. It seems they ask too much of her uncle.

Instead, she lets King Babar leap into her lap and strokes his head so the skin around his eyes widens, then relaxes, over and over. "Hello, my king," she says.

"Look at him," her uncle says. "He was a pasha in an earlier life. He was a rich and ruthless cross-eyed sultan and your slavishly devoted husband."

The dog's head is warm beneath her hand. She kisses the knob on top of his head and King Babar rests his chin on her knee. They sit quietly together for a while, sipping their tea, Sirine's mind taken up with unaskable questions.

*

When Sirine returns to work the next day, Um-Nadia follows her into the kitchen, looks her up and down, and finally she asks, "What's wrong with you?"

Sirine laughs nervously and finishes the last sip of her coffee. "I don't know what you're talking about," she says and leaves the porcelain cup on the counter by the stove. Then she fries the cauliflower, and she has just started layering the eggplant and carrots in the pot when she looks up to see Um-Nadia peering into her coffee cup, turning it and squinting as if she were studying a textbook: looking at the coffee grounds. "Um-Nadia," Sirine says, "no, please . . ." She reaches for it but Um-Nadia has already lifted her round, startled eyes. She holds up the cup and says, her voice hushed, almost reverent, "I never would have guessed it—there's another man!"

Um-Nadia pulls her into the back kitchen. She points to a chair and Sirine plunks down at the table. Her shoulders sag toward the chopping boards, the smells of onion, ginger, lemon, parsley. Um-Nadia draws a chair up close and Sirine tilts her cup, peeking in at the scattered coffee grounds inside the rim, their bits of dashes and curves that remind her of the lines of Arabic. "How do you do that?" Sirine says.

"That's nothing." She flips one hand back, then leans in. Um-Nadia's eyes are kohl-rimmed today with flaring edges. She slits her eyes to long black lines, crosses her legs and crosses her forearms over her knees. "Tell, tell, who have we here?"

Sirine closes her eyes. She stands, takes the cup to the sink, fills it with water, rinses it clean and puts it in the drain, then sits back down. "You can't tell Mireille or Victor." Um-Nadia makes a zipper motion over her lips. "It's Aziz," Sirine says.

Um-Nadia thumps her hand to her chest. "No."

"I mean, it was Aziz for two seconds. I don't even mean that. It was never Aziz. It's just that—I was going through a—a confusion about Han." She closes her eyes, sighs. "Aziz and me, we just had this one little thing just one night—it was so stupid and I wasn't even interested in him and I just... I don't know—he was being so *nice*—"

"Yes, yes, it's always these 'nice' ones."

Sirine traces the edge of a chopping board with her fingertip. "I haven't told Han yet. But I'm going to. I can't take it anymore, carrying the thing around in my head all the time. I'm just going to have to do it—"

"No!" Um-Nadia cries, her voice like a quill. "You mustn't do that at all, at all. It's much too dangerous. If you tell, either it will kill him or he will have to kill someone else."

"Kill somebody? Han?" Sirine says. "No—"

"Habeebti, you would not believe in ten million years what people are still like. Ask me, I know."

Sirine shakes her head. "Not Han. Never."

"Sure, sure, not Han. You think he's special pure. But still, even so." Um-Nadia slides her pack of emergency cigarettes out of the pocket in her housedress and knocks one out, turns it unlit between her fingers. "Remember the story about my friend with the bad husband? You know, where he keeps flying back and forth?"

"Oh, and when he dies of a heart attack, she finds out that he's been keeping another wife and family back in Yemen or someplace?"

"Right, so my friend... what did I say was her name?"

"Uh—Munira, I think."

"That's her. Yes. I remember, she was just exactly like you. You always make me think of her, you know that? She couldn't believe it either. She thought the world was one hundred percent modern. She thought that once you got to America, nothing bad could ever happen again."

"But her husband kept flying around."

Um-Nadia points the cigarette at her. Sirine can see where the shell-pink polish is frayed at the edges of her nails, traces of pink lipstick on the filter. "And you see how that all turned out."

Mireille pokes her head in the door, but she closes her mouth and steps inside when she sees Sirine's and Um-Nadia's expressions. She sits beside her mother at the table. "What's going on?"

"What happened to Munira?" Sirine asks Um-Nadia.

Um-Nadia looks at Mireille for a moment. She puts the cigarette back into the pack. "Well, she died."

"She died?" Sirine feels oddly stricken. "I didn't know. What happened? Was she old?"

"*Tch*." No.

"So—what?"

Again she looks at Mireille. Mireille tucks her chin onto the heel of her palm and says, "Her name wasn't Munira, it was Nadia. That story's about my sister Nadia."

Sirine sits back.

"She died of a broke-heart, a month after the husband went," Um-Nadia says. "She couldn't take knowing what she had to know."

"She had stomach cancer," Mireille says to Sirine.

"Where do you think it came from?" Um-Nadia asks Mireille angrily. "Do you think it just appeared in a puff of smoke like a jinn in a lantern? The husband gave it to her with his sneaking and lying and lying and sneaking. It was like living with a serpent and every night that she slept with the snake he put more of his serpent poison into her."

"Ma . . ." Mireille rubs her face with her hands. "We don't even know if it's true—about that secret family. We don't know if he even knew those people. He didn't have any pictures or letters or any signs of them at all. For all we know, that other woman was just a scam artist who wanted to collect his life insurance."

"I know what's true!" Um-Nadia stands up, scraping back her chair. Some of her hair falls out of its bun, her eyes red and wide, the lipstick edged into cracks around her lips. "I know exactly what's true. Don't you ever, ever tell me that I don't know. I am your mother and believe you me, I *know*."

CHAPTER TWENTY-FIVE

When Aunt Camille was a very, very old woman and I was a very, very young boy, we happened to be on the earth at the same time for a short period. She took that opportunity to tell me about my cousin Abdelrahman. She told me about his drowning career, and her search for her naughty son, and so on and so forth.

She told you herself? But, you mean they're true, those stories?

You're going to get philosophical on me? True, not true, real, not real. Who knows what's what?

But the people—the people in these stories, they existed?

Look at it this way: there is truth inside everything living and dying and more, you just can't always recognize it at first—like the innocent seed that starts the uninhibited *mejnoona* tree.

But Abdelrahman? He survived? He really went to Hollywood?

You know, there's an art to listening to a story—it requires equal parts silence and receptivity. Yes. There was an Abdelrahman; he was your great-cousin. Did he survive? Well, maybe he didn't drown, maybe he did. After all, there is a drop of the drowned Arab in all of us. I know I personally have a great deal of one in me.

So he died?

All right, let's talk about the theoretical end of the story. Since we're talking theory. And since it isn't healthy to abandon a story.

*

Every year at the end of the winter term, the university's Department of Ethnomusicology puts on its concert. It's a major event that draws Arab and American students as well as community people. The program chair, Mazen Mahmoud, is a celebrated Libyan oud player, and the program always features music from several Arab nations, including Morocco, Libya, Egypt, Palestine, and Syria. This year, the program says, the concert will feature instrumentals and singing, as well as classical and popular Arabic music, and concludes with an open dance.

Han and Sirine run into Aziz and Nathan at the auditorium. This is the first time Sirine and Han have seen Nathan since his photography exhibit and for a moment everyone is stiff and uncertain. Then Han holds out his hand and Nathan takes it and bows slightly and with dignity, but he is clearly relieved, Sirine can see that. Nathan's hair is slicked down stiffly—there are still channels in his hair from his comb—and he's wearing a corduroy blazer with suede patches at the elbows. He looks like a boy dressed up for his school picture. Han apologizes for the incident at the exhibit, and Nathan says, aghast, "No, please, it's all my fault," and embraces Han awkwardly, with one arm. Aziz is wearing what looks like a velvet smoking jacket with a tasseled belt and brown suede shoes. "This is me as an English poet," he says. Then he takes Sirine's hand and kisses it with ceremony before she can pull away.

"You know this is an important performance," Nathan says sternly.

"And there's dancing at the end," Aziz adds, showing them the program. "Of course this means we'll have to share Sirine."

She glares at him. "I don't know how to dance," she mutters.

"And neither do I," Han says, putting one arm across her shoulders. "So we're fated to be together."

It's open seating in the auditorium and already crowded but Nathan spots an open row. There's some uncertainty about who will be seated next to whom. They start down the row, then back out twice, switching places. Sirine wants to sit on the outside, next to Han, but she ends up seated between Han and Aziz with Nathan on the other side of Aziz. "When you finish your graduate degree," Aziz says to Nathan, "then you too will get to sit next to the beautiful woman."

Nathan folds his arms and looks away, his face dark.

Finally, the lights fall and the curtain opens, and there is a huge, multi-level orchestra of student and faculty musicians on stage. Mazen Mahmoud faces the audience brandishing a conductor's baton. The audience hushes expectantly.

The conductor swoops his baton through the air and the orchestra launches into the first number, violins sawing, flutes tilted, three men rippling their hands and fingers over their drums; it is pure drama and intensity. There are several instruments that Sirine has never seen before—Han whispers their names—kanoon, rebab, oud. Sirine marvels that these young students are proficient on such unusual instruments. She presses her shoulder against Han's, leaning into him and as far as she can maneuver from Aziz's arm and knee. She feels microscopically aware of both Aziz's and Han's bodies, the nearness of their skin, the rising of the hair on one arm, the invisible touch of a knuckle or an inch of thigh.

But as the night proceeds she is led away from herself, into the music itself. The songs are complicated and rhythmic, and they resonate for Sirine in the depths of her consciousness. She realizes that some of them are songs she remembers her father playing on his turntable, the stereo playing arm riding up and down with the waves in the records, her father singing to the music as the sound rose and fell. And even though she didn't understand the words, she still understood innately that the music was emotional and thrilling. All her uncle listened to was Italian opera, which seems, now that she thinks of it, not all that dissimilar. She sits forward into the listening, captivated by the theater of the performance, the energy of the sound that fills the air and vibrates up the floorboards and through her bones.

For the second half of the program, a young man sweeps onto the stage, receiving a thunderous ovation. The conductor introduces him as a well-known singer of *maqaams*—a traditional Iraqi song style. Han leans over and whispers, "I know his work—he's from Baghdad." The singer folds his hands in front of him, lifts his chin, the musicians wait, and then his song rises from him and shimmers over the audience, iridescent and longing. The young singers' topaz-colored, half-closed eyes seem to float with some inexpressible emotion. The song travels into Sirine, murmuring, blurring the sensations inside her.

As the songs continue they seem to stir up Aziz and Nathan as well. Aziz's knee travels a bit and bumps into Sirine's knee; she shifts both knees in Han's direction. Then there's some rumbling between Aziz and Nathan, their arms and shoulders pulling up; they fidget in their seats. At a quiet moment between songs, Nathan hisses, "Excuse me!" Someone in the row behind them shushes them.

When it's time for the last song, the singer steps forward to the front of the stage; he raises his hands as if cupping them to a candle and his voice rises, lambent, flickering, as if there were more than one voice inside him, as if it were originating from the earth or sky and merely moving through him, his body a flame delivering heat and light. The song is in Arabic, but Sirine closes her eyes and it takes her to a place where the sky is transparent, the trees have branches like black bones and canopies of pointed leaves. And in the distance of the song her imagination is released: she sees colors and shapes, imagines darkened figures emerging from a bend, their faces obscured, golden lanterns hanging from staffs, fireflies swirling over the earth.

When it is finished, she applauds hard, shaken and satisfied. But just as she is about to turn and search out her jacket and purse, the conductor returns to the microphone and says, "And now we will open the dance floor!"

The three men on tablah—hand-played drums—begin their tattoos, the violinists sweep their bows in unison, and the music speeds up. Now the singer sounds jaunty, almost American. Instantly people from the audience are out on the dance floor, their hands and arms twirling over their heads, hips tipping back and forth. One woman brandishes a white handkerchief over her head.

"This is fabulous!" Aziz says. "We've got to go up there. Come on, Han; if you don't take Sirine, I'm claiming her for myself."

"Why don't you leave her alone?" Nathan says.

A young man from Han's Arabic class leans over their row and interrupts, saying, "Professor, see? It's rock 'n' *rai* music." Han laughs and turns to him.

"Oh-ho," Aziz says to Nathan. "So she's bewitched you as well, I might've known."

"What's with you?" Nathan asks. "Don't you have any respect for anything?"

"Now we're on to respect all of a sudden? Please don't go getting religious on me, my friend. I believe you're the one who specializes in covert agent photography."

Nathan's face hardens. "You don't know anything about me."

"Why? What secret files have you opened on me?" Aziz says. "Get any good dirty pictures lately?"

Han veers back into the conversation. "What's all this?" he says.

Sirine swivels toward him and blocks his view of the two men, grabs his arms. "They're just being silly. Come on, do you want to dance?"

But as soon as they're on the floor she regrets it. The lights are sweltering and the audience rises in towering rows all around them. She tries twirling her hands over her head like the other women but feels self-conscious and wooden. Han smiles and claps with the other men; he circles her and doesn't look away. She tries to follow him, watching his feet and his eyes. And after a while she begins to feel easier, her body softer; she begins to think that she can dance. It feels a bit like the movements in her kitchen, flowing from the big stove to the sink to the counter, sidestepping Victor, passing plates to Mireille. She smiles and her anxieties start to subside. Men and women move around them in couples and she sees this is the way the world works—in close partnerships—something she's never really tried to attain, but it has found her anyway. A memory comes to her from far away—of sitting at a weather-beaten picnic table with her uncle, watching her parents dancing on the grass. Her mother's hair and full skirt ballooned around her knees and her father moved back a few steps—just as Han does now—watching and admiring.

She closes her eyes and knows she will not tell Han anything about her night with Aziz, because nothing at all happened. It's over and done. It was a folly, a last fling—before Han there had never been anything but flings. Now, she tells herself, she will learn a new way of being in love. She thinks: everything is going to be just fine.

But when she opens her eyes again, a veiled form approaches just behind Han's left shoulder.

"Hi, Sirine!" Rana calls out. "Hello, Professor! I never thought you guys would be here. Mind if I cut in?"

Sirine feels a thin sheath of sweat turn icy all along the inside of her forearms and down her spine. Han smiles, tilts his head, and looks at Sirine as if to say, well, what choice do we have?

Sirine swallows and backs up; she bumps into a couple of dancers and stops to apologize. When she looks around, Han and Rana have gotten pulled deeper into the dancing crowd, but she has no wish to return to Nathan and Aziz. She moves off the dance floor and watches from the side as Rana grabs Han's hands, interlaces her fingers with his, arches her back, and swivels her hips. Her scarf flies around her shoulders and Sirine notices, as Rana turns her head, that her scarf has an embroidered red border.

More dancers crowd onto the floor and it's harder to see. Sirine squints and lowers her head, peering between the arms and shoulders. A black silk scarf, embroidered with red berries. Her breath speeds up. She frowns, not sure if she's remembering exactly what her scarf looked like. She looks from one side to the other, and walks back onto the dance floor.

She sneaks between dancers, head down, urgent, as if going to meet someone. She catches glimpses of the scarf between the moving bodies, loses sight of it, catches it again. She turns and thinks she sees Nathan and Aziz moving out onto the dance floor. She gets closer, keeps Rana's head between her face and Han, until she is almost directly behind Rana, seeing clearly that it is her scarf, the one she thought she'd lost, draped over the young woman's head, Rana flaunting the beautiful embroidered silk for everyone in the world to see.

And before she can even imagine what she should do or what she might say, Sirine is reaching out—Han spots her then, his face glowing with sweat, a great smile—and she snatches the scarf right off of Rana's head.

Rana wheels around and her uncovered hair fans out, spills over her shoulders. And Sirine realizes, in a moment that seems to go on and on, that this is not her silk scarf at all, that this one is stiff and starchy, a cheap cotton fabric, the elegant embroidered berries just a clumsy print border. She stares at it. And then she drops the scarf on the floor.

And she turns and runs.

*

She runs out one of the side exit doors, the heavy metal bar sliding beneath her hands, and she doesn't stop until she's outside in a narrow alley, a drizzly space with damp brick walls and a concrete floor. She can hear the music and the dancing thumping through the walls of the building, echoing in the alleyway. Breathless, she leans against the brick wall, rubs her palms against the rough bricks. Someone walking by might think she was praying. She feels her heart pounding in her throat. She smells diesel and mud and wet bark. The misty rain fills her hair, lifts it into a frizz all around her head. "Oh God," she says over and over. "Oh God, oh God, oh God, oh my God."

She hears a click then and freezes. She hopes whoever it is won't notice her there. Perhaps they'll think she's just some sort of crazy woman or street person and keep going. She hears footsteps coming closer and holds her breath.

"I gave Han the slip," Rana says. "He doesn't know where we are."

Sirine doesn't respond. She closes her eyes.

"You're wrong about me," she says. "I'm not interested in him. If that's what this is about."

Sirine presses her head in harder, presses her palms against the brick so she can feel the cold all the way up her wrists. "I don't believe you," she says. But then she looks at Rana. "I saw the two of you kissing one night."

"No, you didn't," Rana says matter-of-factly. "No, you didn't."

"I followed you."

She shrugs. "That doesn't matter. For one thing, I'm married."

Sirine drops her hands. "You're married?"

"When I was thirteen. My parents arranged it. And my mother's an American. Married me to my rich second cousin Fareed. They thought he would help curb my wild streak."

Sirine turns sideways against the wall to look at her. "They did? When you were thirteen?"

Rana leans back against the wall as well. "Yup. He was an industrial engineer, twenty-one years older. He worked in the oil fields in Saudi. He was gone for six months at a time, sometimes more. Fareed was a total control freak. He had closed-circuit cameras installed in all the rooms, including the bathroom, so he could keep an eye on me even when he was away."

"You're kidding."

"Oh." She flops one hand at Sirine. "That's just the start. He had locked iron gates around the house and iron bars on the windows—so no one could climb in, he said. But of course then I couldn't get out. There was even a lock on the telephone. Servants had to bring me my food by sliding the plates in under the bars. He didn't trust anyone with a key besides himself."

"How absolutely horrible." Sirine feels like a fool. She looks at the veil in Rana's hand and wishes she could just disappear.

Rana gestures toward the cement steps and they sit down next to each other. "You want to hear all this?" she asks skeptically. Sirine nods. "I don't like to tell my American friends, it just feeds all the usual stereotypes—you know, the sheikh with the twenty virgins, all that stuff."

"Don't worry, I won't think that," Sirine says.

"Well, I'll give you the short version." Rana folds her arms over her chest. "The whole thing was miserable from beginning to end. But one thing being locked up did was give me a lot of time, you know, to think. So I made a plan. Fareed only came for a few days once or twice a year. He would bring his engineer friends from the fields and entertain them. And he unlocked the gates and opened the windows so they wouldn't know what he was up to. The servants would cook and they would eat and drink and pass out on the living room floor. All except Fareed. He never drank. He would take me into the bedroom then and demand that I perform what he called my 'duties.' So gross. I hated it. Over the years, though, I got smarter. One day I waited till he came home and told him I wanted to make him a special dinner myself this time. He was all excited, thinking that I'd actually come around to caring for him, 'like a real wife,' he said. I made him a plate of lamb and rice and soaked the dish in araq."

"The liquor? That's so strong. Didn't he taste it?"

She shrugs. "I just told him it was my first try at cooking and I suppose he wanted to show me his approval. He ate the whole thing and got drunk on the food and then I poured it into his coffee as well. It was a special kind of araq that he kept for his friends. Supposedly it was made with the venom of a kind of snake that increased its potency or something. And makes the man stronger too—if you know what I mean. Some horseshit like that. I poured it into his ice cream and his tea—everything I could think of," she says, laughing. "Then I just poured him a straight glass of the stuff and told him it was fizzy water from France. He barely swallowed a sip before he passed out. His friends were drinking and passed out all over the front rooms and main entrance, so I decided to squeeze my way out the bathroom window, which was the only one big enough to fit through. I was fifteen and a half years old at the time. I knew if I waited one more year I wouldn't be able to fit."

"My God."

"But I did it." She turns to Sirine. Her eyes and hair look like enamel in the dark. "I got away and he didn't come looking. Too embarrassed, I think. The only time I'm interested in men anymore is for the game of it. I'll sleep with one just because I can and then I'll never see him again. Like my poetry teacher."

"You and Aziz!"

She half-shrugs. "He's not so bad, really. Once you get used to him."

Sirine sits with her elbows tucked on to her knees and stares at Rana's scarf. She shakes her head. "Wow."

"Although I'm not sure he counts as a very good game. Some men are too easy. I like a challenge."

"Of course," Sirine says. She wants to laugh but instead she looks straight up then and lets the mist fall onto her face.

They sit like that a moment but the step is getting cold and wet. "Well," Rana says.

They stand, then Sirine thinks for a moment and says, "But, after all that—well, why do you still wear . . ." Sirine looks at the scarf Rana holds crumpled in one hand.

"This?" She shakes it out and drapes it over her head. "This reminds me that I belong to myself. And to God. I still have faith, you know." She smiles. "My dad wants me to get divorced, but I've found that having a missing husband is useful."

"I'm sorry," Sirine says. "I mean—you know—about all of it."

Rana tilts her head; her lips look full and dark as blackberries. She touches Sirine's face with her fingertips. "Actually, I'm pretty sorry for you," she says. "Trying to be with someone like Han."

"What do you mean?"

Rana's eyes are lowered. She seems to be considering something. She ties the scarf beneath her chin and strands of her hair escape. She starts at the top of her hairline and meticulously runs her fingers along the edges of the scarf until every bit of hair is tucked under. Then she says to Sirine, "I think it's better if you try asking him yourself."

Rana offers to drive her home, but Sirine prefers to walk. She wants the slow rhythms of her own movement. Cars whistle past her down the boulevard and a slick moony reflection shines on the street. She passes unlit corners and side streets and a few cars seem to slow down beside her, but no one bothers her. When she arrives home an hour later, the mist has soaked her clothes and she is shivering.

That night Nathan, Aziz, and Han each call her uncle's house, asking to speak to Sirine. Every time her uncle comes to her closed bedroom door, he just stands outside and sighs and she says, "I'm not at home." Sirine stays curled up in bed with the comforter wrapped around her. She's not at all used to making scenes. The experience has left her feeling so embarrassed and exhausted that she feels like she will have to sleep for a long time before she can speak to anyone.

*

Deep in the night Sirine thinks she hears bursts of rain against the wall. She turns over groggily. She dreams that she goes to her window and Han is standing outside under the long, tangling strands of the palm trees, calling to her. She doesn't answer him because if she says anything she will tell him about Aziz. She opens her mouth but no sound comes out. Her spine is stiff and cool, her neck straight. The palms fronds are floating in the wind, the strands flickering. In the dream, she asks him if it's not Rana, then who is it?

King Babar moans and presses against her. The photograph in her nightstand drawer whispers in her ear.

CHAPTER TWENTY-SIX

After having his ears filled with stories by Crazyman al-Rashid and getting kicked out of the mermaids' prison, Abdelrahman caught a camel, a boat, a jeep, and a bus, and slowly but surely made his way to Hal'Awud. Once in America, he learned that the city of Hollywood, or Hal'Awud, was nicknamed *Babylon*, and he realized as soon as he got there that the place was indeed somehow ancient and cursed. He heard the streams of languages and voices in the streets rippling up like the hot air over a traffic jam. There were monuments and sculptures and symbols everywhere, the name of the town written in great and terrible letters on the side of the hill like the Sumerian Ziggurat of Ur. He saw the movie stars in their fur coats, the reporters with their flash bulbs, and Grauman's Chinese Theater where he saw his very first movies. And those colors, those spires, those flashes of light and sound led him to believe that he'd discovered the forbidden Mahram Bilqis—the moon temple of the Queen of Sheba. In a way he had—even though it's hard to think of it that way now. Poor Hollywood with its dirty sidewalks, where you're walking on stars and don't even notice until you drop your gum wrapper by accident and bend down and realize you're stepping on Robert Mitchum—or worse, someone you never heard of, with a name like Martha Gastower. . . . In the olden days, the neighborhood was beautiful and devilish as a woman in a yellow dress. And even with all that he'd seen and done, Abdelrahman Salahadin was still just a Bedouin yokel at heart.

But Bedouin yokels definitely have their place in things: they happen to know, for example, that there is something lunar and eternal about oases—no matter how much people mess around with them. Abdelrahman recognized the way the wind played over the Pacific, just as it did over his Red Sea, and he recognized the healing, astringent scent of the desert as he walked in the city streets. And he took one look at the moon temple of the stars—also known as the Chinese Theater—and he went nearly insane. For the beauty of the Queen of Sheba and her handmaidens was reputedly enough to make someone crazy. He stood in the lobby of the theater, too afraid of the flashing lights to actually go and sit down in the presence of the gods. He watched the movie through a crack in the concession stand door and there he was smitten with the acting bug.

Bitten.

Yes, bitten. He didn't know who those lovely people were on the shining screen or what they wanted or how they'd gotten there. All he knew was that he wanted to be alongside them.

*

The next day, Sirine returns to work. She stirs tabbouleh and drops cardamom seeds into demitasses of black Arabic coffee, as she has a thousand times before. And she prays no one saw her grab Rana's veil at the concert last night. The students come in and while no one says anything, she has the feeling that they're sneaking looks at her.

She plants herself in front of the big cast-iron burners. The burner plates look fierce and black as teeth. She moves the skillets over the flames, shakes them one-handed with her steady forearms, so the onion slices flip and sizzle. Gradually, she loses herself in the rhythms of work, a potful of rice, grilling kabobs, drinking coffee, the flame leaping under a blackened pan. She works until her mind is cool and undisturbed and there's only her hands and six tall blue rings of flame. And she starts to recall her dream, but all she remembers is the sound of rain against the windows—though apparently it didn't rain last night.

The gradients of light alter in the window; time takes on a rare, shapeless form in the kitchen. Sirine is unaware of the customers around her, the hum of conversation, the TV, the forks and knives clattering on the plates, the silver hood roaring over the grill. The lunch rush dwindles away. And Han doesn't come. Sirine hasn't stopped working for several hours when a hand touches her shoulder and a man's voice says quietly, "Chef?"

She turns. Victor Hernandez's white kitchen jacket is buttoned to the neck, his army boots half-tied. He looks down, tentative. "Sorry to interrupt. It's just that, it's just . . ."

"That's all right Victor." She turns away to stir a bowl of parsley, lemon, and tomatoes. "What's up?"

"Well, your friend," he says. Sirine stops stirring, turns to look at him. His long, narrow Aztec eyes. "Han? He came here last night," he says.

"Han? Was here?" She points at the floor.

"He left something for you—in the kitchen. I was working late, this was around one-thirty, two. Even Cristobal was gone. So I heard these sounds on the back porch. It spooked me, you know? So I went to see and it was Han sitting back there on the steps."

Sirine smoothes down the front of her jacket, considering. "Did you talk to him?"

Victor nods. "I thought he'd been drinking. His eyes looked kind of red and his skin was shiny. Though now maybe I'm not so sure if he was. He looked really sad. I sat with him and he said he'd been thinking about going back to Iraq."

She becomes aware of her heart speeding up. "He said that?"

"I almost know how he feels. I mean, I was born here and all, but sometimes I wish I could just go off to someplace like Mexico." He gazes at Sirine a moment in a gentle speculative way. "Anyway, he talked his head off. He said that there wasn't anything for him here in America. He asked me if I ever felt like it was all a big lousy dream."

Sirine presses her fingers over her mouth. A whiff of garlic and hot peppers. "What did you say?"

"I said, no, man! I said, America is most definitely not a dream. But even so, I think he still has that idea in his head. I mean about going back. I've seen it happen a lot, you know—my friends, they get to, like, a certain point." Victor looks around, as if checking for spies. "But, Chef? You cannot let him do it."

She feels her heart thrumming. She studies his face, the bronze, flat sides of his cheekbones.

"You know, he was telling me what it was like where he comes from, about the *guardia* they have there, and their crazy dictator, and it was reminding me of something. And then I remembered it was Cristobal. You know Cristobal is from El Salvador?"

"No, I didn't know."

"They firebombed his whole family. The *guardia*. All dead. They were just little farmers from nowhere. Out in the country. He got out of there, I don't know how. You should see how messed up his legs are."

She closes her eyes.

"Chef, listen, I'm telling you, you can't let Han go back there. They'll kill him for sure. Places like that, people like Han are the first ones to go. They stick out too much and people notice them and start talking. That's how it always goes." He starts to pick up a stack of dishes, then sets them down again. "You know something else he told me? He said that they think that the word *Ole* comes from the word *Allah*. It was from when the Arabs came into Spain a million years ago. I was thinking it could even be true—like, at the bullfights, they always yell *'Ole!'* when they stab the bull, I've seen it myself, and you know, I think he might be right."

After Victor leaves, Sirine goes into the back kitchen. Han's gift is there in a vase on the table—a bouquet of velvet-red roses.

*

The woman in the Near Eastern Studies office says she has no idea where Han might be, but then a slim girl in jeans comes out of a room with an armload of paper. "You're looking for Han? I think he went to the afternoon lecture."

Sirine gets directions to the lecture. It's just one floor down and it turns out to be in the same room where Aziz gave his reading at the beginning of the term, only now the French doors are closed and the carpet looks muted and granite-colored. She can hear the speaker's voice out in the hallway as she approaches; the sound is pleasant and dull as static. All the folding chairs are set up, but there is only a small scattering of people. Han and Nathan sit together in the last row. Han's head is tipped forward, as if he were sitting in church.

The speaker's voice rises and Sirine stops inside the doorway to listen. The man says, "Now, according to UNICEF, fifty thousand Iraqi adults die because of U.S. sanctions every year, and five thousand children die in Iraq *every month* because of the American embargo of food and medicine. The sanctions deny people access to basic health care, clean water, and electricity—they're a systematic violation of the Geneva Convention, which prohibits the starvation of civilians as a method of warfare. In the past few years, tens of thousands of people have fled Iraq—many of them are professionals, trying to escape the terrible economic and political situation." The speaker looks up from his notes and sighs. He looks over the audience and says, "If twenty-five people die in a plane crash in the U.S. it makes headlines. But five thousand Iraqi children? Or a hundred political dissidents? Even if all of Iraq has acted wrongly and belligerently in every way since the day America started selling them arms, how is it possible that the deaths of five thousand children a month is not burned into our minds?"

She hears a murmur: Nathan is whispering something to Han; he turns his head and spots her in the doorway.

Han whispers to Nathan, then slips out of his chair. Behind Han, Nathan turns and waves to her. It's an odd gesture—more of a signal than a wave—his fingers outspread as if in warning, his expression pleading. She frowns and tilts her head, but then Han comes toward her. His face looks gaunt and flattened, blue wings of shadows under his eyes. He approaches her, leans in close, and murmurs, "Sirine, I've been wanting to— Can we go somewhere?" He holds out his hand and she takes it.

The speaker's voice rises and Han turns back for a moment to listen to him. "Let me tell you all something," the man says, his voice charged with emotion. "Let me just tell you this. America simply cannot continue to pillage the natural resources and economies of other countries, to heap its desires and values, its contempt and greed on the backs of others, and not expect there to be consequences. Let me tell you this: there are always going to be consequences. I don't know when or how. But if things continue as they are, there will certainly be consequences. We do not live in a vacuum. We are not the only nation in the world. We have been doing terrible things to countries like Iraq for a very long time. Things that Americans believe they don't have to learn about. You may want to live a life of benign indifference to the rest of the world, but understand that as long as you live here, murderous things are being done in your name. We have a moral obligation—a pact—to live as fellow citizens of the world. We have broken that pact through our indifference to others. And someday, something terrible is going to happen *to us*."

*

Her uncle's house is quiet at four in the afternoon. The late sunlight washes out the brick walls and fades the red tile roofs on the houses around them to tones of peach and coral. Today is the shortest day of the year, the wind is slight and gray as a sigh, and it seems as if the world is easing into a long sleep. Sirine brings Han into the entryway and she feels disoriented, as if she is five years old and encountering it again for the first time: the scent of her uncle's wool and silk carpets, the musty furniture with the cigarette burns, the old oil paintings of fine ladies in filmy dresses and sea captains and men wearing monocles, and the scent of a thousand leather and canvas and paperback books crowding the shelves and the leftover traces of endless pots of coffee and cardamom.

But they don't go into her uncle's library on the right or the abandoned living room on the left, or her bedroom up the stairs. Instead, she takes him in back into the kitchen and sits him at the round speckled white table. She sits down across from him, crosses her hands, takes a breath, and says, "Han, I'm sorry. I'm sorry that I lost your scarf and I'm sorry about making a scene at the dance and I'm sorry—oh, I'm sorry about everything."

His face looks papery and empty, his eyes bloodshot, almost burnt. Sirine feels that all the blood has drained out of her face as well, a thin buzzing fills her ears. "Why, what are you sorry for?" he asks, squinting at her. Then there is a blooming in his cheeks, a color deep as beet juice, red triangles covering his cheeks, and suddenly his eyes widen, he laughs softly, and says, "Sirine, my one true love."

*

They stay at the table for a while, not speaking. Sirine feels a mixture of anxiety and release. She wants things back the way they were, yet everything is not right. It frightens her to sit with him like this, not speaking and not looking at each other, so finally she stands and begins opening cabinets, hunting out rice, onions, and garlic. While Han sits and gazes into his private distance, she assembles a meal: chunks of lamb grilled directly over the gas flame, gleaming skewers of onion, tomato, zucchini, a scent of lavender in the oil. There is a bag of frekeh in one of the cabinets and she considers this for a moment but then shuts the door. The aroma of garlic, grilled lamb, and open fields fills the kitchen. She brings it to the table on a big plate with rice cooked with saffron and toasted pine nuts. She tries to eat a little of it herself, but the meat is tasteless; she can barely swallow it. So instead she sits and watches Han eat, hoping, in this simple act, to draw him in.

When he finishes, she rummages through the refrigerator and finds the tin can of powdered coffee. She pries off the plastic lid and spoons up the slick, glossy ground, adds it to a demitasse of water—a teaspoon of sugar, stirring over heat, waiting for the rise of foam in the open pot. She can't find the cardamom, so she adds a curl of lemon peel. She feels light-headed and overtired, so she makes a cup of tea for herself and brews it in a glass with sugar. It tastes faintly of stone and she thinks it must be old, but she drinks it anyway.

The sun has long since set by then and she watches Han's profile illuminated with the flares of headlights through the kitchen windows—the neighborhood commuters heading home. He fingers the edge of his coffee cup, turns it slowly, and makes a noise.

"What?"

He smiles, then says, "You cook like an angel."

She hides behind her teacup, watches him a moment. He's not in the room, not really. She needs to ask what is wrong. But in truth, she's afraid to know, and he seems to sense this himself. She takes another deep breath, puts down the cup, and leads him up the stairs that rise out of the entryway, with the polished wooden railing and the boxes of street light cast from the panes of glass in the front door. Sirine takes Han to her bedroom, which she's slept in almost since the beginning of her memory. She sits him on the bed with the ivory-colored comforter and the curved dark head- and footboards and she holds his hands in hers. Then she turns to the nightstand drawer and slides it open, and for once she doesn't hear the musical laughter twirling into the air. The photograph is silent as she picks it up, this image she has memorized; she is not sure why she is doing this; it feels as if she is pressing on something, pushing through cobwebs. She hands the photo to Han. He smiles in a distracted way, without looking at it, sits on the bed, and rubs his eyes. "No more photographs."

"What do you mean?"

He holds his hand over his eyes a moment longer and says, "I've seen too many."

Then he lowers his hand. He looks at the photo and his head moves back. "Where did you get this?" The corner of the snapshot trembles in his fingers. He stares at it and she can hear the breath rushing through his body; his expression is clear as a flash of light: it seems as if she can see the intricate workings of his thoughts, vascular and intimate, racing like blood cells. "I lost the only photo I had of her. I never thought I'd see her again." He looks up: his eyes are too bright. "This is my sister Leila."

*

"Before the war," he says. "Before the Americans bombed Iraq . . ." Sirine slowly curls back on the bed, blinking. He leans back beside her. He is going to tell her, whether she wants to hear or not.

*

"My parents sent me to the private boys' school in Cairo," he says. "My American friend Janet sponsored me, covering my tuition and costs, and I entered a world of the mind that I'd never dreamt existed before. I stayed away from my home for five years, spending vacations and summers at the school with the few other children whose parents had essentially abandoned them. I loved my family but they seemed to be of a world I'd left behind. I could have gone on to the University of Baghdad but Saddam took over in 1979, the year I returned to Iraq. In 1980, he declared war on Iran over some disputed territory. Suddenly there were book and paper shortages as well as food and water rationing. Scholarships were nonexistent and my American funding—well, of course it had stopped.

"I came back from Cairo obsessed with just about everything cultural—literature, painting, drama. I wanted nothing to do with what I said were the 'betrayals' of religion and money. I said and did as much as I could to cause my parents as much unhappiness as possible. I was always angry with them—I felt as if I had gone on to a new place in my life while they had remained stubbornly behind. Now I saw our poverty all around us—everything—the dirt floor in our house, the warped glass in our windows—all of it offended me. At night the sky flashed with bombs; it was impossible to sleep. I had nightmares of flying in pieces through the air.

"Saddam started forcing young men to join the army and my parents wanted me to stay at home, out of sight. Instead, I went out late at night with Arif and Leila, visiting our friends, discussing theories about economics and foreign policy and the workings of the world." He stops and looks at his hands a moment, rubbing them slowly together. "I guess that's why I love Nathan's stories about Baghdad—he's had more adult experience of the city, the life that I'd wanted to have, but I was too young when I went away. When I grew older, some of my school friends started saying that America was the great traitor, consuming goods and resources—and never really giving anything back but baubles, cheap entertainment. Smoke and mirrors. And I began to understand. The street signs in Baghdad are written in Arabic and English, and you see Disney characters and American-style T-shirts everywhere. Trinkets. Junk.

"But America had also sent me to my new life and I couldn't imagine turning back from that. I wanted to be a writer and a visionary—like Hemingway—I was excited by the possibilities of languages and world travel. I wasn't any good at stories or poetry, so I sank myself into politics instead, a ragged language, publishing diatribes against Saddam Hussein in underground newspapers. I wrote under a pseudonym, Ma'al—I thought it sounded dangerous and mysterious."

*

Han closes his eyes and rubs at his temples. He lifts his face again, and his eyes are stark. "I let Leila and Arif distribute these newspapers among their friends. I encouraged them to go from door to door handing out mimeographed copies of my articles. They even read my work at public gatherings while I remained 'in hiding'—it was a game. Leila was sixteen and Arif was twelve; both of them thought I was brilliant.

"Eventually, of course, Saddam's security police heard about my writings and learned where I lived—someone tipped them off. They came to our home and pounded on the door. My parents hid me in the olive cellar under the living room. I could hear Leila stop them at the door. They told her they were there to arrest the so-called Ma'al, author of treasonous and defamatory articles that attacked the Iraqi president and supposedly the nation of Iraq. But it seemed this wasn't the real reason they were after me: they said that they had information that I'd had dealings with a certain American businessman—a known C.I.A. informant. My twelve-year-old brother stepped forward and told them that he was Ma'al.

"The cellar was filled with great glass olive jars; my hands slipped over them. There was the bitter smell of the brine mingled with the damp earth of the cellar. The sounds of boots, cold sharp voices over my head, a small sound my mother made in the kitchen before my father hushed her. I could see through a crack in the foundation and I remember how the dust and weeds around our house were all gold and tramped down, everything was so yellow.

"I hid in the olive cellar and let him offer himself; they arrested him. I didn't know what to do. I didn't think they would actually arrest a child. I assumed it was done just to frighten us—that they'd take him in for a short while and then let him go. I was the one they were after. So as soon as the police drove away, I knew that they'd be coming back for me. I left that evening. But they didn't release Arif. I learned later that they came back in the same week and arrested my friend Sami. And a few years later, they came and arrested my sister Leila as well. They said she was affiliated with American spies. They took them all away. The police might have thought that this would bring me back to Iraq, but it didn't. I let the police take them away. Once I was in England, I tried everything I could think of to track them down—calling friends and writing letters—I might as well have been trying to find someone on the moon. I wondered if Janet understood how dangerous it had been for me and my family to be associated with her. It began to seem as if my time at the private school had been a kind of brainwashing, with so much exposure to Western thoughts and values, a glorification of the West. Even after she'd spent all that money on me, I'd never learned Janet's last name or what she and her husband were really doing in my country. But she knew that Saddam Hussein was coming to power. She knew all sorts of things she shouldn't have known. And while I never really learned their motives, eventually I understood that in some way—deliberate or not—they were the ones who'd betrayed me.

*

"Is Leila . . ."
"Yes, she's dead."
"But how do you know?"
"The scarf that I gave to you? It didn't belong to my mother, it belonged to Leila. My aunt Dima mailed it to me after she was killed."

Sirine wraps her arms around her chest. She shakes her head. "Why didn't you tell me?"

He frowns at the window. "I didn't want to frighten you. I didn't think you would wear it if you knew."

Sirine leans forward, takes Han's hand in hers. But something has pulled him away from her again, out of her grasp, as if the story itself has filled his lungs and drawn him under. His eyes move but the light has gone out of them. He's shivering as if with a fever, his skin grayish and the scar at the corner of his eye inflamed and red. She looks at it and his fingers go to the spot. "I got this when I escaped." He fingers the scar lightly. "One of the men helping me to escape suddenly turned on me and tried to steal my father's prayer beads. He saw the way I always carried them close to me and assumed they were valuable. I woke one night while he was trying to slip the beads out of my hand and he struck me across the face with a broken glass bottle. I bled so profusely that it frightened him and he ran away. That night I had to walk five miles alone in the desert until I came into a Bedouin camp right at the border. One of the men there said that he had once been a cook and he said he'd seen so many injuries in the kitchen that he could stitch up anything. He sewed my face with his wife's needle and thread and then they escorted me across the border themselves."

"A chef?" Sirine tries to smile.

But Han doesn't seem to hear—his thoughts are fragments, reflections that flit across the surface of his mind. He frowns and says, "Have you heard of the Evil Eye? You know, I grew up always hearing about the Evil Eye. It's a bad spirit that takes things away from others and makes things go wrong."

Sirine holds his hand in both of hers. It lies cupped and becalmed, palm up between her fingers. "Sure, I know about the Evil Eye."

"I never believed in it until Leila was taken and Arif was arrested. A few years later my father died of a stroke. I think the fear and sadness just became too much for him."

"I'm so sorry."

"You wonder if there's anything you can do. You stay up at night trying to think of the thing that will rescue them." His eyes look dazed and fluid. "What is the thing? What is it? I sent money and letters and never knew if they received anything. I wanted to come back as soon as I heard about Leila but my father said no. He said my job was to stay alive."

Sirine squeezes his hands.

"And before I left to come here, to Los Angeles, I received a note from my mother's sister Dima, who said that my mother had gotten very sick and even gone a little crazy living all alone."

"That's terrible." She thinks, the letter.

He smiles a faded smile, full of rue. "Well, it's all terrible, isn't it? It's why I started to believe in the Evil Eye. Because I couldn't believe that so much bad could happen to one family. But it's happened to the whole country, after all. I wonder if a whole country could be under a spell like the Evil Eye."

She looks away.

"No," he murmurs. "I don't know. It's not right. Things aren't right. . . ." His voice trails off as he gazes at the bedroom window. Sirine follows his gaze and remembers the night that he climbed out the same window. It seems now like it happened a very long time ago. "Things have changed," he says. "I need to return, while my mother's still alive. I want to see her one more time, to be with her—it's something I should have done years ago. I have to go back." His eyes open and shut slowly, as if he's nearly asleep.

"Come on," Sirine says. "Not tonight, okay?"

"Tonight is it," he says. "It's all we've got now." But he slides down under the comforter.

"Han, we both need to rest. We can talk more about everything in the morning." She brushes the hair back from his face. He looks at her once, with tenderness, then closes his eyes. Soon after that, his breath slides into an even rise and fall. He looks young in his sleep, though he is still frowning, a vertical crease set between his eyes, as if he is working on an unsolvable puzzle.

*

The moon comes up in a bare sliver and the room is full of shadows but the air is motionless. Sirine quietly moves to the windows and opens them a few inches. Wind swings through the room, fragrant with the smell of streets and dust and the desert, the last exhalation of the long winter nights. The night sky is silver and spectral, light flares in the windows and bounces off the cars. The breeze feels chilly and she climbs back into bed.

She slips in beside Han, puts her arm across his chest carefully, trying not to wake him, and whispers, "It will be all right, Habeebi, it will all be fine. You'll stay here with me and my uncle. We'll love each other, we'll get married and be happy. Perhaps we can send for your mother somehow, bring her to this country. We'll be together and it will finally be all right." She strokes his hair while he sleeps. And eventually she also falls into a deep, walled-in sleep, dreamless and thick as smoke in her body.

*

She wakes when the room is gray with dawn. She is dressed in her jeans and sweater; things seem vaguely wrong. The windows are shut. Her mouth burns as if from eating too much sugar.

She sits up in bed. The photo is no longer out on the nightstand; in its place there is a piece of paper folded into a sailboat. She touches the blankets and realizes only then that Han is gone.

*

The note says: "Things are broken. The world is broken. Hayati, it's time. I've gone. Imagine that I was never here at all."

*

No one answers the phone at his apartment. Sirine grabs the keys to her uncle's car and drives through the early morning streets just starting to fill with commuters. She lets herself into his apartment with her key. Most of his books and clothes are gone, his suitcase, his toothbrush, his lapis prayer beads. And her yellow hair barrettes.

His stacks of notebooks and writings about Hemingway are also gone: the pages of Arabic handwritten in blue ballpoint on lined white curling pages that were Han's translations. "Big Two-Hearted River," *A Moveable Feast*, and *The Old Man and the Sea*.

She drives to campus but it's winter break and the place is nearly deserted. She tries all the doors to the Languages Building until she finds an unlocked entrance in an outdoor stairwell. But the building is empty, ghostly with the absence of students, the corridors echoing. She walks down the hall, listening to the sound of her footsteps repeating through the floors. She finds Han's office on the third floor, rattles the doorknob, looks at his name stenciled on the glass, and looks at the row of chairs lined up and waiting for him outside the door. She feels a black wave of despair mounting inside of her.

When Sirine gets back to her uncle's house, the sun is starting to rise. Her uncle meets her at the door. "Habeebti, that was Lon Hayden on the phone. He just found out that Han left a message on his office phone sometime last night and he said that he resigns!"

CHAPTER TWENTY-SEVEN

So Abdelrahman Salahadin had enough with drowning. He would try his hand at being a movie star. And even though he'd never acted before and he had started out with only three words of English—*Hal'Awud, Dar'Aktr,* and *Fil'Imm*—he also had devil-man good looks, smooth skin and smooth eyes, and a wide swimmer's back. So he got a few minor roles here and there to start; he played Mexicans and Italians and this sort of business. He gradually got more ambitious, wanting bigger parts, so he started asking around and heard about this and that. He also heard tales about a movie that had been made before his time that was called *El Shaykh.*

The Sheik.

Yes. That. A plum role. Arab incarnate. But they'd given the part to an Italian! Some know-nothing named Rudy So-and-So, because no one in Hollywood wanted anything to do with an actual Arab. Back then the directors and producers didn't think of Arabs as terrorists, they thought Arabs were more like something from the Bible. Of course, they didn't have time for that sort of nonsense. Besides, they thought someone with actual dark skin might run amok, do something unpredictable. So there were other Arab movies with great parts which went to Italians, some Irish, even a Spaniard or two, I hear. There was *The Ten Commandments,* which was shot over by our Aunt Nejla's house. And *Greatest Story Etc.* was done on Abdelrahman's grandfather's farm. And *Barabbas,* in which the director offered the part of a sultan to a crazy blue Bedu, Crazyman al-Rashid, who was visiting from out of town and stole some camera equipment and wrecked it for everyone.

Anyway. It just so happened that there was a new Arab movie starting up. With a famous English director. A lot of money, music, sand, the works. Here, finally, was Abdelrahman Salahadin's chance for something big. It was, in fact, to be filmed in the swirling stretch of Wadi Rum desert, right in the backyard of Aqaba where he had grown up. It was a long shot, he was still an unknown, but you have to understand that even though he'd spent years marinating in the Red Sea, Abdelrahman Salahadin was still young and beautiful. Beautiful. With clear skin like yours and black shining eyes like your father's, with a spine like a dagger and a head of hair as dark as midnight on the Nile.

When he walked onto the stage at the audition, all the Italian actors fell silent. The director was very far away, hidden among a sea of empty seats, and when he nodded, Abdelrahman opened his mouth and cried out, 'A small, barbaric people!'—which happened to be one of the more interesting lines in the movie—and his voice split open the air of the theater like a spear and everyone knew that he would be the star of the movie.

Except, of course, how could he be the star, this Jordanian, Syrian, Lebanese, Egyptian, Iraqi, Palestinian, drowned Bedouin of an Arab?

*

All day, Sirine works with one eye on the front door, as if she were holding her breath.

The café fills with more students than Sirine has ever seen in there at once. Every table is crowded with young men from all the Arab countries; some of them go and borrow chairs from the Shaharazad Drugstore across the street. They're arguing in Arabic. Every single person seems to be shouting, the cords standing out in their necks. Many of them also watch the door, as if expecting Han to appear at any time.

Victor Hernandez stays in the kitchen working frantically with Sirine, doing salads, soups, and dips while Sirine works the grill: Cristobal and Um-Nadia both run dishes to the tables. "What is this?" Victor asks Mireille when she stops to wait for a pickup. "What's going on out there?"

Mireille glances at Sirine; finally she says, "They're saying that Han quit the university and went back to Iraq. They're arguing about why he left, or if he had to escape, or Saddam Hussein was involved or the C.I.A., or I don't know what."

Victor swivels to look at Sirine. "He did it—he went back!"

Sirine ducks her head under the roaring hood. The heat of the grill seems to pass right through her body and the grease chatters and snaps like teeth.

She works without a break, turning out skewers of lamb and chicken, braised shanks, grilled fish, until her arms feel limp and her back is tight. The students stay, making a commotion all day. They eat and wait and argue an hour past closing time, until Um-Nadia takes a broom out of the closet and stands in the middle of the place, shaking the broom and shouting: "*Imshee!* Go home everybody now! That's enough of everything and I got a headache!"

*

Victor, Cristobal, and Cristobal's specially-called-in cousin Eliazer all begin cleaning. Sirine sinks into a chair. She feels translucent, as if she's lost her skin and bones. Her head still hums with the roar of the hood and the din of the arguments. There's a lingering, earthy scent of chopped parsley. She closes her eyes for a moment, listening to the white ringing in her ears.

Mireille sits across from her. "Some of the students were saying he was a spy."

"A spy?" Sirine drops her arms into her lap. "A *spy*? For who?"

Mireille shrugs. "The C.I.A., the Iraqis, whoever."

"That's crazy."

"Someone else thought he was one of Saddam Hussein's secret sons."

Sirine rubs her temples. "Why are we talking about Han in the past tense?"

"Did he tell you anything at all? Is he coming back? Did he really go back to Iraq?"

Sirine looks down, feels her face crack, as if she will cry, but it seems she's run out of tears. She tries to say, I don't know, but there is no air in her lungs. Mireille scoots her chair so close that their knees are touching; she grabs Sirine's hands tightly. "It's going to be all right. He's going to come back, I'm sure of it. I can feel it."

Sirine shakes her head. "I don't know what to think."

"Then listen to me—I know how he felt about you. Any idiot could see it. Maybe he got scared but he's coming back, there's no question."

Sirine stares at the floor. "Got scared of what?"

*

Sirine returns to Han's apartment that night and calls the airlines, dragging the phone into his bed. When she says in a wobbling voice, "Yes, I'd like to buy a ticket. To Baghdad," there's a long pause on the other end.

"I'm sorry," the woman finally says. "There are no commercial flights from the U.S. into Baghdad."

Sirine blinks, squeezes the receiver. "You mean—you mean I can't go?"

"There's a travel ban for Americans. I don't think they would let you in even if you drove yourself to the border," the woman says.

Sirine rubs her hand over her forehead. Tries to think. "What if I was an Iraqi?"

Another pause. "Well, I suppose you could try flying to Europe or a different Middle Eastern country and then fly on one of the carriers that does go into Iraq. There aren't that many. Or maybe you could fly into a neighboring country and drive across. It's very dangerous there, you know," the woman adds.

"Why?" Sirine asks. "What would they do to me?" She looks at his balcony and remembers the night she thought she saw a gargoyle out there watching her.

"I'm sorry?"

"Do you think they would arrest me?" She presses her lips together—realizes she sounds hopeful and crazy.

"Miss—I—I—really don't think—"

Sirine quickly hangs up.

*

The phone is ringing. It is so dark for a moment she can't remember where she is. Even the city lights look dimmer and more distant, blurring through her consciousness as she wakes, her face turned toward the balcony. But she wasn't really asleep, was she? She couldn't sleep. She waits but the answering machine doesn't come on and Han still hasn't come home to answer it. It keeps ringing. She sits up, wondering if he would call his own apartment.

She goes out to the phone in the other room, picks up, and murmurs, "Hello?" But no one speaks.

"Hello?" she asks, more loudly this time.

Still silence; Sirine feels it shift into a silence of waiting or expectation. She hears something tiny, molecular, trickling over the phone line, inside the whorls of her own ear. She exhales, and in that exhalation she murmurs, "Han?" Then instantly realizes her mistake. Her breath feels raw, her heart peeled away as a bulb. There is something unearthly and sinister there, she feels it in the receiver. The monstrous thing, waiting for her, attached to her mind, hanging by the slim line in the middle of the night. She wants to throw it away from her, run, but it dangles there, silently breathing, slithering into her ear. Her mouth tastes burnt and bitter, as if filled with soot.

Sirine closes her eyes and forces herself, shaking, to slowly replace the breathing receiver. It wants her, the quiet thing waiting on the line. She doesn't know why. She looks around the half-empty apartment and it seems in that cool, midnight hour to be filled with ghost-shapes.

She takes off her clothes and pulls on one of the shirts Han left hanging in his closet, then gets back into bed. She curls up in Han's clothes and covers and scent. Her sleep is light, filigreed as lace; she's frightened of dreaming. Sirine tosses and several times she imagines she hears the scratch of his key in the lock. She stares at the dim red light from the clock radio switching the hours. Finally, she falls asleep in the very early morning and then drags herself awake at nine. She's late for work, but unable to hurry, barely able to splash water on her face or to squint at her reflection in the mirror, her eyes aching, as swollen as if she'd been crying all night. She bicycles back to her uncle's house to see if there's been any word from Han.

But there are no notes, no messages on the machine. She goes upstairs to her bedroom and stares at the unmade covers. Then she changes into work clothes, moving slowly but automatically, curling away from thought. Easier to be numb and disoriented. She goes back downstairs, picks up her jacket and keys, and has her hand on the door when something makes her turn around. She looks into the kitchen and sees it, still on the table: Han's coffee cup from his last night there. But for some reason the saucer is inverted over the demitasse, the way it is done for fortune-tellers, so the seer can shake the cup and read the pattern of the coffee grounds after the coffee is drunk.

She gazes at it a moment. She didn't see him cover the cup, but there it is like a sign or a secret message to her. She picks up the cup and saucer, very carefully, in both hands, and realizes she will not be able to ride her bike like this. Her uncle has already driven to school, so there's no car. The city bus is too risky between the crowds and the potholes, so finally she decides to call a cab. The name on the driver's license propped in the window is V.S. Ramoud. He helps Sirine into her seat and asks no questions, driving slowly, eyeing the reflection of the cup and saucer in Sirine's hand in his rearview mirror.

When she walks into work, Um-Nadia spots the coffee cup and immediately she's brisk and intent. "All right," she says quickly. "All right, come back into the kitchen. Right away."

They arrange themselves at the kitchen table with Victor and Cristobal looking on. Um-Nadia stares at the cup and then at Sirine. "Is this your cup?" she asks. Sirine shakes her head. Um-Nadia turns the saucer slowly, scrutinizing it. "Was there a wish?" she asks.

Sirine says, "I don't know."

Um-Nadia lifts the saucer and the cup sticks to it for a moment before releasing with a faint *pock*. She nods. "The wish will come true," she says. She turns the cup, reading the drifts of dried grounds lining the porcelain interior. Her forehead wrinkles with concentration and her lips move silently and Sirine, Victor, and Cristobal all wait. Finally, she looks up from the cup, her eyes fretful and evasive. Then she says quickly, "It's fine. Everything is just fine."

Sirine waits, staring. Finally she says, "That's it? 'Everything is fine'? What about love or journeys or trouble? Can't you see anything more?"

Um-Nadia glances at it briefly, as if she would prefer not to look. "No," she says and sets the cup upright on its saucer. "There's nothing of interest here. Besides, it's all silly superstitions. You should know that. Arabs don't believe in these old-time ways anymore. We're an advanced civilization. No time for the Dark Ages!" With that, she stands, carries the cup and saucer to the garbage bin under the sink, and drops it in. "Lunch rush is coming!" she says and walks out.

The remaining three stare for a moment in the direction of the garbage, then move to their separate jobs. Later, when the back kitchen is empty, Sirine returns and discovers that someone has fished the cup out of the garbage, wrapped it in a dish towel, and tucked it into her backpack.

*

The day is a blank slot; she moves like a sleepwalker, chopping and stirring, lifting the spoon to her lips; but everything tastes like wet cotton to her. It is impossible not to wait for Han, not to be trained on the sound of the front door; she refuses to think that he is not coming back. All around her people are talking, laughing, and eating; their noise and heat swirls up, surrounding her yet apart from her. It seems that the students are already losing interest in discussing Han. Then a family comes in: an Arab man and a fair-haired woman and two pale, dark-eyed children. She lets herself imagine that this is herself and Han and their family, that her life is shared in the close spaces between herself and her husband and children. She closes her eyes and stirs.

*

On her break, she sneaks into the back kitchen and calls the police. Her breath comes in short, tight gulps. She says she wants to report someone missing.

"How long has the person been missing?" the officer asks.

Sirine hesitates, not entirely sure, her sense of time scattered. "I think it might be forty-eight hours." She gives some of Han's background information—identity, appearance, address, profession. She tells the officer that Han is her boyfriend. But she's startled when the officer asks if she has any ideas as to where he might be. She thinks for a moment, then says, "Yes, I think he's gone back to Iraq."

"What makes you think this?"

"Well. He left a note. That's what it said. And he took his things. But it was just so strange and sudden...."

"Why would he go to Iraq?"

"Well, he's from there. Originally. But it isn't safe for him. I think..." Her voice wobbles. "I think they might hurt him."

"Who might?"

"You know—Saddam Hussein..."

There's a pause, then, "You think Saddam Hussein is going to hurt your boyfriend?"

This sounds strange to her. For a moment she's confused. Then she says, "Wouldn't he?"

There's another pause. "Miss," the officer says. "I'm not sure this is actually a police matter."

"Can't you just—isn't there a way for you to still look for him?" *He said that they would kill him.* But she realizes that it is like the other day with the airlines agent, that she is already sounding slightly mad.

"Miss—"

Mireille and Victor come into the kitchen carrying dishes.

Sirine hangs up.

*

That night Sirine stays late at work; she is partly avoiding home but she is also still hoping and waiting for Han. She ends up helping Victor and Cristobal swab and scrape. As they work, she notices Cristobal's fine, smooth hands, their precise fit to the mop, the way his hair falls in glistening black strands into his eyes. Like Han's. There used to be an ongoing procession of new custodians working there, Arab or Asian or Mexican. But Cristobal has lasted for nearly two years already and he frequently appears with cousins or friends who help him clean. He gives them kitchen leftovers and pays them some of his tip money. She glances at him and feels drawn closer, wants to put her hand on his warm skin. She remembers that Victor had said Cristobal was from El Salvador and she would like to ask him: What will happen to Han now? What will they do to him? It seems that Cristobal must somehow know the answer to that. But of course, she thinks, he doesn't; they're from different countries, how could he know such things? Still, she finds herself moving closer to him, almost unconsciously, scraping the grill, wiping the counter, until he looks up at her, startled, and moves away. She waits until he moves into another room and then she puts her hands up to the front of the satiny metal hood and tries not to let herself start crying. If she starts now, she thinks, there will be no stopping.

Finally, there is no more work to do. The chairs are all upended on the tables, the floors gleam, and Sirine has to go somewhere. She bicycles back to Han's building but dreads going into its empty, extinguished rooms. She wheels around to the back of the building where his balcony faces out but there are no lights on there. Han isn't inside. She doesn't even stop, just swerves away, tires swirling in the gravel, and pedals to her uncle's house.

He meets her at the door holding an open book, a history of Constantinople. "Someone in Turkish Studies told me it was good reading," he says. Then he squints at her face. He sighs, puts down the book, and opens his arms. "Come," he says. She moves into them, smelling the good tobacco dust and coffee grounds and crumbly book smell of her uncle. "Ah, Habeebti," he says, "Habeebti, Habeebti."

"He's gone," she says out loud, for the first time.

"I know. I know. His crazy decision."

"What will happen to him?" she cries into his neck.

"I don't know, Habeebti," he murmurs. "That's not a place to go back to. Not now. Not in this world."

"Will he come back?"

Her uncle doesn't answer.

*

She follows her uncle into the library and sits next to him on the horsehair couch. She touches the rough material, inhales the mustiness and weak light and eucalyptus scent. She tries to take it in. She tells herself, I'm home again.

Her uncle rubs his hands over his face. She looks up out of her tears and says, "You're tired."

Her uncle looks distant and contemplative, slightly sadder than he used to be; he folds his hands, then cracks them, pushing out, then sighs. "I grow old." His pants are loose and rolled up above his bare ankles and he has a belted plaid flannel bathrobe on over this.

"No."

"Oh, for certain." He smiles at her and when she seems about to start crying again, he pulls her back into his arms. He smoothes her hair and hums and says, "Your mother was a big crier."

He rocks her a little and lets her soak the corner of his shirt and finally he gives her an old crocheted doily from an end table to wipe her nose on. "Thank you," she murmurs. He smoothes her hair back and she thinks of the way he would try to brush her curly hair for her in grade school: it always got bigger and frizzier the more he brushed, so full of static that it crackled.

He sighs again, then says, "There's no telling about the things in the world. We have to learn patience, Habeebti."

She closes her eyes. "How? How do you learn that?" He pulls an afghan up over her shoulders and she lets herself slip beneath the warm currents of the room, the memory of stories he told her when she was a girl.

"Patience comes from strange places," her uncle says. "From the moon and stars, from sighing and breathing, and from working and sleeping, to name a few."

*

Sirine is almost asleep as he tells a story.

"Not everyone knows this, but in addition to the real mountains there are purplish ghostly mountains that sleep behind them. And you should never look too closely for too long at just about anything unless you're willing to let yourself perceive this other world, the world behind the senses, the world not of things but of immutable, unknowable being.

"This was the way I felt on the day your father met your mother. We had lived in this country together with a gang of other immigrant friends—all of us half-crazy with missing home, our parents, our language, our food. So one day, my younger brother comes home and he says to me: today I was out walking and I met my destiny coming toward me in the street. Well, how do you like that? Even though we were thousands of miles from where he was born—there she was, destiny, waiting! I felt it again on the day they married. You could feel it like something in the air. That was the terrible Day of the Terribly Hot Suits when I sweated all the way through my jacket and down to my socks. I was so sad on that day that I thought I would feel that way forever. I thought I was sad because I would never have such love in my own life.

"Finally, when your mother was pregnant with you, then I understood what the something in the air was. I touched her stomach and I could sense you in there, swimming in your purple fish light. You were such a mystery: I imagined you there with fiery feathers, a face like a gold mosaic. And even though up to that point your mother wanted to call you Maybelle and your father wanted Samar—and I was secretly favoring Dishdasha the Great myself—I knew when I touched her stomach, maybe three inches over your head, that you were called Sirine. And that after you, anything was possible."

*

Later that night, after the stories and feeding the dog and turning off all the lights, Sirine climbs upstairs. She turns down the blankets on her narrow bed, as she has done so many times in the past. But now it feels different. She feels skinless, barely assembled. Everything hurts. She lies in her bed and feels Han's absence open in her like a wound. She shivers; her tears are gigantic, swelling inside her. She has never felt this way about anything before. She pulls the covers up to her ears. Curls knees-first into herself. And just when she is certain that she can't bear it, can't bear any of it, King Babar hops up onto the bed, presses his woolly head to her face, and stretches his body along her chest. And eventually she sleeps.

*

She dreams she is a child again. Her arms are plump and soft, her hair is tangled wild. She and her uncle have just come home from the beach and there is sand, as usual, in her clothes and shoes. It is the day that her parents are leaving once again for Africa. The boxy gray suitcases had to be left open all night to air them out. They stand lined up, packed and orderly as soldiers in the entrance. Her mother's suitcase is small and her father's is even smaller, and both of them contain photographs of Sirine. They always show her the photos before packing them away. "See?" her mother says. "We're taking you with us." In the dream, they are together, her mother crouching to gather Sirine up. Her mother's lilac scent and shining hair falls over her. They watch Sirine's father at the end of the hall, grinning at them and combing his own hair back, hand over hand. "The secret to a good marriage," her mother whispers, her hands cupped around Sirine's ear, "is to never really know your husband. Not all the way." Her mother's arms are long and white like Sirine's, her hair is a shiny auburn flag. Her father comes over and he scoops her up in one arm and shows her how to shield herself in case a bomb ever drops, by putting her thumbs in her ears and covering her eyes with her fingers. She marvels at how smart her father is. His arms are strong and dark as trees and his hair is woolly tight. His chest is covered in curling black hair.

Then the dream goes to the place where she does not want to be.

Watching the two men—now she knows they are newscasters, Huntley and Brinkley—and their theme music that makes her think of slanting rain. She is calm as she was on that day, sitting next to her uncle on the hard, horsehair couch; they are listening to the palm leaves that sound like rain through the open door. The night through the screen is sparked with crickets, warm and mild, even though it is only a few days before Christmas—Christmas Eve Eve Eve, her uncle said—and they've seen the pictures of the snowstorms in another place, cars sliding sideways like toys along white streets. Then there is a commercial for Twenty Mule Team Borax cleanser and Sirine is thinking that next is her favorite show, *Lost in Space*. But then the news is back—if only they had changed the channel, she thinks, perhaps none of this would have happened. The talking men are showing Africa again today. There is fighting there—but there is always fighting in the places where her parents go, or earthquakes, or starving children, or something terrible. There is no place safe except beside her uncle on the horsehair couch. Her father says it is all about oil and greed. Earthquakes are not caused by oil and greed, her mother says. I'm not so sure, says her father. But now Huntley and Brinkley are talking about guns and fighting in the streets and American relief workers. And Sirine knows this part didn't happen exactly this way, but in the strange, terrible dream it is happening; they see it on the news: Her parents are there on the village road. The tribal soldiers in foreign uniforms on the other side, facing them, the guns shining in their hands. Her parents are with their friends, Mohana the engineer, Ruthie the teacher, and Laura the nurse—they are young people laughing and holding drinks on the lawn chairs in photographs. Now they are on the TV and their death is in their faces, five American relief workers, the reporter is saying. A war, they said—was that what it was? An uprising. Were they Muslims? No. Her uncle is saying no. She heard the reporter say it but she didn't see it, not really. But in this dream that she can't break out of or stop or rewrite, it is happening on the screen in front of her: Mohana then Laura then Ruthie. She sees her father hit with a single bullet in the head, a tiny hole. Instantaneous death. And her mother hit with bullets in the legs and wrist; she dies the next day in a village clinic from blood loss and septicemia, blood poisoning. She and her uncle heard it on the TV and in her dream they watched it happen. Her parents went out and they never came home. Their bodies were shipped back in plain board boxes, unopened. But to Sirine, they were buried somewhere in the middle of Africa; she never saw them again.

There was a small will—almost no property or savings. In the event of their deaths, her uncle had been recorded as Sirine's legal guardian. They had arranged it—Sirine learned—in the same month that she was born. As if they had known.

After their deaths, her uncle took her up to the flat roof of his house—two blocks away from the apartment where Sirine had lived with her parents. He said, "This house is yours and you will always be my only daughter and my only child forever and ever." He held her so tightly she could feel his ribs, his slight, perishable frame against her shoulders. She felt that day—she knows as she dreams this—the way she feels this night, thirty years later: mortally wounded, ancient and silent. And all the tears left her body, almost forever.

Until she wakes the next morning and feels the dampness cool as air across her face. And she knows, in her half-awake state, that she has had the forbidden dream, the dream-memory that she keeps shut away. She realizes with a soft pang, like remembering an old loss—something that should no longer mean anything but somehow still does—that she is already ten years older than her parents were when they died.

CHAPTER TWENTY-EIGHT

Back in her hometown of Aqaba, Aunt Camille was pleased to see all the familiar sights and sounds that she'd left years before when she went in search of her naughty boy. Her many sons prepared a welcome-home feast of mensaf, made with baby lamb stewed in onion-yogurt sauce prepared on a bed of rice and bread. They fed their mother as well as the entire displaced tribe of blue Bedu, and they tried to convince the blue Bedu to stay on in Aqaba for good. But the whole point of being a blue Bedu is to drape yourself in sweet incense and to wander around the Dhofar Mountains. So, after three days of feasting and reminiscing, Aunt Camille bade them a tearful farewell at the train that would finally take them home.

She turned and faced her nineteen sons then, and realized that one had brought his laundry, another had some mending, and some others hadn't had haircuts since the day she left town. She sighed and realized that something inside of her had changed while she was on the road: Aqaba looked even smaller and sleepier than she remembered it. It had none of the vivid richness and warmth that her memory had lavished upon it: this was just a place among places. Something inside of her had grown larger, she realized; she thought she'd given up on finding her son, but something was calling her back to the search.

*

One week after Han left, a blue aerogram letter arrives at Sirine's uncle's house, postmarked from London. Sirine immediately recognizes Han's neat block script in blue ink. Her hands begin trembling so that it takes her a minute to slice a serrated knife through the edge. Her breath is seized up and her heart pounds so it feels like a fist inside her chest wall. She sits down and holds the letter in both hands and it takes a moment before she can focus on the words:

*

Between planes–Heathrow Airport, January 10th, 2000.

Dear Sirine,
Can't stop thinking about you. But it seems that I have left my body, my body travels without soul or consciousness, which remains in America, with you. This personal division is the only reason I was able to climb out of our bed and leave you while you slept the other morning. Now I feel like I'm watching myself go. I can't stop myself.

There are many reasons why I have to return to Iraq, though I'm afraid to write them here, afraid of seeing the reasons written down. Just as I was afraid of speaking the other day while you cooked for me and talked about forgiveness. Too soon then.

Is it enough to say that I didn't want to go, that I never thought I could do it, that the thought of leaving you was even worse than the thought of what is waiting for me in Iraq?

Nothing is enough, I know that now, but it's too late for me. I'm driven by the prospect of return: my country won't let go of me— it's filled me up. You know that. And a certain fear–an emotional fear–has suddenly lifted and freed me.

Sirine, I don't know what's going to happen. Would say that I am coming back to you if I thought I could. I'll contact you if there is any way to do it, but this seems unlikely. The most I hope for now is just time—to see my family, our home. Beyond that, I'm afraid there won't be options.

I won't ask for your forgiveness, only that you let yourself remember me and to know that I loved you so much. More than I knew I could.

Always,
Hanif

*

She lies on the bed, the letter in her hand, close to her face. The transparent paper looks blue as a vein of blood. When she exhales, the paper trembles. She reads it over and over, staring at the place where he writes, "I am coming back to you." He says that he loves her, that he cannot stand to leave her: yet he has left. She rereads it until she can't see the words anymore.

She tries to fill herself up with work. The days compress, hard and square as blocks, as if time has edges, and she gives herself barely enough time to move from sleep—which has turned treacherous and untrustworthy—to kitchen. She pedals wildly through the traffic, dodging between cars, turning close enough that she can feel heat rising from their bumpers and metallic hoods. At work, she loses herself in chopping, mincing, skinning, crushing. She stirs without seeing or smelling, and she cooks by rote, never tasting. She knows the food doesn't taste the way it should, but she no longer much cares about food. On breaks, she ruffles through the newspapers the students leave on the tables, looking for news about Iraq, or just looking at the photographs in the Arabic newspapers.

A few of Han's colleagues stop by the café to check on Sirine, and once she thinks she sees Aziz conferring with Um-Nadia out front, but he doesn't come back to the kitchen. Um-Nadia tells Sirine later that she informed Aziz that he was "too much" for Sirine right now. And Nathan never comes in at all. Sirine doesn't want to see anyone but Han. Somehow, seeing his friends presses on a painful, tender spot in her, her guilty suspicion that she didn't deserve his love in the first place. So she tries not to look up from her work at all. She pushes herself until there isn't room in her for thought. After a few weeks she realizes that she is not really waiting for Han. Not in the way she was at first—so consciously and expectantly. And this makes her sadder. When Han first left, she couldn't help herself. In those first days it felt as if her heart might slip out through the center of her chest. But now she can pull herself back from that soughing grief and stay tucked up tight.

*

One night her dreams intermingle with a distant, foreign scent. She's left the coffee too long on the stove and it's burning. Han is there in the room, waiting, but she can't find a matching cup and saucer. If she doesn't bring the coffee soon, he will leave. The cupboards have hundreds of dishes; she hunts and hunts but none of them match and she can smell the coffee burning.

She wakes for good at three A.M., gets up, and when she opens her backpack, she discovers the coffee cup that someone had wrapped in a towel weeks ago. Its grounds are completely dried out now and they've fallen away from their intricate patterns; the cup has barely any scent at all—even when she tips her nose down into it. She goes into the kitchen, with King Babar following, his nails ticking on the floor, and she puts water on to boil. Then she fills the cup, pouring steaming water over the old grounds and stirring until it makes a thin, grayish brew. The flavor is gone: it's gritty and faintly bitter and she drinks it all, gazing into the night in the window over the kitchen sink. Whatever fate was written in his cup, she thinks, she wants to share it.

*

On the day of her fortieth birthday, Han has been gone for two months.

At the café, they give her presents wrapped in shiny paper: a feathered hair ornament from Mireille, a pair of good heavy knives from Um-Nadia, a box of Mexican crushed peanut candies from Victor, and from her uncle, a recipe book from Syria published in 1892, *On the Delights and Transfigurations of Food*, that he accompanied with his own handwritten, pasted-in translations. "Congratulations, Habeebti," he says. "You will always be my little chicken."

She has a slice of cinnamon-pepper-chocolate cake baked by Victor

Hernandez's mother. There are no birthday candles and so no wishes, for which she is grateful. Um-Nadia tells her to take the rest of the day off, but she refuses, saying she would rather work. So they unlock the doors to the café. Sirine cooks breakfast and she sings the birthday song over and over, just under her breath, *senna helwa ya jameel,* lovely year, oh Beauty.

*

That night, after she's done with work and alone in her bedroom, she sits on the bed beside the dozing, dreaming King Babar, and stares at her old Syrian cookbook. The recipes are pared down to the essentials: simple equations, the ideal calibrations of salt to vegetable to oil to meat to fire. They're little more than lists, no cooking instructions or temperatures, but scattered among the pages are brief reflections on the nature of animals, forest, flowers, people, and God. Sirine browses through the book, lingering equally over the reflections and the lists of ingredients, which seem to her to have the rhythms and balance of poetry. There is one for a roast chicken that she decides she may try preparing for a daily special: chicken, saffron, garlic, lemons, oil, vinegar, rosemary. Following the ingredients the anonymous author has written and her uncle has translated: "Praise be to Allah for giving us the light of day. For these creatures with air and flight in their minds if not in their bodies." Is it a prayer or a recipe? She reads it several more times and can't tell.

She puts the book on the floor beside her bed and switches off the light but she doesn't sleep. It feels as if her body is a taut string, resonating with dark music. She lies on her back with her eyes open. She dangles one arm over the side of her bed and lets her fingers brush over the old cover of the recipe book. Tomorrow she will make a new dish. But, she thinks, Han will never taste it. She remembers that she had seen the date of her birthday circled in Han's calendar—her name enclosed with a red heart. She thinks that if he were still alive, he would have found a way to call that night.

CHAPTER TWENTY-NINE

Back in Hal'Awud, the British director, who wasn't rich and famous for nothing, had cast the lead role of his movie: he'd selected a tall, crazy, drowned-Arab of an Irishman with see-through skin and see-through eyes and a voice like water in a well. He was to be the star of the show. And the movie wasn't called *Sherif Ali ibn el Kharish of Arabia*, now, was it? It was called *Lawrence*.

Of Arabia.

Yes! The *Of Arabia* part comes second, you see. No one particularly cared about the Arabian-of-Arabia, they cared about the Irishman who came dressed in Arab's clothing and the English director's idea of desert music, which went like this, ah-ahhh—da-dahh dada dahh-dahh.

And so he *stole* the movie, just like that. Just like real Lawrence stole the trust of the Arab tribes and just like the gringos stole California from the Mexicans, Peter O'Toole stole the movie from Omar Sharif, to whom the movie rightly belonged. Who was actually the true brilliance and beauty and intelligence of the story.

Are you sure Omar Sharif used to be Abdelrahman Salahadin?

Everyone in Hollywood changes their name, right? Look

at Woody Allen. He was called Allen Konigsberg, which, in my opinion, is a much more melodious name.

But are you sure?

Well, one is never sure. The point of everything is that Sharif too was a drowned Arab. Which was what made him so beautiful and tragic. And that once you let them see the drowned Arab in you, then you're lost.

A moral!

Only because you're looking for one, which means that you are looking in the exactly wrong direction.

Well, that is a very strange ending.

Oh no, there's always more to the story of Abdelrahman Salahadin. Don't worry.

I didn't know that business about the Queen of Sheba. That she was so beautiful. That it could make you go crazy.

It was one of her more salient characteristics.

*

The days are a dream of chopping, stirring, and frying, the nights a span of cleaning and talking. Every evening after everyone is gone, the tea is drained and the dishes are rinsed, every night Sirine cries just a little less, a little less, with King Babar's stern and loving eyes fixed on her from the foot of the bed. Sometimes she dreams of a barking dog.

They start to close the restaurant earlier, and every night Mireille, Um-Nadia, and Victor Hernandez come to her uncle's house and they talk until words fill the room like an incense. They talk, Sirine thinks, as if it's very important that she not think about the last year. As if to drive Han out of their memories, as if it didn't matter that he is no longer in the world. Um-Nadia starts to mention handsome customers who've come into the café. Then she raises her eyebrows at Sirine. One day, Victor comes over with his bachelor cousin Alejandro but Sirine barely looks at him as he sits stiffly embarrassed and silent at the counter.

Sirine spends a lot of time alone inside her thoughts. She has started to wonder about things, about whether Han really loved her, or if she'd just been a distraction until he returned to his real life, about whether he chose to leave her or if something had forced him to go. And about what happened to him. And then she wonders if it's somehow worse not knowing these things than actually knowing you'd never really been loved at all. One night she is suddenly so angry at Han for leaving that she thinks perhaps none of it matters as much as she thought it did. Maybe a death is just a death. She didn't betray him—he betrayed her! He betrayed their love, he betrayed her trust and faith. He allowed her to think he would be with her always. She props her elbows on her bedroom windowsill and looks for the crescent moon. There are so many slight things she can distinguish between with her senses: she can smell the difference between lavender and clover honeys; she can feel the softening progression of ripeness in a pear; and she can sense how much heat is rising in a panful of gravy, lentils, garlic. She knows all of these subtle things through her skin, but she doesn't know the simplest things, like—did he betray her?

Of course, she betrayed him.

Sirine can't quite get it; can't completely take it in.

That he is gone, unutterably gone, beyond her ever calling him back to her. She cannot conceive of the sacred, foreign language that has separated them; she no longer knows what Han is. She believes that at one time the elements inside Han and herself had called to each other, like the way ingredients in a dish speak to each other, a taste of ginger vibrates with something like desire beside a bit of garlic, or the way a sip of wine might call to the olive oil in a dish. Now she feels there is no one to resonate to her; that person is no longer on the earth, and the earth has gotten much colder and much more unknowable.

*

One day, she bicycles to work after the sun has come up, and the air is white and fleecy with fog. Everything is so white it makes her think of snow. She thinks she's seen snow once—paper-light flecks that stirred in the air like cinders and vanished before they ever touched the earth, a freakish cold snap, her breath coming in bursts like blooms of steam. Now the fog is so dense she has to pedal slowly, watching the palm fronds and cars looming up out of it like ghosts.

The fog tries to seep inside the café, a filigree around the door, rolling over the threshold. "It's like another world," Mireille says, wide-eyed.

Everything feels softer, all edges blunted, as if magic has trickled into the street. Customers walk in and then turn and look back out the whitened window, staring as if they can't quite believe it.

Sirine ties up her hair, puts on her heavy white jacket and apron. She feels steady and capable—in her element. But her feelings are all contained and held away because there is always, also the feeling born out of Han's absence—nothing is exactly right anymore.

She slices an onion in half, peels away the amber skin, the crisp white body wet between her fingers. She places it face down. She knows how to cut an onion. Or a tomato. Or a clove of garlic. She knows how to cut so the fragrance and juice are captured. She chops quickly, fingers curled in, away from the blade, going fast. The door chimes ring and the door rattles open. And she sees Han come in.

She cuts off the very tip of her index finger. Not much. A sliver of skin, it cuts so easily, like a bit of onion, she doesn't realize she's done it until she looks down. Her breath a ragged gasp. Then she looks back up and it isn't Han at all. It's Aziz.

Aziz cries out, "*Ya Allah,* your hand." There is a crimson thread of blood running down into her palm.

Um-Nadia grabs her and says, "In back!" and she steers Sirine through the swinging door. They run frigid water over the tip until the water blooms red, swirling with blood. Um-Nadia swabs the wound with disinfectant and has Sirine hold her cut hand up while Mireille locates the bandages. "Maybe she needs stitches," Mireille says as they bandage her.

"*Tch,*" says Um-Nadia. "Stitches. Stitches, what for?"

"Sirine?" Aziz says. He pokes his head through the kitchen door.

"Look what you made her do!" Um-Nadia says to Aziz. Aziz looks aghast and teary-eyed. He opens his mouth but doesn't speak. "I told you not to come."

Mireille looks at Sirine. "Should I smack him?"

Sirine shakes her head. Um-Nadia and Mireille install Sirine in a kitchen chair, put her feet up on a stool, and tell her to hold her finger elevated. "I'm fine now," Sirine protests. "Really, it was hardly a scratch."

"You're in shock," Um-Nadia says. "You don't know if you're fine or not or what. I will tell you if I think you're fine. And you're not fine." She holds up her hand in Aziz's face. "Three minutes," she says. "Then *khullus.*" And she goes out. Mireille follows and sneers at him on the way.

"I'm so sorry," Aziz says quietly, standing in front of the refrigerator.

"Oh . . ." She waves her bandaged hand. "Really, this is nothing."

He nods and stares at her hand as if he doesn't believe her. Then says, more quietly, "I'm also sorry about my own behavior. I feel like I let you down. I wanted to come and see you after Han, you know—but I just . . ." He shakes his head, the wings of his shoulder blades bunched up in his back. "At any rate, I was fairly certain you wouldn't want to see *me*. I didn't even leave my apartment for a week, hoping he'd call. I felt immobilized." Sirine studies his hand with the too-tight gold ring. She doesn't say anything. She knows what he means, knows just how he feels, in fact. But she doesn't have the energy to offer him even this consolation. Finally, he lifts his head. "You look tired. Are you sleeping at all?"

"Sometimes. Not often," she says, then smiles.

Aziz sits across from her at the table and settles his chin in his hand. "Yes, I know. No more bad habits for me either—like sleeping. I keep thinking of—God—Han actually going back there—and then I get stuck there in my head too, you know? Thinking it over and under. I still can't believe he did it."

"Yeah." She looks away. "I try not to think about anything at all."

"Yes." He clears his throat, shifts his weight. "Well, I've been wanting to see you, of course, but there's also another reason why I came—I—I just wanted to let you know—my little book and I have been invited to an artist's residency in Italy. It's supposedly some kind of honor. I'll be leaving here for good at the end of the term."

Sirine looks back but doesn't quite meet his gaze. She takes in this news as she takes in most information these days—through a layer of gauze, a muffling silence—it has no real importance or meaning for her. Her grief rests in the outermost layer of her skin, weighing down her features and making her too sensitive to touch. Then she does look at him and now that she knows he isn't Han she barely recognizes him at all. She has to remind herself that they slept together one night; that she once tormented herself over this fact.

"And I thought—this might be ridiculous, I know, but I thought perhaps you might consider coming with me?"

She tips her head, curious, as if he were speaking another language. "Where?"

"Well. Italy. You could stay with me. I mean, we wouldn't have to—to do anything—you didn't want to do. We could just go together as good friends.

But perhaps it would be a change of pace. Something new to look at. Take your mind to a nice, new place. You could stay as long as you wanted."

"You and me—in Italy?" She feels a riffle of something like laughter rising under her diaphragm. She wants to ask: and who are you again? But he looks at her so earnestly and sadly that she squelches it. "That's . . . very kind of you."

"Think about it. You don't have to answer right away."

She shakes her head. "I couldn't leave here. This is my life."

"But perhaps you would care to expand that life?"

She half-smiles. "Not with you."

His expression fades a little then and he wipes his hand along the table. "Of course, I felt you might say that." He looks pensively around the room and Sirine does too, tries to see what he's seeing, but it's just the big bins of plastic wrap and shelves covered with containers. Finally he lifts his chin and gazes at her and says, "There are some things I've done . . . I'm not proud of. I may have done some less-than-noble things in my life. Heaven knows, I'm not Han. . . ." He pauses but Sirine isn't looking at him; she presses her hurt finger against her thumb. "I have to ask you one more thing," he says suddenly. "Han never left me any sort of message or goodbye. I had no idea—none. I thought he and I were good friends, but . . ." He stares at her. "I can't stop thinking about it—I need to know: is it because of what happened between you and me—is that why Han left?"

"Because of . . ." she mumbles, wondering what he's talking about—she's already forgotten again—then she remembers. "*Oh*. No," she says. "No, I never told him. Nothing." Her mouth feels like cotton.

"Good," he says quickly. "Thank God, thank God. Because I couldn't have forgiven myself."

"Hey, Chef—" Victor swings into the room, looking for Sirine, then stops when he sees Aziz. His face darkens and Sirine sits up, the little hairs prickling along the back of her neck.

"It's okay," she says to Victor. "It's fine. I'm coming now."

Victor remains in the door for a moment, eyes narrowed. He bangs back out through the swinging door.

She quickly turns to Aziz. "Well. I'd really better get back to work. Things get so crazy so fast out there. . . ." She pushes on her knees and stands.

"Well, then." He stands, gallant and restored. He kisses her injured hand. "Let me just say, I haven't stopped thinking about you," he says. "About all that we've had together. You can always call me. Consider Aziz permanently on-call."

"That's nice," Sirine says, standing. "Send a postcard when you get to Italy."

He tries to kiss her hand but she turns it into a handshake. Then she waves goodbye.

*

Han left nine months ago. It's early morning and Sirine is stirring lemon juice into a tahini sauce. The café is unusually quiet for September, the start of the school year, the new fall term. She is stirring and a student comes in and sits alone at the counter. He orders coffee, flicks open his newspaper—the one with the pale yellow pages—the *World*—and begins reading.

Sirine barely notices—she might not have looked up at all, but the tahini sauce needs more lemon and the lemon is on the ledge near the counter. When she looks up, the newspaper photograph—smeary, granular, shadowy—of three hooded, barefoot men catches her eye. She looks closer: one man's head is partially revealed, and she can see the sad slip of his eyes, the way the black shock of hair falls over his forehead; and she knows.

"Please," she says to the student, who glances up, pushing on the silver rim of his glasses. "I'm sorry to interrupt. But could you tell me what this caption says?"

He folds the page and reads for a moment. "It's about Saddam Hussein," he says. "This says he has executed these men accused of crimes of defamation and treason. It says they are Western spies and collaborators." And then the student seems to pause for a moment as well, taking another look at the photograph. He folds the paper up neatly and offers it to Sirine without quite looking at her, his voice lowered, saying, "Would you—would you like to have this?"

But she is already walking into the back kitchen, past Mireille and Um-Nadia, Victor Hernandez and Cristobal, off the back porch, across the courtyard, through the screen of leaves, and into the bougainvillea bushes. She pushes into the dense, scraping branches, as far as she can go, so her hair and her clothes are caught and torn, and she sinks her face into her hands and sobs.

*

A week later, a small box arrives at her uncle's house. It is half-crushed and covered with postmarks and cancellations from Tunisia and Yemen and France. Sirine's name and address is smeared, written in English and Arabic, in a primitive, unfamiliar handwriting. She sits down right on the first step of the staircase to open it, her mouth paper-dry and her pulse thudding in her ears. The plain tissuey wrapping paper falls away and she pries open the little cardboard box, hands shaking.

Inside is a blue piece of paper. And Han's blue prayer beads.

The silk cord was snapped and reknotted and it looks like it's missing a few beads. She smells them; they're cool and dimpled and she presses the beads against the side of her face and her uncle finds her like that, in the same place, on the same step, when he comes home an hour later.

"Habeebti," he says and crouches over her, looking at the package. "Oh, Habeebti, now what is this?"

She holds up the blue paper. It is written on in Arabic, the writing has big gaps, most of it has been inked out by a thick black marker. "Please," she says.

He sits next to her, switches his regular glasses for his half-glasses, puts one arm around her shoulders, and begins translating the few remaining traces of the letter: "I knew your . . . here, in this place . . . we . . . he asked me to send . . . he often spoke of . . . you must know . . . and he . . . very, very much." He takes off the reading glasses, slides them into his shirt pocket, and puts on the regular glasses. "That's it."

"That's all it says?"

"I'm afraid it's been rather heavily edited."

Sirine folds the paper carefully, closes her fingers around the prayer beads. "Then it's enough," she says.

CHAPTER THIRTY

The difference between a crazy person and a prophet is that one has followers. So the difference between a waiter and a movie star is fans. And all sorts of fans came to the movie theater to see the ghostly Irishman.

Peter O'Toole.

Yes. But once they got to the movie this other actor, an unknown, burst inside their eyes, this one who carried himself like a palmful of water, whose skin was clear as water, but whose eye was pointed and black as an arrow. When he was Abdelrahman Salahadin, he was little more than nobody at all, but when he became this other thing, a movie actor—

Omar Sharif.

—then he was everything and everybody. In his left ear was the soft inhalation and exhalation of the desert and the susurration of the ocean winds. In his right ear was the sharp metallic din of America. He became what they call *a star* in this country. In his right eye there were parties and girls, directors and scripts, money and fast cars. But in his left eye there was a sort of absence, a nothingness, that he couldn't quite identify. And if he tried to look straight at it, it would just float away in the maddening way that such things have.

Meanwhile, back home at last in sleepy Aqaba where

nothing ever changes, Aunt Camille was concentrating on becoming an old lady. Many years had come and gone since she first set out in search of her lost son and she had finally decided to try and retire. Her other uncountable sons took her for walks, and brought in her mail, and remembered her on Mother's Day. But every night when she went outside and looked at the roving ocean, she wondered about her missing son, Abdelrahman Salahadin.

One day she received a letter with the return address: "East of the sun and West of the moon." She thought it was another ad from the credit card company and almost threw it away. But she realized that the handwriting on the envelope with its odd slant, curves, angles, and funny punctuation looked familiar. She realized it was from her old friend, the mermaid Alieph. She opened the letter and learned that one of Alieph's many well-wishers and devotees had taken it upon himself to purchase and import one of those fancy motorized wheelchairs and had brought it to her in her cave so that finally she could get out a little.

She was crazy about the thing! Finally, no more dragging that great lump of a fish tail around on dry land. But as you might imagine, those jagged rock trails and precipices around the cave were murder on an electric wheelchair. So Alieph decided to put on the *hejjab* for camouflage and moved herself and her wonderful rolling chair out of the mildewy cave and into downtown Cairo.

Great news, but there was more. Queen Alieph was out picking up a few things for dinner just a few nights back—a couple people were coming by her Cairene loft for wine and cheese—and what does she see plastered a thousand and one times up and down the alleyways? Posters covered with the face, ten feet high or more, of Camille's bad son Abdelrahman Salahadin!

Omar Sharif.

Along with the letter, Alieph also included a few of her latest poems, which were going to be published in a certain trendy literary magazine. But Camille didn't have time for poetry appreciation. She whistled for Napoleon-Was-Here, started packing her bags, and she wondered: what were they wearing in Cairo this time of year?

*

The evening after she received Han's beads, Sirine is at work when she slips and drops an entire panful of roasted fish in tahini sauce. The kitchen floor is covered in sauce and fish and Sirine stands in the middle of it, hands out, not breathing. Um-Nadia looks through the swinging door and says, "Habeebti." She comes out with a mop and looks Sirine up and down, then says, "Habeebti, go home before you kill someone."

Sirine doesn't argue. She goes into the back kitchen and pulls her rain slicker on over her chef's jacket. Mireille offers to give her a ride, but Sirine shakes her head. She walks into the cool, glassy air and climbs on her bike. All of the petals have fallen away and the leaves are tattered, but there are still some remaining scraps of the flowers Han wove into her wire bicycle basket. They flutter as she pedals and she realizes she prefers this—the shredded, witchy look of the old leaves—to the new blossoms. She imagines covering her whole bike in torn vines and sailing down the streets with all her trailing twigs and tendrils.

Lately she has started thinking about her last evening with Han, remembering the things he had said and done. The way he covered his eyes when she showed him the photograph of his sister and said, *no more photographs, I've seen too much*. She wonders: why did he say that?

She thought she would just go home, but instead she finds she's heading into Westwood Village. Even though it's been months, she remembers the way through the streetlights and neon signs and shopping crowds and then the village lights taper away and the neighborhoods start along the winding walkways, under the big, arching palms. She rolls down one street, then another. For a moment she thinks she is lost, then she remembers a particular curve in the road, some bamboo wind chimes, a group of banana trees. The night sky is a high, curved vault over her head.

She finds the house with its broken roof tiles and dark windows and crooked door. Slowly, she rolls her bike across the lawn and up on to the concrete front steps. Sirine knocks and calls out, "Nathan!" He hasn't been back to the café since Han left and she wonders if he even still lives there.

She has come hoping for a photograph. It doesn't matter what it looks like. She thinks somewhere in that darkroom there will be at least one more picture of Han. She must reassure herself that he did exist, that she loved him. Almost nine months have passed; last night after she received his prayer beads, she laid awake and realized that she could not conjure up his face. If she could only see him again, study his brow, the line of his mouth, the expression in his eyes, then she thinks perhaps she could find out what she didn't know about Han—what she should have known.

She knocks again and again, and when no one comes to answer, she tests the door and it's open. "Nathan?" she says. She glances around, then enters the dark, jumbled-up living room. "Nathan, are you home?" She feels for a switch and turns on a dim overhead light that makes the room shadowy and that smells of burning dust. "Nathan?" She walks slowly through the room, around piles of clothes and books, rumpled papers, empty bottles. "It's me, Sirine!" But she's having trouble raising her voice. The stillness makes her want to tiptoe. She approaches the darkroom door. The red light is on and the door is partly open, so she pushes softly and peeks inside. It's empty except for the trays of solution and some prints hanging on the drying line.

She looks once behind her, then goes in. Clipped to the line there's a photo of Aziz in his smoking jacket, his face full, sultry, and self-satisfied, his hair tossed back. There is one of Sirine frowning, peering into a crowd of people at the Department of Ethnomusicology concert. She studies that one for a moment—she wasn't aware of Nathan taking that picture. Then she spots a print of her and Han drinking tea in the kitchen at her uncle's house. She pulls it off the drying line, excited, studying Han's face closely. The familiar lines of his face ripple over her skin—the scar at the corner of his eye catches in her breath. *Han.* She turns to the other photos then and discovers there are more surprises: her and Han together in front of the Persian grocery store; outside Han's office; there's even one of her and Mireille watching Han from the hallway as he teaches his class. There's a shot of Han kissing Sirine in the courtyard behind the café, and then there's a shot of the two of them making baklava in the back kitchen. She discovers more shots of the two of them and she quickly flips through them. It is as though the whole of their relationship has been somehow invisibly noted and catalogued. Han is the hero and Sirine the love interest. There are moments she remembers or half-remembers, and others that she doesn't remember at all: her head on Han's chest; a backward look he gave her; a forkful of food he places into her mouth. Their faces are so open, their gestures so tender, she feels her raw grief return—the put-away feeling of the past months—tearing at some hidden place in her body, and the tears that come up so easily these days, waiting for anything to release them. It is a kind of sweetness, molten and overwhelming and filled with flashes of pain. And through this grief, she is stunned by the level of concentration, the sheer amount of stealth and discipline and single-minded focus, that acquiring these images must have required. Somehow, she feels less horrified by these images than she thinks she ought to feel. There's a glow about them, the light caught in such a way that an onlooker might say the photographer was discreet and respectful, even reverential. She never realized before how important Han was to Nathan, or how consumed Nathan was by their relationship. And now that Han is gone, there is something gratifying, even moving, about this attention.

She rubs her eyes and temples and experiences an upwelling of pity for both herself and Nathan, a sense of his loneliness and isolation, lost here among his images. Both of them locked into separate griefs. She grabs a couple of prints furtively and starts to back out of the room. Her shocked grief finally begins to give way to a sense of dread and unearthliness, as if the more she looks at herself, the less it seems that is really her in those pictures, or that anything in the world is the way she thought it was. The way people who've almost died describe looking down at their own bodies as their spirits fly away.

She hesitates in the doorway a moment, frozen between fear and an urgent, insistent desire to sweep up all of the photos to protect herself and Han from this intrusion. She spots another print—Han is holding her, his head propped over hers and his eyes shut. That is the one she wants. She slips back into the room to pick it up and in that moment something comes to her, buried beneath the bitter odor of developing solutions and chemical baths—so faint it might almost not be there at all, but so familiar she can't help but turn her head and inhale—a scent of berries.

Once she steps out of the darkroom, the scent is easier to detect. She moves into the darker back half of the house, the photos in one hand, the other extended; she is listening, inhaling slowly and carefully, tasting the air. She comes to the edge of another door and barely pushes. It takes a second for her eyes to adjust. There's one big uncovered window in the room; the moonlight spills across the floor and illuminates a bed with a motionless form at the center covered head to toe by a large square black scarf. She comes closer, tests the edge of the scarf for its texture, the fine work of the knots. Her heart feels as if it's swelling with blood; a supple throb of pulse throughout her entire upper body, wrists, face. She inhales and the scent is everywhere, an intricate lace of fields and fruit. And now it is the scent of Han himself.

Very gently she begins to pull the scarf toward her, the figure beneath so still, she could be unveiling a statue.

The gauzy silk releases swells of its particular scent of earth and rare rain, infusing Sirine's senses, her memories rising like tea leaves in a cup. The last of the material whispers away from the figure underneath, and Sirine is looking at Nathan, asleep and curled naked on the bed. His skin looks bluish and smooth as mother-of-pearl in the dark, his penis curled between his legs like a seashell. Trembling, she lifts the cloud of material to her face, breathing it in.

After a moment, she realizes she wants to go. She turns and takes a few careful steps toward the door when she hears a sound behind her and turns to see Nathan sitting up on the edge of the bed. He looks at her as if wondering if he's dreaming. "Sirine," he says softly. "I wanted to return it. I really did. I've wanted to return it for months. I couldn't think how." He pulls a bedsheet around his body, turns his face to the window.

She turns and starts to leave, waits, then turns back again. He is still there. Now he looks like a monk—sunken cheeks, hungry lunar shadow eyes, a body inhabited by an old spirit.

She holds the veil up against her chest.

"I recognized it right away," he says. "As soon as I saw it."

Sirine stands perfectly still. "You took it," she says. "Why did you take my scarf?"

"I'd like to explain. Can I at least do that?"

"What do you know about the scarf?"

"I was in love with Han's sister. With Leila."

"Leila—" She stops, takes a deep breath.

Nathan runs his hands over the bedsheets, fingers rippling over the waves. The moonlight filtering through the window hits the tops of the folds so they seem to turn into crests of foam. "I used to read about Baghdad in the *Arabian Nights*," he says. "It was all magic and adventurers. I thought that's what it was like there. And when I got older Baghdad turned into the stuff about war and bombs—the place on the TV set. I never thought about there being any kind of normal life there."

Sirine leans back against the doorframe. She closes her eyes and folds the silk between her hands. She tries to stay calm, to listen to his version of Baghdad unwind in the room: a city with crowded streets and bars and educated young people, and experimental artists and directors, and stylish tourists from around the world. And Nathan standing in the street trying to take it all in. When she opens her eyes she sees old library books lying cracked open face down on his bed, rolled-up undershirts and socks on the floor; she smells, through the berry scent, an odor of old clothes, film canisters, something bitter and chemical in the room.

So she keeps her eyes closed as Nathan talks about Eastern domes beside Western multistory buildings, and ancient ruins and contemporary ruins from the war with Iran and then bombs from America, missile attacks that left huge smoking holes in the earth; she hears about outdoor markets filled with hanging skinned rabbits, lambs tethered to posts, fruit stands stacked high with tiny tart oranges or glowing onions or heads of garlic big as fists, the smoky scent of sesame, of freshly baked bread from an open stall. And outlying horizons of sleeping purple mountains.

Then Sirine hears about the young woman. She was standing at the market with her mother when Nathan walked in. Nathan describes her meticulously: the spill of her black hair, her plummy red lips, the angle of her hand as she inhales a lemon. Knowing that he has to see her again, knowing that he is lost.

Then, after days of searching, he finds her again. She is hanging out laundry in a field as he is walking by. He stops in his tracks. She knows he's been looking for her because everyone sees and talks about the American who is walking all over town, taking pictures, looking for the girl he saw in the market. They think he's a spy.

He approaches her father and younger brother Arif—her older brother is away at Oxford—and convinces them to let him work in their orchards. Her father has come to believe that American wealth and political influence is the Iraqis' only hope for combating the dictator in power. He and Arif are interested in this intense young man with the pale gray eyes and porcelain skin. For some reason, they like him, even with his bad Arabic, his picture-taking and questions and hanging around; they recognize his obvious, helpless love for the girl. They know he's doomed and half-crazy and too in-love; they let him stay there and work, even though they know it's bad luck and dangerous. Americans attract attention. He keeps a tent in the field where the Bedu orchard-tenders work, but at night he hides himself under a ledge beneath the girl's windows and sometimes she comes out and speaks to him.

There's a sound and Sirine opens her eyes. She's back in the close room in America. She thinks she sees a movement in the air around him, a sort of wisp. Or just a trick of the light. He stands, trailing his sheet, bone-white with motes of blue shadow. He goes to a corner and she hears a drawer hissing open, then he returns with an envelope. He pats a space on the bed beside him for her to sit and she thinks about it and then does so, tentatively. He slides out a handful of color snapshots. He hands them to her one by one; they reflect the moonlight, photographs of the simplest images: bare salt-stems of coarse grass; the stone corner of a window; the edge of a plain whitewashed house. "This is where I lived," he says. "For months. This was the whole world. The space below her window." His eyes are closed. "It smelled like olives. And a bit like the sea."

"Han's house," she says softly.

Another snapshot: the back of a man's head swathed in his white head-covering—a kaffiyeh—his hand reaching for a cup on a round brass table.

"I wanted to marry her. But I was just a guest in her world—her parents, her brothers. I couldn't take her away."

More snapshots: trees with glossy branches against a washed-out sky. "The orchard." Pointed leaves bright as coins. Black olives. "My world." Her hand: round, smooth, brown as a loaf. "Leila."

It's a different pose but the same laughing girl, the same curling tendrils and velvet eyes. "Oh yes," Sirine says quietly, holding it up to the moonlight. "I know her. I found her picture under my bed."

He looks startled. "You found the snapshot? I'd brought it at Thanksgiving to show to you. I was planning to tell you about Leila and me. You and Han both. But then I saw you wearing the veil...." His eyes widen. "I got rattled and left. I'd had her photo in the pocket of my coat and didn't realize it was missing until the next day."

Sirine thinks for a moment, then smiles vaguely and says, "The dog—King Babar—he's a terrible thief."

"Could I perhaps have it back?" Nathan asks. "I can't find the negative."

She looks down. "I showed Han the photo right before he left. He took it with him."

Nathan stares at her and she sees a passage of feeling run over him. In the uneven light he looks like a man beneath a river current. He frowns and lowers his head. "Han had no right to give away the veil!" he says intensely.

"He had no right. Not like that. You didn't know what it meant. You dropped it. I found it lying on your kitchen floor.... It belonged with me." He touches the veil briefly, then withdraws his hand. "No. It belonged to Leila. She was wearing it on the last day I saw her."

*

The snapshot—a young man's grave face, black eyes, a horizontal evenness in the gaze, a flicker of Han's features. "Arif knew about my relationship with Leila. He was polite but quiet around me, always a little reserved. He'd been imprisoned and released once already before I'd met him and he seemed older than he actually was. I'd been working in the orchard for a couple months when the men showed up. Arif had come from the house; he was running between the trees toward where I was working. He grabbed me and brought me into a shelter they'd dug out beneath the house for storing roots and olives.

"I realized I could hear everything that was happening in the house: it was all just inches away through the dirt and floorboards. Leila was talking and they were talking, asking for the American who was taking all the pictures. I could barely breathe or swallow; I was terrified, thinking of the stories I'd heard about Saddam's police. But Leila stood her ground and said there wasn't any American, that it was crazy. They started to search the house. I could hear them turning things over while she followed them. She insulted them and cursed the government. I pressed my hands against the dirt of the ceiling in the darkness, praying that she would stop. When they took her away, she didn't make a sound. But later, when we all came back upstairs, I found one of my pictures of Leila lying on the ground by the doorway—it was one of the shots that I'd given to the American man in the business suit."

The photographs in Sirine's hands are dark glass. She slides them back into the envelope and holds them out to Nathan, but he pulls back. "They're all poison," he says. "They're what brought the police."

"Han thought the police had arrested Leila in order to get to him. He felt responsible for that."

"No—he was long gone by then. The police came because the family was harboring an American."

"So the American man you gave the pictures to—was he C.I.A., or—"

Nathan smiles and shakes his head. "I don't know."

Sirine studies him a moment. "Isn't there any possibility that Leila is still alive?"

At first he doesn't respond. Slowly, he slides back on the bed, props his head up on one elbow. "The way it works is that a few days after Saddam's security police take someone away, sometimes they give the family a present. A small sealed box. They tell you that's it, that's the remains of the person they took away."

"Can you look in it?"

"If you're brave enough. But if you don't look, then there's the possibility that person doesn't have to be dead."

Sirine drifts her fingertips over the scarf.

"This arrived with the box," he says, touching a corner of the scarf. "An artifact. The parents must have sent it on to Han while he was in England."

Sirine looks at the scarf; it feels like skin, like melting butter; a puddle in her lap. "At first he told me it belonged to his mother," she says. "Later he said he was afraid I wouldn't have worn it if I knew the truth."

"Would you have?" Nathan smiles at her. Then he turns onto his back and gazes up at the ceiling. "Sometimes I think it was a dream, but I'm inside the dream as well. For days after the police came, I was so frightened that I stayed hidden in the cellar, the rest of the family living and talking and moving over my head. But on the morning they brought back her scarf, I came out and took my camera and walked down the main street of the village. I wanted someone to arrest me and take me away. But no one came. It seemed as if no one saw me at all. That helped me feel better. It was like I'd already become a ghost, like Leila. I hitchhiked back to the city and a few days later I talked my way onto a plane. I came back to the States. I was a ghost—I felt like I could walk through walls, like I didn't have any body at all.

"For years after that, all I could do was work, look at things, photograph them. I couldn't think about anything. But when I heard Han was coming to teach here, that was when I started to suspect that I was still alive."

"You'd never met him?"

"No, but for the whole time I knew Leila, she never stopped talking about this older brother in England, how smart and brave he was, how he'd won scholarships to important schools. So then I was working for a photography studio in Glendale and an Arab client mentioned that Hanif—the famous translator—was coming to campus. I couldn't believe it. I drove out to Westwood to see if it was true. He was giving a talk—it was part of his interview for the job. At first I could hardly look at him, he reminded me so much of Leila. It was the oddest sensation, like blood coming back into your body after you've had frostbite—a terrible burning all over, starting in my gut, going all the way out to my skin. I felt awake again for the first time in years, I wanted to be near him every second."

"You must've hated me," Sirine says. "Taking him away."

"I didn't!" Nathan protests. "At first it was—strange, but then I started to feel like you were a sort of gift. I was getting to relive my old love by watching you and him together. That's why . . ." His voice trails away and he closes his eyes.

"All the photographs you took," Sirine says. She holds up her handful of prints. "Like a photo album."

"That's not all," he says. Nathan rolls over so he's facing away from Sirine. A car passes the window, so close its headlights scald the room, the photographs flaring in Sirine's hands. "I told him everything, you know." He swallows; she can see his throat moving. "The night before he left."

She thinks. She remembers finding Han and Nathan on campus, the talk: *five thousand children die in Iraq every month*. She remembers Han's expression as he came to her; his silence. A feeling of dread climbs over her. "Nathan, what did you tell him?"

He doesn't answer right away. She can see his throat working. "It's been so painful to live with these secrets," he says. "You have to understand. I never realized that Han held himself responsible for Leila's death. I should have guessed it, I suppose. They say that for some people, the guilt of surviving the people they love is worse than death itself. All this time, I kept quiet about what really happened—I thought of that as my own punishment. To live like this—shut away from everything, and to never, never tell anyone what happened. I couldn't stand the shame of it. I couldn't stand myself. I thought of killing myself but living seemed a better punishment. I'm responsible for Leila's death. My carelessness drew the police to her. When I met Han, I saw inklings of Leila again. I wanted so badly to be close to him, I would have done anything to keep him from knowing what I had done."

"But then—that's what you finally confessed."

Nathan closes his eyes. "He came to my house—it was very late, a few hours after the Arab music concert. He was upset after you'd left. He blamed himself for dancing with that student. He said you'd refused to speak with him when he called you at home afterwards and then you ignored him when he came over to the house."

"When he came over?" She frowns, then remembers: dreaming of rain—the little stones he threw at her windows.

"He started blaming himself for all sorts of things. He brought up Leila. He told me that he was responsible for her death. And that's when I told him the truth. When I told him, I had a feeling, almost a physical sensation like the air itself was shattering. I no longer had to carry that knowledge around by myself. Han didn't believe me at first. He kept saying, 'They took her because of you?' I thought he would kill me—I thought that he would hate me. But he just looked confused. He said he was going to go home, he said he had to think about what I'd told him. He even thanked me. I think in some way he might have been feeling freed as well."

"Freed to go back to Iraq." Sirine glances toward the window, the wet sidewalks and long moon-cast shadows. She can sense her feelings shifting. Nathan turns and looks directly at her, and she feels a premonition. "There's more," she says.

His gaze retreats; he shakes his head. "I didn't want to—I swear, Sirine. I never, ever would have hurt you deliberately. Never. I never meant for any of this to happen."

She tries to swallow, but her throat feels tight and swollen, a current races from her scalp to the base of her spine. "Tell me."

He shakes his head again. "It was after . . . all this—after I'd told Han what had happened between myself and his sister. He said he didn't blame me. He even said he thought of me as a brother. I don't know. I suppose I was careless because I had finally told my secrets. I felt so much lighter. I told Han I wanted to give him copies of the shots I had taken in Iraq. I invited him into my darkroom. There were prints in the chemical bath. I'd lost track of what I'd been working on. You know, I never label anything. And he was standing there while I was going through some folders, and when I looked back, he was staring at a photo in the rinse bath. I'd forgotten all about it. . . ." His voice withers.

"What photo?" Sirine asks softly.

"Of you." He nods. "And Aziz."

Sirine goes very still, so quiet she can feel the pulse in her neck and temples. She can hear the blood in her head. She watches as Nathan stands and pulls another print out of a pile on his dresser. He walks over and silently hands it to her, then sits. "I followed you to the beach. I shouldn't have, but I was worried. I didn't trust Aziz. But that was all I did. After the two of you left the beach, I didn't follow you—any further." His voice is prim and discreet.

Sirine turns the print so it catches the light from the window. She sees herself and Aziz at the pier: they lean into each other, their faces so close, about to kiss, his hand on the back of her head; her face is open, drowsy; she looks as vulnerable as a child. "Oh God," she whispers. "He saw this?"

Nathan rubs his face with his hands. "I shouldn't have taken it, I never should have taken it. I knew that at the time. But I did—I took it. It's like an instinct with me, when I see something . . . striking. It was the only one I took. I regretted it right away. I meant to destroy it."

"But here it is."

"I forgot about it—honestly."

Sirine looks toward the window. From the street, the headlights from a second car fill her eyes; she doesn't blink; she lets the light burn all the way through her head. She feels it pass through her to the opposite wall, passing through her skin like thought. *Han saw this.*

"I knew he would go back to Iraq eventually," Nathan says. "No matter what anyone might have said or done."

"Did he—did he say anything? I mean, when he saw this picture?" Her voice is faint.

He hesitates a moment, then says, "He said he'd had a funny feeling. . . ."

"A feeling."

"He said he felt somehow that it didn't mean anything—" He hunches over. She waits for him and he lifts his head. "But that he still didn't know if he could forgive you."

Neither of them speaks. Sirine reminds herself to breathe. She looks around the room. She considers trying to explain herself to Nathan, why she went off with Aziz, but there's no point to it now. She finally lets herself look at Nathan's face again: it's like crepe, crumbling inward, as if there were no substance behind the surface. "This is why he went back to Iraq," she says flatly. "This picture."

He reaches over; his fingers graze the back of her hand. His skin feels cool and dull as wood. Then he touches her hair, slides his fingertips along one curling lock. "It was Han's choice to go."

She looks away toward the windows; there are silver ropes of rain under the streetlights; the moon whitens the sky. She stands and moves toward the door, then stops and places the scarf on the bed. "Please keep it," she says.

He picks it up slowly, as if frightened of it, and looks at her.

"It belongs with you," she says.

He holds the scarf to his chest; she turns away.

CHAPTER THIRTY-ONE

Back in the Forbidden Temple of the Queen of Sheba—also known as Hollywood, California—Abdelrahman Salahadin was tiring of pretending to be a movie star. Forty years of movies had come and gone and he was tired of women who were sparkling in the evening but crumpled in the morning light. He was tired of playing Russians and Frenchmen, tired of Italians playing Arabs, tired of tall white actors playing short brown Mexicans. He was tired of electric lights that never turned off, of noise that never gave way to silence, and tired of money. Yes, if you can imagine: the man who'd sold himself a hundred times and more for a bag of gold coins was finally tired of money itself.

He was getting older and he craved the comforts of home and family. He couldn't find anyone to have a cup of tea and play a game or two of backgammon or bridge with. All these Hollywood people did was throw their crazy parties and drive their shining cars around in circles. One night Abdelrahman was attending one such event. Everyone was there—Frankie, Sammy, Jerry, Dino. Abdelrahman liked Dino—he'd looked deep into his bloodshot eyes and seen a drowned Arab there. As usual, though, Abdelrahman quickly tired of the party and he stepped outside for some fresh air. He stood by the kidney-shaped pool where blond girls were swimming naked in champagne, but he was looking up at the night. His left eye was blurry and his left ear heard a whispering sound. Suddenly there was a thump on his back and a white face with waxy black hair was looming over him. Dino. Abdelrahman Salahadin could smell lethal waves of alcohol radiating from the man's skin. His eyes were unfocused, and they swam in a way that reminded Abdelrahman of the eyes of the Crazyman al-Rashid.

"Hey, what's shaking, daddy-o?" said Dino.

Abdelrahman merely smiled. He let his gaze drift back to the night, and slowly, gradually, the first breath of a sliver of the crescent moon emerged from the darkness.

The crescent moon is an important symbol in the Islamic faith. Many mosques are crowned with a crescent moon, in much the same way that churches are adorned with crosses. The Prophet Muhammad, peace be upon him, told his followers to time certain rituals and activities according to the new moon. The first sighting of the new moon marks the beginning of each Islamic month and it marks the end of Ramadan—the great and pious month of fasting—which closes with the 'Id-al-Fitr, the Feast of Fast-Breaking, when everyone dresses up in new clothes, goes out visiting and eating!

So Abdelrahman was very excited. He knew the significance of the crescent—the reward to the patient, the watchful, those who are willing to wait. His eyes filled with tears and his hands shook. He reached up to point it out. Dino stared and squinted and swayed and finally he said, "Buddy, I don't see anything."

Abdelrahman Salahadin was the first person in the world to see this particular crescent. It hung over their heads, slim as an eyelash, bright as quicksilver, emanating faint music from the cosmos. He smiled happily and Dino, seeing through his drunken haze this tender, yearning smile—the first honest smile he'd seen in years—bent over and whispered to his friend, "You know, sometimes a fella's got to know when to go home."

That night, Abdelrahman sent a telegram to his friend, the Egyptian director Jaipur al-Rashid—also known as Crazyman al-Rashid—who was beginning auditions for his production of a play called *Othello* written by a mad Englishman. Al-Rashid was going to translate the whole thing into Arabic with an all-Egyptian cast, and he was going to have the actor playing Othello powder his face white. Abdelrahman wrote to his old friend, asking him to save him a part in his revolutionary production: he'd always wanted to try his hand at legitimate theater. Little did he know that al-Rashid had already put up posters advertising his famous friend in the lead role as a publicity stunt. He had been planning to tell the Cairene audiences every night that unfortunately Abdelrahman Salahadin was sick and that his part would be played by the understudy. So this all worked out very nicely.

And neither Abdelrahman nor al-Rashid had any inkling that, having seen the publicity posters, two special women would be in the audience for the opening night: a mermaid poet and a proud mother. And, well, what can I say? The rest was history.

So what happened?

Oh, all sorts of things happened!

But I want to hear about their big reunion. What was it like? What were they feeling?

Habeebti, here is something you have to understand about stories: They can point you in the right direction but they can't take you all the way there. Stories are crescent moons; they glimmer in the night sky, but they are most exquisite in their incomplete state. Because people crave the beauty of not-knowing, the excitement of suggestion, and the sweet tragedy of mystery.

In other words, Habeebti, you must never tell everything.

*

One year later, Sirine is starting to feel like she can breathe again without wanting to cry. Mostly she feels the neutrality of absence—neither happy nor sad, apart from sudden surges of feeling that lick through her, quick and electric as nerve synapses. Only when she cooks, in those moments of stirring and tasting, does she feel fully restored to herself.

She has started to taste her own cooking in a professional way again. Detached, critical, and overly scrupulous. It tastes somewhat different from how she remembers it. Her flavors have gotten somehow stranger, darker and larger: she stirs roasted peppers into the hummus and apricots and capers into the chicken. And she walks into the basement storage room one day and discovers Victor Hernandez kissing Mireille on the butcher block table among the onion skins. Mireille, then Sirine, burst into laughter. Later, Sirine realizes it's the first time she's really laughed in a year.

A month later, Mireille is engaged to Victor Hernandez and Victor moves in with her and Um-Nadia. He makes three different kinds of mole sauces for their wedding dinner, and chocolate and cinnamon and black pepper sweetcake. Mireille gives Sirine, as a bridesmaid present, a book about a woman who cried into her cooking and infected her guests with her emotions, and this story, somehow, gives Sirine a kind of comfort. She thinks about it for weeks afterward and wonders if it is possible to do the same just by standing near the food. Her customers—the young Arab students, professors, and the families—seem more serious than before, more given to brooding, hugging, and thinking. And on several occasions someone—usually a student—has burst into tears while eating the soup or tearing the bread. Um-Nadia wants to send Sirine to the big school, the culinary institute up in San Francisco, to make her into a master chef, to learn to cook, she says, "French things." Sirine isn't sure she wants to do that. She suspects that Um-Nadia just wants to give her a vacation and get her to meet new men. But the only thing that gives her any pleasure is stirring and tasting and swimming back and forth from the back kitchen to the front.

*

For her forty-first birthday, her uncle and Um-Nadia—who, Sirine has noticed, have started to bump their shoulders together when they stand side by side washing dishes—give her a new set of prayer beads. They're irregularly shaped bright blue stones with gold flecks and a gold silk tassel. She fingers them. "Thank you," she says, clicking the beads together. "They're lovely." Her uncle and Um-Nadia look emotional, the feelings close and crowded in the room. "It's a reminder," her uncle says. "So you don't forget to say your prayers."

"They're lapis," Um-Nadia says. "Like the sky."

"A beautiful thing," she murmurs.

That night she takes Han's prayer beads out of her pocket and kisses them and then puts them in the drawer of her nightstand, along with her new set, and slides it shut.

*

Early in the morning after her birthday, while Um-Nadia and her uncle are drinking tea and talking downstairs, Sirine lounges on her bed, poring over the *Kitab al-Wusla Ila'L-Habib*, or *The Book of the Link with the Beloved*—another birthday gift, which her uncle had left wrapped in shining paper outside her bedroom door during the night. A translation of a medieval cookery book, the book itself seems five hundred years old—each of its brittle brown pages crumbles a bit as she turns them, giving off the scent of dust. The recipes, which include all sorts of extinct wild game, internal organs, molds, and fermentations, intrigue her. She is studying a hare stew when there's a noise at the door downstairs and then the sound of Um-Nadia's laughter, which is softened in such a way that for some reason the skin on the back of Sirine's neck stands up in pinpricks. The laughter scrolls up through the floor, filling the air around her.

Sirine eases to the door gently and puts her ear against it, pressing her face against the recessed wood panel. She doesn't know why she's being secretive. She opens the door then and looks down the stairs. Um-Nadia and her uncle are standing by the half-opened door, their faces silhouetted by the gray early morning light. Um-Nadia is laughing her musical, three-note laugh and Sirine sees her hand move forward to touch her uncle's face. Her uncle catches the hand then and kisses her fingertips. Sirine, who was about to call to them, stops herself. She feels waves of heat and then cold passing over her.

She carefully slips back into her bedroom, to her cookery book, and lies on her stomach, a heavy, inevitable feeling rolling over her. She doesn't open the book; instead she runs her fingers over the cover stamped with the title, the gilt lettering all worn off. There's a tap at the door and she puts her face down on the book and says, "Come in."

Her uncle stands alone in the doorway; he blinks and looks around the room for a moment, then at Sirine. "I guess that was you just now? On the stairs?"

"I'm sorry." She rubs her nose. "I didn't mean to spy."

Her uncle gestures to the armchair as if asking for permission to sit, then he simply sinks down on top of all of Sirine's discarded clothes on the seat. "Sorry—my back." He folds his hands. "So you saw." He looks at her out of the corner of his eye. "Are you shocked?"

At first she thinks she is, but when she studies his soft face, she knows that she isn't shocked at all, that she is happy for them. Just like she is happy for Mireille and Victor. And that all of this happiness is touching a very sensitive place. She leans back against her sloping headboard, trying to think how to explain herself. Finally she just sighs and says, "It's . . . Han."

Her uncle nods. "Please tell me."

"There's something . . . bad—really bad—that I did." She stares at her knees. "I didn't want him to know. I tried to keep it from him, but he found out and that's why he left." She presses her lips together tightly, squeezes her hands flat between her knees. Finally, she glances up without raising her head.

Her uncle sits back, taps one finger on the bridge of his glasses. Then he says, "You know, for the longest time I felt like I'd betrayed your father."

"You—how?"

"It was my idea to come to America. Not his. I wanted adventures and sightseeing and all this sort of thing. Your father wanted to study engineering in Baghdad and stay out of trouble and work for the city. Nice and plain and simple. He never liked to leave home. He was quite happy where he was. But oh no, I couldn't let it go. I talked and talked and talked about America until he gave up and said, fine, enough, okay, let's go. It turned out once we got here that I was the one who stayed home and he had the adventures. It turned on some kind of big switch inside of him. He and your mom were always traveling everywhere. And you know, that's why it happened. That's why they died," he says softly. "Being somewhere he wasn't meant to be. I've often thought—maybe, if I hadn't talked him into coming here in the first place—maybe he would still be alive now."

Sirine tucks in her chin. "But you don't know that. Anything could have happened. And if he hadn't come here—then I probably wouldn't be alive now."

"Yes. You see? That's how these things go. I finally had to decide for myself that that was what was meant to be." Her uncle shrugs. "The way I look at it—you should feel glad that Han found out about the bad thing. It's the only way to know if someone can love you—if they still love you even after they know about the bad thing. Or the twenty-eight bad things. All of it."

"But Han is—" She stumbles over it, the word. Instead she says miserably, "Han isn't here."

"So you do it. I'll help. You can know about the bad thing and I'll forgive you."

"Do I have to tell what it was?"

He rubs his chin. "I don't know. Do you?"

"I don't know," she says. She rolls to one side, props her head on her hand, and tries to think about it, but her head feels fuzzy, her thoughts confused. She tries to imagine Han forgiving her and is washed over by a sense of loss. "I can't," she says quietly.

"Then let me make a suggestion—let's eat breakfast."

She nods, relieved, and slides off the bed and the two of them go out into the unlit hallway. It's so early the house is still dark and when she looks toward the window above the front door, it looks like the city lights are out.

They go downstairs, the lit doorway from Sirine's bedroom sliding over her shoulders as she descends. The night fills the rooms of the house, tidal and oceanic. Across the room she sees her uncle's night-blooming flowers are fully opened.

Sirine turns on the kitchen light. There's a recipe from the medieval book that she wants to try—an omelet fried in oil and garlic, a stuffing of crushed walnuts, hot green chili peppers, and pomegranate seeds. She goes to the cabinets and the refrigerator and begins to work while her uncle sits at the table and opens his history of Constantinople. She stands at the table, peeling and mincing onions, then fries the omelet lightly, turning it once, and its aroma is rich and complicated. Then Sirine and her uncle sit together in the library and eat.

The dish is sweet, tender, and so delicious that it's virtually ephemeral, the eggs dissolving in their mouths. Sirine is hungry; she eats more than she has at a single meal in over a year. It's good—she can taste that. For the first time in over a year, she can taste her influence on the food. She licks her fingers when she's done. Her uncle puts down his napkin, says, "*Alhumdullilah*, thanks be to God." Then he nods, points to the empty plate, and says, "The eggs have forgiven you."

CHAPTER THIRTY-TWO

So Abdelrahman performed in the greatest role of his life on a rickety unknown stage in Cairo with a faceful of white powder, under the guidance of a half-crazy director. He was a great hit—no one actually expected the famous American movie star to show up for a play in Cairo. But then his face was painted white, so most of the audience didn't recognize him. But his mother did. Abdelrahman fainted at the cast party when he saw his mother for the first time in forty-one years. Aunt Camille approached him, tall as a door, her every finger glittering with sea-colored gems purchased for her by her other sons. And there was the Covered Man—now the mermaid Queen Alieph—in an electric wheelchair behind her. Camille was so proud of her son. She realized that he'd spent his whole life acting: first as a drowned Arab, second as a drowned Moor.

They hugged and kissed and laughed, and Abdelrahman forgave the mermaid Alieph for bewitching him, and she forgave him for being a bad prisoner. And in the end, this is also a story about what a good thing it is to forgive—a relief to the one who did the bad thing, and a great relief to the one who gets to forgive! And they all moved into a nice flat in Cairo, playing backgammon and drinking sweet mint tea and reading poetry. Aunt Camille and the jackal-eared dog grew ancient together—one more miraculous than the other—and they died, one at sunup the other at sundown, on the exact same day. But in this story they're not dead yet. In this story, the dogs and the mermaids and the mothers and the sons all lived together forever. Until the next big thing came along.

There. Are you happy now?

*

It is a cool morning for late spring. Sirine stands near the grill as it heats up. One by one the lonely students filter into the café. There are birds arguing in the trees over the window, above the kitchen sink. Victor, an official sous chef, is chopping onions and garlic; Cristobal is now a line cook, and a kid from Senegal named Percy is the new cleaning person.

It is almost two years since Han has left and he has started to recede from Sirine's dreams. They weren't even together that long, she tells herself, a matter of months. But she still sometimes looks for him, unconsciously scanning the crowds.

On this morning, however, she is remembering a dream she had that she could breathe underwater. She recalls the pulse of ocean currents in her head, her arms soaring, a dizzy happiness in her chest. Now the dawn is saffron-colored in the windows and the café is glowing. She is stirring a pot of leben yogurt, which is heated slowly, carefully, tenderly, and hopefully, layered with butter and onions and heady and rich as a high summer night. She cannot stop stirring because it is a fragile, temperamental sauce, given to breaking and curdling if given its way. So she must wait and stand and stir and stir and stir and look and look. And she is standing and stirring and looking out the window and then toward the dining room.

One student sits at the counter and flicks open his paper. Sirine doesn't read the American papers, but she still turns reflexively toward the Arabic papers—especially the ones printed on the soft green and cream-colored pages. On this morning her gaze brushes over the front of the student's newspaper, and when she sees the photo, she barely registers it. But then something makes her look again. And then, for the third time, she blinks and looks closer and it's a photo of a man who resembles Han, but cannot be Han.

"Excuse me, please," she says to the student.

He curls the corner of the paper in to look at her, then sees that she's looking at the photo on the opposite side.

"Can you tell me what that is?" She points.

He patiently turns the paper over and reads the short article, whispering to himself in Arabic. He shakes his head and laughs and says, "It's a crazy story. It says this guy's a political prisoner who broke out and then escaped from Iraq by following the migration of these animals across the border into Jordan. He says he's on his way home—I don't know where."

Sirine looks at the photo again and now she sees a blurry deerlike animal in the background—it looks rough, and wild, with a pair of great carved horns.

The student brings the paper close to his face and examines the photo for a moment. Another student gets up from his table to peer over the first one's shoulder. He points at the image: "See, that's—that's a gazelle."

"That's no gazelle," says the seated student. "That's a—what do they call them in English? Elks?"

"It might be a mountain goat."

"That's not a mountain goat, you idiot," says a fourth student.

"It's an oryx." Everyone falls silent for a moment and turns to look at the speaker—it's Khoorosh, who is looking at a copy of the same newspaper and eating a plate of eggs and lentils. "*Oryx.*" He goes back to his eggs.

She looks at the student. He's tightly wound and wiry, his eyes glimmering with humor. She stares hard at the paper. "What's the man's name?" she asks, pointing now. "Does it say?"

The student turns back to the paper, studies it a moment. "Here it is." Then he looks back at her. "Abdelrahman Salahadin."

She feels a blast of cold wind like a shout of laughter. A wild wind like the wind off the ocean's back. Her knees go weak and her mouth dries up. She lifts her hands but there is nothing to grab.

"Chef?" the seated student says. "Are you all right?"

The young men scramble to get her a chair but Sirine shakes her head, takes a rocky step back. "I'm—I'm okay. Can I just . . . " she reaches weakly toward the paper. The student hands it to her. Sirine lifts it and says, "Just need a little air."

She walks out back to the courtyard. Then she stands there, trembling, and takes a deep breath before she looks at the newspaper. Sirine lifts it to her face and studies the photo closely, first the details of the animal, its splendid horns and almond eyes, delaying another look at the man. And then finally she lets herself look—slowly, gradually—at the man. His clothes are in tatters, his face is covered with about a week's worth of stubble; he stands in an open field as if he'd just washed up there. She tries to focus on his face. The photograph is composed of tiny ink dots and Sirine's eyes burn as she stares at the newsprint. She closes her eyes again and tells herself, relax, and she opens her eyes.

Han.

It cannot be, but of course it is, it undeniably, certainly is.

She stares and stares and stares, the photo filling her up—the soft shape of his eyes, the sweep of his hair, and the crescent-shaped scar at the corner of his eye.

And then things are shivering loose inside of her, large plates of ice shifting and breaking. She drops the paper on the stairs and walks across the courtyard to the *mejnoona* tree and grabs hold of its flaming, blooming branches; it sways all around her, a conflagration; she holds on as if it were the only thing anchoring her to the ground. Han is alive. Han is alive in the world.

"My God." She looks up to see Mireille standing on the back porch, staring at the newspaper Sirine had dropped. She holds it up. Her voice shakes. "Is it?"

*

Sirine remains in the courtyard after Mireille has gone in to tell her mother. She can hear the life of the kitchen and the café through the walls. She sees reflections swimming in the back window.

She feels it again. Swift and sharp as physical pain, like the blood returning after frostbite: the thought—*Han is alive.* After so many months of waiting and mourning. She is almost calm among the papery bougainvillea—the madwoman tree and all its finery, once again, inside the courtyard, this mosaic of light and plants and wind.

She thinks of the story of Abdelrahman Salahadin. Sometimes, in the months after Han left, when she was falling asleep she got confused and couldn't quite remember if it was Han or Abdelrahman who loved her, if it was Han or Abdelrahman who dove into the black page of the open sea. Was it Abdelrahman who had to leave her, to return to his old home, or Han who was compelled to drown himself, over and over again.

She imagines him, tangling in the water, in the long, black-tongued weeds that grow up for miles from the bottom of the sea floor. Was he afraid at that moment or had he long ago given himself over to the seaweed and fish? Had he already dreamed of such a death so many times that, in the end, it was as natural as going home? He returned to Iraq knowing that they would certainly kill him. Somehow they have not. For some reason—she thinks—they've been granted a reprieve.

In a single moment, it's as if all the months and months of separation that have gone by have disintegrated; years collapse.

Um-Nadia appears in the doorway and looks around as if she were shy. She is holding the paper. She smiles, brushes the hair from her face, and closes her eyes.

The wind picks up and the two tall palms make the shivering sound of rain. From all the way down the street, Sirine can hear the impassioned bark of a little dog at the limit of a short leash. The trees and the bushes all start to sway and Sirine notices the pomegranate tree has finally borne the starts of a few fruits.

Inside the kitchen, the phone starts to ring.

Sirine waits, buttons her jacket a little higher, and then someone is calling her name. She runs inside. Victor Hernandez is on the phone, saying Han's name and looking at her. He stands beside the front stove stirring the silver cauldron of leben, the big spoon tilted in his hand, the burners flickering with blue flames. She presses her hand against her mouth and takes the phone.

permissions

Extract from "A Dream for Any Man" in *The Pages of Day and Night* by Adonis, English translation copyright © 1994 by Samuel Hazo. Northwestern University Press paperback published 2000. All rights reserved.

Extract from *Love, Death, and Exile* by Abdul Wahab Al-Bayati, copyright © 1991 by Bassam Frangieh.

Extracts from "Leavetaking" by Ibn Jakh and "Mourning In Andalusia" by Abu il-Hasan al-Husri in *Poems of Arab Andalusia*, copyright © 1989 by Cola Franzen. Reprinted by permission of City Lights Books.

Extracts from *Open Secret: Versions of Rumi* by John Moyne and Coleman Barks, copyright © 1984 by John Moyne and Coleman Barks. Reprinted by arrangement with Shambhala Publications, Inc., Boston, www.shambhala.com.

Extract from Jaroslav Stekevych, *The Modern Arabic Literacy Language*, copyright © 1970 University of Chicago Press.

Extracts from "The Ode of Tarafah" by Ibn al-Abd from *Anthology of Islamic Literature*, edited by James Kritzeck. Copyright © 1964 by James Kritzeck. Reprinted by permission of Henry Holt and Company, LLC.